Royals of Sondmark
Book Four

The Dandelion Princess

KEIRA DOMINGUEZ

Contents

For Maren, our golden maknae

Prologue

September

ELLA

I draw my knees up to my chest and hunch over my cell phone in a shapeless hoodie. The pose gives me the appearance of one of the fearsome gargoyles perched along the roof of the Grousehof, but my mind is a storm.

I frown at the screen. Seong has been rocked by a natural disaster, and the rubble is still smoking. It's the right time to send a message, but Smart Ella is shouting at the top of her lungs that I should go through official channels. I can help in a thousand ways that don't involve personal contact. I don't need to pick old scabs. Idiot Ella is half out of her mind with worry. I have to know that Marc is safe.

My thumb hovers over a tiny icon—a tiny photo of him and me, cropped from a larger group picture—and the name underneath reads "My Brother's Best Friend".

I release a breath and type quickly.

Marc?

Send.

This is a mistake—such a mistake—and I look up to calculate the time change. Soft morning sunshine glows from the edges of my drapes, but it's almost midnight in East Asia. He's probably dead asleep and won't see the message for hours. Maybe it's not too late to—

Incoming text bubbles begin to bounce, and I jerk upright.

Ells. Still breaking hearts in Sondmark?

My scabs feel the sharp sting of fresh air and I screw my eyes shut. This hurts in the exact way I knew it would.

No. I shake my head. I'm going to be fine. I lean against my headboard and take a slow drag of air. I am a princess of Sondmark, not a teenager with a crush, and I am definitely, for sure this time, going to fall out of love with Marc van Heyden. It has been 287 days since I sent him a cat meme. I deserve a sobriety pin.

There are no support groups for falling out of love with your brother's best friend. I've known him as long as I've been alive, and his little sister is my bestie. Disentangling my life from his feels as impossible and painful as shrugging out of my own skin. Still I try. When our paths cross at royal engagements, I maintain a friendly distance. If he closes the distance, I try to drive him off by being as boring as possible. This is a Herculean task, but it is also how I found out I can talk about historic cufflinks for twenty-three uninterrupted minutes.

For the last year, I have kept myself busy, fulfilling royal assignments and fighting with my mother over her narrow interpretation of "appropriate footwear". I wrap myself in the cozy sanctuary of online fandoms. Still, the effort of *not* thinking about Marc every minute of every day feels like holding one of those impossible yoga positions—the kind my twin, Freja, manages so easily. I am aware of every passing second, breathing a prayer that in another month, or the one after that, this pathetic, one-sided crush will wither and die.

I enable voice-to-text.

I've been praying for you, I tell him, my throat stiff with emotion. *I want to do something for Seong. What do you want? A boatload of bottled water? Someone screaming at the NGOs to get busy? Can I throw money at your problems?*

Since early reports of the disaster reached Sondmark, I've spent every spare minute glued to the screen, absorbing the photos and video feed pouring out of East Asia. Marc and his mother, a Seongan native, were on the ground in less than twenty-four hours, providing key aid in the aftermath of an earthquake, a tsunami, countless landslides, and the suspicious rumblings of a nuclear reactor.

My life in Sondmark stands in sharp contrast. I've worn a succession of ball gowns, trotted from museums to embassies like a royal show pony, and smiled at dozens of cameras. All the while, Marc has been in hell.

"Trust me," I whisper, frowning at the text bubbles hopping on the screen. "I can help you."

His answer to my string of questions comes as a pat on the head. *That's sweet, Ella. You've got enough on your plate.*

He adds a finger heart emoji to soften the blow, and I pass my thumb across the tiny graphic, forcing myself to stop reading something into it that isn't there and won't ever be.

I type out a message.

Be safe. *heart-hands emoji*

I toss my phone onto the bed and reach for my laptop, a stubborn tilt to my chin as I begin to type. "Nearest mainland port to Seong."

Marc is getting help whether he wants it or not.

1

RESPAWN

APRIL

ELLA

"The princess is the worst," I insist. "She should get a job, contribute to society, and maybe rescue herself for once."

The voice of Staggering_Indifference, an American graduate student, comes through my headset. "Without the princess, we have no game," she insists.

"Yes, but a princess?" I scoff. "In the year of our Lord—"

"A princess trapped in a garden is an archetype. She's not helpless if she's able to inspire the worthy to perform noble sacrifice."

No one can see my eye roll to this Medieval Studies monologue. I could teach my own college course on what a flaming pile of garbage the idea of princesses are in the modern era. "Yes, but—"

Staggering_Indifference squeaks her surprise when we are suddenly ambushed. "Maybe let's cut the philosophizing?"

I unleash a wave of arrows and, once I find a rhythm, my attention bounces across several screens. Dialing the volume of the game down, I boost a playlist featuring the music of BLUSH, a favorite Seongan girl group. I sing along, too low for my headset to catch it.

Kiss me like you mean it...unintelligible Seongan lyrics...Kiss me like you mean it

"On your left," I say, guiding my squad through the ruins of a castle.

The members fall into formation, sights trained on the dense tangle of briars. LoveShush is on my right hand while Staggering_Indifference, dragonslayer2, and BeastlyDutchOaths guard the rear flank, firing as needed.

"Panda," LoveShush shouts, her avatar crumpling to the flagstones. The skintight bodysuit with strategic cut-outs was not, it turns out, as strategic as my flak jacket and tactical gear.

The ruins erupt in fire and my eyes dart across the screen. "Follow me to higher ground."

BeastlyDutchOaths is fatally hit during the retreat, but we all respawn on the top of the rise, watching clouds of smoke between us and the horizon, our avatars bouncing gently on the balls of their feet. For today, the princess is on her own.

A notification pops up on my screen. "Group Torture, 10 AM."

I frown, tapping it closed. I've got at least fifteen minutes before the weekly Wolffe family meeting, and our life points are in the red zone. "We have to do a side quest," I suggest.

BeastlyDutchOaths has a hard timetable he can't squeeze another minute out of.

"Sorry guys," dragonslayer2 says. "My sister is going to rain hellfire on me if I don't clean Boris's enclosure. I'm out."

I roll my eyes. Boris the box turtle would be thrilled to paddle around in his own waste for the next hour, whereas our team will have to disband and go through the hassle of reorganizing if we don't at least make it back to our raiding ship—part Viking longboat, part time traveling device. "Dragon—" I plead.

"I'm gaming before noon, Panda. She hates that. If I can't contribute to the 'health and wellbeing' of my family, she'll confiscate my best controller and *SquadRun* figurines." He aims at me, delivering a kill shot to a lone knight just over my shoulder. "Again."

Staggering_Indifference pops in. "My boyfriend has a paper due about constitutional monarchy for his civics class and I promised to help. Panda, can you proofread it? You said—"

I try not to think of how many campaign points we're shedding as we speak. "Of course. Send the file over the Friction server when you finish."

Their avatars shimmer on the hilltop, disappearing as their life points are drained from our stats.

"You have somewhere to be, too," LoveShush reminds me. She's the only one of our squad who knows who I am beyond my gamer tag. In real life, she's Alix, my oldest friend who actually thinks skintight bodysuits with strategic cut-outs are reasonable fashion choices. She knows me as Her Royal

Highness Princess Ella, Duchess of Sorstorm who showed up to kindergarten with monogrammed bib overalls and a security detail.

I glance at the clock and swear under my breath. "I'm not bailing on our team."

Sometimes I worry that people on *SquadRun*—and a whole fetid raft of tabloid reporters—will find out who I really am, but I need this outlet. Half the team is American, I reason. I'm not sure they could find Sondmark on a map.

"You go," Alix says. "I'll stay behind and pick mushrooms and sorrel until our life points are restored."

Tedious. Glacial. And Alix has enough to do, keeping her family's stately home afloat in the absence of her family.

"No," I decide, "we're going after the abbey. We'll grab a relic—in and out."

"There is no in and out with murder monks," she warns.

I ignore her negativity and begin to race across the boggy ground in the direction of the massive abbey grounds.

"I wanted to ask you something," she says, shooting a flaming arrow into a grove of trees. "My mom and Marc have been in Seong for ages."

His name is like a tiny, pale sliver under my skin. Marc has been gone for seven months and thirteen days, but who's counting?

"I need your help."

"What is it?" I answer, swinging a grappling hook from the base of a tower wall.

"I'm getting married on July 12th," she says, cutting off my scold. She already knows I think it's insane to plan a massive wedding in three short months, and her voice is determined. "If you're not going to be my maid of honor, I just won't have one."

I vault over the top of the tower wall, slashing through a couple of waiting sentries. Their blood splatters in elegant arcs. Alix is my best friend, but she has no real idea of how stressful the last year and more has been. My family is in disarray and she's only seen glimpses of the mounting pressure.

I would love to be her maid of honor, showing up for more than a group photo on the big day, but—

"You know it's impossible," I say. Mama will never say yes. "We're stretched thin. There's the Ragnar Prize banquet coming up as well as a couple of royal tours, and Freja has practically abandoned us." I swallow away the knot in my throat. My twin's sudden elopement last Christmas made everything harder. "Alix, you have a million friends."

"Only one *best* friend," she reminds me. I can hear from the tone in her voice that she's all big eyes and quivering lips, but I can't see a way to say yes. "Just think about it, will you?"

We grab a relic—the sacred elbow joint of an evangelical saint—fending off attacks from a dozen lethal monks on our way back to our ship. As we push into the current, I review our new stats and stretch hugely. This session was ugly, but our team has been saved to fight again another day.

Mid-stretch, my eye catches the time on the screen. 10:13. *Stultes es.*

With a yelp, I rip off my headphones and dive into the closet. Hasty hands clatter hangers together as I fumble for clothes. In a saner world, Mama would be glad I haven't run away from this royal prison, but I don't live in a sane world. I live in the heart of my mother's kingdom, behind the high, gated walls of the Summer Palace, and she demands perfection.

I'm leagues from perfect when I stumble into the family meeting, smelling of hastily-applied deodorant wipes and wintergreen gum, but I aim a brief curtsey towards my mother—my queen—and drop into my seat with a thump.

"Thank you for blessing us with your presence," Mama replies, her voice dry. She checks her wristwatch with a frown. "We expect," she says, employing the majestic plural, "to be blessed, hereafter, with your punctuality."

I adjust my glasses and send her an affable smile. "Punctuality from the personality hire? That's a big ask."

"That will do, Ella," she bites.

I shoot Clara a look and mouth the words, "What did I miss?"

She picks up a red leather portfolio and tips it discreetly. "Crown Estates."

Ugh. Time for Noah's quarterly financial report from the Crown's agricultural concern. I flip past tabs reading "Media Mentions" and "Marriages and Succession Act (1798)" to locate my brother's precious pie charts. One of the pages contains a graph showing how many more kilos of free-range venison were sold under the House of Wolffe label than last year. A red line on a chart shows an uptick. An orange line moves sharply down, and I consult the key.

Oh. Pity about the sugar beets.

My mind wanders as Noah drones on. If he were reporting on the state of our family, what would he say about our lines careening in every direction? My gaze slips to Mama at the head of the table and Père on her right hand. Has she apologized for commanding him to skip his father's funeral on political grounds? Has he agreed that Grand Père's tolerance of a fascist regime was problematic? My parents are so correct in public, so careful of their image as a well-oiled machine, but everyone knows that they haven't shared a bed in more than a year. Still, the Great Hall has stopped echoing with their shouts, so that's a win.

What of Clara? Last year our youngest sister took up with a naval hero and launched a privacy lawsuit against a tabloid. Only time will tell if her surprising knack for performing her royal duties will make up for the headache she is causing my mother on other fronts.

My gaze slides along to Alma, my oldest sister. Mama got her most dependable child to agree to an arranged marriage, but then everything blew up when her fiancé, Pietor (lying scum of Himmelstein), cheated on her. Now she's secretly seeing the future king of Vorburg—Sondmark's nearest neighbor and oldest rival—and no one knows what to expect.

The next chair is empty and belongs to my twin, Freja, who performed a swan dive into royal irrelevance by eloping with an immigrant on Christmas Eve. Officially, Mama was thrilled to welcome Oskar to the family and said so in her yearly broadcast. Unofficially, she's probably grinding her teeth in her sleep from the effort of dealing with the fallout of a princess who got married without asking anyone for permission. There are strict laws about that kind of thing.

Where is the legendary discipline and deep bench of reliable working royals the House of Wolffe has been known for?

I glance at my brother—at home in his suit and tie, dark hair waving from his brow as he warms to the subject of cost-cutting like a total loser—and grab my phone, typing out a chirp from my secret alt account.

@trashpandaprincess: The Wolffe princesses could breathe if Crown Prince Noah would finally get married and have babies. Round up foreign brides of distinction! Throw a ball!

I smother a wicked grin. If I'm lucky, the chirp will find its way into our next family meeting under "Media Mentions". Mama, frowning, will use it as an example of how fickle public opinion is, but the subtext to my brother will be, "Just say the word and I'll hire a DJ and order the booze."

Mama would love the positive press of a royal wedding. Alas, Noah's pulse is as flat and bitterly cold as the Sondish lowlands, apparently unmoved by the dozens of models he cycles through each year. I am convinced that getting him to the altar will require an act of divine intervention.

He pauses briefly as Mama's secretary, Caroline Tiele, supplies me with an updated agenda with notes written in the margins in her clear, precise penmanship. Only after she skirts past him, raising her arms and taking careful steps to avoid a collision, does he continue.

With half an ear on the rising price of fodder, I leaf through the other tabs.

"What's this?" I blurt, derailing the gripping topic of large-scale food production. "What happened to my assignments?" I hold the folder open on a nearly empty page.

Mama folds her reading glasses with an irritated snap. "Do you think it is likely that *Vrouw* Tiele forgot to include them?"

"Helena," Père scolds.

I sweep a finger up and down the blank page. "This makes it look like I'm being held for ransom somewhere. Are you busy sourcing the funds to be delivered by a black ops team?"

"Nonsense," Mama says, adding absentmindedly, "I don't negotiate with terrorists."

I arrived at the family meeting, prepared to fight about wearing nylons and high heels to track and field exhibitions, or about how arriving to a morning kindergarten read-aloud in full glam terrifies the children, but I would have gone to both events, in the end, dressed in the only way my mother can imagine is appropriate.

Outside these walls, I'm still doing the princess thing. Can't she trust me?

I consult the list. There's a STEM event I could do in my sleep, a film festival appearance, and a few cocktail parties where I'm expected to be just a warm body.

What is Mama thinking? My stomach tightens with pain. My mother is running low on reliable princesses, but I'm like a misshapen carrot selected for those delivery crates meant to combat food-waste. Odd but edible. She can still use me.

"You will be otherwise engaged," the queen says, whisking her glasses on again. "Alix van Heyden has accepted a proposal of marriage from Mr. Thomas Farrell of the United States of America."

It's impossible not to laugh when she speaks like that. I shove the pain into a tight little cubbyhole and let out a giggle.

"I know. Alix told me months ago." I knew she was going to marry Tom when she asked me to conduct a little light reconnaissance on his old girlfriends, sending this request via an upside down video chat in the middle of her garden pilates. "*Vede*, the whole country probably knows by now. She put it on the Saint Sissela group chat."

Clara snorts. Our all-girls private school was named for a nun, but it wasn't exactly a bastion of maidenly discretion.

"*Vrouwheid* van Heyden called me this morning and made a rare personal request," Mama says. "She asked if I might spare you to be Alix's maid of honor."

My smile tightens. "I already said no."

I hate living this way, desperate to escape this royal straitjacket, daily abusing the soft creature of my flesh by pouring her into suffocating shapewear, forcing her to hold her breath, her tongue, and her appetite. I live under my mother's rule but, for once, I beat her to the punch.

"You will say yes," Mama commands. "I've cleared your schedule as much as possible."

My eyes narrow and I fall against the back of my seat. "You said what?"

"The van Heydens are nearly family," Mama replies. "While *Vrouwheid* van Heyden is in Seong, she will be unable to support Alix as much as she'd like. Sparing you to be her bridal attendant is the least we can do."

It sounds reasonable but unease feathers over my skin. 'Reasonable' is not in the vocabulary of Queen Helena of Sondmark. "You're not going to be short-handed?"

Mama holds my gaze. "You could use the rest."

"I *could* use a rest," I answer, my voice nothing like the clear, declarative tone drilled into us from infancy.

"Excellent," Mama nods.

I sit in shock through the rest of the meeting and, as my siblings file out, I realize that the prison doors have been thrown open. I take a breath, trying to adjust to the idea of an entire spring dedicated to being young, healthy, and rich.

A moment later, I'm on my phone, rising from my chair, tapping out a search for sequined bachelorette party rompers.

"Oh," Mama says, turning from the door. Caroline halts, too. *Here it is,* I think, my finger hovering over the 'Buy Now' button. *The catch.*

"There's something the Saint Sissela group chat might not know... Marc van Heyden is coming home."

She sweeps from the room, and I plop to the seat. My stupid heart is galloping like I haven't aged one *flamen* day in ten *flamen* years.

I focus on a mediocre landscape painting hanging on the opposite wall and inhale. Nothing has changed. I exhale slowly. Marc is back, but I nursed that crush along like a *SquadRun* team for too many years. The castle is a smoking pile of ruins and I'm out of arrows. It's time to call it quits.

Past time.

2

FRIEND ZONE

MARC

Noah sinks a three-point shot over my outstretched hand and jogs backward, taunting. "When did you get old?"

"Do you know what time it is in Seong? I should be asleep." I roll my neck and pass the basketball to a teammate before posting up under the basket. Thor Brosemann, Ella's usual security detail, shoulder-checks his guard and drills the ball into my hands. I roll it in for a soft layup.

It's not enough to win.

"Your crown," I say, lobbing a towel at Noah's head at the end of the game.

He rubs it over his hair as the others—an under-butler, a couple of guys from palace security, and a pastry chef—make their way to the showers. Amidst the distant clink of weight machines and classic rock, I wipe my face with the edge of my tank top and sink onto a bench.

"Are you going to give me your report?" Noah asks, throwing back a swig of water.

He's not only my best friend but my future king. The noble families of Sondmark are still required to take an oath of allegiance to the monarch, and I, as the current holder of the van Heyden title, will bear the sword of state when Noah is crowned. When he asks a question, I have to answer.

I flick the rubber lip of the water bottle. Open. Closed. Open. Closed. "It's worse than the press reports show."

My words are a meager portion of the truth and a line forms in my brow until I work out why. For months, I have been reporting my daily observations to another member of the House of Wolffe. They belong to her.

"The press is reporting significant progress," Noah prods.

I lift my shoulder and repeat the words of my government report. "Urban centers are beginning to take shape. Farther out, we established temporary shelters and a reliable supply chain for food and other necessities, but Seong has a lot of people scattered in upland villages. Even in the capital, it's one step forward and two steps back. Inflation is rampant, and it's hard to get anything but shelf-stable food."

His tone sharpens. "Is there a risk of famine?"

I shake my head. "Without regular shipments, maybe there would be."

Noah tosses the ball between his palms. "Glad to be back?"

"Of course."

My answer is brisk and certain but my thoughts stir with complexity. I close my eyes, blocking out the opulence of the palace gym, trying to tap into the single-mindedness I woke up with every day in Seong. Most of the time was spent getting supplies to outlying islands and organizing donations. During what were supposed to be periods of rest, I donned a hard hat, work gloves, and face mask, clearing villages of rubble and debris.

I open my eyes to the painted ceiling depicting the old Sondish myth of the Dragonslayer and the Maiden, the apple-cheeked girl nestled in the curl of a scaly tail. The knight, clad in his requisite armor and carrying his requisite sword, is left to handle the beast on his own.

I am here, but there is another me still in Seong. Still living the story of aftershocks and refugees returning to ancestral villages. Still living the story of a whole country being stretched and stretched until everyone has a place to spread a sleeping mat.

This is Sondmark, I remind myself, where the prime minister is calling for stricter immigration controls, afraid that I will be a bridge between my mother's homeland—a place that is stamped on the shape of my eyes and the warmth of my skin—and the country of my birth.

Vailys.

"I don't know how you did it," Noah says.

"With my favorite chainsaw," I answer.

Noah palms the ball. "You didn't have to return."

"I can't neglect my business any longer, and Alix is about to be married." I smother a yawn as jetlag has its way. "She needs to step back from helping so much with the estate."

Though I am a hereditary peer of Sondmark, I learned about duty from my mother.

My father's greatest love was himself, followed closely by every illicit drug known to man. When he met my mother, a Seongan student and model, I'm convinced that her primary appeal for him was how much she would shock the family.

After he popped off to that great ayahuasca afterparty in the sky, everyone expected my mother—*Amma*—to auction off the collection of family portraits by Oppeger the Younger and retreat with her regrettably half-Asian children to London or Singapore to live off the fumes of the van Heyden fortune. Instead, the trophy wife dug in her heels and kept Lindenholm afloat, transforming it within ten years into a brand of organic agricultural goods. It drives Noah crazy that the Crown Estates haven't quite caught up in terms of quality, even if they dwarf us in market share.

Because my mother devoted herself to Lindenholm, I was able to grow my startup, Han Heyden from an idea scribbled on a legal pad in a Stanford dorm room to the thriving tech company that now forms the backbone of Handsel's reputation as the Silicon Sea.

"*Amma* wants to relocate to Seong," I say. "I can't count on anyone else to shoulder my responsibilities, and it's time to get serious."

Noah gives an approving nod. "You know your duty."

"I thought you knew yours," I smile, "but I hear you're still chasing models."

"I have a type." Noah breathes a silent, bitter laugh.

I'm not the only one holding back. My oldest friend still won't talk about the moment almost three years ago when he revealed what his type was. We had run out to Outingen Huis after he returned from an assignment abroad and spent the day riding over fields, ending up on the beach with a bonfire. One beer had turned into two, and then three.

After a few reckless years, he was finally beginning to understand that there would be no true escape from being the next king. For me, my father's drug-fueled stumble from the cliffs of sobriety was my own personal cautionary tale. We weren't there to get drunk.

I had asked a question I'd been holding on to, waiting for the right time to deploy, annoyed that I couldn't seem to just toss it out. "What's Ella up to these days?"

I felt myself hold my breath, waiting for his answer.

He stared at his hands so long that I was about to repeat the question. Then, "There are people we can't be with."

I closed up tighter than a spinster's night robe and a response squeezed from my throat. "A crown prince can date anyone he wants."

"Not anyone." He tossed his beer aside and it landed with a thunk into the soft sand. "Your sister." He snapped his fingers like he was trying to remember her name. "Alix. I can't date her."

I smiled against the lip of my bottle. "I already gave Alix the talk about you."

"Deal." Noah didn't slur but his words were overprecise. "If I can't date your sister, you can't date any of mine." He grabbed my hand and shook it, sealing the contract before I could read the fine print.

He went on, staring hard at the sky. "Employees are off-limits, too."

"Obviously. I'm not going to start pinching your maids."

"Can't call them maids," he corrected. "Housekeeping staff. I didn't mean them."

"Do you mean what's-her-name? *Vrouw* Tiele?" His mother would go through the roof if she thought either of us were chasing her administrative personnel. The power imbalances alone were enough to make me keep my distance even if I was ever tempted by the terrifyingly self-composed secretary.

"Caroline," he clarified. Her name was as soft as the bonfire hissing against the damp sand and his gaze shifted to the flames. He must have been silent for a full minute before he added, "Promise me you won't date her."

"Noah—"

"Promise."

"Yeah. She's not my type."

With that, he got to his feet, tossed his shirt aside and ran into the dark waves.

He never said a word about it again, but that was the night I discovered that, as surely as *Karlswagon* rolls through the night sky, every model since then was just for show.

Noah bounces the ball between his knees, catching it, spinning it. "You've got a type too," he says. My stomach clenches but he goes on, "I read about your dating scandal."

I lift my eyes to the dragon and the maiden, shaking my head with a measure of relief. The stupid peculiarity of Seongan celebrity culture is that it's a scandal that a grown man of more than thirty summers is dating at all. The scandal is amplified by the fact that the girl in question is a member of BLUSH, the biggest pop group to come out of East Asia.

"Is there any truth to it?"

"We did some volunteer work and went to a few fundraisers," I say, grabbing the ball out of his hands and sinking it into the basket.

"There's something you're hiding," he answers.

"When you're ready to tell me whichever chain-smoking model you're ready to make my next queen, I'll tell you about Jang Mi."

I roll the ball from my fingers and toss it to him. He takes my spot, but the ball dings off the rim. "S."

"Speaking of fundraisers... Tell me how to thank your sister. Ella drove a lot of donations to Seongan relief." I am trying too hard to sound casual, and I throw an unforgivably wild ball, missing an easy jump shot.

He makes a layup. "She had me call in a lawyer to work out the tax implications. Her single-mindedness has been driving our mother insane."

I follow him, but the ball rebounds off the rim with a thunk.

"S," he says, grinning.

"She didn't just cut a check. She rounded up well-connected friends to spread the message—and then there were all those social media posts..." Her help extended to sending late-night texts back and forth with her brother's oldest friend, listening to my worries, offering practical suggestions for broadening our media reach. Noah wants to know how I spent my time in Seong? *I* know.

I clear my throat and check the heavy locks on the area in my mind designated "Friend Zone". I simply want to make sure Ella gets credit with a family that never seems to give her enough. "I owe her one."

Noah stands at the free throw line and it swishes the ball through the net. "Yeah? Can I call in a favor?"

"You're not Ella," I say, dribbling the ball to the line. My mind flinches away from thinking about all the ways his sister is different.

"It's *for* Ella."

"Ask." I position my throw, square up. I dribble and adjust my grip.

"How do I put this?" Noah wonders. "She's struggling."

The ball stills in my hands. "Is she still mad?"

"Hey," Noah breaks my concentration. I look up. "What makes you say that?"

I blink and I'm back there, crawling into my bed at the end of every day, scrolling through her messages.

*Ella: *covert picture of Noah in front of a slideshow* Can you talk him out of being SO excited to discuss venison harvesting on the Crown lands? *Bambi emoji, skull emoji, vomit emoji**

Ella: I got you a chainsaw. (An entire shipping container of chainsaws, tbh, and enough petrol to power them for a year.) Yours is hot pink. Happy birthday!

*Ella: *edit of NGO directors skipping down the street tossing money out of their baskets* Hope tomorrow goes well! I'm praying.*

Ella: Merry Christmas! Don't ask about Freja. I saw that photo of Amma in muddy overalls and red lipstick when she met the U.N. aid envoy. Was he checking her out?

I blink and the memories retreat. "Of course she's mad," I answer, rolling the ball in my grip. "Her twin got married without her."

Noah laces his fingers behind his head. "Freja is the only thing she'll admit being mad about." He glances over to a couple of the housekeeping staff doing pilates and drops his voice. "Things are bad. Mama and Père are still—" He makes a slicing motion with his hand. "All our sisters are pairing off. She and I are the last survivors, and there's a lot of pressure on the both of us."

I dribble the ball. Keep my knees soft. Stay loose. I feel it in my chest—the way it tightens when I think she's sad or hurt or worried. "What am I supposed to do about it?" I aim, bouncing on my toes.

"She's been relieved of official duties this spring in order to be your sister's maid of honor."

Hell. *Flamen* hell. I need to keep my distance. "Can you afford that?"

"I don't think we can afford not to. It's not a punishment, but my sister has always been a loose cannon and I've never seen her so upset. In this state, she could do anything—run off with a footman, start a revolution—and my family doesn't need another PR crisis right now."

My grip on the ball hardens. "What does this favor involve?"

"Nothing much. Since you'll be so close, you can keep an eye on her for me—keep her out of trouble..." He grins. "Maybe let us know when to pack her off to a nunnery."

A favorite Wolffe family solution. I dribble, every nerve in my body screaming for rest. It's more than jetlag. Maybe I'm coming down with something.

"What do you say?" he prods. "Be her big brother?"

3

OFFICIAL PORTRAIT

ELLA

Alix's hair is the color of pink cotton candy. She jumps off the edge of the fountain outside the gates of Aldo Gardens and hauls me into a fierce hug. My best friend is model-slim and striking, one of the rare private school girls to shake off the title of *nepo baby* when she became an international fashion muse.

She doesn't hug like someone who has a luxury handbag named after her. (The Alix is as surprisingly capacious as her heart.) She hugs like she did in kindergarten, squeezing the breath out of my lungs, and squeals into my ear, turning us into a spectacle for a crowd of onlookers.

"Alix," I protest, words muffled.

She leans back, holds my chin, and tilts me this way and that, finally uttering a guttural sound at the back of her throat. "It's a crime your mother doesn't permit you to wear winged eyeliner everyday." She frowns, glancing over her shoulder. "You're not wasting all your hotness on one of these inbred aristos are you? I won't allow it."

"Hotness?" I dimple at her generosity. Tonight I'm wearing a cropped sweater, distressed jeans, and a comfortable pair of trainers. Tortoiseshell glasses perch on my nose and a leather cross-body bag is a callback to my favorite Seongan anime, *Roar's Mansion*. Calling me hot is ridiculous, but my standing policy is that I'm never too good for compliments.

I peel out of Alix's arms and get a peek at her other guests. An odd mix. Modeling friends pose for selfies on the other side of the iconic fountain, making the most of long legs and good angles. Girls from Saint Sissela's gossip languidly behind expensive sunglasses, cigarette smoke wafting gently above their heads. There is the usual assortment of weedy men from old families wearing high-waisted cream trousers and silk shirts open to their pasty chests, prepared to behave like cads given the smallest encouragement.

Loud American men who look like the only time they read is to skim the AI search results on Performance Maxing are engaged in a pull-up competition in the branches of the trees lining the grand avenue. What if I brought home a Tucker or Brody to meet my mother? A giggle escapes me. She would die. With gleaming eyes, I adjust my bag, not at all opposed to being very foolish with a man in chinos and a fleece vest. I've spent eighteen arduous months trying to find a new type. Maybe tonight is the night I finally do it.

"Ready?" Alix asks, halting my prowl.

"Did you really rent out the whole park?" I ask. Royals are rarely allowed to indulge in lavish gestures without an opinion piece in *The Holy Pelican* decrying the waste, and I feel a pinch of jealousy.

Alix nods. "We gave away a thousand tickets to low-income families for the mid-term holiday. Tom's idea." That would explain the noise coming from the amusement park.

"That's very sweet."

"He got a group discount. Tom is very good with money, even though he has none of his own."

I choke. "Alix, he's an investment banker and you met in the Hamptons. He's not exactly—"

"He's not lavish, I mean. His car is a used 2006 Toyota Corolla, and he went to an actual junkyard to find a replacement motor for the passenger side window when my blowouts kept wilting." She looks over my head and finds Tom in the crowd. When he gives her a wave, her whole face lights up. "His love language is informative YouTube home repair videos," she hisses. "Don't tease him about it."

"You wound me," I reply. The weather on this April night is cool but dry, and a light breeze ruffles my hair, sending thousands of fairy lights dancing. "If he has a brother, set me up."

"He has three sisters," Alix laughs, tugging me up onto the edge of the fountain. A summer dress skims her bare legs and I worry for her. She's the kind of person who trust-falls into relationships, and I wonder if Tom has learned to bring layers.

"Do one of your big whistles," she asks. I pinch my fingers against my lips and let out a piercing sound, cutting through the cigarette smoke and ennui. More than five hundred heads turn in our direction and Tom threads through the crowd, reaching for Alix. I see that he is wearing a sensible sweater and carries an extra jacket slung over his arm.

She catches his hand and laces her fingers through his. "We are sharing the park," she calls. "If anyone acts like some spoiled princess— Oh, no offense Ella."

"None taken."

She continues. "—you're dead to me."

As one body, the crowd surges towards the open gates, weaving around the fountain like fish in a stream. My security officer, Thor, is keeping his distance, and I take my phone out, framing the bright lights of Aldo Gardens, my best friend, the ridiculous crowd...

Alix pauses at the gates. "If any of you gets into a scrape, don't come looking for the bride," she laughs. "Find Ella or Marc."

At the sound of his name and the implication of his presence, a crisp, electric current prickles along the back of my neck. Marc? I hunt the streaming crowd for a familiar figure, half Sondish, half Seongan. I go up on my toes to look, my fingers working through my curls, and brush away the sensation.

"I'm right here, Ells."

My heart stops and I close my eyes, hoping for a reset.

This nervousness is just my limbic system. Those early-formed neural pathways always herd me toward specific reactions like a rabbit following a game trail through a forest. It's science, and when I turn around, it's going to disappear. He'll be what I have decided he should be—Noah's best friend.

I turn, full of resolve. It melts slowly away when Marc emerges from the shadows of the tree-lined avenue wearing a dark Henley, the sleeves pushed up his muscled forearms. He holds a light jacket in his fist, a pair of jeans emphasizes his long legs, and a rigid gold circlet bands one wrist, kissing the base of his thumb.

When he gets closer I will note how his eyes are dark, fringed with lashes that make old women hold his chin and mutter, "Wasted on a man." I will observe that his lips are full, curving in a gentle but unmistakably sensuous line. I've known him so long, I tell myself, that everything about him is old news.

Still, my cheeks flush. My fingertips itch to touch him but I press the sensitivity away, urging myself to have some sense.

He's leaner than he was last summer, his jawline more pronounced. I notice that, too.

He stops maybe three yards away, looking at me—lips slightly parted, teeth set, eyes intent and appraising. Some profoundly adolescent part of me rips the clinical clipboard out of imaginary hands and scribbles her own observation. Marc looks like a powerful nature spirit, assuming human form to tempt honest maidens with the promise of ruin.

Damn limbic system.

I grip the strap of my bag and summon Smart Ella from the basement where she's lying bound and gagged. "You didn't say a word about coming back."

"You didn't ask." His glance flicks down the length of me, making his own observations.

I fidget under his leisurely inspection. "I'm still as short as I've ever been."

He gives a low laugh and I close my eyes, repeating the mantra I use when I'm in Mama's jewel vault. *You can't afford it.*

"Welcome me home," he commands, holding his arms wide.

I take a breath, and it comes with a painful hitch. This is the reason I had to fall out of love with Marc van Heyden. Every time he throws his arm over my shoulder or kisses my temple, the simple, careless affection feels like turning a screw into my skin. It's easier to shut away the part of me that wants complicated, grown-up things, because she is forever doomed to be disappointed.

I hop into his arms and he rocks on his feet. The smell of his cologne, a mix of pine and magnolia, drifts between us and I push out of his hold. I want more than he can ever give, and pretending things haven't changed between us since I was fifteen is safer.

"What did you bring me?" I demand, putting out my palm.

He clicks his tongue. "I wasn't on vacation. There was a lot going on—"

I pinch his waist. "Cool story," I reply, my hand still out.

He places a gauzy parcel on my palm. "Someday I won't bring you anything. What will you do then?"

"I'll have more room on my bed, for one thing." Thanks to Marc, I own more than a dozen stuffed raccoons.

"This won't take up room in your life at all."

I work the bow free, and a thin gold chain strung with tiny golden racoons falls into my hand. My mouth tucks with a smile. "This is a high-class way to call me a trash panda," I say, winding the chain around my wrist. It's way too big. No matter. "I can get it shortened."

He takes it out of my hands and propels me backward until the edge of the fountain hits me on the back of the legs. I sit abruptly, fighting off a storm of hormones. Residual attraction. I can't expect it to go away all at once, just because I told it to.

"You will not." He sinks down on one knee, lifts my shoe to rest against his thigh, and turns his attention to the clasp, warm fingers brushing against the delicate bones of my ankle. He adjusts the chain, lightly tickling my skin, and looks up. "Do you like it?"

My cheeks are on fire and I look away from his steady gaze. "It's nice."

He winds a finger through one of my curls, and tugs it—a silent reproof for my apparent lack of enthusiasm. If I was fifteen a few minutes ago, I'm twelve now. By the end of the night, I fear he'll be feeding me fish crackers from a snack baggie.

"Ready to have some fun?" He puts a hand on my back to lead me through the delicate lacework of metal vines embellishing the front gate, and when I shift, his fingers brush my skin. He pulls away like I'm made of magma.

I grip the strap of my bag. "I have substantive, serious-minded questions about your time in Seong, Marc. I really do."

"But?" he laughs, leading me down the promenade.

I fist my hand under my chin as though I'm holding a microphone. "Are you dating Lee Jang Mi of BLUSH?" I don't give him a chance to answer before I fire off a few more questions, mimicking the insane coverage of a man whose only mission in Seong was humanitarian. "Are you prepared to apologize to her fans? What is her skincare routine? When can we expect a fourth studio album? Can you confirm or deny that the lyrics of *Third-Generation Rich Man* are about you?"

I tilt my hand under his chin and he captures my fist in a light grip. Ducking his head, he brings it closer to his lips. "Those lyrics would be?"

Marc's warm breath on my skin sends a wave of heat through my veins. "He looks like a billion/It's not his billions/No ATM at the minute/All I want is to get it, get it, get it." I clear my throat. "Those lyrics."

His eyes dance. "She uses Blossom & Branch skincare." He releases me. "I brought some for you...for all of you."

Oh. I halt for a beat, letting the bomb spiral through my belly that Marc and Jang Mi aren't just a fevered invention of the Seongan press. They're close enough that he knows about her morning makeup routine. They're really— Oh.

I inhale sharply. This was always going to happen, and it's going to make everything easier. In desperation, I hail some friends and drag us into a loud, laughing group that runs from the merry-go-round to the Stop and Drop. The din of laughter and screaming almost drowns out my thoughts.

At the top of an enormous pink slide, Marc, arranged on a rectangle of burlap, hooks an arm around my waist and hauls me in front of him. "Ready?" he asks, mouth by my ear, holding me close. When we cross the finish line, I leap up like I've had a scalding.

"Gravitron?" somebody suggests, and the group goes off. When Marc moves to follow, I grab his arm.

"Are you insane?" I ask.

"What?"

"Allow me to take you through the dark forest of memory—"

"Stop," he smiles.

"—when riders of the Gravitron—a harmless ride, beloved by all—were terrorized by one Marc van Heyden."

"I had an upset tummy."

A masterpiece of understatement. "The ride was out of commission for the rest of the night and *Amma* had to settle the cleaning bill for an entire row of girls on the other side of the wheel. I still don't understand the physics of that."

"One time. I can't even believe you remember."

I shake my head. "Remember? I'm haunted. I used to think you were kind of cute, but that was the night that killed my crush forever."

Yes. He knows about the crush, and he knows it's something to laugh about. I admitted to a tiny, toss-away, years-old infatuation for the same reasons a magician uses a leggy assistant and a smoke-machine. It's a misdirection so that Marc won't see all the years I've spent wishing he was mine.

We pass a shooting gallery where some of Tom's American friends are having a quick-draw competition. It's not too late to find my Tucker or Brody.

Marc catches me looking at them. "The sights are faulty," he tells me. "You won't hit what you're aiming at. Where are we going next?"

"No spinny rides."

He grins. "You'd think I'd outgrow it."

My lips tighten. "There are some things you don't outgrow."

We continue up the midway, parting around families, casually keeping eye contact as we walk in tandem on either side of the crowd.

A group of teenagers knocks into me, and Marc shouts something I can't hear over the sound of a calliope. I shake my head and he tries again, this time with gestures. Finally, he cleaves his way through the stream and herds me through a low doorway, pulling a curtain closed behind him until we're squeezed in a photobooth so tightly that there's nowhere to look but right at his collarbone.

"Let the crowd pass," he says, his throat working in a swallow. "We can get a picture."

I hold my phone up. "There are hundreds of pictures of us."

"So we'll give one to Alix," he says, tapping a credit card to the reader. The screen powers up, framing us inside a tiny digital box. "Smile."

I push the curly hair out of my face and look at the unblinking lens as a countdown beeps. *Click.*

The bench is narrow and Marc throws an arm around me. "This isn't a royal portrait," he chides, brushing his fingers against my waist. Even the suggestion of being tickled has me squirming. *Click.*

"You're wasting the film," I say, smacking his hand. He drags me closer and my blood thickens. *Click.*

"Hand heart," he says, lifting his hand to form half the heart—fingers curled over, thumb forming the point. I lift my hand and it's comical how small my side is. *Click.*

"We'll give her that one," I say, scrambling to my feet. I trip past him, but we tangle and he catches me on the narrow bench, bracing his hands on my waist. *Click.*

"I thought it was over."

"Looks like we got one more shot," he answers. His hands haven't moved.

The silence stretches and he takes a breath. Before he can speak, he's pushed from behind and I'm squashed into the corner, saved from a parade of a couple of Saint Sissela girls by his forearm braced against the wall.

"...an actual photo. So fun," one says, peering over Marc's shoulder, pushing him against me. "Ella! You escaped!"

Yasmin is not the brightest bulb, but she also thinks the fact that I have to show up to community centers on snowy Tuesday mornings in heels and stockings is hilarious. I love her.

Marc dips his head, breath stirring the hair near my ear. "Isn't that the one you put in a headlock?"

She called Freja The Hunchback of the House of Wolffe in the first week of school. My cheek brushes his and I whisper, "Just once. She made a handsome apology."

"Ella?" Dahlia, a bubbly brunette whose romantic decisions might be a form of self harm, squishes into the booth. The last boyfriend was an aide to the prime minister who treated her like the hired help.

I make a muffled answer and feel Marc's chest shaking with laughter as the camera clicks through a series of photos. When we finally emerge from the booth, Dahlia turns to Marc, her eyes wide and her lashes fluttering. "Welcome home, *Neerheid* van Heyden. Are you back for good?"

He reaches into the photo depository to retrieve our strip. "That's the idea," he says, ripping off the photo with my uptight expression. He hands it to Dahlia. "Compliments of the Crown." He puts the remaining photos in his wallet, nods his farewell to the others, and takes my hand, guiding me to a picnic area to catch my breath. Marc doesn't have to be told that I don't love crowds or tight spaces.

"Stroopwafel?" he asks.

When I nod, he leaves me on a bench under a tree that glows with fairy lights and shivers with soft pink blossoms. Soon he returns with a flat, syrup-filled waffle as big as my head, and he devours the piece I tear off for him in one bite.

The sound of Alix's unmistakable laugh carries over the distant music. "I like him. Do you?" I ask. "Tom."

The edges of his mouth pull in thought. "Alix doesn't always think when she's throwing herself into one of her passions."

Marc isn't wrong. Being a muse isn't a full-time gig. My friend has dabbled in being a Pixy influencer and a pop singer, hiked one of the lesser Alps for charity, and now works as a social media manager for the van Heyden estate. She ran Lindenholm when her family was gone. By some miracle, the place didn't burn to the ground.

"Are you worried she doesn't really love him?"

"I'm worried she's not using her head."

I let the syrup dissolve on my tongue and offer Marc another portion. "Who thinks when they fall in love? No, don't answer that. I can't imagine you or Noah being carried away by something soft and feral."

He swallows, the muscles of his throat working, and my pulse lifts. I shift my gaze to examine the stroopwafel, torn in the shape of a ragged heart.

"Well," he whispers, giving my hair a brotherly tug. "You'd better not be carried away. I won't have you running off and getting engaged, too."

4

SPEEDRUN

MARC

"Never say never," she says.

Ella's silky curl rolls between my thumb and forefinger, wrapped in the scent of blossoms and warm sugar. "Hmmm?"

"I hope 'She horrified the government' is on my epitaph."

She looks up, and her green eyes, crinkled with laughter, catch the light. Her freckles and a soft blush are just visible under a dusting of powder. I know this face already, but I hardly hear her for how intently I'm tracing the lines of it. I know her brows are soft to the touch and that her chin narrows, following the shape of a heart. I know that her mouth is expressive.

Kissable.

"The opportunity to cause a national scandal was wasted on Freja," she continues. "You should have been here to see it. When she eloped, it was on the front page of every newspaper and all over those trashy podcasts. Comments sections were ripping her to pieces and she was completely unbothered. If it had been me, the flame wars would have been visible from space."

I release a sharp breath, her curl slipping from my fingers. I don't like to talk about Ella's eventual marriage. I don't like sitting this close to her, noticing everything from the way her tongue sweeps up sweet crumbs at the corner of her mouth to the way she shakes her curls out of her face. I don't like how empty my hands feel.

I blink. It's jet lag, the way my mind rocks between hyperfixation and the inability to focus where I need to. Just jet lag. I've only been back five days.

I reach for another piece of stroopwafel, but Ella holds it high above her head, just out of my reach. "Ask nicely."

Doesn't she know me? We tussle for a brief but intense moment, her laughter turning into a piercing yelp as my hands band the sensitive skin at her waist. Her great weakness.

She lands a hard blow against my chest with her elbow but I narrow the gap in one quick jerk, reaching for her wrist. Gently, but firmly, I drag the stroopwafel between us and take a huge bite, wolfing it down.

"*Whui-ho*," I taunt, brushing the tip of my tongue along my lip. It's a Seongan phrase, meant to encourage. *You can do it.*

Ella shoves my chest but I don't budge. "You're a pest."

"You never win that game. I don't know why you play it."

She slides me a look. "You're going to lose a hand someday. And you'll deserve it. And I won't cry when we give it a Viking burial. I'll shoot the flaming arrow myself."

"Ella," I admonish, resting my arm across the back of the bench, playing with her curls again. Technically, we're in public, and this is where Noah specifically told me I was to get Ella to behave.

I grip the wooden slats and try for another piece of stroopwafel. She's faster this time, slapping my hand, capturing it, lacing her fingers through mine. I don't even try to twist out of her grasp.

After she polishes off the rest of the treat, she releases me, brushing her palms with exaggerated elegance, and flashes a look of triumph. Holding a small fist between us, she gives me a tart smile. "*Whui-ho.*"

My stomach tenses with desire. Just a flash. Nothing particular to her. In the past months I haven't had time to think of women, and this must be a sign that I finally do.

I'm no danger to Ella—Noah made me promise to keep clear of staff and sisters, and she is no danger to me. Even before I left for Seong, Ella and Alix started spending more time in Handsel than Lindenholm. When I visited the Summer Palace, I would see flashes of her on her way out the door, and it's obvious that she makes no effort when I'm around. One time she went on about cufflinks so long I started to wonder if kissing her would make her shut up.

On the whole, however, Ella has made it as easy as possible to keep my hands to myself. A furrow gathers on my brow. Why is it that I never have to calculate how easy Freja, Alma, and Clara make it?

I locate a rational answer, looking to dissolve these unsettled feelings. For months, we've been almost as far apart on the globe as two people can be, but Ella was the first person I messaged when I woke up in the morning and the last person I texted before going to sleep. Of course there's an added frisson of awareness when I am right next to her. Eventually, I'll get used to it and we'll figure out how to go back to the way things were.

The furrow deepens. The sight of her figure poured into curve-hugging jeans isn't helping.

She wonders if I've ever been at the mercy of something warm and feral?

Yes. I've acquired some recent experience, princess.

My friendship—a brotherhood, almost—with Noah is the closest relationship I have, outside my family. He warned me away from his sisters in direct, straightforward words, and this is nothing but jet lag—this night that seems to be nudging categories and definitions sideways.

I lift my hand to brush the curls within reach, so softly she can't feel it. In Sondmark, public opinion polls can't agree that the sun rises in the east, but they all agree that Ella is everyone's favorite princess. Statistically speaking, these feelings I'm trying to tamp down are nothing special.

She leans forward, her curls spilling out of my hand. "It's time to ask you those substantive questions about your time in Seong," she smiles. "Do you want to talk?"

I shake my head, then I nod.

This week, I gave a brief report to Queen Helena and the Secretary of Foreign Affairs that amounted to a series of facts and proposals. Ella doesn't need that. She was there with me every day and knows more than anyone. A memory edges through my mind and my mouth tucks with a smile.

Ella: Do you think I won't notice that you haven't sent me a check-in photo in six days?

Marc: Hey, Ells. Busy here. Relief workers belonging to the Seongan Statebuilding Party were found misappropriating funds and funneling them to supporters. My mother is on a tear.

Ella: Check-in photo, Marc.

*Marc: *photo of the left side of my face, grubby with upland dust**

Ella: I could text Amma, if you want, and force it out of you.

*Marc: *photo of the right side of my face—faded bruise on my cheekbone, and a new chunk taken out of my right index finger with a grimy, bloody trail down my wrist* A tree trunk rolled the wrong way. I didn't want to worry you.*

Ella: Not worried. I'm certain you're communicating to me from the line outside the infirmary.

My next photo was of a clean bandage and a clean face.

There's nothing we left out of our texts, but I find myself talking, telling her again about the mad scramble for supplies and order in those early days and all the ways Seong is still in trouble.

"I'm glad to be back," I say at last, watching Ella, her chin tipped toward the fairy lights and the blossom-laden branches. "I am."

"But?" She brings her gaze down to mine.

"But I was able to hop a flight and get out of it. For those with deep roots, there's nowhere to run."

She reaches for my hand, holding onto it in silence. Eventually, she turns it over, inspecting the right index finger and the slightly wonky fingernail, and grunts when the healing meets with her approval.

"Now you," I say, liking the way she cradles my scarred hand. "Tell me about Freja."

She shifts her weight and rocks forward but I hook a finger through her belt loop and anchor her to the bench.

Her muscles tense, and from over her shoulder, I catch a glimpse of an illuminated sign on the midway. "Try Your Luck."

"If you run, I'll chase you and we'll end up wrestling in the grass." I crane my neck, gazing doubtfully into the gloom. "You look too cute in that sweater to ruin it."

Her cheeks pinken and a sudden wave of definitely jet lag rolls through me. Looking at Ella that way is a mistake I won't make again.

"What do you want to know?" she asks.

I give the loop a little shake. She'll tell me everything. Alix is her best friend, but the first time Ella ran away from the palace as a ten-year-old princess who talked the palace chauffeur into driving her to Lindenholm with a pile of bespoke luggage and her favorite gaming console, she ran to me. I was the one who carted Ella off to the stables, where she groomed the goats, told me how her mama was "going to be gone for three whole months this time," and cried her eyes out.

I was the one who fixed it so that she could stay with *Amma* instead of her nanny. I was the one who made a pinky promise that she could come to us every time Freja was in the hospital or the queen was on a diplomatic mission. I remind myself of this past, using the solid wholesomeness of it as a shield to keep my thoughts in line.

Ella shifts sideways on the bench, folding her arms over the backrest, and leans her chin on top of stacked fists. "I don't have the right to be mad. Freja's happy—more than happy. She's," her brow gathers in thought, "radiant. What kind of terrible person can be mad at radiant?"

A smile teases my mouth. Ella is radiant when she's not even trying.

"Are you mad about *who* she married or *how* she married?" I ask. I stretch my legs out, crossing them at the ankles, and fold my arms over my chest. No more touching.

"Oskar's fine. He's got great hair. He frowns an unholy amount, but he feeds her when she's hungry. I mean, he's not my type, but I get it."

Wait. "You have a type?"

She ignores my question and closes her eyes briefly, curly lashes resting on her cheeks. "I don't even mind the elopement, in theory. No one was invited but—"

"You're her twin. She might have made an exception."

"Thank you." She pounds my arm to emphasize the point, adding, "It's wild that Mama isn't out for blood, but of course there's one rule for Freja and another for me. Can you imagine her city-leveling wrath if I eloped?"

"You are not going to elope," I snap. A brief silence follows and I clear my throat. "I'm surprised you've held onto so much righteous fury for so long."

"Four months is no time," she mutters.

I think of the friend she once put in a headlock. "You're bad at holding grudges."

"I'm trying to hold this one."

I nudge her shoulder with my own. "Have you talked?"

"We see each other probably once a week. I'm not giving her the silent treatment."

I read between the lines, a power I only have when it comes to Ella. "Let me guess: you're always in a group. There's always a show on in the background. You can't talk. You've got a meeting in five."

A dimple tucks the softness of her cheek. "It would do terrible things for my grudge if I let her have her say." Then her smile fades. "It feels like I've been trying to get close to Freja since we shared the same womb, but I exhaust her, she thinks I'm too loud, and her hugs last microseconds." She swallows hard. "You know she doesn't flinch away from Oskar?"

This is worse than a grudge—Ella has a bruised heart. But when the distant sound of a rollercoaster rumbles across the park, she claps her hands, clearing the air. "It's fine," she says, an expression she uses exclusively when it's *not* fine. "I'm just ticked off at her for messing up my exit plans."

Not this again. My hand lands on my chest and I groan. "How old are you, woman?"

"I'll be twenty-seven next month."

"Is your plan still in a fuzzy unicorn binder with a tiny brass lock?"

She snorts. "Give a girl some credit. My digital records are encrypted and stored in an external hard drive."

When she scoots closer, a spark of nervousness rolls through me like a chunk of glowing coal. Her voice drops into a conspiratorial whisper. "Here's the plan. I'll take a sabbatical from being a working royal to pursue a graduate degree in computer science, and my mother can temporarily split my patronages between my siblings. When I finish, Mama will try to force me back into tights and tiaras, but I'll be like, 'Okay, but my research is literally saving the world.' And then somebody anonymous," she laces her fingers over her heart and I look away like I've touched a hot stove, "will leak the details of my heroic saintliness and Her Majesty's hands will be tied."

I clear my throat. "Quick question, Ells. How are you going to literally save the world?"

"Maybe I'll create an ultra-efficient kidney donation database or configure AI tools to track endangered species." Her eyes glint with unrealized schemes, and the sight hits my heart like a bird of prey zeroing in on a field mouse. "What do you think my mother is going to do when faced with a choice between letting entire coconut crab populations die off or forcing me to give a speech to the Association of Medieval Heraldry?"

I touch the tip of her nose with a bent knuckle. "This is the face of a woman prepared to devote her life to saintliness?"

In a flash, her posture becomes prim. Well, as prim as she can manage with all those curves. "After a year of good deeds, I'll renounce my place in the line of succession with profound regret, set up a trust for Sumatran orangutans or something, get a sprawling, modern place on a sun-kissed coast with excellent internet speed, and become a lady-recluse."

I lift a brow. "It sounds like a Bond lair."

She lifts a brow. "If people leave me in peace, I'll ditch the moat of laser sharks. You're invited to drop in anytime. You'll find me on the beach wearing sunglasses that cover half my face."

Another image walks out of the sea and into my head. My mouth dries up. "And a bikini with a utility belt?"

She flicks my arm. "I'll be so far away that even if I forget to use a compostable bag to carry my groceries, the editorial board of *The Holy Pelican* will have to step all the way off my case."

I listen to this crack-pot scheme tracing the freckles over the bridge of her nose with my gaze. Ella has been coming up with plans to run away for as long as I've known her. I see it for what it is—a security blanket, something to wrap herself up in against the pain of being treated roughly by the people who are supposed to love her best.

"You think you could follow through?" I ask. Research for Noah.

"Thanks to Freja, my timeline has to be reworked, but I'll never stop trying to escape this funhouse of horrors."

When I watch the light play over Ella's face, I feel a seismic rumbling in my chest—the kind that used to send me diving under a table. Signs that the ground beneath our feet is shifting.

"Speaking of," I say, standing abruptly and striding off. She catches up to me and we pass Thor, her security officer, attempting to hide the fact that he's standing exactly twenty meters from his asset by holding a massive bag of cotton candy as he sweeps the perimeter. "We're headed to the funhouse, but we'll come back this way," I tell him. "Ten minutes."

He nods.

I keep talking, trying to avoid the kind of dangerous silences that give my body too much time to react to her. "You've done a lot of fashion diplomacy," I say. Even tonight, her *Roar's Mansion* purse will get a mention in the fashion press once Alix releases photos of her party, bringing the topic around to Seong. No one in Sondmark has been as focused on the ongoing crisis as Ella. "I wanted to thank you. I'm sure it was tricky."

"You know how much I love disappointing my mother," she laughs, dismissing my gratitude. "Anyway, how am I going to get my Seongan dramas if the studios can't rebuild? There it is," she says, outpacing me. I have to break into a jog to keep up until we arrive at the funhouse entrance, blinking with garish green lights.

"Speedrun?" she challenges.

I scope out the dim interior and the angled mirrors. "How about we take things slow and steady?"

She makes a face. "Boring."

"Safe," I counter.

"Same thing. Ready?" The tip of her shoe digs into an invisible line. "Set." She turns her brilliant eyes up at me and I promise myself that tomorrow I'll start watching her in ways Noah would approve of.

"Go!"

5

No Filter

ELLA

I shoot through the funhouse maze with crisp certainty, detecting false reflections, and building up speed as I go. Light flashes across my eyes in a dizzying kaleidoscope of color, but I keep running.

I don't see the mirror until I slam full-tilt into it, cracking my head against the surface. I reel back while the surface flexes, distorting my shape—short, tall, short, tall. Pain splinters through my brain and behind my eyes, and I sink to my knees.

"Ella? Ella!" Marc sounds far away but closing in fast.

"I'm dying," I gasp.

"Keep talking." His voice bounces around the glass and metal. "I'm coming. Is there blood?"

I lift my hand and groan when I see the slick surface. Mama is going to murder me.

"Ella?"

I've got a little cry in my throat when I admit, "I need medical attention." *Vede.* There's a goose egg rising under my hand.

Marc slips through an opening I was certain was a dead end. "Let me see," he commands. Gentle fingers prod the skin, and when I flinch, his mouth presses into a line. "*Elskede,*" he murmurs the common endearment. His mouth is tense, and I think he would rather be swearing. When his hand cups the side of my face, I grit my teeth. "Let's get you out of here."

We make it into the fresh night air, and he consults the park map for the first aid station while I take a long breath through my nose. Hot and cold waves flash through my body in sickening succession. My head spins, but he crouches in front of me, presenting his back. "Hop on."

No. Not that. Marc has carried me on his back when I reeked of the muddy patch in the bottom of the kitchen garden or was bleeding from some scrape with a farm animal who didn't want to be hugged. But I'm a grown woman, or so my mother attempts to drill into my throbbing skull, and I do not ride piggyback.

"You look like death," he says, merciless in his honesty. "Hop on."

I grip his shoulders and he eases me up as gingerly as a blossom falling into a palm, stepping away in a swift, soft-footed stride. We skirt the noisy midway, and sooner than I hoped, he settles me into a reclining chair in the brilliantly-lit first aid station. He perches on a stool while the nurse attends me.

"How were you injured?" she asks, examining the wound, tipping my head back and forth. My brain feels like a bucket of wet sand and I want to throw up on her shoes.

"We were in the funhouse," Marc starts.

She rips open a package, extracting a sterile swab. "Are you under the influence, Your Royal Highness?"

I groan. "Only of my own poor judgment."

When the ointment hits the scrape, I suck in a sharp breath, and Marc's large hand settles on my ankle, rolling the thin chain under his thumb.

"Ice for now," she says, stripping her gloves off and handing me an ice pack. "*Neerheid* van Heyden—" she murmurs, eyes lingering on Marc in clear violation of ethical standards.

"Have we met?" he asks, gently curious.

Her cheeks flush. "You were just voted the Hottest Man in Sondmark. There's a copy of the magazine in the breakroom." She jerks a thumb toward the doorway and I emit a sharp double cough, recalling her to a sense of duty. "Are you responsible for her?" she asks.

He frowns at my forehead, hardly sparing her a glance. "Definitely."

The "trained" "medical" "professional" sighs. "I don't think it's a concussion, but let's be on the safe side. No driving. A good night of sleep is fine, but I'd like someone to keep an eye on her for the next twelve hours. If the headache gets worse, seek further care."

Marc's pocket buzzes. "It's Thor," he says, checking his phone, "wondering where we are."

I lift the ice pack. "Gimmie."

He surrenders the phone and I angle my body so that it looks like Marc and I are standing side-by-side. I snap a photo and engage speech-to-text. "Ella wants to head home. I'll drive. Can you send someone from the palace to collect her car?"

He looks over my shoulder. "Did you seriously crop your wound out? He'll think—"

I toss him the phone. "I learned from the best."

My head throbs all the way across town and up the hill to the Summer Palace. When we enter the Great Hall, Marc hands his keys to the night footmen while I frown at the velvet treads of the marble staircase.

"Do you need another lift?" he asks.

"I'm fine," I grit out. It might be true.

He ignores me and slides his hands around my waist, lifting me against his chest. We're halfway up the stairs before I work out that being carried with my nose pressed against his collarbone is much worse for my peace of mind than being transported piggyback.

"You're going to drop me," I insist, shifting my weight.

I receive a slap on my bottom. "You're being carried up the palace staircase by the Hottest Man in Sondmark, as determined by the discerning readership of *Vrouw WOW* magazine. Enjoy it."

I fumble for my remote key. "I knew you could tell she was checking you out."

He pushes through the door of my suite. "I'm not blind."

True. He isn't blind to other women. Only blind to me.

He sets me down, peels my bag away, and drops it on the sofa. "Are you good?" he asks, standing too close as he examines my bump.

"Perfect." I step away too quickly, and he steadies me with a hand on my waist.

Taking a sharp breath, I paw through my hard-earned wisdom like a woman digs into her purse for a pain pill. Marc is a dead end. Falling out of love with him has taken every ounce of discipline I'm capable of. I can't go back. I won't.

So it's just friendship—a relationship status as simple as water. That being the case, I allow him to steer me into the bathroom and deposit me on a stool. He opens and shuts a few drawers, and hauls a low chair over so he can work a fluffy, pink headband around the bruise.

"Ells—" His thumb traces the raised edge.

"I'm fine," I insist, even as my vision slips sideways.

He starts removing my make-up and I surrender. The truth is that I can't lean over a sink in this condition and the sooner he gets me into bed the happier I'll be.

My brow furrows. No. Wait.

"Stop thinking so hard," he says, smoothing the furrow. I close my eyes against his face but I still smell his scent and feel the dizzying sensation of his fingers on my skin.

He rubs in a night serum, the last step in an abbreviated skincare routine, and I force myself to my feet—away from his closeness. A wave of nausea shudders through my frame.

"Whoa, I got you," he says, hands splayed across my back.

I shrug his hands away and edge toward the closet. "I just moved too fast."

"Yes. And if you do that, you'll fall over. Can I help with the pajamas?" he asks.

I grip his arm and say, deadly serious, "I would rather die."

His eyes dance. "You need eleven more hours of observation."

I turn him to the door, ignore the throbbing of my head, and push against Marc's back. He plants his feet like a Seongan statue of an ancient warrior prince. Immoveable. Freakishly hot.

"Doctor's orders," he says, spinning. I land into him with a thud and he holds me steady. My defenses are down. My judgement is sketchy. My hands are on Marc's rock hard chest and he needs to leave.

I push again. "I'm not sure she was even a nurse."

He shrugs and my hands move up and down with the play of muscles. *Dominanstid.* I shove myself away, will the rocking in my head to subside, and retreat to my closet for a pair of flannel pajamas. "Figure out where you're going because you can't stay here," I call.

"It's a palace—I can find another room," he says. "I'll just text your mother—"

"Traitor." I poke my head around the door, faster than is wise, and blink against the pain. "You wouldn't."

He lifts his phone, finger hovering perilously near the green call button.

"There's nowhere for you to sleep," I return to the closet, wrestling with my pajamas. A light sheen of sweat glistens on my misshapen forehead. Even the exertion of carrying on a conversation with a closed door is exhausting. Still, I persevere. "You're, what, 190 centimeters?" I sound offhand, but I know exactly how tall he is. "Too tall for the sofa."

When I emerge, he's sitting on the edge of my bed, bouncing lightly. Testing it.

"*I'm* not taking the sofa," I say. The only other option is a hammock chair. He'd be crippled for life.

He smooths the bedding. "Your bed is big enough for two."

Oxygen vanishes from the room. This is what comes of maidens consorting with forest spirits. This is what comes of being carried in the arms of the man you used to love when you're not in your right mind. Trouble. "We're not sharing a bed," I snap.

"You'd rather die?" he echoes with a little laugh.

There's nothing to do but turn it into a joke. "Worse. We'll fall in love," I say, giving a horrified shiver.

He grins, running with my tired Seongan drama plot line. "Our families will fight in the Great Hall."

"Your mother will slap me across the face with spicy fermented cabbage and scream about how I corrupted her treasured son."

"Corrupted?" The word is soft, barely audible. Then his eyes narrow. "My mother would never scream at you. *Amma* loves you and your mama loves me," he says, giving another bounce on the mattress. "They'd have us married before the month was out."

There's a sharp pain in my lungs, but I excise the feeling and replace it with cold-blooded reason. "See? Disaster. There's not room for you, me, and all those stuffed animals."

He leans back, palms against my coverlet. "We could build them into a wall."

I do a hot word problem. How many plush racoons would it take to form a wall tall enough and thick enough to keep me away from Marc in my bed? Answer: Infinity of them.

"No," I clip, alive to the possibility of danger. "No sofa. No bed. You have nowhere to sleep."

Marc pushes off the mattress. Instead of heading to the door, tossing health warnings over his shoulder, he opens an antique linen cupboard and digs out a thick coverlet and pillow.

"When I'm in Seong, I often sleep in the traditional way," he says, spreading them on the floor along my side of the bed. He looks up with a taunting smile. "Give up, Ells. I hate to lose."

I release a shaky breath. "I have an extra toothbrush under the sink."

We brush in silence, but I feel as though I've stepped into one of those slice-of-life movies that throw the beauty and tragedy of ordinary things into soft relief—the peeled tangerine rind catching the light, the wind blowing papers into the ocean, the ice cream offered to a crying child, a solitary dinner eaten under a cruel light. Beauty and tragedy. I listen to the rhythm of us and wonder which this is.

He wipes his face and catches my eye. I return a strained smile. I was good. I was good for so long. I was good when I made promises to Future Me and My Lutheran Babies that I'd cut out this fruitless love for the man who had zero interest in being their father. I was good when I focused on self care and my exit plan.

There is evidence that I wasn't good all the time. Things between Marc and me got muddy over text these last months, but he was more than 8,000 aeronautical kilometers away. When our teasing tipped into flirtation, it presented no real danger.

I close my eyes and remember how Marc would send me a snap of himself hiking through a forest in traditional Seongan workwear—baggy pants, a utilitarian button-up shirt, a hot pink chainsaw hooked to a utility belt, and a dusty face mask covering his nose and chin. He would type a caption: "No filter. What are you wearing?"

He always seemed to send these when I was still in bed, but I'd send him a selfie, no matter what. Would I angle myself out of the morning sun? Yes. Would I rake my hair in order? Also, yes. He said no filter, but he didn't say no judgement.

I step over his pallet and slip into bed, the sheets cool and soft against my skin. My hands grip the edge of the blanket and my eyes bore into the ceiling as I prepare to count off every second of this long night.

With the flick of the light switch, he settles on the floor.

Perhaps he can sense my restiveness because he begins to talk, his voice warm and dark, bridging the distance between us. He tells me stories about clearing roads in Seong—of the endless wreckage caused by the earthquake and tsunami, of whole houses carried off their foundations. He speaks of ancient characters found deep in the hills—mountain gods in the form of goat farmers scouting for survivors and castaways, and friendly fire spirits tending their woks, feeding the volunteer force day and night.

We drift off to sleep like that, laughing softly back and forth, and I dream that he rouses me hours later when the night shadows have deepened and the palace is at rest from turret to dungeon.

"How's your head?" he asks, cupping a hand around his cell phone flashlight, shielding me from the sharp glare.

In the dream before this one, I was wearing a fluffy pink cupcake dress, surrounded by fortress walls, a churning moat, and canons belching balls of flame as a hero hopped inexorably in my direction.

"The princess is the worst," I grouch.

He pushes the hair off my forehead and I feel myself slipping back into cupcakes and fire canons. Cool lips touch my forehead and his whisper reaches me on the frontier between these dreams. "Not my princess."

I wake to Clara leaning over my bed, her nose scrunched up. "You look awful."

I sit up, clutching my head, and my gaze drifts to the floor. Marc left no sign of his stay.

"What are you doing here?" I ask.

"Marc van Heyden knocked on my door around seven. He said you needed to be checked at," she looks at her watch, "nine. So how are you?"

Clara is clad in workout attire and her high ponytail swings as she adjusts her laces. It takes a second to realize that the faint irritation I feel is being cheated out of brushing my teeth with Marc this morning and roasting him for how anxious he was.

"The headache is manageable." I reach for my forehead and feel the stomach-sliding sensation of encountering skin where there shouldn't be.

"Great. Now, on a scale of one to ten, how excited would College Ella have felt about Marc sleeping over?" My sisters know about the old crush, too.

I don't even consider telling her the truth. "Negative four. I almost barfed down the back of his shirt."

"Ew. Are we hiding this from Mama?" She looks doubtfully at my forehead.

I reach for my phone and scroll to my calendar. "My next engagement isn't for days." We might be able to keep this secret.

"Alright," she agrees, stretching her quad, "I never saw you. I was never here."

Clara jogs off and my phone vibrates. I swipe on Marc's text and grin.

"No filter, Ells. What are you wearing?"

6

No Choice

MARC

The Han Heyden office tower casts a long shadow. An armored Mercedes pulls up in the chilly forecourt, and when Thor opens her door, Ella steps out. The way she does it isn't like any other woman in the royal family—neutered, bloodless, brisk. Ella moves like Italian cinema.

She waves, setting off a cheer from the small crowd gathered outside, and I take a long look. *Vede.* She's dressed wrong. I know the palace dress code as well as she does. I know that white trainers, glasses, a tailored jumpsuit, and a navy blazer breaks it in a dozen ways. And I know that I like it.

It's a good thing that she doesn't work for me. It wouldn't take more than a week of steady employment before there would be meetings organized around getting me to stop leering at the new web dev. My VPs would stage an intervention, demanding that I keep a two floor buffer zone around her cubicle.

I bow over her hand.

"This is new," I murmur. It's been a long week, every second filled with meetings and emails to get me back on track after my leave of absence. I've barely had time to catch my breath, and when she looks up at me, I can't breathe again. "Did you have to scramble over the palace wall to avoid Queen Helena's inspection?"

"Mama is busy," she answers, smiling her princess smile. It has ceased to be strange to me, this habit the Wolffes have of transfiguring into living embodiments of the nation in the blink of an eye when the cameras demand it, but I miss my own, personal Ella.

After greeting a row of giddy executives, I escort her down a wide, wood-panelled hall where a line of script reads, "The Story of Han Heyden". What follows is a series of quotes and photos charting the progress of the company over more than a decade. Ella halts in front of an enlarged image.

"This is new," she says, eyes roving over the picture of four recent Stanford alums standing in a spray of champagne, celebrating their first venture capital deal. I'm holding a yellow legal pad and I've got my arm around a girl who disappears into the frame. The only sign of her is a shoulder and a sliver of a hip.

"I didn't crop you out," I say.

She laughs. "I'm not offended." She points to one of the figures in the background. "Isn't this that awful girlfriend you had? What was her name? Maple? Evergreen? Something unshaved and smelling of patchouli."

"You know it was Willow. And I *didn't* crop you out."

The dimple flashes. "I don't blame you. I was more harm than help in those days."

I point at the frame. "I had them print the whole picture but wrap you around the back to preserve your privacy."

Ella glows with pleasure and moves on to another photo. "I wasn't expecting to see you here."

"I own the place," I answer.

"Aren't you too busy for these kinds of things?"

I am. My responsibilities are as loud as the dull, heavy drone of bees over a lavender field in high summer—ever-present, un-relenting—but standing with her now, everything quiets.

"We'll get a nice tax break for sponsoring this event."

Ella continues up the hall, smiling and nodding her head at doorways crowded with curious employees. "The brief said I was to be escorted by the Director of—"

"Human Resources and Recruitment." I nod. "Val's daugh-ter is sick and she asked me to step in."

This is a lie. Not about Val and the kindergartener with the croup. That's true. But when the position opened up, I shook off a meeting with a fleet of executives to be here.

I can't afford this, but my eyes linger on Ella's face, looking for traces of the goose egg. My muscles tighten, maybe a sign that I haven't been getting enough sleep.

When we come to the end of the hall, a line of primary-aged girls trails obediently after their teacher. The first one spots Ella, and bouncing on her toes, reaches out for a high five.

Ella nods politely, decorously, to the teacher and then locks in. Twenty-two high fives and twenty-two new monarchists later, she glances over her shoulder.

"Coming?" she laughs, and I lead her off to the conference hall, humming with noise.

"Your Royal Highness," I say, leading her to one of the dozen circular tables, following the set script. "We're building egg-drop devices using recycled items collected in the past month—cardboard boxes, interlocking bricks, tongue depressors..." Ella's eyes glint with silent laughter.

"Not every design will be a success," she muses, glancing around the room. "I'm sure the early days of Han Heyden taught you a lot about failure."

Ella was there at the birth of Han Heyden as a freshman at Stanford with some practical knowledge of software development. Several times a week, she would crowd into my tiny apartment to perform QA tests, writing automation scripts to try to break the software.

I had my work cut out, keeping my engineers from glitching out in the presence of an actual human woman, but she worked for free, happy to take compensation in the form of late night bowls of ramen and Han Heyden merch—mousepads, low-quality pens, and hoodies she'd wear all year round with a pair of tiny shorts.

Stultes es. I haven't thought of those shorts in years. I hook a finger behind the knot of my necktie and tug it slightly. Maybe I'm having a medical event.

"You'll work here," I say, nodding at a pile of garbage. My voice drops to a whisper, "A trash panda in her natural habitat."

She kicks me under the table and I smother a grunt, moving out of the way when she introduces herself to the others. A pool photographer weaves around them, capturing the right shot of interest or surprise. Later, she gives a short speech to introduce a pioneering physicist, and finally adjourns to the lobby for the egg drop finals.

"Sir, the senior executives are restless," my assistant, Werner, warns. "If you had hinted that you would be attending—"

"I didn't know I'd be attending," I say, following Ella with my eyes.

"There's still time to catch the end of the budget meeting." Werner offers this thrilling prospect, and the noise of my responsibilities—Lindenholm, Seong, Han Heyden—comes roaring back.

Ella steps into the elevator with members of staff and gives me a nervous little wave from the back. She hates tight spaces, and I return a reassuring smile.

"Sir?" Werner prompts.

"I'll work late." I always work late. "All night if I have to."

My assistant gives a resigned sigh. "I'll let them know that instead of reviewing our technical infrastructure needs, you've elected to...watch eggs as they are flung from the mezzanine." Werner places a microphone into my hands.

Any regrets I may have are silenced when Ella leans over the balcony. "Stand free of the blast zone, *Neerheid* van Heyden.

From what I understand, the tabloids have dubbed you the nicest face in Sondmark."

Brat.

She continues. "Shall we endeavor to leave it as we found it?"

"Marc," I say, flipping the microphone up. "Anyone about to pelt me with eggs should know my given name, Your Royal Highness."

"Ella," she corrects. "Our first contestant is," she bends over to hear the shy voice of a future scientist, "Mia. What was your method, Mia?"

The short, tow-headed girl speaks in a tone of breathy excitement. "I used an inflatable neck pillow wrapped around a shoe stuffed with newspapers holding the egg."

"An excellent use for newspapers, Mia. Let's see if your meal will be scrambled."

Over the side it goes, right on target. I tuck the microphone under my arm, unwrap the package, and hold the intact egg aloft. See, ladies? Science is fun.

Ella continues through the queue, meeting triumphs and disappointment with the same cheerful energy. At last, an egg—wrapped in an orange peel packed with confetti and tucked in a nappy—explodes across the floor, spattering my leather shoes in yolk.

"There goes my lunch," I laugh, taking the sting out of a failed attempt. The young scientist giggles.

"Who's next?" I ask.

Ella leans over, her red curls falling forward, as breathless as a teenager. "Me. I'm the last one."

"What do you have, Ella?" I ask.

"I folded three origami wings and bound them with painter's tape. In the middle, I've cocooned the egg in slightly inflated surgical gloves."

I retreat from the blast zone a generous step.

"Want to make a friendly bet?" she asks, lifting her package over the railing. The crowd screams its approval and her eyes dance. "I'm hungry," she says. "Are you hungry?"

I don't have time to be hungry. "I'm hungry."

She smiles. "If my good pal, Eglantine, makes it," she bounces the egg lightly in her hands, "you have to feed me lunch. Agree?"

The crowd, scenting romance, goes wild. Suddenly, I want to send up some bubble wrap tied to a bouquet of helium balloons, and lay down a nest of pillows. Our good pal is not going to make it.

"Agree."

When she drops it, I feel a dog of hope sit up in my stomach, paws restless, chin raised in expectation. The paper wings set her packet spinning in an elegant dance but when it lands an ominous pop echoes through the lobby.

Before I can confirm the outcome, she breaks in. "If you don't open it, we never have to know if the egg broke."

I lift a brow. "You want me to falsify test results in this Temple of Reason?" I ask.

"Falsify? You wound me, Marc. No. We'll put it to a vote," she says.

I grin. "Ella, this is not how scientific consensus works."

She ignores me. "Those who say the egg is broken..." A few scattered claps serve as the only memorial to empirical evidence. "And those who think it's intact..." The lobby shakes so hard that government scientists are registering signs of volcanic activity.

I'll tell Noah I *had* to keep her for a lunch date. It was for science, after all.

"Let's see it," I say when I finally get her to my office. I set aside the wrapped sandwich from Bette's, and she lifts her hair away from her forehead, allowing me to brush my fingertips over the slight swelling. "Good makeup. Are you having any lingering headaches?"

"Do you count my mother? She marched me down to Doctor Frum's surgery when she saw it. I swear, the woman has eyes like a hawk. Anyway, I got the usual lecture," she says, spinning her hand in the air, "about how I'm not fifteen anymore and she's juggling several reign-ending catastrophes at once. Can't I just be easy so she can focus on Freja? All of it."

I hold Ella's chin in my hand, tilting her face into the light. She's not made of glass, and her doctor is one of the best in the country. Still, such knowledge doesn't shorten my inspection.

Finally satisfied, I relax onto the leather sofa, overlooking the city's historic skyline. Ella kicks off her trainers and tucks herself into the corner.

Why am I worried about her? The question has the rough heft of a brick, and my mind hastily boards up its windows. The answer is—must be—that I am her friend and protector, I think as I pick up one of the white trainers. Those rigid roles protect us both. "Was this on Her Majesty's list of approved wardrobe choices?" I ask.

Ella reaches for a sandwich, but her face wears the same look it does when she's left one of the pasture gates open and all the cows have wandered out. Ask me how I know.

"Approved?" She chews her liver paste on rye. "Mama doesn't have time to monitor every little thing, and I took a chance." She meets my gaze from the corner of her eye. "No. I already know what you're going to say. Don't. You can't imagine living every second of your life policed by a loving but tyrannical despot."

My lips twitch. "She's going to be annoyed that you're not wearing contacts."

"My eyes were itchy this morning."

I look deeply into her brilliant green eyes and think traitorous thoughts. Her Majesty is more short-sighted than her own daughter. She doesn't see that Ella is the kind of person you have to allow to be twenty percent unruly unless you want the whole one hundred.

"I put my glasses on in the car," she admits. "She's busy trying to find a loophole in the Marriages and Succession Act."

"Are you worried?"

Ella arches her back, stretching her arms wide, and my thoughts unravel like a sweater caught on a rusty nail, random facts spilling into my hands. Ella has a brilliant mind. Ella taught me how to level up on *Killer's Sun*. Ella likes Vestfyn. Vestfyn. I cling to the word, rocket out of my seat, and cross the room to retrieve a bottle from the mini-fridge.

I hand her a bottle and sit, wrists on my knees, tracing the wood grain on the coffee table with my gaze. I am not okay.

"I'm not worried. My sister's problems are not mine," she says.

I snort. She probably thinks she means it, but I have the receipts to prove otherwise—a text thread more than six months long detailing an actual wrestling match she engaged in to get Clara to admit her feelings for Max, social media tutorials to help Freja bring more visitors into The Nat, and endless video games played with the crown prince of Vorburg to deal with his frustration over not being able to spirit Alma across an international border and keep her for his own.

"I've never met anyone more involved in the lives of the people she loves," I counter.

"I'm turning over a new leaf," she says. "The only thing that worries me about Freja is how I'll ever get out if she doesn't stay in."

"You're throwing off your mother's concentration with stunts like this." I nudge the sneaker with the tip of my shoe. "And this." I touch a light finger to the frame of her glasses. "And this." I raise my sandwich and feel heat rise up my neck.

"Asking me out during a public engagement, forcing me to feed you... A number of those girls are going home to write fanfic about us."

Ella's eyes light up. "Do you really think so?"

Anxiety swims through my blood. "You're not still writing on that old account?"

She works herself into the couch cushion, bracing her feet on the coffee table. "I ought to finish *Temptation of the Elf Prince.* It was some of my best work." She bumps my shoulder and the air vacates my lungs. We're too close and she can't keep doing that—touching me. My skin vibrates with the need for more.

"You should stop worrying," she continues, reaching for a pickle. "We aren't exactly the type of people to inspire fanfic. When was the last time a tabloid put us on the same page? Honestly, Marc, we could be caught swimming in Handsel harbor in our under-crackers and everyone would be like, 'Trusty Marc van Heyden, liegeman of Crown Prince Noah, gives an impromptu water safety course to Princess Ella.' Not one newspaper would waste a drop of precious ink to document how not into each other we are."

Ella nibbles on the pickle, her lips pursing at the taste of sour juice. A line runs down her wrist and she kisses it away.

I hook a finger around the knot of my tie. I should stop wearing these *flamen* things—become one of those tech CEOs with a closet full of organic cotton t-shirts and flat-front khakis. In the meantime, I force myself to remember that I am a dutiful son, a respected business leader, and a loyal friend who made promises to his crown prince. I can't afford to explore why or how much I hate her construction of our relationship.

"Anyone could mistake friendly banter for flirtation," I grit out. "Be careful."

She lifts her eyes to the ceiling. "You could have been giving me mouth-to-mouth and no one would have blinked."

The mental image kindles a fire that spreads heat along my veins, until Alix bursts through the door, trailing a gust of expensive perfume.

"I cannot believe my luck, finding you together," she claps, dropping her immense bag on the coffee table. She ransacks the contents, tossing aside tubes of skincare, a packet of flossers, and a carabiner of scrunchies, finally unearthing two embossed invitations. "I can choke two sea birds with one herring."

"What is this?" I ask, taking the card. My heart has not found a steady rhythm.

She swipes the card away, bats me on the top of my head, and hands it back. "I can't believe you've forgotten your only sister's engagement party."

"*Third* engagement party," I grunt. "There was the intimate dinner at Minty's, and then Aldo Gardens for everyone you had ever met, and—"

"This is for Tom," she cuts me off, stuffing her purse again.

I flick a glance to Ella. "Not for Tom," I mouth. She catches her full bottom lip on a laugh and I want to push Alix out the door or off the roof. Time alone with Ella is precious, and my sister is burning it up.

"*Amma* is in Seong," Alix wheedles, "and you're busy with your company and the estate, but this is important. We have to knit ourselves into a proper family before the wedding."

"Knit?" Ella laughs. "What do you know about knitting?"

Alix takes Ella's invite and bops her on the head with it before handing it back. "Remember when I spent a summer in an ashram? There was no internet, and I made you a potholder."

"I thought it was half a bikini top," Ella muses, turning the card over. "What's the theme?"

Alix wiggles between us on the sofa, pushing me away from Ella—from some reckoning. There will be no balance until I pay a price for looking at her the way I do. Pay again for the way my heart can't calm down, even when we're not alone.

"It's a costume party," my sister says.

Ella doesn't hesitate. "I'm in."

Alix turns to me. "And you?"

I don't have time for this. I'll have to work late tonight—and every night—to earn my rest. My duties are demanding and clear. But another thought chases this. I promised Noah I would keep an eye on this princess. I tell myself I have no choice.

"I'm in."

7

Collecting Myself

ELLA

It's as though my mother is running one of those mouse colony experiments.

She furloughed me for a season and gave me everything I thought I wanted—abundant, nutritious food, modern heating and cooling, all the high-speed internet a girl could ask for, and vast oceans of time. As a result, I'm about to go out of my ever-loving mind.

In the week after the STEM event, I amuse myself by firing off anonymous chirps criticizing the government. I lead virtual campaigns to capture a castle, a relic, a crown... I may be having an existential crisis, but my *SquadRun* numbers have never been better.

Each day is as smooth as a dish of Pankedruss, until one evening my doorbell sounds. "Dragon, you're in charge," I blurt, tossing down the gaming controller. I race to the door rather than buzzing my guest in.

"Clara," I say, pulling her across the threshold and through to my office with a galloping dance. *A person.* An actual, flesh-and-blood person.

My little sister's hair is silky smooth and smells of peaches. She perches on the edge of my gaming chair wearing stilettos and a cocktail dress, looking me up and down, and I can see her swallowing her words. "How much do you love being off the clock?"

I sniff, wadding up an empty Spicy Ostepops package and pushing it deep into the waste bin. The air smells as stale as a sealed crypt after a plague burial. "Living my best life."

She glances at the monitors, seeing a *SquadRun* campaign and several ReadHe threads. "Marc nudged me to check in on you. Are you plotting the revolution?"

I perk up. "Where did you see Marc?"

"He came to one of the Ragnar Prize lectures last night."

He could have texted. We used to text everyday. I tell myself that I'm off that drug, but my biofeedback loop must be broken, because when I scratch the surface of my thoughts, Marc turns up every time—deep in the soil, impossible to sift out. There are so few topics I can think of without thinking of him.

With desperate energy, I twist my hair up to fasten it with a claw clip. "I could use some fashion advice, if you have a sec." I drag her chair around to face the computer screens properly. "Alix and Tom are throwing a party and I have to find a costume."

"Pull up ThumTac," she commands.

"There's no reason to stick with humanoids," I say when the lifestyle site pops up. I navigate to a board dedicated to the cosplay of my favorite fandoms and tap on the picture of a calico cat in the shape of a bus.

"Um... That's ambitious," she says. "You do know that most of the girls will be in lace masks and skimpy outfits. It's okay to just want to look hot."

"This isn't my first Viking raid," I mutter.

"Okay, well, what do you want to achieve?" she continues. Such a princess thing to ask.

When the event is one of my royal engagements, the answer is easy. I want to defy my mother and move the dial on what constitutes acceptable behavior for a princess of Sondmark.

"I don't want to steal the spotlight from Alix or anything, but a princess doesn't get to dress like a cat bus everyday." I sweep some crumbs off my desk and into the bin.

After the STEM engagement, Marc and I barely made the news. The caption of a single photo on page five read, "Old friends reunite to share science message". Still, there was some fallout.

"Did you see that Mama is back to checking my wardrobe when I represent the Crown?" I ask, my tone level. "Maybe she won't freak out when I'm at a private event."

Clara touches my arm with the same sympathetic gesture we use when we are tasked with managing public grief. "We should do a movie night soon. I know I've been busy. We're about to break ground at St. Leofdag's for an interactive garden, I'm taking on new patronages, and then there's—"

"Max," I finish.

Her lips twist in silent apology.

"Don't feel guilty for being happy," I say, putting my hands on her cheeks and forcing her face to the screen. "I'm glad when any of us escapes the spreadsheets."

Mama's spreadsheets have been a sword hanging over my head since before I could toddle. The story goes that because Mama found her match in a marriage carefully arranged by her parents, her children will benefit from her guidance to find theirs, thus avoiding a host of calamities that have befallen other royal houses in modern Europe. (Here, Mama's story digresses to go over specific examples of infidelity, treason, and best-selling tell-alls.) Her spreadsheets, they say, are filled with the names and net worth of the only people in Europe worth marrying, and they go on for pages.

Instead of selecting matches from this list, my sisters have chosen an officer, an immigrant, and the heir to a hostile kingdom. All the pressure of upholding tradition and supporting the Crown lands at my feet and Noah's. I have to break free while it's still possible.

Clara taps the cat bus again. "I'd very much like you to close your eyes and visualize trying to pee in this. Let's veto all costumes in the form of a vehicle."

"Bummer. My backup plan was going as a white box truck with dramatic brake failure. What about this one?" I point to a drama that features a girl wearing a massive red scarf that swallows half her head.

Clara looks heavenward. "I am begging you, with tears in my eyes, to choose something hot. You haven't dated in so long. Please give me a crumb that says you want to."

I catch my bottom lip between my teeth. Marc is everywhere and Clara is right. "There's this drama about an ancient Seongan king and the mermaid who lives in his fish pond, but—"

"Mermaid? Perfect."

Clara does not care to hear a comprehensive exposition of the characters and plot, instead navigating to a high-end shopping website. Eventually, she lands on a vintage Schiaparelli number on the back of a willowy model. If you squint, there's something fishy about it.

Reason raps her knuckles on the desk. "I am too short and I have enjoyed too many laminated pastries to make that work. Can you imagine how many fashion historians would release unhinged video essays if I tried to squeeze into that? We've only got a week and I have to be realistic."

"Realism is for people with a mortgage," Clara counters. "I'm not going to entertain a negative attitude from the same girl who wanted to whip a whole cat bus together with a glue gun and piano wire."

My eyes gleam. "When it falls apart on the dance floor, it's going to be hilarious."

She shakes her head and puts her finger under my nose. "No. No. We're not going to play this game where you make yourself into a joke just to avoid people seeing there's something you really want and can't have."

Her incisive appraisal lands like a stab in the back. "I don't—" But I do, so I shut up.

"Caroline will source any fabric you need," Clara continues.

"Caroline? You mean *Vrouw* Tiele?"

She nods. "We'll do the mermaid."

"I can't be a mermaid," I protest.

"Give me one good reason."

I would pay serious money if she let this drop. Going through puberty on a global stage teaches you to play the cards you're dealt, and I've got a lot of amazing cards. I'm cute. I'm playful. I'm clever and approachable. But it has never occurred to anyone in our nation of 5.8 million citizens to describe me as sexy.

"Here are two good reasons," I say, waving my hand over my considerable cleavage. "Look at all this business. My clamshell bra is going to look like it was cultivated downstream from a nuclear power plant."

Clara's laugh comes through her nose. "Now you have to do it. Marc would die."

There he is again. When other girls practiced writing *Vrouw* [frothy first name] [surname of Global Shipping Dynasty] in their composition notebooks, I was scratching out the Chinese characters of his Seongan name, Jun Hao—handsome, vast—and telling the other girls it meant 'peach tree fate' or 'hot soup'.

"Marc?" I whisper.

"What Marc?" Clara echos, searching images of mermaid costumes.

"You Marc-ed first," I say. "Why is he going to die?"

She makes a few keystrokes. "Oh. He really likes your...business."

Time slows like a spaceship failing the jump into light speed. *Woooooooom.*

Be cool, Ella. Be very cool.

I remember the very minute I tipped from hero worship into love. It was at Saba Hofstein's sixteenth birthday party and Marc had come back from Stanford for Christmas. He was networking with the grown-ups and wearing his hair long enough to tie into a loop. I kept telling myself that it did not make him look like an ancient poet-warrior. I told anyone who would listen that it looked dumb.

But by the end of the night, my cheeks were beet red and my gaze refused to lift above his chin stubble. He tugged on my hair and asked how it was possible to develop a case of crippling shyness when I could parade myself in front of half the county during Queen's Week without making it a big deal. I dug my toe into the carpet said that I was still getting over the flu. I've been lying ever since.

The shock of finding out that Marc has ever looked at me with anything warmer than brotherly affection must show on my face, because Clara glances at me and her fingers slow to a crawl. "I know what I saw. He was checking you out."

My mouth is dry. "When?"

Her brow furrows, "Last year? We were at Outingen Huis. You were wearing that striped swimsuit Mama got so mad about, and when you tossed your wrap," the memory makes her giggle, "Marc looked like he'd been punched in the teeth."

I fear my face is frozen in a critical error screen—blue and blank—because Clara bumps my arm. "It wasn't weird. I'm sure he knows Noah really would punch him in the teeth if he made a pass. I just thought it was funny."

She's wrong, I think, shaking feeling into cold fingers. If Marc had ever given me the smallest sign that he was interested, wouldn't I know?

"Are you okay?" Clara asks, touching the back of her hand to my forehead.

I lift a shoulder. "Maybe he had a bad clam."

"Speaking of clams," she replies, clicking on a brilliant fabric of green sequins. "If you wore something like this and took the scales all the way up your bodice, you wouldn't have to bother with the shells. Get Mama's seamstress to whip up an ocean-inspired headpiece."

"With a lace mask?" I laugh. "Hotness is basic and men are overrated."

Her lashes flicker. "I can assure you that the right one is not."

I only have a week, but miracles are wrought with unholy amounts of money, royal privilege, and Caroline Tiele.

On the afternoon of the party, I run out to Lindenholm, breezing through the front doors of the massive old house where the symbol of the van Heydens, a pair of wild stags locked in eternal combat, is carved into the ancient woodwork at the head of the stairs. Dust motes dance in the light and I lift my nose, scenting beeswax, fresh mown lawns, and old, old books.

Alix races into the hall and scoops me into an embrace and, half-throttled, I smile at Tom over her shoulder.

"This looks promising," she says, tugging the zipper of the garment bag slung over my arm.

I pass it off to a member of the housekeeping staff and wonder if I will lose my nerve. "Have you been decorating?" I ask.

She nods. "And I'm famished." The comment has the color of a complaint from the Middle Ages—the kind where bothersome archbishops get murdered and the king can say his hands are clean. Within moments, a girl brings a tray of coffee and an assortment of tiny sandwiches into the drawing room.

"Thank you...Cora, yes?" I say. The staff member nods and smiles, before taking herself off. "Where is *Amma*?" I ask. I don't remember a time when I called her *Vrouwheid* van Heyden or Madame Han Lan Hua.

"My Ella," a voice with a faint accent calls from the doorway. *Amma* hugs me like an oversized cardigan folded over her chest. In reality, she wears brilliant red lipstick and clothes designed to cow financial wizards into releasing enough funds to put a new roof on crumbling ancestral piles. Though this is not her home, she fought for it. When a wild princess was put in her care, she fought for her, too.

"You didn't hug me like that," Alix laughs.

Amma talks over my head. "You never stand in one place long enough for this kind of hugging."

"I'll hug you, Ali, even if I have to chase you down." Tom picks her up and carries her across the hall, her shrieks of laughter trailing behind them.

The room falls into silence and *Amma* brushes back my hair with the palms of her hands, giving me a long appraisal. "You look tired," she pronounces.

"There's no reason for it. My mother wants to keep me out of trouble, so I'm on a sort of administrative leave." I laugh, though it sticks in my throat. "Anyway, it's a rest."

Amma doesn't laugh. "I see how it is. When you can least be spared, you have been pitched from the palace like a pest." She shakes her head and exhales her frustration. "She mishandles you."

I am vulnerable and transparent under her sharp gaze, and wish I could drag a curtain between us. She probably sees that, too, because she turns the topic, grilling me about my patronages, and ends by telling me to get a Seongan facial.

"Have you met anyone worthy of you yet? No, I can see that you haven't." I wipe my face, trying to get whatever she sees off, but she lifts her voice. "Has anyone seen my son?" she asks.

The footman answers at once. "He is at the west boundary, ma'am, but promises to return for the party."

Amma shakes her head, earrings flashing brilliantly in the light. "Promises," she mutters. "He'll come back, reeking of filth." She gives me a kiss and checks her watch. "Run down and collect him, my Ella?"

I am at home here, so I dig out an old coat and boots by the kitchen door, roughly my size, and find a key from the row of hooks in the stables. Matching one to a quad, I am soon bumping over the muddy track, the fresh air tearing through my curls.

In the east fields, I find Marc in a ditch with local laborers, covered in dirt and sweat. I hail him from the top of the hill. After he shakes every hand and slaps every back, he makes his way to me, the wind playing through his hair up the steep rise.

At the sight of him, a length of tension spools out of my shoulders, and then I catch myself. Marc is not my lover. These worries I have—about my mother, about my sister—are mine alone. I tug them back again, tucking them under like a circle of dough.

"Climb on," I say, when he's close enough to smell. I should mind his musky scent but I don't. I glance away, remembering Clara's words, and blush hotly. *He was checking you out.*

If it were true that he was gripped by a momentary attraction, he had a year to do something about it. I crush the green shoots of hope, ruthlessly ripping them out by the roots. Hope hurts.

I brace myself as he mounts the quad behind me, settling his hands on my waist. Heat flares up my neck, and I thank the brisk spring wind for having already put some pink in my cheeks. I wish he looked like a troll.

Who am I kidding? Marc would make a hot troll.

I drive the quad back, but my stiff posture makes riding double a punishment. The second time I crack his jaw, he scoops an arm around my waist, anchoring me against his chest. I wish he didn't make me feel warm and safe. As soon as I reach the old stables, I cut the engine and scramble off the quad.

"*Vede*, Ells." He laughs and reaches for me. I steady myself and put distance between us, speeding along the kitchen path. If he asks me what's wrong—

"You had to pick today to fix the drainage?" I ask, filling the silence, pregnant with his curiosity. "You have the money to hire out."

"No one is that rich." His eyes narrow and he closes the distance between us, raking his fingers through my hair, putting it right.

My hand chases his like a good Sondish housewife, shooing her guests away from the dishes. *Don't do that. It's my job.* Our fingers tangle and he pulls away but I am warm all over.

Han Heyden isn't hurting for money. "I read *Businessmen's Quarterly*," I say, turning toward the house.

"For the articles?" He winks as he takes my coat with his, hooks them inside the mudroom, and shucks his filthy boots as I shuck mine. I catch our reflection in a fly-specked mirror and see the reassuring sight of a pair of old friends with dirty faces. We will never be more to each other than we are. I have made my peace with that. If my rosy cheeks tell another story, I shy away from reading it.

"If *Amma* moves back to Seong," he says, his shoulder brushing mine, "I'll have to run Lindenholm. No amount of money will replace being on good terms with my neighbors."

I hook the heels of my shoes with my crooked fingers, slip them on, and retreat to the doorway. I pause there and lean against the jamb. "You could meet them at farming conferences and invite them over for cocktails. You don't have to meet them in the mud."

He pauses in the too-small doorway, too, curving his shoulders to fit against the other side of the frame. I look away. "You love our mud. I used to catch you in it all the time. This deep." He reaches out and brushes a line under my chin, gently drawing my gaze back to his.

I look at him as long as I can—almost three seconds—before averting my eyes to the brick floor. I trace the nicks, uneven lines, and the irregularities of a surface that hasn't been forced into consistency—training my attention on those gaps instead of the tiny one between us.

He touches my cheek, but I don't look at him this time. "They have to trust that I will have their backs." His hand drops and he suddenly shifts. "You remember our college days? Everyone wants to come for the party, but only your real friends will come help you move a couch."

The quarter hour chimes with a gentle bong and he hitches away from the doorway. As he goes, his wide shoulders crowd the narrow hall. My mind travels to a Saturday morning with a tall graduate student and his vegan leather sofa. A short princess, unwisely wearing flip flops, shouts curses on his children and his children's children as they load the truck.

8

LITTLE INCLINATION

MARC

I peel out of the muddy clothes and step into the shower, allowing the hot needles of water to wash the grit away. I can't wash away the image of Ella calling to me from the top of the hill, her wind-knotted hair bright against gray clouds, a heavy black turtleneck sweater framing her face and the old coat giving her no shape at all.

I kick the thin film of standing water, lace my fingers behind my head, and lean into the wall, breathing in and out, steam bringing clarity with each breath. She's Noah's sister and Alix's best friend, and those things are too important to dismantle for...whatever this is.

Soapy water runs down the drain far more easily than it ran down the hill on the west boundary. There we trained it to flow down a particular slope, building up earthworks with the hope it will hold. These reactions, sudden and unwelcome, can be trained, too.

My costume for the party is a lucky choice, reinforcing the importance of discipline. Dressed in the long flowing robes of a Seongan nobleman, I wear a transparent, wide-brimmed hat with a high, thimble-shaped crown, secured with a loose strand of bone and glass beads hanging against my heart. A plain undergarment with a stiff white band settles across the back of my neck, and the overrobe of silk gauze is stitched with our mother's family name, *Han*, along with the insignia of the Seongan national flower: a common dandelion—the first flower to return to our ravaged country in the wake of a crisis.

Alix frowns when she sees it. "You're not wearing a costume. You're wearing an heirloom."

Through the wide open doors of the ballroom, I see superheroes and fairy tale princesses—an assortment of costumes wide enough to include powdered wigs of the Hannöversch Era and armored breastplates from the Ostphalians. I am hardly out of place.

I kiss her cheek. "That's not a minidress. It's a handkerchief," I tell her.

She spins. "Lars and Bianca's wedding was an iconic moment of Sondish history," she says, pointing the tip of her boots. She reaches blindly for Tom before she can confirm that he's there. He takes her hand.

"You know Lars and Bianca?" I ask him.

"I know my girl is letting me wear a frilled shirt in public," he grins, a vision in powder blue.

Suddenly Alix gasps, gripping my arm. "Marc!" Her eyes glisten with unshed tears. Not unusual. Alix is a crier. "I'm sorry I dragged your costume. Did you coordinate with Ella?"

"What did they coordinate?" Tom asks.

"I'm never asking for another present again," she lies, rushing past me to a figure descending the stairs. It's all a blur of color and motion until I register who it is. Then I am caught like a portrait of a Seongan king, frozen on silk, lined in ink, kept in holy silence. Ella has arrived, and my mind slides a door between me and my gut reaction with a hard crack, containing it behind a thin, translucent barrier. The sound of the party retreats and my heart thunders in my ears.

I arm myself with familiarity, trying to force what is breathtaking into something that feels commonplace. This is just Ella. We've attended birthday parties, rugby matches, cocktail events, and bonfire nights, and this is not the first time I've seen her in a gown. But the door between what I feel and what I'm supposed to feel glows as warmth and light bleeds though, overtaking cold reason.

This is not just any gown. The green, figure-skimming dress rests on the points of freckle-kissed shoulders, and light ripples as she walks. Her crown is made of sea glass, shells, and tiny pieces of driftwood, the net sweeping over dark eyes. Her skin— My rigid collar presses into my neck and the knot high up on my chest holds me together. Her skin is lightly dusted with iridescent scales painted down her arms, across her collarbones, and up the delicate cords of her neck.

Alix threads both her arms through Ella's and mine, smiling up at us in turn. "There was this drama I was obsessed with, years ago," she explains to Tom. "I made it my whole personality, and," she hugs my arm closer, shaking it with the intensity of her feelings, "these are the characters: the King of Seong and the Queen of the Ocean. I'm dying. Dead. You're going to marry a corpse bride."

"I'll get us adjoining graves," he smiles.

With Alix's explanation, my confusion clears.

Mermaid in Moonlight was twenty-four episodes of implausible romantic slush that nevertheless caught fire with international audiences, setting off the Seongan Tsunami—a tide of cultural influence carried by artists and performers across the world. It told the story of a mythical being who, for the love of a king, pledged to live as a queen by daylight, retreating each nightfall to the rocky pools of Gongboja Palace. In the end, her longing for freedom consumed her royal lover, and he slipped into lapping water to join her world.

"You planned this?" Alix asks.

"Of course," I smile, looking over at Ella. *Play along.*

Ella shakes her curls off her shoulder and she gives me a glance that makes my tongue stick to the roof of my mouth. *You think I'm new here?*

"Tom," she asks, leading them into the ballroom, "did you have to glue on all that chest hair?" I watch them go, my eyes tethered, possibly forever, to the swish of her hips.

Ella was supposed to arrive as a cat bus or a formless, wandering spirit, shrouded from head to toe in a black cloak and porcelain-white mask. Why isn't she a formless spirit? Where is the costume that was supposed to create a perimeter? What is happening to me? I rake through my robes, locate my cell phone, and stab out a reckless message to Noah.

Who in hell let your sister out of the house looking like this?!?! You wanted her to stay out of the papers? Someone should be fired or sent to prison.

My thumb hovers above the send button and I wrestle with my longstanding commitment to female empowerment. I growl.

Delete, delete, delete.

I grab a bottle of soju and a shot glass from the bar and escape through the long windows to the cool terrace. It's quiet enough that my thoughts catch up to me, demanding my attention. I toss back a measure of alcohol, the taste at the back of my throat sharp and bracing. I fill the glass again.

My heart slows. These reactions I keep having to Ella aren't jet lag or heart disease or lightheadedness. They won't disappear with a workout or a baby aspirin or drink of water. They've been there for maybe years, I recognize. Background noise, suddenly boosted.

The rough stone balustrade bites into my palms and the stars blink fitfully through threatening clouds. The fact that she is Noah's little sister seems to matter far less than how much I want her for myself.

Hell. I close my eyes.

It's attraction.

This much truth squeezes through my defenses before I pull the drawbridge up, put my back into it, and cut off an army of more dangerous thoughts clamoring at the gate. I pass a shaky hand across my mouth. It's just attraction. The green sequins sway in my memory, clouding my judgement. *Significant* attraction, I amend.

This is the moment Noah prepared me for with his two commands: don't date his sister, and watch over her as he would. I can't wish away this attraction, but Ella is my unwitting ally when it comes to keeping my thoughts to myself. My stomach tightens as her words echo in my mind. *Not one newspaper would waste a drop of precious ink to document how not into each other we are.*

Right. It's as clear as day that this...interest I have for her will have to pass. I've been gone a long time, and there are other attractive women in the world. I crane my neck, look through the window, and try to find one. Just one.

The room is dark, and I'm on the wrong side of the glass, but Alix must have invited everyone in Sondmark with a Swiss banker and boarding school trauma to this party, so—*whui-ho*—time to find some other girl to think about. I'm sure it can be done.

My quest is interrupted by *Amma*, who waves me into a circle of neighbors and local business leaders. Her hair swirls high on her head and she wears a lavender cloak, brandishing a wand like a laser pointer.

The talk is of crop yields and zoning laws, but my gaze rakes the crowd for someone I can whip up a hormonal, adolescent reaction to. Anyone.

Literally anyone at all.

Ella laughs.

I tug at my rigid collar and feel *Amma's* eyes on me.

"*Jinwohasu?*" she whispers.

I nod. I'm fine. But the next time I hear the laugh, I turn. The sight gives me no joy. Ella is surrounded by a knot of worthless *adel*, and I feel like I did on the Gravitron all those years ago—sick, disoriented. This is the price of soju on an empty stomach. She should know better. The men crowding around her, all titled and landed, know too much about how the monarchy works.

It's easy to guess that they want something—an order from their art gallery or a photo with Ella, snapped by the photo-journalist roving through the party. Men like these wouldn't allow themselves to get serious about her. People who fly their dogs across international borders for pet grooming appointments don't know how to make the kinds of sacrifices being the husband to a royal princess would demand.

She laughs again, and my eyes linger on her face, tracing the lines I know by heart. Ella hates crowds.

My mother nudges me. "Marc?"

"Excuse me," I murmur, bowing slightly. I make my way across the room, cleaving a path through the guests.

"Ella," I say. Even amid a mind-numbing techno set, she hears me.

She smiles and I clasp my hands behind my back, just to be safe. "I came from *Amma*. She wants…" I trail off. I didn't come with a plan.

"Of course." She twists out of the tight circle and aristocratic fingers fall from her arm. When the fabric of her dress hitches on her curves, she smooths it. I frown.

"What does she want?" Ella asks.

"Who?"

"*Amma* sent you," she laughs.

"Did she?" I scoop an arm around her waist, shielding her from an enormous paper mache lion headdress, and half carry her out of the party. What sent me to her side was a consuming desire to break *Neerheid* Kaas's fingers, but I can't say so.

I don't stop until I cross the hall and push through another door. It's a shock, going from the thumping intensity of the ballroom to the cozy warmth of the library. The floor is scattered with well-worn rugs, and it's quiet here, save for the gentle crackle of the fire and the rain beating on the glass. Ella slips out of my grasp and wanders over to one of the Oppeger portraits of a young Renaissance *vrouwheid*, glowing under a gallery light. I watch her with an expression that runs the entire emotional gamut between ravenous and starving.

Stultes es.

She glances at me over her shoulder and my face shutters. "Thanks. It was getting crowded in there."

Silence settles between us, a thread of attraction pulling the easy weave out of shape.

"It's raining," she says, crossing to the window. She steps out of her heels, hitches her dress—sequins sparkling in curious waves—and plants a knee on the cushioned bench, trying to winch the old casement open a few centimeters.

The window sticks and I brush her hands aside, forcing it open.

Her scent mixes with the smell of rain, and she sinks back, a smile playing on her mouth. There is no sign that she is trying to tempt me, but the way I feel doesn't need an invitation.

"Were you getting bored of playing the lord of the manor?" she asks.

I settle on the end of the narrow window seat, braced against shelves holding all the ancient wisdom of my ancestors.

I glance down, the string of beads shifting against my heart. "I *am* the lord of this manor."

She leans forward, peering under the rim of my hat with eyes that narrow in silent laughter. "And I am a princess of Sondmark. That's not all we are. What happens to Han Heyden if you devote your life to Lindenholm?"

"I might hand the reins to someone else." I watch her reaction.

"Your baby? Please."

I feel the hard, uncompromising shelf at my back. There's no room to retreat. "I know what the title of *Neerheid* van Heyden means."

"It means sacrificing a brilliant life on the altar of tradition." She gives a puckish smile and tiny prismatic rainbows dance against the smooth wood paneling in a kind of halo. "The thing about hereditary titles is that everyone knows what they're supposed to do, but no one is having fun."

"You're not having fun?" I ask, nudging her foot with the tip of my shoe. Even that much touching is a mistake.

She leans against the casement, catching a few raindrops in her hand. "This isn't a vacation. I'm working on a new app," she says. "I've binged a few dramas, gamed with internet strangers, trolled—"

She snaps her mouth closed, then covers it with the back of her hand and turns it into a yawn.

When her arms stretch wide, I imagine pulling her into my arms on the narrow bench and tasting her lips. *Vede.* I glare at the ornate strapwork on the ceiling. In another time, I would be drawn and quartered for these thoughts. Even so, I know what I heard. "What have you been up to?"

"Nothing." She hops off the bench, scoops up the heels, and tries to run. In two long strides, I catch her hand. "Ella."

My hold is loose but unyielding and she turns, tossing aside her shoes to peel my fingers back, one at a time. She makes no progress.

"Tell me you got rid of that Chirp handle," I demand. "*Tell* me you're not still trolling the prime minister's posts."

Her cheeks flush through the iridescent scales, and the set of her chin is obstinate. "What I do in my free time is none of your business."

"Ella." I shake our hands and her brilliant green eyes turn on me. *Vede.* My heart beats a hard, uneven rhythm. I cover it with worry and anger. "Is that what I told you when you wanted to help with Seong? That my business is not your business?"

"Many times."

"Did you listen?"

She aims a blistering look at our hands. "No one knows it's me."

I tug her forward and she tips against my chest. "*I* know."

If she surrenders here, her face tilted up to mine and her curls brushing against my skin, I am lost.

But she never surrenders. Instead, she twists away and traps my arm against her ribcage. My hold is gentle but she tears at my fingers. For the second time today, I cradle her against my chest, but this time I steady myself with a palm against her half-bare shoulder. So much of this is childish but too much of it is not.

"It doesn't matter if *you* know," she grits out. "You won't expose me to the press."

"What about all those men back there in the ballroom?" I ask. The flash of jealousy, hot and uncontrollable, blazes through me. "What if you let it slip to one of the *adel* that you call the prime minister—"

Her back thumps into my chest. "Those guys are my friends as much as you are. There's no difference."

No difference? A new source of frustration erupts from me. "You can't count on those bottom feeders. Unless you promise to give a man like that something that makes dating a princess worth it, you are radioactive."

Ella bites my index finger and I release her with a manly yelp.

She rounds on me, her wide green eyes full of hurt. "Radioactive?" she whispers.

Dominanstid. What the hell did I just say? My finger throbs but I hardly register the pain. It's not too late to beg for forgiveness.

No. No. I'm only doing what Noah charged me with—looking after her as I would my own sister. She needs to see the danger she's in.

"This isn't a joke," I say. "If it leaks that there's an actual royal behind @trashpandaprincess, it could damage your whole family."

She shoves my chest and I tip off balance, taking her with me, cushioning her as we fall in a heap of silk and sequins. The brimmed hat spins away but I am lost in the sensation of Ella in my arms, her mouth pressed into the crook of my neck. It will take a month in a monastery to find myself again.

I feel the surprise in her exhale and her breath warms my skin. Six months. Nothing less.

Ella scrambles upright, straightening her crown, and I wedge myself up on my elbows.

"*I'm* not any danger to my family," she rages. "*I'm* not throw-ing away a decades-long marriage like it's nothing. *I'm* not suing the press. *I'm* not running off to get married. *I* didn't fall in love with a stupid foreign prince. *I* don't go around with models when my only job is to secure the succession."

She gives me a swift kick and I rub the spot, watching as she scoops up her heels and balances her way into them.

"Everyone treats me like I'm a disaster waiting to happen," her voice shakes. "I never thought I'd hear it from you."

9

CHIFFON CASCADE

ELLA

Talk to me, Ella.

I spend the week not replying to his single, not-an-apology text, angry that he put me in a position where I had to defend slope-shouldered *adel* from the charge of not taking me seriously. I know they don't. Few men would. Who is going to swallow the poisonous pill of marrying a royal princess in exchange for hostile media coverage, intense governmental scrutiny, and the chance to escort me to endless state functions?

No one who isn't wildly into me.

Alix and I spend a couple of days shopping for bridesmaid gifts. I feign interest in her brilliant idea of setting Yasmin up with one of Tom's friends. I don't feign hard enough, because she asks why I look like I want to lead a cavalry charge through the East Gate. I tell her Mama is driving me crazy.

It's not entirely a lie. Amidst a firestorm of family scandal, she still finds time to inspect my attire in the Great Hall. My opportunities to look and act like a normal human girl are few. Maybe this is why, on the day of the Handsel Film Festival when she's attending an economic summit, I take a gamble.

"I need your help," I tell Mama's dresser, Analiese, poking my head around her office door, a garment bag draped over my arm.

Her brows gather. "You never need my help," she says, hooking the hanger on the wall and tugging the zipper. "What is this?"

A custom-made dress spills from the garment bag, a dream of soft lavender fabric and dandelions scattered across the gauzy material, the seeds representing hope and resilience, Marc once told me. Devotion and love.

Marc. My lips firm and my eyes flash. Nevermind Marc. Seong deserves my best.

I brush my fingertips across the silk skirt. It's just a gown, but Seong is falling off the front page, and this may be my last chance to make an unequivocal statement for its further financial and social support. Mama might lock me in a tower on a ration of bread and water for this stunt. It is this worry that brings me to Analiese. I am determined to look the part of a dutiful princess in every other way Mama would wish.

"You're going to let me do your hair and make-up," Ana says, setting me in front of a mirror. "You're going to wear high heels. You're going to thank me for not making you wear stockings. You're going to say, 'Yes, ma'am. Thank you, ma'am. Anything you say, ma'am.'"

My lips twitch but my voice is humble. "Yes, ma'am. Thank you, ma'am. Anything you say, ma'am."

Over the course of several hours, she turns me into my mother's dream, wrestling my hair into loose waves and raking it into an up-do. She zips up the dandelion dress, and I survey my reflection with the knowledge that I have never looked better.

I walk the red carpet of the festival and, by the time I enter the packed theater, the fashion press has identified the silent message stitched into my dress. When Pixy adds a button on every repost, directing readers to charitable organizations, it doesn't matter how much trouble I'll be in. Helping Seong is worth it.

A thunder of applause follows me as I make my way through the royal box, and on the edge of the balcony, Mikkel Dorsgard bows over my hand. The actor is handsome in a bleak, Scandinavian way. Hollywood uses him when they need a hot Amish farmer or a hot Cold War spy or a hot Danish philosopher, and it's a shame my type is a man who is half Seongan, half Sondish, and equally conversant with technology and royal protocol. Bonus points if he owns a palace.

We watch one of Mikkel's films about early industrialization, filled with artistic jump cuts of a hard rain and a swelling river. A downstream narrative follows a childless widow cleaning her antique coffee service and tenderly placing it in a box under her bed. His signature smolder is a look I've witnessed in at least three movies, and it's present and accounted for as he takes his shirt off to scythe her wheat field. I roll my eyes.

Against the flickering lights of the film, my mind drifts back to the single, spare text. *Talk to me, Ella.* Despite our hard words, I remember how gentle Marc's hold was, the imprint of skin on skin. I blink when the lights come on and the curtain falls closed. The audience rises, and I stand with them to give Mikkel's abs a seven and a half minute standing ovation.

We adjourn to a large glassed-in garden for a cocktail party and photocall, and I am drawn away from a conversation with Jeneke Stennum, Yasmin's mom, to have my picture taken with Prime Minister Torbald. "Your Royal Highness," he murmurs, frowning at the Seongan dandelions dotting my dress, "I didn't realize you wanted to dabble in politics. I'm sure your mother will be thrilled," he adds, words laced with acid. "I'm happy to give you some tips if you want to try your hand at winning an election."

I smile at the bank of photographers and try not to fidget. "I've never asked; how does it feel to enter a room without the fuss of applause?"

A photographer shouts a direction at me, and we turn as a pair. "It's a novelty finding you doing some actual work," he replies.

"I suppose I *could* be harassing a pair of newlyweds for the crime of getting married."

Torbald's jaw sets. "I sleep very well knowing that the country is about to have one less princess propping up an outdated institution and draining the state treasury." He trades a jovial shout with a passerby and I know the effect will be a dynamic picture. He's good at this. "Freja is going to destroy herself, which leaves me plenty of time to focus on Alma."

"What do you mean?"

"The story the palace told about her broken engagement doesn't add up. I think she was playing around and got caught."

I inhale sharply. He's too close to the truth, and I am boiling with rage. If I stay here another minute, I'm going to push him into the buffet. I straighten my shoulders, sending a brilliant smile to Mikkel Dorsgard.

"You called, goddess?" the actor says, crossing the red carpet. As ever, he smolders.

I manage to get through the rest of the event without doing violence, but as soon as I walk through the doors of the Summer Palace, Mama orders me to her office. I stand at attention in front of her desk as she scrolls through *PAPZ* updates, pushing an aggravated finger across the screen. The headline is, "A Match for Ella?" and she lands on a picture of Mikkel looking down on me like I've been captured in the tractor beam of his personal magnetism.

"This is when and whom you choose to date?" Mama asks, the words dropping like hot irons into cold water.

I roll my eyes. "We're not dating."

The way Mama inhales makes me think I'm going to give her a stroke. She is tired, and I look away. "Your sisters peddled that line three times in the last year. I am no longer in the market for lies."

"We're not," I insist.

She pulls up the photos. "Whatever the kids call it. Hanging out. Talking stage. Hooking up."

I grimace. My mother shouldn't even be in the same galaxy as those words.

She lands on a shot of my dress, the dandelions rioting over chiffon, and releases a ragged breath. "And this. This was deliberate."

I swallow tightly. "No one was here to inspect my clothing."

Mama closes her eyes and rubs her temple. "I don't have time for this, Ella. I'm... just—" her hand punctuates the air as she searches for words, "stay out of the spotlight and focus on the wedding."

When I depart, I turn and stare hard at her closed door. I knew that dress would displease her. I knew it, but I had to take the chance to help Seong one last time, even if it meant facing her wrath. I close my eyes. Evidently, she can't even muster that anymore. She's had enough of me.

I scurry off to my suite, and Clara is hard on my heels. "Come for dinner at Max's cottage," she says. "It'll be nice."

"Who's coming?" I snap.

"Max and me, Freja and Oskar, Alma and Jacob."

The name of every couple is like a giant pendulum, swinging back and forth, trying to knock me off a rickety rope bridge. I'm bobbing and weaving, but between the prime minister's threats and Mama's dismissal, I'm too upset for manners. "You want to turn me into a charity case? A..." I count in my head, "...seventh wheel?" I push the door of my suite open. "Pass."

"It's not like that. Please," she says. "If he's free, you can bring Mikkel."

"I am *not* seeing Mikkel," I insist. When she scurries out, I throw a stuffed raccoon at the door.

I slouch into my computer chair, doom scrolling through rh/RoyalsofSondmark, one of the ReadHe threads dedicated to my family. Each comment throws another log onto the blazing fire of my emotions.

@RoyalWeddingRiot: The queen must be out of her mind. Discipline among the princesses has broken down completely. Lawsuit, elopement, cheating allegations...

@King_of_Fromage: Princess Alma is a crushing disappoint-ment. I thought she was going to keep it together. AT LEAST?! Have I been stanning a family of losers?

@Morrissey_is_Murder: Ella is our only hope.

If I'm their only hope, we have drifted too far from divine light. Alma is the best of us, while I can't wear stockings and heels without moaning that it's a human rights violation.

I anxiously tap on my keyboard, changing my playlist in a fitful attempt to calm down, but the words turn over in my mind. *Ella is our only hope.* The dam holding back big feelings swells with hard rain.

Over the last year, I have pushed, cheered, and life-coached my sisters towards their happy endings, all while trying to put out this torch I've been carrying for Marc van Heyden. Their success made me wonder if happiness might be written in my stars, too—but no, Marc reminded me that I'm untouchable to men of his class. My mother couldn't even waste her time correcting me, the prime minister insinuated the downfall of two sisters, and internet randos—dispensing judgment and correction for even the most upright and circumspect among us—have driven me to the edge of a cliff.

I close all tabs and open a new one. I scrutinize my login information, running a finger under the code and saying it out loud like a pilot with a preflight checklist. Remote VPN? Done. Alt account? Done. Plastic slides over all my cameras? Done.

When I feel safe, my fingers fly over the keyboard. I take screenshots from the Wolffe sisters' group text, "No, I'm the Favorite", lifting photos of Pietor, Alma's one-time fiancé, with his hands trespassing the bikini zone of an Italian model. My sister never thought to delete them because she is a good person and lacks a diabolical imagination. I suffer from neither of these things.

A decorative sign hangs on the wall over my computer depicting a sword dripping with blood. In a runic script, it reads, "What Would Queen Ageltheld Do?" My royal family has held the throne of Sondmark for 800 years through merciless warfare, strategic poisonings, and more than one dagger to the throat. I was not bred to sit back and swallow the lies filthy little gossip-mongers dish out.

I run the images through an editing app, blur Gabriella's face out, add a timestamp, and circle identifying details. Ask some other princess to ignore her hot Viking blood when her sister's character is called into question. *I* won't.

I upload the photos to a ReadHe thread—rh/AmItheJerkwad—under the username @trashpandaprincess and compose a post that seems to pour out of my fingertips.

I (m35, nepo baby, narcissist) abandoned my fiancée (f30, perfect, blameless) for over six months to row a tiny boat across the Atlantic, wear tiny-brimmed hats, and post philosophic dude-bro affirmations on my socials. Though Fiancée was busy running her family business, I had an interest in exploring ethical non-monogamy and social media influence. (Those shirtless beach pics won't upload themselves.) Now, I know what you're asking. Did we discuss my research into utilitarian romantic situationships before I left? Answer: No. (My bad) But I live by the rule that what happens in one hemisphere stays in that hemisphere.

In the middle of my soft launch for an open marriage (see pics), Fiancée called off the wedding, leaving me to deal with disgruntled bankers. My family's company, Schmimmelstain, is restructuring and needs an infusion of cash from her family's larger and more successful conglomerate. Returning home to negotiate a new settlement, I discovered that Fiancée had cut me out of her life with the same ruthless precision a dermatologist uses to slice off a skin tag.

When ambiguous photos of her standing with an unidentified man surfaced, was I the Jerkwad to let everyone think she was the cheater?

**Edited to add, Yes, I wax my body hair.*

I smile—not the smooth, royal smile of a Sondish princess working a rope line, but the murderous smile of a raider with a longboat full of plunder—and hit send. I never consider what might happen downstream.

Two hours later, I am running an intense *SquadRun* campaign when the disaster breaks. My phone blows up, and by the time I pause my game, there are nearly thirty missed messages on the sisters' group chat.

Freja: *It's you. We know you posted Alma's problems all over the internet. How could you hide something of this magnitude from us?*

I lift my brow. *I'm* hiding from *her*? Be for real.

Alma: *You better pray Mama doesn't find out.*

You'd better pray no one finds out.

I'll help where I can but you have to understand how much hellfire you are manifesting.

Clara: *Dominanstid. We found your Chirp archive, too.*

My stomach drops, bouncing into my throat.

Clara: *What in KING FREDERICH'S literal dungeon were you thinking?*

Your fingerprints are everywhere.

You have to take this down.

You have to do it now.

You should consider joining the Broederschap.

No screens. No wi-fi. Start a life of simple subsistence farming and prayer.

She wants to punish me via Anabaptists? Clara—of all people—should know that no one takes ReadHe posts seriously. There's so much garbage in there.

I throw my phone into my room and return to my game with the obstinate certainty that, eventually, my family will thank me for finally hitting back. I am not going to apologize to my sisters for this, and I won't pretend I'm sorry for Pietor's exposure either. Still, as the campaign wraps up, a slow-growing unease chips away at my peace. Until this afternoon, no one except Marc and Alix knew anything about my secret accounts.

A knock on my door pierces my thoughts. Releasing a muffled curse, I hit a button to open it, but keep my eyes on the computer screen.

"It had to be done," I start with a defense I've been planning since I got their texts. "The prime minister has his sights set on all of us and plans to weaponize Alma's supposed lack of character. I neutralized him. You're welcome."

"Ella." Marc's voice, soft and low, makes my heart fall into my toes. He leans around the threshold of my office, slowly taking in the surroundings. He brushes the edge of a bulletin board with a finger. The cork board is more than a decade old and pinned with lists of Seongan dramas in an attempt at an early ranking system.

His hair falls over his forehead and I fight the feeling of how much I missed him this week. Marc bumps away from the door jamb and retreats to the main suite, removing his suit coat and slinging it over the back of the sofa. He works the tie loose and twists two buttons undone. Slowly, he rolls his cuffs up like he plans to stay.

"Are you here to call me names and remind me I'll die alone?" I ask, scooting past him. My gown brushes his legs in a chiffon cascade.

He catches my wrist as I pass, his touch feather-light.

10

STUPID GAMES

MARC

Don't touch Ella.

This is a recent rule I have imposed upon myself. As soon as I break it, I remember its wisdom.

All week I've been fighting to get away from the moment I tumbled to the floor of the library, Ella in my arms, alive at every point of contact. It comes rushing back with all the speed and punishing strength of a rugby tackle. I thought I'd achieved something—peace, stability, perspective, whatever—when I finally admitted to myself that I was attracted to her.

It was like a pagan offering to the gods, a hedge to keep them from taking more. *See what I'm giving you? See how much it costs?* The sacrifice was supposed to buy me something. Rest. Indifference. Critical detachment. Gripping her wrist in my hand, my thumb brushes the delicate bones.

How much would I offer for the chance to act on the attraction?

Everything.

The word passes through me like a ghost, insubstantial but chilling. Ella pulls her wrist free, breaking the connection, and I brush the prickling sensitivity from the back of my neck.

"It's only been a few hours and Alma is all over the news," I say.

Ella curls up on her green velvet sofa and tosses me a game controller. Firing up *Runaway Wagon*, she toggles past the princess, selecting the bandit as her avatar. Typical.

I don't want to play games, but I take the floor at her feet and choose to be a melon farmer whose goal is to get my crops to market. Her skirt brushes my shoulder, her bare foot swings down, and I see the thin gold chain around her ankle within easy reach. I lift my hand, but she nudges my shoulder as the countdown begins.

Three...two...one...

"Alma is in every headline and you are cited in every article," I say, muscle memory taking hold, guiding my hands through a rapid series of moves that propel me into an early lead.

"No one has any idea who the leaker is beyond a ReadHe handle," she counters. "Anyway, don't you have better things to do on a Friday evening than monitor gossip sites?"

Werner is waiting for me to review a financial statement. The rest of the night was supposed to be devoted to reading reports and contracts, some from Han Heyden, others from Lindenholm.

"I set a notification for 'trashpandaprincess' this week to keep up on your illicit activities," I tell her. I set notifications for "Princess Ella" to keep up on everything else. I'm not sleeping well.

Ella swerves into the forest, overtaking my melon farmer, and I slow my progress, looking out for traps. "When the news was picked up by the national press, I thought my phone was going to catch fire."

"The post escaped containment," she says, giving a little whoop when my wagon slams into her net. My cargo cartwheels through the air and shatters on the road.

Round one to Ella.

Her stomach growls, and she frowns. I head to a sleek Scandinavian sideboard, retrieving a butane stove and a gold aluminum pot from a cupboard. In another cupboard I locate her stash of ramen. "Spicy Hot Chicken or Golden Shrimp?" I ask.

"Hot Chicken," she answers, shifting a pile of manga and a well-thumbed copy of *The Joy of Coding* from the coffee table. She sets out two pairs of chopsticks while I fill the pot with water from the bathroom tap.

"You want extras?" I ask, putting it on the heat and rifling through the sideboard for some bowls.

"Is this a question?" she replies, arranging the spoons on the table.

I place an order for the palace kitchens, and a servant delivers two soft-boiled eggs, a few slices of *chasu*, chopped green onions, a lump of chili paste, and sheets of *nori* almost as soon as the water begins to boil. Ella slips two noodle squares into the liquid.

"You should change," I say, my throat constricted, watching the sway of her hips and the soft lavender point where the bodice ends in a narrow ribbon. I catch one trailing strand, my hold too light to hold her. "You shouldn't slurp ramen in something so expensive."

When she turns to face me, the ribbon slides through my fingers. In another life, I would catch it, feel a tug and release. Narrow the distance between us.

"Dripping is for civilians," she says, slipping around me, heading for the closet. "I was trained by a British nanny."

"You were her worst student." I lean against the console, crossing my arms, keeping them to myself. She returns with her phone, checking messages while we wait.

When the noodles are bouncy and translucent, I prepare the bowls and carry them to the coffee table.

Tucking loose strands of hair back, she mixes the ramen and brings a twist of noodles to her mouth. No drips. I thought I was being rational, admitting to an attraction. I could keep it penned up that way. Domesticated. That's what I thought.

Vede.

I stare hard at the steam coming off my bowl. Nothing has to change between Ella and me. We've gamed like this a thousand times. I taught her which buttons mapped to which functions on her first controller. It's nothing new.

I drag the noodles into my mouth, scalding my tongue. "That actor," I say, stabbing the ramen back and forth. The sunset casts a brilliant glow in the room, on the edge of day and dusk. Nothing stays the way it always was. Not even the light, shifting every second.

She laughs. "Mikkel?"

I grip the chopsticks in my fist and blow on the noodles, cooling them.

"Mama probably wishes she could send me to a convent, but our ancestors were too quick to welcome the Reformation." She winks. "Sucks to be a Protestant queen."

"Lutherans have nuns," I mutter. A few. I might be able to sleep again if Ella is bound to vows of chastity, poverty, and obedience.

The light piercing the windows looks like a ripe peach, and I wish I could hold it in my hands, saving it for a dark hour.

"I'm not a nun," she says.

I close my eyes and find a thin slice of pork, swallowing it down. The taste is simple, nothing like the depth of flavor you get when the ingredients have time to sweat and steep. Time is the thing. Maybe that's the potent ingredient to this attraction, too. I've known her forever.

She tips the bowl to her lips, swallowing the last drops, her soft throat working.

"Did he ask you out?" I'm not proud of these words.

"Several times." She dabs gently at her lips and gives me a dimpled smile. "No drips."

She invites me to inspect the immaculate fabric of her bodice, but I look at the ceiling. I spend a lot of time looking at ceilings these days. "You can't go out with him."

I did my research. Noah would want me to warn her that Mikkel abandoned a long-time partner amidst rumors of an affair with his most recent co-star. He'd want her to know about Mikkel's closest friend doing a stint of community service for a minor charge of drug possession. He'd want—

"Not you, too," she releases a breath. "You can't tell me who to date."

The part of my brain belonging to some wise, ancestral warrior-prince tells me that I'll lose this battle if I fight it.

But my ancestor probably doesn't know that I've got an unbeatable opening line like, "Be reasonable, Ella."

"Reasonable?" she squeaks.

I squint slightly. That wasn't the top-shelf opener I thought it would be. "His reputation is rough and his PR firm probably told him to find some willing woman and—"

"Marcus van Heyden." She straightens. "Did you come to insult me for the second time this week?"

"Ella, he's not—" *A good person. Good enough for you. Going to love you until his last breath.*

I push the coffee table back and kneel at her feet, fisted hands pressed into the sofa, bracketing her hips. I meet her stormy green eyes. I could say a dozen more things that would get me in trouble, some of them she hasn't even thought of yet. The possibilities gather on my tongue until the ancient strategist chases me down and holds me at swordpoint.

"I'm sorry," I say, clamping my lips shut. "Of course you can date who you want to."

She accepts my surrender. "I told him no a half dozen times. He's not my type."

Don't touch Ella. I have to remind myself of the rules. "What's your type?"

I follow the slow flush blooming up Ella's cheeks. "I—"

When her phone pings, she reaches for it, falling across one of my arms. When she sits up again, I leave my hand at her waist, and shamelessly read the text from Clara upside down.

"We found your Pixy account, too." This is accompanied by a rage-face emoji, pursed Pavian fingers, and a knife.

"Ells," I say. Peace was nice while it lasted.

She tosses the phone to the other end of the sofa and grabs her controller. "Another round?"

Vede. No. I battled rush hour traffic to be here as soon as the first news dropped because, whether she knows it or not, Ella has kicked a hornets nest. "Did you ask Alma before you pushed her into the news?" I ask, reaching for more noodles. "Did you run things past your mother?"

"What business—"

I give her a level look. "We've been friends longer than you can remember. Your business is my business."

She sets her controller aside. "Torbald has a plan that goes beyond raising so many questions about Freja that she's forced to beg Parliament to approve her marriage retroactively."

My brow lifts. "Beyond that? He said that to your face?"

"Don't you believe me?"

"I believe you." I brush her ankle, hooking a finger under the chain, and release it. *Don't touch Ella.*

"Do you remember the summer our nanny taught me to curtsey properly? Remember how bad I was? I got a sound effects clicker so I could let off belching noises when I bent down. I nearly drove her into an insane asylum. Marc, I am literally the worst princess in the history of Sondmark."

She can't be. Not when she's my favorite.

Ells continues. "But Alma is perfect. She hits every mark. She does everything Mama asks. She wears what people tell her to. She says all the right things."

"No one is perfect."

"She's within kissing distance of it."

I know someone else within kissing distance. I draw back, putting more distance between us. The light, shifting so slowly I didn't notice, is now heavy and blue.

"The only thing she's ever asked for is Jacob. Is her punishment going to be losing her role as a working royal?" She reaches for the end of my tie, threading it between agitated fingers. "Torbald has nothing on her as long as we could establish that Pietor was the one who cheated. So I did."

I like the way she rushes in to help, but— "You used a sledge-hammer on the problem. The government now has proof that your sister—and possibly your mother—was lying to the public for weeks about her engagement. When the prime minister finds out that you were behind the account that leaked the photos—"

"He's too much of an idiot to find me," she says.

"You're too smart to believe that. The prime minister is dangerous, and you can't be playing games at this level. They will catch you."

And, *vede*, what if they do? I lift my hand, letting it fall before I touch her again. I can't handle the consequences of touching her. She already has me on my knees.

Ella turns her stubborn face away. "I've covered my tracks. Remote VPNs, site-specific log-ins, software patches. I'm constantly running too far out of reach."

I lean into her line of sight. "Unbreakable cyber security is an illusion. You know that. I suggest you follow your mother's lead when it comes to protecting your family."

"She's doing such a bang-up job; you should ask my father how it's going." Ella's tone is blistering and bitter. "My mother protects the monarchy first, *Neerheid* van Heyden, and our family last."

The fire in her eyes is supposed to run me off, I suppose. I release a ragged breath. I wish something would.

"Your family and the monarchy are the same things, no matter how much you wish they weren't."

Ella lifts her chin, determined to shut me out, but I see an ocean of hurt beyond the stubborn pose. My voice softens. "Do the responsible thing, Ella. Back off from this fight. Delete the post and your accounts."

Ella stands up and tosses the remains of our meal onto a tray, carrying it to the door. "I won't keep you," she says, as I get to my feet.

Her delivery is excellent—queenly and rippling with fury—but her timing is ruined by the automated door, swinging slowly open. She waits. The dishes clink together. She waits, and my lips twitch. I can't rob her of the satisfaction of throwing me out.

Finally, the door opens far enough to scoot the tray through and she sets it in the hall. "You have enough on your plate," she says, "being the golden boy of two countries. You don't need to worry about me."

11

FAMILY MENACE

ELLA

I hold my breath as he passes and grip the door. It resists me when I move to slam it because of the automatic mechanism that I, in my great wisdom, installed. I jump for the metal latch on the top of the jamb but my fingers brush the air. I jump again.

When Marc laughs in my face, it will be what I deserve.

He doesn't laugh. He brushes my hand aside and presses the release, his breath stirring my hair. When he goes, he'll deliver a final lecture, getting in a parting shot, and I'll just have to stand here and take it.

He drops his arm and the air thickens between us, the narrow space crowded with memories and desires. I hate how much I always want him. In a panic, I push him out of my suite. I grab the door and swing hard, the sound of the slam echoing in my chest.

Vede, that was satisfying.

But the longer I stare at the raised panels, the more blurry my vision becomes. I bite my cheek. Tears are for people without a plan, saints on their pyres, and love-tossed sisters. They are not for me.

I sink onto the arm of the sofa, the heels of my hands pressed into my eyes. Why didn't I change when I had the chance? The first rule of Seongan dramas is that the frothy wedding hat gets flung off as soon as disaster strikes. You can't monologue with bouncing feathers. I look ridiculous, being sad in a dress as sweet as a cupcake.

The sound of muffled voices carries up the hall, and I brace my feet. My sisters. *Flamen hell*. They will descend upon me like Valkyries.

There is a list as long as my arm of mistakes they've made this year, so I stand with my shoulders back and chin up, not above fighting dirty. I stand there for what feels like forever, but the noise rises and falls like a wave, soon followed by the reasonable, muffled sound of doors closing.

They're not coming? I bite hard on my lip, eyes stinging with unshed tears. They're not coming. They don't care enough to be mad and fight it out and hug and cry? None of them? I wait and wait, but the Summer Palace's ancient bones are silent, filled with the sound of every one of us going her own way.

I blink rapidly. Leaving my royal life behind is more vital than ever. I could do it tomorrow, channeling my energies into peddling mid-level mustards, weight-loss pills, and family secrets.

Still. I thought they would care enough to fight—to send a delegate, at least, to shout my ear off about what I owe them. I glower at the door and turn, barking my shin on the coffee table that isn't where it should be. At my cry, Marc barges through the door. He kicks it shut, tosses his jacket aside, and gathers me into his arms.

"Are you hurt?" he asks, pressing a kiss to my temple. "Or just feeling sorry for yourself?"

It's embarrassing, needing him as much as I do. "I thought you left."

"Do you still want to take my head off?"

I burrow into him as his arms tighten around me. "I couldn't do that to the women of Sondmark. *Vrouw WOW* called your face the best thing that has happened to this country since we deepened the harbor."

I can see Marc's smile even without seeing it—the cocky tilt of his brow, the divot in his cheek—but when speaks, his voice is gentle. "I'm sorry for being a jerk about those guys at the party. I don't know where that came from."

Under my hand, his heart beats out a steady rhythm.

I lift my head, catch my reflection in a mirror, and recoil. My mascara is thumbing a ride to Paris, my lipstick has vanished, and I look like I need a rabies shot.

"I am not radioactive," I say, rubbing my eyes.

"Of course not." He pushes a handkerchief into my hands.

I mop up, and he tucks me closer. I say, somewhere from the vicinity of his shirt pocket, "You're right. I didn't think about the mess it was going to make for Alma."

"You apologize to your sister and we'll figure the rest of it out," he says, stroking my hair. "Are you going to delete the accounts?"

"I'll think about it."

Finally, he nods. "I'm sorry if I sounded like—" He tightens his hold.

"An overbearing brother," I force myself to laugh. "I know it's difficult to remember I'm a grown up."

Marc stills, tense as an animal at the sound of an unknown footfall. "It isn't."

The words deserve attention, but I'm too intent on managing my reaction to his nearness to parse out the meaning. I shouldn't be in his arms, curving my body against him like it's as easy as breathing. This is the danger of Marc. This is why I love him. *Loved* him. This is why I cut myself off, limiting myself to a smile and a wave at tiara events. *Everything* with Marc is easy.

I glance up, and his gaze holds mine. I blink and it shifts from my eyes to my lips. It's a tiny movement, over in a microsecond, but my stomach takes a sudden dip and my reflexes slow to a crawl.

I told myself that Clara was wrong about Marc noticing me because I have never seen a speck of interest from this man I've watched with all the passionate absorption of an engineer with his battle robot.

Until this second.

His soft fingers trace down my spine and stop at my waist. My pulse leaps in my throat and I feel like a lost motorist, caught in a fog with no maps or familiar signposts to chart my course, my phone uselessly pinging out a cell signal. *How do we get out of here?*

He inhales suddenly and his hands lift away. He rubs the back of his neck. "See you next week?" he asks.

But I'm still lost in the fog. What just happened? "Next week?"

"Alix's party," he says, looking over me, around me, above me. "The camping thing."

"Glamping," I say, taking refuge in a laugh.

When he retrieves his jacket, I shake my hands out in an attempt to get the circulation going. The old, dead crush was firmly one-sided, but this is... I don't know. I don't know anything.

He straightens, tipping his chin up with a smile that draws me under a cloak of normalcy, warm and protective. "She says she wants to celebrate Tom's traditional culture."

"Finance bro?"

"Pennsylvania Boy Scout. But you know Alix. She can't resist personally-branded sparkling water chilling in an antique bird bath, so..." He pins me with a look. "Are we good?"

I try for lightness, but my pulse still hasn't settled. "We're good. When I see you next time, I promise not to be such a brat."

He grins, walking backward to the door as he shrugs his jacket on. "Don't overshoot the runway."

I don't sleep. I lay in my bed, wondering if I imagined Marc's eyes drifting toward my lips. When the night is darkest, I remember that Marc's first instinct after that infinitesimal lapse in absolute moral rectitude was to ignore it and run like hell.

It's a brutal reminder that I have to get over him. Someday soon, I'm going to get on one of those apps and keep swiping until I find someone to make out with me. Someone who holds me by the waist and keeps on holding.

I rise the next morning, a squished bean of exhaustion, determined to face the music. I stand, hesitating, on the threshold of the breakfast room, when I hear a voice.

"Looking for Mama?" Alma asks. I emit a tiny squeak, but she breezes past me to the sideboard. "She's absorbing the news that I am no longer a scarlet woman in the press. I wouldn't put it past her to launch an investigation into the identity of our leaker."

Mama has little use for me on the best of days, but if she found out my online identity, a swift murder would be mercy. I place my laptop on the table and return with a cup of coffee, a dish of fruit, and Pankedruss.

"Are you mad?" I ask. Better rip the sticking plaster off at once.

"Yes." It's all the more devastating that she says it so plainly. I think I'd rather be screamed at or wrestled with. She reaches for a stack of newspapers, and I see a little nervous hitch in her throat. "Shall we see how bad it is?"

I've already seen the digital edition of PAPZ. The online tabloid placed the most lurid photo on the top of their homepage and cheerfully reproduced the entire @trashpandaprincess post from ReadHe. The headline read "SON OF A BEACH!"

Alma pushes each newspaper across the table as she finishes them. *The Holy Pelican* reprinted a timeline of events, though it's sequestered on their social pages where it can't infect the real news. *The Daily Missive* proclaims, "Handsy Hereditary Himmelsteinian Hooks Humanitarian Hottie in Hinterlands".

The prime minister has weighed in, expressing sympathy on one hand while making a deadly knife thrust with the other. "Though our hearts go out to Her Royal Highness, it makes one uneasy to consider the extent to which the palace successfully hid key details from the public during an important state event. The implications of such control..."

My lip curls. "He's such an eel—"

Alma bends over her phone, tapping out a message. Texting Jacob. I can tell by the little smile playing around the edges of her mouth.

"Alma," I prod.

She clears her throat, turns her phone over, then scoots it far out of temptation. "I'm ready."

"I didn't expect things to blow up—" I begin.

Her brow lifts. "No. You were angry at the prime minister, you reached for a weapon, and you didn't care who might be hurt."

"He said terrible things about you."

She touches the edge of a newspaper and her chin quivers, almost imperceptibly. "Now the entire North Sea Confederation gets to join the conversation."

I feel the pain of my own carelessness, made worse because she's right.

"How did you know it was me?" I ask. Despite Marc's warnings about digital security, I am certain I covered my tracks.

"Jacob connected the dots. You have access to photos of my ex, you're an online creature, and you have a creepy raccoon collection." She brushes the polished table with a row of fingertips. "It's not just affecting my personal life."

She tosses me the front page of the *Sondish Worker*. "Pietor's Crimes: Paternalism, Colonialism, Carbon Waste." The headline is paired with a picture of Pietor in a blindingly white dress shirt, surrounded by grubby children from a Lijuelan slum. It's certainly a look.

I flip the fold down to see another headline. "Locke vs. Hobbes: Ten reasons to abolish the monarchy," and work my way through the lede. "In light of recent events shaking the House of Wolffe, the editorial board of the *Sondish Worker* will begin a ten-part philosophical deep-dive on the subject of royalty and revolution..."

I bite my lip and close my eyes, hoping that if I screw them shut tightly enough, maybe I can go back to a time before I lit my family's future on fire. To a time when my great failure was a burp curtsey.

I hear Alma rise, and when she reaches me, she tucks my hand in hers. I'm hit with a wave of memory. *Keep track of Ella.* That was her job. She was barely twelve when Mama put her under oath to keep the family menace from falling into canals, launching herself over balcony railings, or dashing under horses hooves.

I open my eyes to meet my sister's steady, reassuring gaze. No matter what disasters befall, she always dusts me off and puts me on my feet again. I feel all this at the same time as the realization that her love doesn't come with a permit to run roughshod over her boundaries.

"You were wrong to drag me into all this," she says, "and I expect an apology."

I take a breath. "I'm sorry. You've had a hard enough time this year, and I made it harder. That wasn't my goal—I won't do it again."

She lets me dangle over the burning hot coals for a few moments before giving me a brisk nod. When she offers her pinky, I wrap it with my own, sealing the vow. It feels like time travel, this way we promise, taking me back to when my heart had never been broken and my family was still strong.

"Okay." Alma taps the table. "I'll leave you to get on with your computing."

She let me off too easily. "It wasn't so long ago when you held the indisputable title of Sondmark's Perfect Princess." I buck my chin at the papers. "They've always loved you. I undid that."

Alma tucks her hair behind her ear. Looking at her now, wearing a seasonably appropriate sweater set and a skirt it would be a crime to wrestle in, I could believe that she had a divine mandate from heaven to wear tiaras and sashes forever.

"I bored everyone to tears." She rises, tipping her cold coffee out and refilling the cup. "It's what I prefer. Flying under the radar makes it easier to get things done when you don't have to fight off an angry press. Ella, don't make that face. I'll figure out how to go back to boring everyone again."

"You're not boring Jacob," I say, flashing her a lopsided smile as she returns to her newspapers.

I navigate the source code for an app I created years ago to quiz my sisters on the names, faces, and achievements of world leaders, and wonder if *I* should try flying under the radar. I type a few lines, hearing Marc in my head. *Do the responsible thing.* He lives by that motto. He probably has a tattoo of it somewhere.

I was there when he first told Noah about his plans to attend Stanford. I was there when he plotted his approach to venture capitalists on a pad of yellow legal paper, explaining it in terms I pretended to understand. I was there when his startup took off and he kicked around the pros and cons of relocating to Handsel on that same yellow legal pad. He's half wildly ambitious risk-taker, half dutiful son and scion of his ancestral house, but he's always done the responsible thing. I try to peer into his future and wonder if he will always bow to duty, spending his life bending through thresholds that hardly fit him.

My throat is thick, but Alma breaks in.

"You'd better stay out of Clara's warpath," she warns. "But Freja— Can you remember that she's not the only one who kept secrets from the rest of us?" Alma grips her cup in both hands, unused to having a conversation about feelings, even with me.

"Oh, and thank you for all this," she says, glancing at the newspapers. Color rises in her cheeks and she swallows. "I didn't want anyone blaming Jacob for breaking my engagement when we decide to go public."

I lift my brows. "*When*?" For a princess of Sondmark to date openly is as good as a ring and a wedding date.

She smiles into her coffee. "*When*."

I release a breath, thankful I haven't ruined everything. "I thought you were going to beat down my door and haul me before a tribunal."

She shakes her head. "Clara was out for blood, but Marc wouldn't budge until we promised to leave you alone until morning. He said—" She laughs. "He said that anyone who made you cry would answer to him."

His name is like one of the palace ghosts—warming the room despite a draft, secreting little treasures behind decorative urns to be discovered in a time of greatest need. It warms me now, pinking my cheeks.

"He's a good friend to us." Alma brushes my sleeve as she goes. "Be sure to thank him."

12

SERVING S'MORES

MARC

A noise startles me awake. My eyes jerk open to chinoiserie wallpaper, the vines and flowers climbing up to the high ceiling, bathed in moonlight. I'm at Lindenholm and I throw a switch, groping for my phone.

I swipe up to be greeted by an animated genie who shares Ella's playful expression and curvaceous figure. The sticker nods and winks, arms folded over her chest, while a ponytail bounces over her shoulder. I scrub my face with my hand and text dots bounce.

I'm granting you three wishes, her message reads. *I apologized to Alma and she has no plans to murder me. Henceforth, I promise to do whatever you say.*

I jerk upright. It is barely five on a Monday morning and I am suddenly wide awake with ideas invading my mind, jostling for supremacy.

She adds a rider. *Sorry. Hit send too soon. Promise to do whatever you say so that I can help my family out of this mess and move on with my life.*

I shove a pillow behind my back and command my heart to slow down. If Ella needs help, I help.

I sigh, hitching myself up on one elbow. *This again? You aren't a quitter.*

Don't you remember driving us to ballet lessons? I didn't last a year.

I grin. If I recall correctly, the lessons were taught by a ruthless Russian instructor who spent weeks shouting at Alix to put her shoulders back so her dead ancestors might rest free from the fiery, eternal torments of family shame.

You were good, I type. I'm not sure that's true. Most of that year I spent slouching in a corner, trying to improve my grasp of English by binging *Chicago Law* and thumbing through vocabulary books.

I'm not interested in your lies, Ella declares. *Madame Nikolaevna called me a dumpling.*

A long-buried memory surfaces and I laugh. Any other princess might have thrown a tantrum and dropped the name of her mother's legal team, but Ella started wearing shirts printed with anthropomorphic dumplings over her leotard and making disconcertingly aggressive eye contact while rotating through each ballet position. She would still be at it if Alix hadn't decided that being a prima ballerina wasn't the vibe.

Back to these wishes I'm granting you, she types. I feel a sharp pain under my ribs and frown it away.

How can I fix this situation for Freja? This is quickly followed by, *For my family?*

This is the reason Noah asked me to keep an eye on his sister. The monarchy needs Ella to blend into the background, but a question nags at me. What does *she* need?

I glance at the hand-painted silk wallpaper. One-of-a-kind. She was not born to blend in.

I type. *First wish: Don't start fights when you don't have to.*

She responds with a string of question marks.

You go to war over stupid things, I clarify.

Such as?

I can hear the irritation vibrating between the satellite signals, but I fire off a list. *High heels, stockings, trousers, contact lenses, trainers, make-up, tiaras, orders. I can go on...*

Her answer arrives. *Stockings are symptomatic of more serious concerns.*

A pair of stockings is a pair of stockings. I haven't been able to shake this attraction yet, but that's not the only thing between Ella and I. We are friends. Old friends. I care about her happiness, and don't simply want to force her into acting in ways her mother finds agreeable. *When you fight, it needs to matter.*

The thread goes slack between us and I wait until the bouncing dots appear. *Your second wish?*

Two: Do the best you can with the job you already have.

I accept the incoming video request before I think, and frown into her sparkling eyes. "You are abusing your right to call me whenever you want. What if I wasn't alone?"

"You're adorable," she laughs, shaking a ponytail over a bare shoulder. She's in the small private gym set aside for the Royal Highnesses, and the spring in her curls is explained by the sound of a treadmill. "To have a girlfriend, you'd need to spend time with actual women."

I raise the lights in the room. "I spend—"

"Employees don't count," she says, dragging me as cheerfully as a kid with a cricket bat. "What do you mean 'do the best you can'? Have you seen my public approval numbers? You're looking at Sondmark's favorite princess, eight years running."

The polls could reverse tomorrow. She'd still be my favorite.

I stretch, folding my arm behind my head. Her face tips away and she emits an exasperated growl. "*Stultes es*, Marc, can you put on a shirt?"

I grin but reach for a robe, propping the phone up on a side table. Once covered, I sink against the green silk headboard the same color as Ella's eyes. Above it, contrasting fabric is gathered in a sunburst, and when I settle myself, it sets the tassels on the canopy lightly swinging.

"I like your room," she says. "I like how old it is."

"That's silly. Parts of the Summer Palace are a thousand years old."

"Yeah, but my things are all modern. My bed is huge."

"Oh, *now* it's huge," I taunt.

"I've always wondered how you manage to sleep in an antique four-poster at your size."

I grip the sheet. We can't be talking about sleeping accommodations. We're friends. Friends.

She goes on. "You'll have to change it out when you do find a woman."

"I'll get one who likes to snuggle."

Her cheeks flush, washing pink through her freckles. "Be serious, Marc. What do you mean 'do the best I can'?"

She's the only one who ever scolds me for not taking things seriously enough. Everyone else expects me to carry the burdens and risks, to have the answers, and know what to do. To them, I'm as funny as a stroke.

I clear my throat. "The press loves you. You give them all kinds of copy being the rebel of the royal family, but how often do they talk about your work?" I burrow into the pillows and a line forms between Ella's brow. If she were here, I'd smooth it away with my finger. I'd chase it with my lips.

"I've been working for Seong—"

"Beautifully," I break in. "You've been creative and unorthodox, and it's paid dividends. But have you ever given that kind of energy to the Queen's Animal Trust, Fairy Godmothers, or the Veterans of the Motovian War Society? Your patronages deserve your best."

"I thought you were going to help me with the succession crisis?" She bites her lip.

Dominanstid. I force myself to concentrate. "Your mother would have more bandwidth to deal with Freja if she didn't have to worry about you."

I roll over, propping my phone on the silk sheet, and stuff a pillow under my chest. Ella mirrors me, hopping off the tread-mill, and perches her phone on the ground to do some stretches on a yoga mat.

"Your wish is going to turn me into a robot," she grouches. "Why bother showing up for engagements when royalty-trained predictive text would do a better job than I do?"

I gaze upward, my eyes catching the riot of stripes, flowers, tassels, and fringes, each surface decorated with unnecessary pillows and ornate molding. Above the bed, there's a cupola carved in wood and covered in gold leaf. It should be eye poison. It should be frilly and excessive. Too much.

I wouldn't change one stick and, heaven willing, when I have lived to a great age, I hope to draw my last breath in this room.

I wouldn't change Ella either.

An eternity sinks between one breath and the next. It's not as simple as what I want. Ella isn't just Ella. She is also Her Royal Highness Princess Ella and she has to make her way in the life she was born into, not run away to some other life, forever out of reach.

I flick the screen "You asked for my wishes."

"You want me to give in to them."

"Your family isn't the enemy."

She moves briefly out of frame to adjust her pose and replace the camera. "Agree to disagree. I'll try to do better with my assignments," she says, returning, slightly breathless.

Her bright green eyes catch me by surprise, the shock of them landing hard against my heart. I have to brace myself for her now. Every time.

"What's your third wish?" she asks, reaching her arms above her head, hooking her fingers in a deep stretch.

I open my mouth to answer but the words won't come—would be wildly inappropriate if they did. Saying what I want would be like shattering a porcelain dish on a cool tile floor. Something priceless might be lost and there would be no putting it together again.

"When I think of something I'll let you know," I answer.

I spend my week thinking about ways Ella is already perfect while she sends me screenshots of the deleted home page on Chirp. Her comments on Pixy disappear, leaving empty spaces in their place. Notifications still ping on my phone, but these are mentions of her handle on ReadHe or PAPZ, speculating about her identity.

Noah accompanies me to the Grousehof when I report to a government agency on conditions in East Asia, claiming his prerogative as the future head of state. He asks about Ella, but I shrug, heading him off with a question about Himmelstein's financial woes. Ella sends me cat memes and progress reports.

"I wore a pair of heels to open a community garden and didn't fight my mother," she says, expecting praise.

I spend a concerning amount of time choosing a congratulatory GIF that says "I'm proud of you but you're also a grown woman who can make her own decisions but also I wasn't checking out your legs when you showed me your stockings unless you're into that and, if so..."

On the morning of my sister's party, I schedule a breakfast meeting with a team of VPs and skip lunch to field questions about long-term budget forecasting with an investment group.

"I'm reminding you that you're clocking out at four," Werner murmurs, slipping me a protein bar in the middle of the meeting, along with an updated cash flow statement.

We both know a real break is impossible. Han Heyden is hungry, always demanding everything I can give it.

I am alone in my office, going over a list of action items, when my tablet flashes a silent reminder. 16:00. Lindenholm.

"It's time," Werner puts his head around the door. "You made me promise to kick you out," he says, yanking the tablet out of my hands. "You said to remind you that Alix won't be in Sondmark forever and you'll never get this time back. So I am."

As helpful as Alix has been this year, I know my sister. She will run away from Lindenholm again with Tom running after her. I have to give her a weekend. I nod. Another alarm seems to silently flash on the edge of my vision. I'll be seeing Ella, too.

In forty-three minutes, I turn from smooth asphalt to well-groomed gravel, the Mercedes slipping underneath a canopy of ancient trees. In the distance, the windows of Lindenholm glow amber in the sunlight, inviting me home. The

Neoclassical lines are softened by exterior walls painted a deep, butter yellow, and it nestles into the grounds like it grew there. Two centuries have passed since the third *Neerheid* van Heyden built it, his wealth accumulated in ways that don't make for clean, heroic stories. Still, it's beautiful.

Amma used to tell me that the U-shaped building made her feel at home. That she knew her old hearth goddesses held her in their hands when, in the earliest and most disappointing days of her marriage, she was blessed to find an echo of a traditional Seongan courtyard house in such an unlikely place.

Alix, her hair an orange sherbet this week, races down the porch and drags me through the hall and into the east wing, past a dizzying string of unused suites. She steps over an extension cord as she strides beyond the threshold, and we are greeted with the sound of an electric drill.

I cock my brow. "What's this?"

She smiles. "I got a VIP RSVP. You'll never guess who. Okay, I'll tell. Mikkel Dorsgard," she squeaks her excitement, fingertips prancing on my arm. "The actor. The *abs*."

His name lands like a left hook.

"You know—" Alix drops her voice into a husky whisper, imitating the famous delivery. "'Your heart is all I wish for, Majesty. Today, tomorrow, forever.'"

Oh, I know it. I fight a gag reflex. All of Sondmark knows it. It won the man his first Oscar nomination and a lucrative ad campaign. I couldn't be more pleased that my sister invited him to come and emote all over the property.

"I didn't know you knew him," I murmur, approaching an arched stone gate.

A giggle bubbles from Alix. "Not know-know. But I know him from his brooding in movies."

"Brooding? What's brooding?"

"Thinking plus hotness," she says, supplying a definition. "I contacted his people as soon as the articles about Ella and him dropped. She looked interested, right? I thought so. I wanted to get her a present because she never meets actual men."

"She meets men." I glower—thinking plus jealousy. She meets too many.

"She meets useless *adel*," she scoffs. We're useless *adel*. "No Sondish aristocrat is going to get serious with a princess. You wouldn't." My skin vibrates in answer. My little sister doesn't have the first clue about what I would and wouldn't do, but she rattles on. "You know too much about the royal clockworks. You've seen under the hood. No," she steps into the garden, "it's better to shop at a new market when the first one doesn't have the right fish."

"Ella's not shopping—"

"Look, look, look." Alix sweeps her hand in a wide arc.

I want to put her straight but she's been busy. The modest 'camp-out' she first conceived of has materialized as crisp canvas tents set on wooden platforms, dotted among blossoming fruit trees. Strings of lights crisscross the garden, and fire pits and lawn games fill open areas, cleverly turning the rigid ornamental walking paths into gathering points. Thick blankets drape over deep outdoor chairs, set in clusters throughout. In the center, a statue of Atlas, covered in lichen and moss, observes the changes but stands resolute, holding the world on his back.

"Marc." Alix tilts her face up and I answer her summons, kissing the cheek she presents. "Don't ask how much it cost."

"I won't," I answer, bumping her shoulder with my shoulder, "but, *jagi*, did the platforms *have* to be engineered so precisely? They're only going to have to come right down."

Alix fidgets, shifting her balance from one foot to another. "When you have a minute, I have this brilliant idea."

"All your ideas are brilliant." Ella. I brush a hand over my arm when she walks through the gate. "But I think your brother is clutching his bank balance."

I should be immune to seeing her in a hoodie and jeans by now. Bored with it. Instead, the sight of her releases a sharp kernel of frustration that rolls under my skin, demanding my attention.

"This is dreamy," she pronounces, eyes lighting on Alix's elaborate preparations. At the look on her face, accountancy flies out of my head.

"See? It's dreamy." Alix elbows me.

I rub the spot and Ella points to the new construction. "You had this planned to the last nail. Who else is coming?"

"No one special." Alix smiles widely and squeezes my arm. "I might slap on a little more eyeliner if I were you."

Ella sends me a look. "Isn't this a camp-out?"

Alix tucks her arm into Ella's elbow. "Yes, dearest, but you should always be prepared to meet your fate. I love this," she says of the hoodie and jeans, "but it's giving s'mores when it could be giving, 'Meet me in the woods.'" She waves a hand at the small wilderness beyond the wall.

Ella rolls her eyes. "For the love of Erasmus's cap, you're not matchmaking, are you? I refuse to make out with a groomsman on the grounds of your ancestral home."

Good. Good for Ella. She has a sound mind. I will devote the next hour to picking out a supportive GIF.

"He's not a—" Alix shakes her head, sounding affronted and sisterly. "I'm just asking if you brought a cute top." I never knew what a dirty liar she was until this moment.

"I'm dressed for a campout," Ella shoots back, shouldering her overnight bag.

Alix directs Ella to her quarters and I watch her go. Too jealous. Too hungry.

Ella climbs the shallow steps to her tent and I can't look away, no matter how much I want to. I make one last bid to resist temptation. "I could use tonight to work," I murmur. "I'm not in your wedding party—"

"You're the one walking me down the aisle," Alix counters, tripping away. "Don't be stupid."

I grip my bag and take a breath. *Don't be stupid.*

At dusk, guests begin to trickle in, fires are lit, and I'm dragged into an unserious game of *stikubb*. When Ella launches her baton into a fountain, I stand at her shoulder, modeling an easy swing. "Like this," I say, straightening her wrist, taking my time. I try to ignore that my heart is beating like I'm one of those software engineers with a dating profile that reads, "I own thirty-three snakes."

"Ella," Alix calls, her voice slicing through the soft evening air. She stands alongside Mikkel Dorsgard, king of the Sondish screen. He's framed in the arched gate, his hair ruffling in the breeze, comically photogenic. "I found you a friend. Come say hello."

Ella's voice is so low I hardly hear the murderous threat. She gives me a tight smile and drops the baton on my foot before jogging to Alix's side. He's not her type. This is my refuge.

Then he kisses her hand and I feel a direct, uncomplicated emotion, mostly in my fists.

When the night grows dark, we gather around the largest bonfire, dragging chairs from the shadows in a loose circle. Alix starts a Seongan drinking game which gets ever more ridiculous and, when a row of empty bottles have been lined up on the edge of the fountain, she hands Ella an old school photo. I lean over to see a snapshot of several Saint Sissela girls dressed up for a dance, posing like supermodels.

"You took this picture," Ella says, glancing up at me, a soft dimple tucking her cheek. "You threatened to cut off Alix's allowance when we wouldn't stop laughing."

Mikkel crowds her other side. Would it delay his next shoot if we got in a fist fight? In the event of a lawsuit, Han Heyden would suffer. "What is money for?" *Amma* likes to ask.

"Look at the youthful passion in your eyes," he says.

"That's not passion," she scoffs, passing the photo around the circle. "That's cheap mascara."

Alix crashes into them from behind, wrapping her arms over both their shoulders so that they look like a couple. My sister lifts her chin and says, with the firm resolution of the slightly drunk, "Let's play hide and seek."

13

VERY UNCOOL

ELLA

"The boundaries are the garden and the woods." Alix gives me a hopeful little push toward Mikkel and closes her eyes to begin the count. "One, Dragonslayer. Two, Dragonslayer. Three, Dragonslayer..."

Dahlia darts behind a statue with a groomsman while Yasmin, in fur boots and skin-hugging athletic-wear, crouches in the middle of a path and puts her hands over her face. Two more groomsmen scramble into fruit trees, raining white blossoms as they shake the boughs.

"I know a good spot," Marc says, dragging Sondmark's most famous actor to a cluster of topiaries by the back of his collar.

Amateur hour. I don't waste time on the manicured confines of the garden, but shoot through a stone gate and into the woods. I know this ground, having traveled every meter of it during my misspent youth. Still, it's May and the ground is wet. I slip up a rise, tripping over heavy roots coiling across my path.

"Forty-seven, Dragonslayer," Alix calls, continuing her count. "Forty-eight..."

I brush my muddy knees and take a sharp turn. It's here, somewhere. Doubling back, I see the familiar silhouette of a particular tree, and slide into its large hollow. I stand with my back against the trunk, slip a shoe off, and shake a twig out. It's wonderfully dark. My heart thumps with excitement and air burns through my lungs. Above the wall, the bonfire casts the faintest light into the woods.

When I hear a soft rustle of underbrush, I hold my breath and shrink against the tree. So help me, if Alix sent Mikkel my way, I'll bribe her colorist to turn her hair lime green.

The figure passes, checks, and changes direction, eventually blotting the light out entirely. I hold my breath until I hear the hushed whisper. "Ella, it's me."

I grab a handful of flannel, hauling Marc into the shelter. "You know this is my hiding spot," I hiss.

A low chuckle vibrates against my chest. "I know it's big enough for two. Were you expecting Mikkel?"

I drum a fist against his chest. "Did anyone follow you?"

Marc lightly grips my upper arms and leans his head out. He's been in a strange mood all night, frowning and silent. His thumbs press into my upper arms, and heat radiates from his touch as from a small pebble thrown into a smooth pond, ripples colliding against every obstacle. I shake my head. When Marc is in one of his protective moods he's always grumpy.

"One hundred!" Alix shouts, her voice muffled and distant.

At first, Alix and Tom collect the easy prey—friends whose commitment to the game lasted only as long as it took to step behind a decorative urn. The losers return to the fire, and their conversation lays down a soothing murmur, punctuated as the minutes pass by shrieks and shouts when other guests are flushed from hiding spots.

All the while, Marc and I stand in silence, his thumbs gently brushing my arms. His breath stirs my hair and his scent is a mixture of soju and subtle cologne. I stare straight forward, resorting to an old trick to hold myself together. *Harald, Frederick, Frederick II, Frederick III...*

He looks up and drops his head, no sooner settled than shifting again. "You still have a trash panda account," he says.

He can't see my furrowed brow. "No, I don't. I sent you screenshots—"

"*SquadRun*," he cuts in.

That. My body eases. "Nobody knows about that."

"Ella."

It hurts when he says my name, but I want to lean into Marc, punishing myself for the sin of wanting him. I swallow thickly. I want gravity to work differently than it does—to push us together no matter which way we sway. I want to kiss him and bear no responsibility for it. It will just be one of those things that happen. One of those things that can't be helped.

Louis, Malthe, Malthe II... I whisper my answer. "I've had that account for more than eight years."

His hands begin to trace a pattern up and down my arms, slow, soothing passes. "I know. You took that handle in Palo Alto when you discovered that raccoon who liked to raid the trash bin," he says.

I smile at the memory. "I was so freaked out that I climbed you. I had a leg hooked over your shoulder."

He laughs, the soft sound wrapping me in a pleasant warmth. His next words bring a chill. "You have to get rid of that account, too."

How can he ask this? The palace is a fishbowl, but against all odds, I created a community lasting a miraculous eight years. Does he think it happened by accident? Online friendships are delicate, hardly able to sustain an altered time zone or a change of relationship status—I've listened to boyfriend woes, offered free tutoring, and blown off all manner of deadlines to preserve this sanctuary. If I abandon it now, my team will disintegrate, reforming in some fashion, perhaps, but never the same.

"Anything else," I bargain. "I'll cram myself into a tight little royal box and make myself fit. I'll be perfect," I say, shoving his chest, practically granite under my hand.

Instead of cool stone, he's warm flesh, and my old crush pushes through the surface like a tulip before a hard frost. It's the wrong time to be raising its thick head.

Marc doesn't budge. "What are you trying to do?" he asks, unbothered.

I push harder and try not to enjoy it. "You're in my personal space."

"You once climbed me," comes his reminder. I can hear the laughter as he exhales, narrowing the tiny distance between us. "Freja and I have personal space. Alma and Clara and I have personal space. You and I don't have personal space."

Rough bark bites into my skin as I attempt to fuse with the tree. "Why can't—"

His hand covers my mouth and his body settles against mine, head dipping to my ear. I freeze. "We have company."

Alix and Tom stumble through the underbrush, laughing. The pitch and weave of their cell phone lights tell a story of tipsiness, but when they move off, narrowing into distant pinpoints, Marc drops his hand. I draw a shaky breath. My nearness doesn't mean anything to him. He builds walls between himself and his best friend's lovestruck little sister like he's been training for it his whole life, and I try to drill it into my stubborn skull that he's not making a pass. This is just his competitive streak and he's trying to keep us from getting caught.

"How do you think you could be more perfect?" he prods, voice rough, resuming a topic I dropped alongside my sanity.

I bless the darkness. "I'll read my speeches exactly how they're written for me. All my opinions will be laundered through the administration wing. Inflation? Hate it. Literacy? Big fan. Teen pregnancy? Won't someone think of the babies?" A silent laugh hitches his chest. "I'll order clothes that make me look like Alma."

"You mean those straight skirts and sort of filmy blouses?" I can hear his gathered brows. He's trying to imagine it. "That's a terrible idea."

"Why?" I ask this focus group of one.

"It won't work. They won't look the same on you as they do on your sister."

My cheeks flame as I parse out his meaning.

I know what I look like. I can't walk into or out of my cursed palace without passing full-length mirrors in every direction, and it would take an idiot to miss the fact that I don't have Freja's delicate elegance, Alma's stately majesty, or Clara's enviable measurements. I have to shrug off being called stout by boutique owners, described in the press as having a sturdy figure, or praised (in an actual speech with an actual transcript you can access on the actual government website) by the National Farmer's Guild for my fine, buxom appearance.

For all that, I'm remarkably well-adjusted. I like the way I look, even if I am fairly short and all business. But having Marc point out all the invisible ways I fail to measure up to perfection feels like being in a boxing match and having my cornerman deliver an uppercut. I expect him to send me back in the ring, patched up and ready to fight, but since he returned from Seong he hasn't been able to keep a civil tongue in his head.

I punch him in the arm—light and teasing despite the way my heart stings. "Are you calling me a dumpling?"

"What? No. I said you won't ever look like your sisters," he corrects, catching my second fist before it makes contact.

A sharp breath escapes me. "Do you even hear yourself?"

"Oh," he says, pushing a thumb into the fist and breaking it up, lacing his fingers through mine. Despite all the pain and irritation, a tiny lightning storm sparks through my veins. "I see the problem."

I tug my hand but he holds it firmly. "You can wear those kinds of things if you want," he tells me. "Just know that everyone will lose their damn minds."

Soju has possibly knocked the corners off my ability to bring his meaning into focus. "Explain it to me like I've just sustained blunt force trauma."

His gaze swings away, silvery moonlight touching the side of his face. "She asked," he says, speaking to his ancestors, maybe. His gaze swings back. "She asked."

He slides his arm around my waist and pulls me up on my toes. There is nothing brotherly about his hold, and the shock of it evaporates the air in my lungs.

"That third wish," he says, gaze dropping to my mouth, leaving me in no doubt about what he wants.

He searches my face for some sign of assent and I only have a millisecond to think. This isn't love—it just isn't—but my mouth tips with a smile, and the voice in my head is dragon-slayer2, shouting amid a hail of enemy fire. *Take the shot!*

"Yes," I whisper.

Marc draws a ragged breath and drops his head, fisting his hands in the thick cotton of my hoodie. As soon as his lips touch mine, I stop caring that this might be his way of delivering an inspirational message on body-positivity. His mouth is warm and mobile and...

I sigh, our breath mingling, as he takes control. I am intimately aware of how rich and full his life is, but he kisses like a gamer with a hyperfixation. Like someone who has been cooped up in a basement for months, planning every move, playing and replaying this moment until the muscle memory is burned into his soul.

When he gathers me closer, destroying my peace from now until the day I die, a thread of panic races through my nerves. *Oh no, oh no, oh no.* I had convinced myself that kissing Marc van Heyden would be like wearing a pair of espadrilles—something nicer in my head than it could ever be in real life. But the reality of Marc's lips on mine is much better than even my best attempts to imagine it. He is not a disappointing kisser and I am in serious trouble.

I grip his shoulders, fragile with the desperate hope that he won't see all the years I've spent wishing for this and hiding it. *Vede*, this is going to hurt. He must sense some withholding because he gives me a frustrated, coaxing shake.

Okay.

I release the tight grip on myself and pull him into me, tracing the scar in his hairline, down to his earlobe. When I brush it, a shiver travels across his shoulders and he holds onto me like I'm the only thing keeping him upright. For a few moments, I think it's true.

He pauses to breathe, the drag of air coming with a shudder, and I smile against his lips. Marc is being very uncool.

I didn't know. I didn't know it was going to be this good. It was supposed to be an adolescent crush, as dead as a felled oak, hauled out of the woods. Now that same ground is sprouting fairy rings—new magic growing from the roots of the old. What am I going to do?

Before I can hazard an answer, a crash breaks us apart. I stumble against the tree just as a pair of bright flashlights pierce the dark sanctuary.

14

Ove! Ove!

ELLA

I squint away from the harsh points of light and hastily scrub my mouth.

"The game is up," Alix laughs, hauling me out of the cleft, unaware of the terrain. I twist my ankle on a thick root and bite back a cry as I join her on the path.

"Didn't you hear my 'Ove! Ove! Pen up the cows'?" She sends Marc a scathing look as we go. "I found Mikkel right away."

At the campfire, Alix pushes me into an empty chair next to the actor. For the rest of the night, I catch Marc gazing at me from across the fire, his face grave.

It's not that serious, I want to say. It was one kiss and we satisfied our curiosity.

My throat vibrates with a rueful laugh. That wasn't one kiss. It was a nine-part miniseries with subtitles, musical numbers, and a dramatic cliffhanger setting up season two. It's all I can do to answer questions and nod along to conversations while that kiss plays and replays in my head.

The party begins to break up. Some guests head to their tents and others to smaller fire circles, filling the night with low voices, interspersed with apologetic bursts of laughter. As the maid of honor, I do my part to keep the party going, hampered by Mikkel who won't shut up. The pain in my ankle turns into a dull throb and I listen with half an ear, wishing I could go to Marc. I want to reassure him that nothing can change our friendship, but a worm of anxiety chews away at the soft flesh of certainty.

"I would have said no to the prosthetic ears but the money was insane," Mikkel says, speaking of his role in an American blockbuster, firelight flickering over his chiseled features.

I tip my head back, following the smoke into the night sky. "There's Ulek the Bear," I cut in, pointing to Ursa Minor. Marc taught me to identify him and *Karlswagon*, The Woodsman and The Herring Net.

Across the fire, Marc stills.

"I read a script about a nuclear physicist on a doomed mission who falls in love with a nebula he imagines as Audrey Hepburn. We're getting AI to recreate her role," Mikkel persists. Pressing his palms together, he closes his eyes briefly. "Such an honor to work with her."

Eventually, I give up any thought of outlasting Mikkel. I retreat to my tent, gritting my teeth against the twinge in my ankle. When the flap drops closed, I collapse onto the bed, finally allowing the enormity of the night to crash into me. I kissed Marc. It wasn't some delusional, self-insert fanfiction vomited into a Notes app by a fevered adolescent mind. I peel off my shoes and go over it again a few more times just to be sure. He knows I was into it. I flop back and cover my face with a thick pillow. *Dominanstid*, he could see how much I liked it from a mile away. It was as obvious as a monster destroying whole cities, burning everything in its path with fiery breath.

No matter how soft the Turkish rugs or how smooth the Egyptian cotton, sleep eludes me. At the break of dawn, I shrug on a flannel layer and stumble from the tent, my hair a fury of curls.

I follow the smell of woodsmoke and have a tiny, Girl Trackers freak out about leaving fires unattended all night next to historically significant stately homes. I break into an awkward run, skidding to a stop when I see Marc add another log into the blaze. He lifts his eyes and drops the piece of wood. Sparks kick up, flying skyward in a whorl of smoke until they flame out.

"I thought—" I stumble into a low-slung chair, watching him.

"There's water. There's a rake. There's a four meter perimeter," he answers.

I nod. My heart won't settle. He takes the chair next to mine, leans forward, running a finger along my uninjured ankle, and hooks the slim gold chain. "Ella—"

"Ove! Ove! The cows are out," Alix shouts, hopping from her tent, hair wrapped in a pink plush headband with a bow in the front. "Breakfast!"

Marc's fingers slip away and I scramble to my feet. "Where does she get the energy?" I mutter.

Marc grunts a laugh.

"You look like you've gotten a telegram that all the young men of your village have been wiped out in the Great War," Alix says, greeting her brother. "What happened?"

He gives her a great hug and me a look. *Don't you dare.*

Doesn't he know me at all?

I won't tell Alix. I can't. After long hours of reflection, I arrive at the conclusion that it appalls me, what we've done—what I've done. I dragged Alix along when I got my first bra. We played pin-the-tiara on the eligible bachelor when we tried to guess who Mama had lined up to be Alma's future husband. When Tom wanted to propose, he came to *Amma* first and then to me.

She doesn't know how long I was in love with her brother, but she does know every boy I've ever kissed. If it had been Mikkel in the woods, I would have already dragged Alix off to my car, where I would have ranked his performance on a well-established scale between Tobias, the Unexpectedly Capable Stanford Beatnik, and Cameron, the Handsy Junior Diplomat.

I can't lie to Alix, but neither can I bring myself to look at her. This is the hard truth. Marc and I are connected by invisible threads of kinship and history running back and forth in a water-tight weave, and the kiss is already snagging those irreplaceable strands.

Breakfast is served in a small courtyard where heating towers provide an umbrella of warmth and a long table is set up in the center. It's decorated with crisp white linens and careless wildflower bunches that have me wondering how early some servant was up, raking through the meadows for the delicate arrangements.

The wedding party straggles in, bleary-eyed but conspicuously chic. A princess, aware of the professional photographer prowling on the perimeter, has to be careful about how she publicly interacts with wealth, but Yasmin's hair is in effortless disarray and money drips from her wool blanket, patched tweed jacket, and vintage cowboy boots.

Alix butters a roll and hands half to Tom. He hands her the jar of preserves, their exchange deft and wordless. "I want reviews," she says. "Did you all sleep well? Marc?"

I glance up to find her brother looking at me.

"Marc," Alix snaps her fingers.

"I stayed near the fire pit all night."

She makes a sound of annoyance at the back of her throat. "Is that where the wi-fi was strongest? You're going to give yourself an aneurysm if you keep going at this pace." She pats Tom's hand. "A wise man turns his life into a temple and finds better things to worship than work."

Marc's gaze drifts to me with a look that steals my breath, looking away only when a servant leans over his shoulder and speaks in a low voice. Marc strides away, and when he returns, I almost tumble off my chair. The spectacle of glamor rounding the high hedge on his arm is wearing the shortest miniskirt I've ever seen in my life. Long black hair moves like strands of glass and her baby-smooth skin appears to be experiencing sun for the very first time.

I bolt to my feet and Alix grabs my wrist, her voice coming out in a breathy squeak. "Ella. Is that Lee Jang Mi?"

I nod and look around the table, waiting for these dummies to get it. A member of the Seongan girl group BLUSH is standing in the garden. This beauty ambassador for Chloe. This pop queen. This singer of such iconic lyrics as "Blow up my phone like dynamite. Blow up my life, let's do it right" with accompanying iconic body roll.

She greets Alix with a soft bow and elegant hands, the epitome of Seongan formality under Marc's approving eye. Though I want to lean into the delightful fandom of it all, my heart stops. She's here because of Marc.

This was always going to happen. Someday, a girl would come into Marc's life who suited him in every way. Someday is today.

I want to run out of the garden and have a good cry, but a lifetime of wrestling tender feelings into submission serves me well. I send a message of silent gratitude to my mother. My face clears of everything more complicated than how much I am

BLUSH's number one fan and I rake my unruly curls over one shoulder, smiling widely.

Marc watches me. "Lee Jang Mi, meet your most die-hard fan, Her Royal Highness Princess Ella of Sondmark."

Her expression is one of gentle curiosity.

"Just Ella," I correct. "I'm so excited to meet you that I might die. I really might. Am I dead?"

The goddess looks to Marc for a translation. He speaks to her in Seongan, a string of syllables too fast for me to parse out with my limited vocabulary. Besides, his hotness is extremely distracting. "My pleasure to meet you," he coaches her.

"My pleasure," Jang Mi murmurs, mangling it, giving Marc an adorable look of confusion.

I curl my fingers in, the nails biting into the soft flesh of my palm, but Alix grips my fist, too overwhelmed to notice. "Would you like to join us for breakfast?"

Jang Mi halts over her words, drawing an invisible string connecting her to Marc. "We have business."

Marc leads her back through the break in the hedge, and Jang Mi turns her head to look at me, slipping her hand through the crook of Marc's elbow. I frown, thinking of a famous Sondish expression from the Cold War. "When you meet a Vorburgian on the street, punch him in the mouth. He'll know why." Some things you understand without the need for words. Jang Mi wants me to know about her relationship with Marc. *Stay clear. This is mine.*

Alix rocks me side to side. "Did you know a member of BLUSH was coming?" she asks. "Marc is killing it with his surprises these days."

I reach for a blanket, covering my sudden wish to burst into tears in the dousing weight of wool.

"And did you see that miniskirt?" She laughs, taking a strawberry cut in the shape of a heart from Tom.

I nod. "The dating scandal isn't the only thing that has legs."

15

LITTLE CREATURE

MARC

"It's good of you to come," I say, reverting to my mother's tongue.

"I'll go anywhere you ask, *Marcus-shi*," she says, tagging my name with a Seongan honorific.

We pick up her breakfast smoothie on our way through the kitchens. The slurry looks like the underside of a boat dock, but she swears by it, happily sucking the straw as we adjourn to the library.

I hold the door but my gaze locates the exact spot where I tumbled to the floor with Ella in my arms. Was it only last week? I look at the window and the woods beyond, but there is no safety there. I might have to burn the little forest down.

I let Alix think I was industriously working last night, shooting off emails and outlining productivity schedules. Instead, I tore through her aesthetic piles of wood until they were reduced to a few bark chips, and cursed myself in every language I know.

Stultes es. Lines were crossed.

Ever since I returned from Seong, I haven't been able to speak to Ella like a normal person, and it's not her fault she has become my own personal kryptonite. When did that happen? Erasmus knows.

I should have backed away last night and explained with clinical precision that I didn't mean she wasn't as appealing as her sisters. The problem was that I meant that she is much, much *more* appealing than her sisters. Other people have different, worse opinions, I'm sure. There were no words that were going to help me with that one.

So I kissed her like I was on the seventh round of a hot wings challenge and she was the last glass of milk. Desperate. Insatiable. My stomach tightens and I feel my heartbeat everywhere. If Alix hadn't found us when she did, I might still be kissing her.

"Why do you look so tired," Jang Mi perches on the window seat, "when I'm the one who took a red eye?"

I sink into the sofa and close my eyes for a moment. I bet Ella slept deeply. I bet she had her hand crooked under her chin at an impossible angle, cheeks flushed with sleep. I don't have to wonder if she likes to push her icy feet under the nearest warm body. I know she does.

Jang Mi glances out the window and I sit forward, clasping my hands lightly as I remember how Ella kissed me back and the brush of her fingertips against my ear. A satisfied shiver carries through my shoulders, but cold reason grabs me by the collar and hauls me back onto the crumbling ledge of reason. Noah asked me to watch his sister and it's my job to keep her out of trouble.

It's not as simple as that. Even now, the memory of that kiss kicks me on the back of my legs, forcing me to kneel before it. Honor makes me frown.

Noah would send a hit man if he knew, and for the sake of the many ties that bind us, this lapse of judgement with Ella has to be regrettable. It must be viewed as a mistake. I rub a hand over the sudden pain in my chest.

"Did I understand correctly, Marcus-shi?" Jang Mi says, stretching to see the corner of the garden from the window. "Was that little creature really a princess?"

Little creature?

Irritation works under my skin as I translate her meaning. Seongan can be a formal language, layered with sharp, Confucian boundaries delineating old from young, king from subject, teachers from students, constantly reinforcing hierarchies. 'Little creature' is a Seongan idiom and not as bad as it sounds in Sondish, but it firmly places Ella in the realm of children and much-loved animals—something to be protected rather than someone who could wreck me.

"Explain yourself, Jang Mi-yeo," I charge. It doesn't matter that she's internationally famous. In the rules which govern our shared culture, she must give way.

Jang Mi crosses her long legs and takes a sip of her smoothie, eyes searching my face. "I was surprised after you described her.

I was expecting one of the Four Ancient Beauties, but in the morning light, your princess has spots all over her face." She gives a shiver of distaste.

"Freckles," I correct. They make me want to run my fingertips along the ridge of her cheeks and plot them as carefully as ancient mariners mapped the stars. "They're cute."

Jang Mi pouts, her eyes open wide and innocent. Her hands are wedged under her chin in a kind of frame. "Aren't I cute? Aren't you happy to see me?"

This kind of performative flirtatiousness is common in Seong, but it doesn't have the same effect in Sondmark. Despite my father's attempts to purge the bloodline of sobriety, I'm probably too Lutheran to succumb to it. "Of course I am. I hope this stop means you're accepting my proposal."

She drops the wheedling tone, emits a little sigh, and shifts into being the entertainment mogul she is. "I ran your idea of a benefit concert past the other girls and our manager. Even with a stripped down production, it means diverting considerable resources from the tour."

"Think of what all that charity will do to your public image," I counter. "You'll be the saviors of Seong. Your career might even survive an actual dating scandal."

"Is that a proposition?" When I make no answer, she releases a sigh and sets her smoothie aside. "If certain conditions are met, we'll consider it."

"And those are?"

"Don't rush me," she says, kneading her neck. "The flight was exhausting."

Negotiations move slowly in Seong. There are layers of ritual to be observed, and her reticence is not really about being too tired. The rigorous Seongan idol system is meant to weed out mere mortals and I'm certain that Jang Mi could pop and lock from her deathbed. No, she simply wants priceless treasures set at her feet and to be wooed with a ceremonial cup of tea as an ancient zither echoes across a formal Seongan garden. Slowly. Formally.

Her eyes flick up and she smiles. "When you needed help, your first thought was of me. Was it your idea?"

"It was Princess Ella's."

As soon as the words leave my mouth, I recognize it as a misstep. Jang Mi may be a hardened professional, but she still needs to have her ego stroked.

I would never have thought of appealing to pop stars. It was Ella who recognized their potential as a driver of charitable donations. It was Ella who worked out the logistics of where and when it would be easiest for BLUSH to take a four-day halt from the tour. She spent weeks spamming me with Pixy shorts, and I dutifully watched each one, lying in my bed at the end of long days, until I finally gave in.

I give her the same smile I gave early investors. "This can't work with anyone else. Why don't we join my sister's party and I can spend the day helping you make up your mind," I add, getting ahead of an outright refusal.

Jang Mi stands, taking in the distant view of aristocrats milling about the walled garden in vintage silk pajamas and quilted robes. "I refuse to dress like a peasant."

True to her word, when Jang Mi joins us at the stables for a group bicycling excursion, she's wearing a mini jumpsuit and oversized jacket, paired with blindingly white high top sneakers.

She tugs on my shirt tails, shy when out of her element. "I haven't ridden a bike in forever, Marcus-shi."

"We're going to ride tandem," I say, pointing to the elongated bike.

Ella brakes next to us, tires biting into the gravel. Her hair has been caught back in a ponytail, and her clothes—a pair of cuffed jeans and a boxy top—should not be making me fight for air. *Vede.*

"He will go too fast down the hills and around the turns." Ella smiles, slowing her English words, and looks directly into Jang Mi's face. I can't detect a speck of embarrassment or awkwardness. I could convince myself last night was a hallucination if I thought my imagination was that good.

Her nose wrinkles with silent laughter, freckles scrunching together. "If he gets carried away, be sure to pinch him."

"Pinch?" Jang Mi echos, elegant even in her confusion.

Ella clips my waist, and I catch her fingertips without thinking. "Stop it," I whisper. I release her, but not before the flame of attraction burns me again.

Tom, wearing a helmet like a good American, leads the party down the long drive and out onto the country road, Alix at his side. Soon, we are strung out along fields newly sewn with barley and oats, a fresh wind at our back. Up ahead, I see Mikkel flirting with Ella, making her laugh by pretending to lose control of his bicycle.

I increase my pace and Jang Mi pinches my side.

"Stop that," I say, lapsing into Seongan.

"Slow down, Marcus-shi," she counters. "This is not a race. What's the hurry?"

I feel her weight shift to one side and I counter it by leaning in the opposite direction. "What are you doing?"

"I'm looking at something," she says, rocking back into place. She pinches me again.

"Ow. What?"

"I didn't know you were in love with someone."

"I'm not in love with anyone."

Jang Mi pinches me again, harder this time. "Does she know?"

We're speaking in Seongan and there is a measure of relief when I stop guarding my tongue. Stop pretending I don't know who she means.

"Her brother is my best friend. I'm looking out for her."

"As you would look out for a 'little creature'?" Jang Mi lays a palm against my back and pats slowly. "Does *she* know?"

Sunlight touches Ella's hair and the ridge of her cheek when she turns her gaze on Mikkel, a man famous for smoldering in high definition. When she glances back at me, something shifts. Her chin dips and she swallows, looking away.

"It's not love," I insist. "Maybe."

Jang Mi reaches for my waist but I bat her hand away before she can do me any more violence.

"Maybe, Marcus?" She drops the honorifics but I let her get away with it for once. "'Maybe' is not the language of the Hanaya Clan," she says, calling forth my ancestors whose rites I perform each season. "'Maybe' is not a word used by people whose ancestors buried their enemies up to their necks in the sand and waited for high tide. Tell me then, do you like her?"

Joaen. Like. The Sondish translation is unsatisfying. We 'like' the color of a new car or the taste of Pankedruss. We would say "I like that girl" in the moments before we make our move, and be speaking of an emotion as thin as tea.

In Seong, *Joaen* isn't a settled emotion. It's not love, but it leads there. It's craving. Worship, almost.

The line of bicycles begins up a long rise, and my chest constricts with the effort it takes to admit the truth. My eyes fasten on Ella and I accept that there's no 'maybe' about this.

"*Naui ta joaen*," I say. I like her.

I feel a sudden boost of power as Jang Mi begins to pedal, putting all her effort into the mechanism. She laughs as we begin to pass the others, flying down the hill on the other side, and when we coast to a stop near a quiet village pub her eyes are sparkling.

She dismounts and slips into my arms for a fierce hug.

"What's this?" I ask.

She shakes her head. "You have given me a treasure, Marcus-shi. This little piece of your true heart." She slips an arm through mine and looks up. "I'm ready to talk about the concert."

16

THAT GOOD

ELLA

I smile at Mikkel because, when I do, my head is in the correct position to overhear the conversation between Marc and a beloved Seongan pop idol.

Did it have to be Lee Jang Mi? Did it have to be the woman whose solo hit, "Heart (Suffocating in a Rice Chest)," became my anthem when I decided to beat this one-sided love once and for all? For months I did a whole morning cardio routine to it.

Flamen hell.

Mikkel is midway through a story about the harms of seed oils when I train my ears on the riders behind me. You would think I would be nearly fluent in Seongan, considering the number of hours I've spent reading subtitles, but I only know an assortment of words. *Hello. I'm okay. Are you insane?* But then I hear Jang Mi say *'joaen'*.

"It's more than liking," Marc once explained. "It's more like an emotional crash out. There's an element of submission."

Marc repeats it back and my hands go hot and cold, my heart thundering in my chest. Did it have to be her? Did it have to be now? Did I expect Marc to live as a monk, forever devoting himself to the sacred texts of software code? No. Marc is a profoundly eligible, landed *adel* and tech mogul. Jang Mi is part of the unstoppable pop juggernaut currently smashing global records. The headlines write themselves. In Seong, they're already written.

Vede.

"Maybe you've got a seed oil allergy, too," Mikkel says, jerking me out of my thoughts.

It hurts to breathe, but I force words from my throat. "What makes you think so?"

His finger, hovering in the air, sketches out a path across my face. "Your eyes are red and there's a little..." He brushes his jawline, "puffiness, around here. I had my suspicions about breakfast so I kept to the fruit. One should never to consume a sausage of unknown provenance."

When we arrive at the pub, Alix races across the forecourt, holding my handlebars as I dismount.

"Mikkel is being attentive," she whispers, speaking English for Tom's benefit.

"He thinks I have an allergic condition. Honestly, he's not my style."

She makes an irritated sound but her mood shifts like a dust mote catching the sunlight. "Oh well. Did you see where Jang Mi went?"

I focus on my kickstand. "Marc led her off to inspect the millworks or 'inspect at the millworks'."

Alix laughs. "I've been manifesting my future as an aunt to little BLUSH babies for hours."

"Babe," Tom says, sliding an arm around Alix's waist. He spares me a glance. "You can't count your chickens before they hatch."

"Is that one of your Amish phrases?" she asks, following him into the pub, swinging their hands together.

Meanwhile, I glower at the trailhead where Marc disappeared. As a matter of dispassionate ethical inquiry, I wonder if a man who has just wholeheartedly kissed someone should have to undergo a period of suspended privileges before he can start kissing someone else. A make-out moratorium, if you will.

"Ella." *Neerheid* Kaas, Auden to his friends, throws a careless arm over my shoulders. He's been flirty since the night of the costume party. Dark glasses shade a hangover and his white-blond hair sticks up in boyish tufts. "I know I'm on your mother's list. When are we going to start testing our compatibility?"

My mother's spreadsheet of eligible bachelors is a comedy bit to everyone who doesn't live under the crushing weight of it but I play along. "I thought you'd never ask."

He dips me over his arm and plants a sloppy kiss on my neck. I suppress a shudder until suddenly, Auden's support disappears. My stomach clenches in a panic, but Marc, appearing out of nowhere, catches me.

He releases me with a stern look and marches Auden into the pub, past the huge, bottle cap portrait of my mother, and into the common room where he plants him in the midst of a group of men. I settle onto a long window seat with the other girls, and when Jang Mi returns from the washroom, I squeeze another space for her next to me.

We trade smiles over lunch. I spread cheese on a savory cracker while she nibbles on a pickle until she finally leans forward, silky hair falling off her shoulder.

"Pardon. May I ask for a translation?" I nod. "What did he mean?" She points at Auden "He is on a list?"

For the last eight years, BLUSH has consumed me like a case of the hives. I've watched scores of interviews, dance practices, and game show clips. The other members are fluent in English, having been scouted abroad, but Jang Mi learned English from a private school and tutors. She speaks slowly, her words hesitant.

"My mother is the queen," I say, flicking a glance at the impressive portrait. Never mind the humble materials. The artist caught her unconquerable spirit. "I must make a good match."

Her brows barely gather. "Match?"

"A good marriage. She wants my husband to be suitable."

"Suitable?"

Each new word is a rabbit hole into the dark underbelly of royal priorities. "Rich, educated, titled…"

"Oh. *Neerheid* van Heyden. *Neerheid* is the title?"

I choke on a swallow of coffee. "Yes. In English, they say 'Lord'."

Jang Mi tears off a strip of pastry, carefully avoiding the wells of butter and sugar, and when she catches me watching, an apologetic dimple peeps out. "Too sweet."

It would be nice to hate her but she's perfect.

"Is Marcus-shi," she shakes her head, "Marcus on your marriage list?" She asks this during one of those odd silences every large group will sometimes have, and the question lands like a splash.

A hot flush climbs up my cheek. "He's on everyone's list," I say, laughing off the implications. "You've seen his house."

"You *must* marry from this list?"

My throat feels tight, but Alix leans across. "Ella would never get herself trapped like that." She places her flattened palm under my chin. "Behold the pride of Sondmark. The Rebel Princess of the House of Wolffe."

The table erupts into laughter, and before I can head them off, tales of my youth are shared with a shocked Jang Mi. Idol training is rigorous. It begins young, eats up an inhuman amount of time, and leaves little leeway for misbehavior. Jang Mi and I should have that in common, but I also have a bent—some might call it a genius—for criminal mischief.

Alix raps her knuckles against the table. "Do you remember the time you climbed in through the headmistress's window—halfway up a turret tower—to wipe Bodil's cell phone before her parents could see it?"

I lower my voice, inviting Jang Mi to understand. "Bodil chartered a helicopter on her parents' credit card to meet her boyfriend in Vaado."

Alix breaks in. "Ella was so determined to keep Bodil from being kicked out of Saint Sissela's that she performed this death-defying climb twice—once up and once down." She giggles. "When she was caught, she had to clean the washrooms for a month."

I grin into my coffee. "Yes, but Bodil got to stay, and I know how to scrub toilets."

Eventually, the conversation drifts into other topics and Jang Mi leans close. "Does this mean you *have* to be with Marc or you cannot be with Marc?"

Marc's voice echoes in my head—the tone and intensity. *Joaen.* She's only trying to find out if she has a clear path, but I feel a flash of resentment. If I were Jang Mi—if I'd heard my crush say that word in that tone of voice right to my face—I would know he was mine.

I inhale a sharp breath. Marc has never felt a speck of romance about me. Things have gotten a little playful in the last couple of months, but I can't allow him to pass Jang Mi up just because he got carried away by boredom or proximity or the soft night sky, his protective instincts activated by the need to make me understand that he didn't call me a troll.

I would never ruin this for him.

My smile feels like tearing a piece of paper from a notebook, following the perforations until a fiber catches and the line swerves across the page. I press my shaking lips together.

My nose wrinkles with theatrical distaste. "My mother would celebrate if she thought I was getting serious with Marc, but I refuse to marry anyone she thinks is appropriate."

My delivery of this shocking lie is pretty good, but pressure builds behind my eyes. I want to run to the ladies' room to, I don't know, take up smoking or have a cry or text Clara to call me about a family emergency. Maybe there's some animal shelter needing an urgent, royal dedication. The citizens will find it charming when I burst into tears while cuddling a lap-full of emotional support puppies.

But Jang Mi glances up and touches my arm.

"Marcus-shi," she says, making herself even smaller, and dragging me closer, "sit, sit."

Blood drains out of my face. It makes more sense to slot him on the end, but a too-small canyon opens up between me and Alix. He can't fit. He can't possibly—

I close my eyes as his long body wedges between me and his sister. The minimal amount of room on the window seat means that we both turn sideways and I'm backed up against his chest while he rests his arm along the back of the bench. When he releases a breath, it stirs my hair.

"How did you become a fan of BLUSH, Your...Princess..." Jang Mi is as anxious as I am to move away from the topic of how I would rather die than give my mother the satisfaction of marrying Marc van Heyden.

I tell her about hearing their debut in the trailer music for *Yakuza Bloodbath: Battle for the Cabaret Club*, and Marc murmurs against my ear. "You shouldn't have been playing that."

Jang Mi begins to speak rapidly in Seongan. After a tiny pause, Marc begins to translate, his lips almost brushing my ear as he tells the story of their earliest projects.

I hold myself as stiffly as I would in a Queen's Day parade and feel Marc's amusement threading under his words. I'm not about to relax if it means more touching.

"I saw you when you played Gongboja Palace," I tell her. "I had to promise my mother straight As for an entire year, but it was the best night of my life."

"Best?" Marc whispers, reaching forward to swipe a piece of cheese, nearly enveloping me. This gets no translation and I freeze, reanimating only when Jang Mi makes eye contact.

"You will come to the Concert for Seongan Relief?" she asks.

The fan girl takes over, and I forget the complicating undercurrents, wrapping my hand around Marc's forearm. "Has it been decided?"

She nods, gracious as a queen. "At Lindenholm in August." She shifts gear again, switching into Seongan, making it impossible to avoid the sound of Marc burrowing deeper and deeper into my brain.

We resume our ride, and soon I'm peddling hard up rises that look like nothing from a distance. The pain in my ankle starts as a twinge and turns into a throb as we reach a trailhead, its entrance dark and cool.

A servant hands out hiking sticks and collects the bicycles, loading them onto a lorry. We are, Tom tells us, to return to Lindenholm in minibuses. He has planned our simple country outing better than some military campaigns, and I like the future Alix has chosen for herself. She is a starter and he is a finisher. He's never annoyed that she runs on vibes.

Jang Mi begs Mikkel to show her the proper way to hold hiking sticks, and they set off into the woods at a brisk clip. I follow more slowly. Despite the tight lacing on my boots, a dull pain grows in my ankle as we tramp over the uneven ground, and my pace drags with each step.

The nearest members of the party become distant flashes of color as the trail bends back on itself, the sound of laughter muffled against tree boughs and dense earth, and Marc falls back, following me up the path.

"What's wrong?" he asks from behind me. I carefully step over a tree root. "You're usually a good hiker. Is it your ankle?"

I would rather drink poison than admit it is. I'm not mad at him, I tell myself. He's done nothing wrong, but I have spent every measure of nobility I have so he can run off with his pop goddess. There is nothing in my bank but pettiness, clinking around like loose change.

He catches the hem of my shirt. "You don't have to go on."

My eyes close on a tide of feeling. Sooner or later, we'll have to talk about the kiss and my noble resolutions. I will never be more ready than now.

I toss the hiking sticks aside and lean against the trunk of a fallen tree. "Alright. Let's talk."

He crouches down. "You should see a doctor about that ankle. What if—"

I shake my head, dragging my boot out of reach. I can't do this if he's touching me. Caring. "Let's talk about that kiss."

Kiss. The word has a definition so broad it's useless. It encompasses the ceremonial greetings I extend to Mama's cabinet ministers at a state banquet, as well as what went on and on and on last night, ebbing and flowing in intensity, delivering a million data points on all the ways I hadn't known Marc before.

He looks up. "Are you upset?"

"Do I sound—" I clear my throat, ironing out the irritation, and lie right to his face. "I'm not upset. My ankle is sore, and you look like you've been dying to reach for your label maker."

"Label maker?" he laughs. He knows what I mean. When I got to Stanford, I luxuriated in untidiness for the first time in my life, tossing ready-to-wear clothes in a laundry basket in my dorm room, free at last from the rigidity of the palace. Marc's tiny ranch house was different. Because it doubled as a living space and a start-up office, organization was key to optimization. When I got him a label maker that first Christmas, I thought he might kiss me. *Vede*, how long was I chasing that high?

Now it's time to put Ella in her place.

He stands and leans against a trail marker. "It wouldn't hurt to be on the same page about it."

I suppress a bitter laugh. Marc might as well whip out the tiny keyboard, typing, "E.L.L.A = F.R.I.E.N.D."

"First of all, it was great." He doesn't look at me when he delivers this gem, but it's a nice little box neatly checked, a compliment firmly delivered. When I don't readily agree, his jaw works, and I take pleasure in derailing this brisk exercise in self-control.

He tips his head back, exposing his throat. His teeth are set and he releases a ragged breath. "Two. You and Alix have been friends for a long time. So have Noah and I."

"So have you and I."

He nods. "You get it. There's a lot of history between us, and we have a lot going on right now. We can't afford distractions." The label maker whirrs to life, the device spitting out a sticker.

I don't disagree with him. I don't. This painful stabbing under my ribs is just the fading specter of adolescent Ella having a fit. If he wants me to recite all the reasons we can't be together, I know them by heart.

"You're running a multinational business, busy taking over the reins of Lindenholm, planning a benefit concert, in the midst of a dating scandal with a world-famous pop star..." I pick tufts of moss from the notch of the tree and cast them into the underbrush, blinking away the stinging sensation. Allergies are hell this year.

His tone is clipped. "You've got a succession crisis to navigate, your family to hold together, your exit from the monarchy to plan, and all those appropriate men to avoid."

I grip the moss. Marc heard me, back there at the pub. I brush my hands together and hop off the log, absorbing the pain radiating from my ankle. Good. I don't look nearly as pathetic.

The air is so still I feel the weight of it on my skin, holding me down, rooting me to the ground. Last night was a dream, but you can't live in a dream. My parents are proof of that, surely.

"I want to make sure we're good," he says. I imagine him affixing the label to my forehead, sliding a thumb across the surface to make it secure.

"I'm good. And now we know." I grab the hiking sticks out of his hands.

"Know what?" he asks as I turn up the rough track.

"That we weren't *that* good." The lie scratches its way up my throat.

It takes every bit of royal training to make it look from the set of my shoulders and the angle of my head that I'm fine, navigating this trail alone. I ask him about the concert, the logistics and details—everything I can think of to keep him talking—but, as we near the waterfall, I can't hide how much my ankle hurts. He slows to match my speed but doesn't say anything.

Dominanstid, I'll explode if he does.

Ahead, Alix hails us from the top of a large boulder. "Ella," she shouts, "you look like you want to do violence. Has my brother been lecturing you about decorum?"

"I wouldn't dare," Marc calls. Even without turning around, I know he looks like something out of a high-end recreational clothing catalog. Perfect hair. Muscled forearms exposed, his tanned skin clean and dewy.

I'm red-faced and sweaty, my hair a frizzy halo. Anyone can tell, just from looking, that we don't match.

Alix hops from the boulder. "Seriously, Ells, this is supposed to be fun. We could take the shortcut to the road and send you back to Lindenholm. Marc, why haven't you put her on your back?"

He moves to crouch in front of me but I stride past him, pride carrying me where my ankle won't. "I'll rest up ahead."

"Ella, you're going to hurt yourself."

Somehow his consideration makes it worse. "I'm going to make it," I clip. "I just had to stop pretending this isn't a big deal."

17

ONE RULE

MARC

Lines of pain bracket her mouth, and by the time we get back to Lindenholm, she's gone silent. It serves her right. I offered to carry her on my back. I packed in the Seongan gummy candies she likes and an extra bottle of water which she refused. I noticed she took Mikkel's protein granola, though. I identify a perverse satisfaction within myself, knowing she hated it.

I retreat to my office with Jang Mi, taking a call with her manager, making notes about the technical needs of an event of this scale. I work from the outline Ella suggested long ago. Festival accommodations, licensing rights, general ticketing, concessions, and facilities. From time to time we pause our work, and Jang Mi shakes her head, muttering, "Aiiiiii," a Seongan sound at the back of the throat that is half word, half bone-deep exasperation.

Afternoon shadows gather and a hard rain pelts the expensive roof of the old house. Auden takes Jang Mi for a short tour, and

I wander to the kitchen, passing Tom on my way, his Pennsylvania accent echoing down the hall. He's in the alcove where Dad used to store his hookah, *Amma* told me, and when Dad passed, she replaced the soft furnishings and got HAZMAT cleaners in.

"Don't be a freaking jago—," Tom cuts off and nods at me. The Bluetooth earpiece is jammed in one ear, and he holds his phone in both hands, fingers tapping the screen. "We gotta do a risk assessment. I'm not budging until we get it. Yeah, I'll call you. If you press that button, I'll use your guts to hang my laundry. No. No. Don't be a moron. Monday morning, I'll call you."

He taps his earbud but his fingers keep going. "Hey, Marc."

"Are we keeping you from work?" My future brother-in-law is of average height, carries a little extra weight around his middle, and seems unconcerned by the retreat of his hairline. I'm not entirely sure what Alix sees in him.

Tom grins with the aura of a man who measures his home office for precise and transparent tax valuations. "I'm just happy to be here."

"I could find you a real office," I offer. "You can touch base before markets close."

"Markets aren't open on weekends," he reminds me.

I shove my hands into my pockets and tap the wainscoting with the tip of my shoe. "That's not how you guys treat it."

Tom's eyes narrow. He leans back, sets the phone down, and crosses his arms, seeing that I'm not quite shooting the breeze.

"One of my biggest clients wanted to move his entire principle into crypto. I figured I should take the call."

I nod an apology.

"Before I let her sign up for this, I told Alix my job was gonna drive her crazy," he admits. "Finance isn't summer camp, but we made a deal. When I work, I work. When I'm home, I'm home." He glances across the hall. Alix is organizing a watch party for *Marathon Bride*, a romcom about a distance runner who refuses to marry anyone who can't beat her PR and the baker who supplies her with pre-race carbs.

I like their deal, but I think of Atlas, holding up his globe in the garden, bowing under the weight of it. "Can you put them in separate boxes?" I ask. It's satisfying to think you can control everything by keeping things tidy.

"Nothing is that clean. I mean, I had to take this call tonight." He swipes up the phone and starts tapping. I'm amused to see that he's playing *Creature Catching*, a gentle little game built around running a farm. One of Alix's favorites.

He flicks me a glance. "I'm competitive as hell, so when I tell you that nobody's going to make Alix happier than I will, you can believe it."

I lift an eyebrow. "You're marrying a model/influencer you met in a hot tub. That doesn't exactly scream casserole dinners and weekends at the lake."

Tom's head swings away with a smile. Like, *Give me a break with this guy.*

"I can make a casserole." He watches Alix who is delivering a speech about where *Marathon Bride* fits into the cinematic legacy of iconic romcom pairings. "All that matters is I found my girl."

I wish it were that simple.

I head back to the library and think about the mess this weekend has been. What did I expect after kissing my best friend's little sister? Simplicity? Did I want her to throw herself into my arms and tell me that I was the only thing that mattered? That she wanted to renegotiate her relationship to the spreadsheet?

When I inhale, it hurts right up under my jaw and down my throat.

"We have to get this nailed down before I fly out," Jang Mi says, standing in the doorway of the library. Her eyes shift past me. "Hello, Ella. Are you going?" Her English is as formal as a textbook.

I watch Ella's progress, eyes trained on the ankle. My housekeeper brought her ice and a stool when she got back from the hike, and now the limp is barely noticeable. She swings a weekend bag in her hands.

"Are you leaving?" I ask.

"Clara needs me to fill in for an engagement tomorrow." She flashes a brief smile, and shows me a text screen full of prayer hands and crying emojis.

I spot her tells: the toe of her trainers kicking against the tile floor, the proof already in hand. Who marshals answers to questions I haven't asked? A liar. That's who.

"I don't like the idea of you driving through this weather," I say.

"Thor will be in the car ahead of me and we'll be in constant contact. I know my way blindfolded." She turns to Jang Mi. "How goes the planning?"

Jang Mi tucks Ella's hand into the crook of her elbow and urges her into the library. "We talked of much... Much. Let me say how much."

Ella listens and offers a few sensible suggestions.

"The launch, though," Jang Mi concludes. "I worry. We have a few months, I want fans to know, but marketing?" She lifts her hands, a gesture that indicates that we are completely at sea.

"You could start by giving your Pixy followers a clue," Ella replies. She crosses the room and flicks a switch, turning on the spot lights illuminating a display case built into one of the shelves. Jang Mi squeaks but I grin.

There are two van Heyden family tiaras. One is a heavy, diamond-encrusted garland of scrolls and lover's knots. We keep it in a bank vault in Handsel, and it is passed down to each *neerheid* for their wives. It's full of history and tradition, but it's also induced countless migraines for two hundred years. It's currently being cleaned for Alix's wedding.

And then there's this one.

"The Dandelion Tiara," I say, glancing at Ella, seeing her plan before she even speaks it aloud. "Posting about it would get people thinking about Seong and Sondmark together."

Jang Mi leans over the heavy glass, inspecting the dandelion motif. "The diamonds are tiny," she says.

Ella leans with her. "No diamonds. No gems at all."

Jang Mi looks at me. "But it sparkles."

"My father had it made when he married my mother," I say. It was almost the only romantic gesture he ever made. "The material is cut steel. Gold-plated and incredibly light."

"There are dandelions for Seong," Jang Mi smiles. "It would look very good on the princess's head."

Images of the Dandelion Tiara perched on bright curls flood my mind. At Ragnar banquets, state dinners, at my dinners, in the tub, around the house...

Ella's cheeks burn red, and she waves her hands at the thick security glass the way you would wave off a charging stag. "I don't dream about tiaras. The less I have to do with them the better."

Jang Mi shifts to Seongan. "How are you going to talk her into owning this one, Marcus-shi?" she murmurs. I grip the back of my neck, fighting the urge to push her out the door and lock it.

"That's not on the table," I reply.

Ella waits for a translation but Jang Mi reverts to English. "You suggest a photo?"

Ella nods. "Your fans will do a reverse image search, which will lead them to *Vrouwheid* van Heyden and Lindenholm. If you'd like to wear it, I can help you put it on."

Some visceral reaction threatens to break through my neutral expression. No. No one else wears it.

Jang Mi glances up at me, cutting Ella out with Seongan. "Look at her face, Marcus-shi. So much control, but she is upset by the idea. You could—"

"It's too complicated." It is. The risk is high and I stand to lose too much. This friendship kept my head above water this year. It kept me sane.

Clearing my throat, I shift from Seongan to English. "Jang Mi says she couldn't possibly wear it."

Jang Mi sighs, tucking her hand into Ella's. "The dating scandal would..." Her free hand performs an explosion. "So annoying. I do not know where it came from."

"You did volunteer work with my team," I say. "If I had known the fuss it would cause—"

She ignores me to train her attention on Ella. "Marcus and I are friendly, yes? But no." She shakes her head at me like I'm gross. No need to be so emphatic.

Jang Mi produces a sunny smile. "We take a picture and I will tell my agency to deny the rumors."

I toss Ella the keys to the case when my phone buzzes. "It's Noah. The crown prince," I add for Jang Mi's benefit. "I have to take the call."

Jang Mi laughs. Seongan again. "Set me up on a date with that spicy rice cake if you really want to make me happy about interrupting our tour."

"That's a dating scandal you want to avoid," I say, crossing to the other end of the room. "Hey, Noah. What is it?"

"The Handsel Dragons are playing the Djolny Resistance this Wednesday. I need you there."

I watch Ella remove the tiara from the case, holding it carefully in her hands. I hardly breathe as Jang Mi directs her about lighting and angles. "Is it box seats and blue blazers?" I ask.

"Definitely not. I need it to look like a casual outing."

Look like. There's always a royal angle. When Noah plays the game, I'm his right-hand man.

"What's up?"

"I'm bringing Freja's husband Oskar and Clara's boyfriend Max—"

"The national hero?"

"That's the one. Crown Prince Jacob will be there, too."

"From Vorburg? Is this diplomacy?"

"No. Has Ella said anything about what's going on with Alma and him?"

Ella hasn't been telling me nearly enough. "I've seen the gossip about them in the papers. I hear the overheated prayers of half the country hoping they'll get together. Is your mother really going to press for a match?"

A pause. "It's not my mother and it's not gossip. Alma created this problem all on her own."

My gaze lifts to Ella and I parse out the implications at once. The queen is in a tight spot. If her other daughters can't be counted on to carry on the family tradition of loveless, strategically beneficial marriages, her pawns have been whittled down to Noah and Ella.

Stultes es.

"My mother wants them to go public all at once," Noah continues. "She thinks it'll help to rip the bandaid off until someone produces a grandbaby and the topic changes."

"Won't I be a distraction?"

"You're not in love with one of my sisters, are you?" He answers his own question. "Having you there will make the narrative a little less obvious."

Ella, having returned the tiara to the case, has her thumb in the divot of her chin and another finger between her brows. She's explaining the correct proportions of wearing a tiara, and Jang Mi mirrors her with a laugh. I brush the damask cushion with the tips of my fingers, following the sinuous curves. If I'm going to say something about my shifting emotions, now is the time. The words crowd my throat.

"Marc?"

Maybe we can do this. Maybe Noah wouldn't mind me dating his sister. Maybe Alix wouldn't resent me for making her wedding season all about me and what I want. Maybe—

Ella hugs Jang Mi. She picks up her bag and gives me a quick, perfunctory wave and then she's out the door. She's already moved on.

I release a breath. "Yeah. I'm free."

The favor isn't even going to be difficult. Ella won't be there. I won't have to fight to control my expression or my devouring gaze when the camera is trained on our seats. I can sacrifice a little privacy, complicating the press narrative of what is—what did Ella call it? A soft launch.

"Send me the details," I say. "Later." I hit a button and look up.

"Does the prince know?" Jang Mi asks, suddenly near. "About you and his sister."

"There's nothing to know."

Jang Mi twists her lips, skepticism in the crooked line. "But you said—"

"I'm not a lovesick teenager," I cut her off. I'm not going to lock myself in my bedroom and write bad *changga* inspired by how much I want Ella.

We rest under a velvet black sky,
Two hands dipped in a river,
Dragged by a single current...

I reach for the switch and plunge the illuminated display case into darkness.

"This will be over before summer."

18

Juicer Stories

ELLA

In the darkened cinema room of the Summer Palace, light shifts over my face. I am fully prepared to enjoy the football match, wearing teddy bear pajamas and snuggling under a lap blanket decorated with the faces of Seongan leading men. The rest of my family watches the screen in the same way our ancestors watched the horizon for signs of an invading army—with impeccable posture and grim determination.

The motor of my reclining chair whirrs as I extend the footrest, listening absentmindedly as the sports presenters add color commentary to the pre-game warm-up. For the rest of my family, this isn't a game.

Clara squeaks. "There they are. There they are."

When the camera pans follows a line of five men making their way to their seats in the stands, I cross my legs and sit up, watching them shuffle into their row, seemingly unaware that they are being filmed. Everyone in the Summer Palace cinema room sits up. *Vede*, I bet most of northern Europe just sat up.

"It's as we planned," Mama says, her attempt to settle herself down is disguised as settling us. "The royal party has been noticed."

The whistle blows and the game begins, but the camera keeps returning to the row of men. When Sondmark finally scores, everyone but Jacob jumps to their feet and joins in the drinking song, weaving their arms over each other's shoulders, the camera shaking in the pandemonium of joy. My sisters try to gauge the effect, commenting back and forth, but when the camera pans to Marc, nobody says a word. I hug my knees.

To my family, he is simply a red herring, blurring the narrative that every man in this row, aside from their dumb brother, is the prayer of three princesses of Sondmark made incarnate. I daresay, he's not even a bullet point on Caroline's exhaustive agenda.

I reach for my phone, as I did every day he was in Seong. Can I still do this? We've cleared the air. We ought to be able to text.

I like the jacket. Did Noah send you a mood board? I hit send before I can think twice.

Though Marc made such a big thing about it, the kiss hasn't stopped me from switching out my dresses this week for the kinds of clothes favored by Alma—fitted skirts and silky blouses, my hair twisted up in a semi-tidy bun. My own take on these rigid uniforms is to give them a tiny nod to *Military Sun*, an iconic fantasy anime filled with wide-legged, high-waisted trousers and over-the-knee hemlines, touches reminiscent of the Great War. It gives me the illusion that I am getting away with something.

This change has been mostly unremarkable. My mother is quietly pleased about the clothes, and it comes as no surprise that the only time I seem to get her approval is when I fall in line. There has been some social media chatter about the shift, but nobody has lost their *flamen* minds unless you count the tabloid website PAPZ who pronounces me, in one headline, "Princess Va-va-voom". There are other, juicer stories for the press to cover. Three of them are on screen now.

Marc replies. *Mood board? Yeah. Something like that.*

I almost drop my phone when the camera pans to Marc. He rubs a thumb across his lower lip in an absent-minded gesture, giving the camera a look that says, "Hide your daughters." I press myself into the seat, gripping the armrests.

Marc crosses his thumb with his index finger, forming a tiny, Seongan finger heart no one in the entire stadium would even notice. Even my family, picking apart the performance and spooling out each positive and negative consequence of this appearance, hasn't clocked it. My cheeks flush, and I uncon-sciously push my fingers into the same shape before the camera flashes back to the pitch.

The figures blur on the screen as a thought slinks up to me, as stealthy as Freja's cat. I'm jealous of my sisters. I've never wanted to trade places with them, but now... I grab onto the safest idea and hold it fast. My sisters are forging their own paths.

Fighting about the dress code is child's play compared to what they have achieved. Mama wanted to match us up with margraves and hereditary princes, but Clara fought her way into relevance and fought for Max, too. Freja struck out on her own, Oskar firmly at her side, and declined to ask for the right to choose her own happiness. Alma has steadfastly refused to turn Jacob into a pawn.

My mother, heading off more serious rebellions, has granted each of my sisters her blessing to move forward with their choices. My jealousy makes sense. I've wanted to get out of the monarchy from the time I could articulate the divine right of kings.

That explanation doesn't settle neatly into the space I've carved out for it, and I watch the remainder of the game with a furrow between my brows. What else is so upsetting?

When the game ends in a shootout, the Dragons eking out a narrow victory, Mama walks to the front of the room. The meeting may come to order. Each of us offers opinions, but in the end, Mama looks beyond my shoulder.

"Caroline. What are your thoughts?" she asks.

"Rumors concerning Crown Prince Jacob aren't going away, but public opinion seems to be on his side."

"The crowd was booing him," Mama counters.

A ghost of a smile brushes Caroline's lips. "He took it well, and it was polite of his home country to lose the match."

I choke on a laugh, but Caroline continues. "It was wise to invite *Neerheid* van Heyden to round out the party."

"Why?" I challenge. The question leaps off my tongue and I want to drum my mouth with the flat of my fingers.

Her eyes meet mine squarely. "He's a well-known fixture at your family events, and the press stopped matchmaking him with members of the royal family some time ago, " she replies. "With *Neerheid* van Heyden, we can expect no surprises."

She's wrong. A few days ago, Marc pulled me into his arms and kissed me so hard my brain went numb. There's no telling what he'll do.

"And Noah?" Mama presses her secretary. "What was your sense of him tonight?"

Caroline gathers her thoughts before she answers. "His Royal Highness is good with people and it shows. He behaves just as an heir to the throne is expected to."

"Excellent." Mama strides towards the door and we follow like a line of magnetized toy train cars with me as the caboose. Père catches her hand and we bump to a stop. In one motion, a frisson of hope electrifies the line. Père touched Mama on purpose.

"How do *you* feel it went?" he asks, brushing his thumb over the back of her hand. Can you make a pass at someone you've been married to for thirty-five years? That's what it looks like.

"It went well." Mama lifts her chin, but she doesn't withdraw her hand. "The lieutenant commander was particularly impressive. I welcome a deeper association with him, Clara."

Mama moves on, but Clara turns around and walks backward, her face frozen in a silent scream, her fist shaking in the air. National hero Lieutenant Commander Max Andersen has finally breached the walls of the Summer Palace.

Alma passes her with a congratulatory touch. Her turn will come. The crowd at that game, heckling him and having more fun than they'd ever had in their lives, want Jacob to try and win their princess. They're dying for him to get on his knees and beg for her.

"I still expect the highest degree of comportment when you're outside the palace walls," Mama commands. "It would take nothing for us to be in an all-out war with Prime Minister Torbald."

"War?" I lift a wicked brow as I follow. "Don't threaten me with a good time."

Each day is warmer than the last as we slide into the final days of May. Water pours from the mountains, swelling rivers and streams, and topless sunbathers begin to dot public parks on the best days. The time until Alix's wedding is measured in weeks.

I represent my mother at the Motovian Embassy, where I sign a condolence book for the grandmother of the present king in my best penmanship, attend a concert at a primary school, and open a charity bazaar. Light duties. In my other life, I lead some of my best *SquadRun* campaigns and help BeastlyDutchOaths map out a syllabus for teaching the War of the Amber Cross. "I know about reluctant students," I tell him. "You have to start by telling them about the pig. Always start with the pig."

Alix gets around to sending me sketches for bridesmaid's dresses, and I pretend to have strong opinions about centerpieces and playlists. Jang Mi releases the photo of the Dandelion Tiara and online speculation goes wild. Official denials mean nothing. News about the benefit concert trickles in from Marc's occasional texts and Alix's gossip.

And, all the while, Marc's kiss lingers in my head like a dream, and I feel like a prophet, trying to work out its meaning.

Yasmin and Dahlia invite me to meet them for lunch at Minty's. The private club, located in a sprawling townhouse and built during the reign of Magda the Great, acts as a bolt hole to some of the most scandalous people in Sondmark. If secrets slip through the heavy black doors, they say, they're strangled to death in the wine cellar and buried in the yard, never to escape Minty's again.

Arne, the head waiter, a slight man with thin hair and a professor's face, escorts me to a table on the garden patio, where the afternoon sun warms my curls. Carefully pruned trees canopy the dining area, dappling the light, and my old schoolmates tilt their heads up. I give them air kisses before sliding into a chair.

"The gauntlet was thick," I say, referring to the line of paparazzi waiting on the curb. "Is there someone famous here?"

"Lev Kepler," Dahlia says, adjusting her massive sunglasses and pointing to a distant table, "the model in all those shirtless Calvin Klein ads."

"Most people think of him as the Dragons' best striker in a generation," I say, craning my neck for a better look.

Dahlia gives a throaty laugh. "I don't."

Who can blame her? Thanks to the twenty meter ad covering a whole building in Frederickplatz, the entire country knows the precise shape of his innie.

"He's with Simone Bissette."

"Where do I know that name?" I ask, no good without the app I developed to quiz me on foreign dignitaries.

"Noah took her out a few times last year," Yasmin adds, lighting a cigarette and blowing away the smoke.

I roll my eyes. Arne sets a tall lime and Vestfyn on the table and waits, his very aura coaxing me to make an order worthy of the chef. After I do, Yasmin and Dahlia catch me up on their season.

These friends of mine move through the world wearing expensive clothes to polo matches in California and cricket matches in Mumbai. They give generously—and photogenically—to charities around the world and never wear the same bikini twice. When Yasmin slithers out of a club at 3 AM, no governments topple.

"We haven't seen you in ages," Yasmin says, nibbling a vegan microgreen salad with probiotic dressing on the side in between taking long drags on her cigarette. "Your new look is— What is it, Dahl?"

Dahlia tips her sunglasses down. "Sexy. Is Queen Helena allowing you out of the house like this, or are you changing in the bathroom like you used to at Saint Sissela's?"

"It's not sexy," I say, glancing down at the fitted skirt. "It's nearly the same stuff Alma and Clara wear." Freja's off in her own fashion fantasyland, and where she goes, few mortals dare follow.

"It doesn't look this way on Alma," Dahlia observes. Yasmin nods.

This is the same dispute I had with Marc—I shy away from the memory of where that ended up—and I frown into my fizzy drink. "It's just PAPZ being PAPZ. When they quit with that silly nickname, people will get used to it."

Dahlia waves her hand up and down my figure. "You underestimate the male brain, Ells."

Arne arrives, unveiling a dish of fresh cod with fennel, buttery smashed potatoes, and coarse mustard. "You are a delight," he tells me, his expression one of beatific pleasure. "If there is anything else you desire, Your Royal Highness..."

"You will be the first to know." I sniff, inhaling the sharp tang. "Have a potato, Yasmin. You remember potatoes, don't you?" I say, sliding it off my fork and onto her plate.

She succumbs to temptation. "We've been helping," she says between chews. "Have you seen?"

I've seen. My old friends have been speaking nonstop about the Seongan Crisis to anyone with a microphone. *Oh, you wanted to talk about runway fashions? Just a sec. Here's a hashtag you can follow to make donations! Peace sign. Pose. Pose. Pouty lips. Philanthropy is sexy.*

"I can't believe you actually got one of the hotel heiresses to get a tattoo with the Seongan flag. I couldn't have asked for more," I tell them.

"You could, you know," Dahlia says, suddenly serious. She bites her lip and lets it go. "If it hadn't been for you—"

"How is the perfidious ex?" I cut in.

Several months ago, Dahlia had the girls over for a movie night. Searching for a snack, I had found a half-empty jar of strawberry preserves in her fridge—the kind that gets tossed into a gift basket without much thought. I asked her about it, knowing she doesn't do jam—and that Edward, Prime Minister Torbald's longtime aide and Dahlia's weak-chinned *adel* boyfriend of nearly a year, has a violent allergy to strawberries. I know this because it's one of the details included in the bio I compiled for my Notable Public Figures of Sondmark and Northern Europe app.

Dahlia had burst into tears, and the movie was forgotten as I mobilized a team to crosscheck his socials, uncovering a curious pattern of likes and posts during times when Dahlia was out of the country on shoots. We found a girl in his 'Close Friends' list with a series of Xs and a row of courgettes in her Pixy name. She'd posted a photo of the breakfast tray her sometime hookup made for her—complete with preserves—on a countertop. We adjourned to the kitchen to discover that the distinct marble veining matched Dahlia's perfectly, and that was it—Dahlia didn't have to wonder anymore, and her sleazeball boyfriend was history.

I am wasted as a princess.

"He's so far in my rearview mirror he's not even a speck," Dahlia smiles, gripping my hand.

"Nobody makes a Saint Sissela girl cry and gets away with it," I say.

She nods and we move on, the bright sound of a fountain drowning out our gossip.

"What's next for you?" Yasmin asks.

My lips pull in thought. I'm researching graduate programs and have real estate notifications pinging in from around the globe. "I'm determined to be a very good girl for the time being."

"Ooh!" Yasmin half-lifts out of her seat, raises her hand, and waves. "Marc."

Like an expensive gas range on a cold, winter morning, my nerves spark to life. Being a good girl just got a little bit harder.

19

QUEEN AGELTHELD

MARC

When Jang Mi posted the Dandelion Tiara on her Pixy account, it broke the internet. Search results for "What is a Neerheid?", "Lee Jang Mi dating scandal", and "Marc van Heyden hot model pics" shot way up, but so too did "Lindenholm, Sondmark", "Seong Crisis status update", and "BLUSH charity concert". We are sold out of jars of Lindenholm honey for the next year.

Though I told her it wasn't necessary, Alix makes herself in charge of fielding press inquiries. She briefs me each evening from the gym at Lindenholm, the phone perched on a treadmill, while Tom lifts weights in the background.

I have dinner with the Seongan ambassador, and we settle on a strategy to woo the Sondish government into giving us the necessary permits and visas for the relief concert. I am stretched as thin as the silk stockings Ella abhors.

For Han Heyden, I am caught up in the final details of an acquisition, lunching at Minty's with a husband and wife who built their business one server at a time. Though they stand to gain a fortune, I deliver soft, diplomatic reassurances that my conglomerate won't rip the heart out of their life's work. We were rivals, but we can be allies.

There shouldn't be room in all this to think about Ella—but she takes time, whether I can spare it or not. There have been a few mentions of her in the traditional press detailing the odd engagement or royal function. Thin morsels, hardly enough to satiate my hunger. One of the reporters at PAPZ, however, is unhinged about her new look, inciting grass-roots social media commotion.

It has me feeling like a college-town record-store clerk, following my indie band from gig to gig—standing in the front row with my lighter when they were still playing pubs and selling t-shirts out of the trunk of a car. Now that everyone else is catching on to how hot Ella is, tickets are hard to come by. Suddenly I'm jostling elbows in the nosebleeds with fanboys who don't know her B-sides from her deep cuts.

"I'll send Werner the amended contract over in the morning." One of my lunch companions breaks through my thoughts, dragging my mind back to the bright courtyard patio with the splashing fountain. To the negotiations.

"Perfect," I breathe, smoothing my tie. I stand to send them off and type out a quick text to my office, when I hear my name.

I glance up to see one of Alix's bridesmaids from Saint Sissela. The girl in the headlock.

"Yasmin," I call, making my way through the densely-packed patio to greet her. A glaring sun is in my eyes, but I recognize the girl at her side. Her name is some kind of flower. Daisy? Delphinium? "Dahlia. Are you meeting anyone? Is Ella—"

Ella leans forward, emerging from deep shadows. "I am." At the sound of her voice, I feel an intense ripcord pull of attraction yank my whole body and all at once I'm fighting for air. Can I not just be normal around this girl?

Dahlia slides a glance back and forth between us. Finally, she whacks Yasmin in the arm and rises, grabbing her jacket and bag. "We have an appointment at Esther Hong's ten minutes ago," she says, pushing her friend ahead of her. "Toxins. Pores."

Amidst the flurry of their departure, Ella and I stare at one another, just looking. No harm in looking at the curve of her cheek and the tilt of her eyelashes behind tortoiseshell frames. I don't know what I want, but if Noah walked in right now, he would see his oldest friend and his little sister standing in a public space, a whole meter apart.

I've been on my best behavior since that kiss. No late-night texts. No calls. No asking Alix where they're meeting. I've been holding my breath. My eyes trace a trail over her face and my fingers itch to touch her skin. Is this what fate feels like? I imagine a thin red string tying her wrist to mine. I imagine ravelling it into my hand, pulling her closer and closer.

"Can I join you for a drink?" I ask.

Her freckles wash with a rosy blush, barely visible in the shifting light of the tree cover, but she nods. Arne, always watching his domain, brings a pair of drinks consisting of soju, cranberries, soda, and salt, disappearing again.

"We haven't seen much of you," I say. We. I drag Alix and my people at Lindenholm in front of me like a shield.

"I've spoken to Alix everyday, either in Handsel or online, being the best maid of honor a girl ever had." She shakes her head. "Only Alix could plan a wedding this way—"

"What way?" My thumb brushes a bead of moisture from the glass.

"When there's no money, people kind of wing it. The DJ is a playlist. Someone gets a case of cheap beer and maybe a fight breaks out. If there's a bit of money, people start freaking out if their second cousin sourced a similar napkin."

"And you?"

She taps the table. "I'm a special case. A princess has to be dragged before Her Majesty's government and bow to ancient laws."

I grunt, amused. This feels like it used to...if I ignore the tightness in my stomach and the fever in my head when I think about Ella's wedding.

"You have to be precisely as rich as Alix to throw a wedding together like she is."

"Like what?" I just want to hear her talk.

She stretches her neck and a jolt of electricity sparks along my skin, "Like, 'Babe, let's ice skate down the aisle in midsummer.

It'll be a metaphor.'" She laughs. "I like that she's having so much fun."

I wish I was having fun. Instead, I have grown philosophical. I imagined putting Ella aside like a smooth stone at the beach, picked up on a whim, rolled between two palms for the novelty of it, and hurled back into the waves.

If wanting it could make it so, we would have greeted one another with the vague warmth I feel for her school friends. I have tried to bring it to pass. Since the day in the woods, I have lived the life of an ascetic, daily praying that we could get back to our old footing, or close enough. To want anything more is dangerous.

I slip a pair of sunglasses on, trying to mute this stirring of attraction. Stirring. A silent sigh escapes. We are beyond that. I thought it was simply a matter of exposure, of building up an immunity to it and developing a reliable course of treatment. It would take patience and exposure, but the effects would dwindle in slow and easy stages.

Kissing her compounded my problems, and now the only way out of it is through it. Her head tilts away. I feel the shortest reprieve known to man until my eyes fasten on the soft hollow below her car.

"I've been remaking myself into a perfect princess," she reports, expecting praise. "The new me wears sweater sets and sensible heels."

I've noticed. Someone on social media made a fan edit of Ella set to "Hot Walk". It's just her, walking to and from several different events, the new silhouette swaying side to side. I'm on season thirty-seven of that particular Pixy short.

"This is your idea of working your way out of the monarchy?"

Ella pinches the frame of her glasses, pushing them up when they slip down the bridge of her nose. "I'll lull everyone into relaxing their grip. It will get very quiet, and when I sense an opening—"

I loosen my tie. "It's never going to work."

She purses her lips around a straw and kicks me under the table. I grunt.

"Have you been in touch with Jang Mi?" she asks.

"Of course."

"I've been thinking about the logistics—what a nightmare the north meadow can be," she says.

"What makes you think I chose that location?" I break in. "Alix doesn't even know."

"It's got the best access to the main road. It has a gentle slope and good drainage, even if the electricity will be a beast to route around the orchard, and, if you position the stage just right, Lindenholm will be lit up in the background." It's like she's been crawling around in my own head for the last week. "Oh," she digs in her purse. "I got *Vrouw* Tiele to give me the name of a former palace secretary who is looking to do part time work in the private sector. She can help with advance work."

She slides a card across the table and I place it in a pocket. We're back to pretending that things between us are normal, but it feels like a wild stag is charging around the cafe tables and our only protection is that we're not making eye contact with it.

"Thanks," I tell her.

"You told me that you like it when everyone wins." She twirls her hand, spooling out an imaginary bow. I want to catch it. Kiss the tips of her fingers.

I hold her gaze until Lev Kepler lopes by in rough, oversized denim with a model as slim as a scarf draped under his arm. Piano music plays from an open window, mixing with the sound of birdsong and distant traffic.

"You have too much going on this summer," Ella says. "The wedding. BLUSH. Have you made any progress with the wearable electronics people?"

How does she have the bandwidth to remember my problems? The stag is sniffing loudly, shaking his mighty head, and his rack of antlers threatens to sweep away the cutlery in a clatter. *Dominanstid*, I can't look away from her mouth. "We'll sign by the end of the month."

Her fingertips run along the glass, tracing watery patterns. "I should start a consultancy business, getting landed *adel* out of hereditary inheritances. You can be my first client. I'll have you hand off the title to Cousin Eckhart and negotiate to keep a suite at Lindenholm so you can throw yourself at Han Heyden full-time. Think about it."

I grip my glass. I've been drowning in work. I barely have time to hear myself think. And when it does...Ella. "I have a duty to my family."

The light in her laughing eyes fades. "Duty is for suckers."

My gaze takes in the tamed curls, the stand-up collar with the tiny ruffle, and the sober-colored skirt. Ella looks like an electric current crackling through an insulated wire, but, as long as she holds perfectly still, you might forget how dangerous she is. "Your brand messaging points to a different conclusion."

"It's a means to an end." Her smile is back. "I only have to turn myself into a dish of plain Pankedruss for another year, long enough for my family to settle down. If I survive the ordeal with my personality intact—"

"That's not funny," I bite out.

"It's a little funny," Ella counters. She rubs her arm against a sudden gust of wind. "Jang Mi is scheduled to start filming a drama next year. There's already talk about how much chemistry she has with her co-star."

I inhale a deep breath. "I don't care what happens with her co-star. I'm not dating Jang Mi. I don't want to date Jang Mi."

Ella shades her eyes, a dark shadow slanting across rosy lips. I know the taste of them, and the longer I watch her, the louder my pulse sounds in my ears.

No matter how steep and narrow the track my ancestors have set before me, I've climbed it, keeping my father's wildness penned up. But sitting this close to Ella, I feel his reckless blood seep into my system, drop by poisonous drop.

The trace of wildness becomes a trickle and I close my eyes for a brief moment, trying to collect myself. I should get out of here. I have work to do and can't afford to waste my time. She'll understand.

I open my eyes to find that the trickle has become a rivulet. Idiot. I know the way she kisses—willing, sweet, stealing my breath. Ella takes a pull from her straw and a flood crashes through my veins, knocking my resolutions aside like *stikubb* pins.

Forgive me, ancestors.

"We have to go," I say, dragging her to her feet and through the maze of tables. No one notices a pair of old family friends, even when they're holding hands.

"Where—?"

We cross the threshold of the club, stepping into the long, tiled lobby that stretches to the front doors. Beyond the brilliant rectangles of light, there are paparazzi, waiting for something to happen so they can splash it across every news outlet in Sondmark. Too public. I glance at the shallow, richly-carpeted stairs, leading to the private suites. *No.* My brain shouts the command. *Too* private.

I urge her into the lounge with a hand to the small of her back, burning up the last of my self-control to keep it from wandering. The interior is dark, the brass fittings gleaming with a rich, dull finish, and near the bar, a few older members gather to talk about monetary policy. I propel Ella past them, beyond the potted plants and the scattering of chairs and tables.

I think of the football game I attended with Noah, full of noise and confusion, the players diving with false injuries to win an advantage. At the end, we hunched over Affelworst and beer in some pub as Oskar patiently explained our national obsession to a baseball-loving Jacob. "Here it is. Here's the one rule." My translation was crisp. "Football is what you can get away with."

Noah isn't here to tell me what the rules are. I steer Ella toward a shadowy alcove at the back where dim light reflects off a black marble tabletop, and deposit her on the leather banquette.

I follow after her, sliding along the high curved back. "We need to talk."

"So shoot me a text," she says, brow knitted as she scoots down the bench. She thinks I want room. I catch her wrist and drag her into my arms, brushing her lips with the pad of my thumb.

Ella takes a shocked breath and presses her palms against my suit jacket. "Marc, you said you didn't want—"

"Forget what I said."

This time, I don't have the excuses of too much soju and the rowdiness of a midnight game. It's not a sudden impulse, either. I've been thinking of kissing her every second since it happened.

My mouth settles on hers in the way an ice-whipped prow of a Viking longboat noses out to rough seas, carrying fur-clad warriors beyond the comforts of hearth and hall. Resolute. Relentless. Quickened with the thought of treasure.

She hardly hesitates before pulling me closer. The knot of my tie presses against the pounding pulse in my neck, and I recognize that Ella lied to me. We are very, very good.

After the first rush, I inhale against her skin. *Vede.*

A pair of pleasant bongs echo across the lounge, resonating through my bones. My mind dimly registers that it is 2 PM on a Wednesday, steps away from where I negotiate some of my most vital business interests and meet for afterwork drinks with her brother. This is a place where people have the highest expectations of me—but a shaky breath breaks from my lungs. I left those shores long ago.

I resume kissing her—slower this time—and taste the lingering trace of cranberries on her lips, bitter and sweet. The soft touch of revelation tents her fingers against my chest. For the rest of my life, when I taste cranberries, I will think of Ella and this kiss.

I nudge her chin into a better angle, and erase the spaces between us. Since birth, I have been steeped in the duties and rituals of two cultures, but even my most righteous ancestor would not blame me for this.

She makes a soft noise, and the seemingly impossible issues that separate me from her feel as thin and insubstantial as a paper door on a lattice frame. Light glows on the other side—muted brightness and tantalizing shadows. It would take nothing to push the door back and cross the line forever. Nothing. I would simply present myself on my knees, head bowed, fisted hands resting on thighs. Your humble servant. Yours.

I catch my reflection in the antique glass—the disheveled tie, my hand splayed across Ella's back, holding her in place. *Vede.* I drop my head again, nosing her chin up, kissing her neck. She shivers and I grin against her skin.

"Admit it," I whisper. "Admit it was good."

Suddenly, Ella bolts upright. She slaps at my hands, peeling them away.

"Arne is coming," she squeaks, adjusting her cuffs. I fumble for her but Arne is closing in fast. I don't know what to do with my empty arms. I cross them over my chest. I drop them at my side. One elbow on the table…

Arne gives a brief bow, his gaze scrupulously neutral. "Your Royal Highness, while you were," he gives a discreet cough, "otherwise occupied, the prime minister called an impromptu press conference. It has been picked up by all news outlets. You may find it noteworthy."

He bows again and departs, not before giving me a reprimanding eyeball. I want to point at Ella as exculpatory evidence, waving a hand up and down her person. *How could I resist?*

Meanwhile, Ella digs into her purse for her phone. She looks to be completely recovered from my attentions, but my arm settles around her waist, hand on her hip. I haven't moved on from this. I may never move on.

"What in the *flamen* hell?" she cries. I look over her shoulder, inhaling her scent. She points to the news chyron, running along the bottom of the screen.

"PRIME MINISTER INTRODUCES BILL CALLING FOR THE REMOVAL OF PRINCESS FREJA FROM

SUCCESSION. CITES MARRIAGES AND SUCCESSION ACT (1798)."

Ella cranks up the volume until the prime minister's mumbling tones reach our ears. "Sondmark has rich natural resources and a deep pool of talent, engaging in commerce around the globe. Because of our strong, unified culture and adherence to the rules which bind us as a people, we are consistently rated as the Happiest Country in the World."

"I'd like to take a look at that research model," Ella spits. She looks like an angry little dragon and, with a shadow of a laugh, I gather her close.

The prime minister goes on. "When we flout accepted norms, this precious unity is damaged. Though we wish the young couple every happiness, it is with a heavy heart that I announce an official inquiry concerning the removal of Her Royal Highness Princess Freja from the royal succession, following her illegal marriage to *Neer* Oskar Velasquez."

"Illegal?!" Ella slaps the table. The men anchoring one end of the bar look up. I pull her into the shadows.

"Only as it applies to the Marriages and Succession—"

Ella elbows me. "It was perfectly legal."

"Not for any princess in the line of succession," I say, pushing a roll of cutlery out of her reach. "It'll be fine. I know your mother is consulting lawyers."

Ella rolls her bottom lip, biting it. "His tone, Marc. I don't forgive his tone."

"Again, your mother has a plan to handle it."

"Handle," she scoffs, pointing at the screen. Torbald is taking questions, his attitude reading as sorry for the whole affair. "I don't want this handled. I want him destroyed."

Ella exists within the fiction that she's nothing like her royal ancestors, but the edge of her voice is as bloody as Queen Ageltheld's sword. She slips out of my hold, bouncing along the seat until she comes out the other end of the curved bench.

"Ella. Wait." My hand chases her. "Your mother—"

Not three minutes ago, those lips were slowly driving me insane, but now they press into a firm line. "Her Majesty is going to do what she always does—be very, very apologetic as she allows the government to grind her family into dust. She'll tell us her hands were tied. That we should brush ourselves off and say a prayer of thanksgiving that the monarchy was saved."

Ella closes her eyes for a moment, and pain is carved in the gentle lines of her face. Does anyone else see this side of her? She doesn't cry often. When she's upset, her emotions take another path to the surface, erupting as caustic humor or aggression. In one fluid motion, I escape the booth and pull her in my arms.

When I promised Noah I would look after his sister, what did we imagine? That she would say something outrageous in public? Her expression promises an apocalypse.

"You're not going to do anything rash," I declare.

She looks up, steel in her eyes. "You're not the boss of me."

20

Dancing Bear

ELLA

Marc rushes me to the elevator and dials up my security detail. "Thor, I have Ella. We're coming back to the palace. Side gate. Look for the black Ferrari." A pause, and he checks his watch. "Ten minutes."

Heat radiates from our clasped hands, but my mind is as messy as an unlicensed circus. The dancing bear has snapped his leash and charges the stands, the dazzling lady tightrope walker is hanging by her fingertips, and a death-defying motorcyclist is trapped in the metal cage of that kiss, racing in circles at a dizzying speed.

What kind of lesson did Marc want to impart to me this time? And, *Dominanstid*, how did he get so good?

I twist out of his grasp. "You don't have to drive," I say, striding into the tiny elevator, four people deep, one and a half people wide. I hate these things, and the walls seem to close in on me as I try to untangle my emotions. "I'm not your responsibility."

Marc locks the ornate metal door and presses the button for the underground garage, crowding me into the back. The deathtrap shudders and the lights dim but, before I can climb out of my skin, he reaches for my hand again, lacing our fingers together. My breathing slows, matching his. *Stultes es.* I'm going to have to begin again to get over him. But not yet. I close my eyes.

"You're wrong," he says, brushing the pad of his thumb across my skin. "Didn't you listen to your mother's Christmas message? It was all about brotherly love. The whole human family bound together in goodwill and peace. We belong to each other. All of us."

Marc doesn't tease my sisters. Not really. His affection for them is as straightforward as a blue sky. He saves this side of himself for me. The elevator emits a death rattle when it reaches its destination, and Marc crashes the door open. I take a deep, clean breath as we exit.

"She didn't mean a word of it," I counter. "Freja had just eloped with a Pavian immigrant, and that was my mother's attempt to head off a national meltdown."

"Cynic," he answers, stuffing me into his car, ducking back in to press a leisurely kiss on my lips.

We're still doing this? I thought the next order of business on his agenda was to give me a talking to about borders and boundaries and neat little boxes. It's an unusual day, though. Maybe the kiss is meant to calm me.

He closes the door with an expensive thunk, and the caged motorcycle in my mind is deafening, my brain filled with melting rubber and blinding smoke. I move to buckle my seatbelt, halting when I see an ornament swinging from the rearview mirror. I cup the gold chain with the row of tiny raccoons.

"It was a deal. Two for one," he says, sliding into his seat and clearing his throat. His eyes never shift from the windshield, but a wash of red stains his neck.

Caroline meets us in the Great Hall with a quick curtsey. "You're the last to arrive, Your Royal Highness," she says, leading the way to the administration wing. The worst possible news has hit my family, yet I hardly register it as strange that our first impulse isn't hugs and tea in a cozy tangle—it's a meeting in a war room.

"It's going to be okay," Marc murmurs. Okay or not, I hold onto him with a death grip. When we enter the room, I curtsey. Marc gives my mother a respectful bow.

"Caroline," Mama says, expecting to be instantly understood. Without fuss, the secretary arranges a chair slightly behind my customary seat. Marc is to stay.

I take my place and fidget with a pen and a notepad, drawing patterns on the page. Across the table, Freja and Oskar carry on a low-voiced conversation, the two of them in a small, self-contained little world.

Mama calls the meeting to order, appearing as the reassuring monarch rather than the anxious mother. "Allow me to misquote Job," she says, slipping into her seat. She perches her reading glasses on her nose. "'The thing which we greatly feared has come upon us.' Caroline."

Caroline clicks on the projector and strides to the light switch. Noah beats her to it and she bumps into him just as the lights blink off. Peeling out of Noah's steadying hold, she walks through the shifting, camouflaging light. "We are here, ma'am," she says, touching the flow chart projected on the wall.

She begins to describe the meandering path of destruction. Freja's legal matter will begin with a formal investigative committee and debate between parliamentary members on the floor of the Grousehof.

My stomach slides. Open Access broadcasts these exchanges on municipal planning disputes and marginal tax rates, and they usually put people to sleep. The idea of my sister's private life being served up for public consumption makes me physically ill.

Caroline continues. "From there, this matter lands before a body of judicial lords before being presented for Her Majesty's royal assent." She clicks through to another slide. "Once the committee begins an investigation, members of the royal family and royal household will be called to give evidence."

Mama tips her head. "I am surely exempt from the summons of a minister."

"That is technically correct, ma'am."

"But?" Mama prompts.

I feel a stirring of envy, listening to the deep respect—even affection—between the two women who work so closely together. To my mother, I am a headache and a pest. Her secretary is her right hand.

"You will pay for it, ma'am. There are risks of appearing as though you are above the law," Caroline replies.

"I know," Mama breathes deeply, and my cynicism returns. "The law flows from me but I cannot use it for my own ends." This is the groundwork for "*so sorry, but my hands are tied.*"

"Helena." Père's voice is soft, though he has been the greatest casualty of this policy. He half-reaches for her, but receiving no encouragement, his hand settles on the table in a loose fist.

Caroline clicks to another slide. "Technically, these interviews are confidential, but Your Majesty should expect damaging leaks. Personal texts and emails swept up in the official inquiry will be made public. If a member of the royal family is less-than-enthusiastically cooperative, it will appear in the press via unnamed sources." Caroline indicates a footnote on her slide deck. "Information about who is testifying before the committee on any given day will be included in the prime minister's diary of events."

"Who is privy to this information?" Mama is in command again.

"The entire country, ma'am. It's posted on a website, usually a week in advance."

It's going to be a feeding frenzy. I grip the edge of my seat and Marc collects my hand, holding it between his cool palms while my pulse steadies. Across the table, Oskar opens a small bag of crackers and places them in front of my sister.

Clara sighs. "Anyone coming and going from the Grousehof will have to walk past a million photographers. The optics won't be good."

The House of Wolffe has produced some monumental optics this year. Clara tipping over Max on Queen's Day and conducting her romance in a variety of picturesque wilderness locations. Freja's breathtaking wedding photos (I'm still salty about it, but I'm not blind), and all those social media videos with Oskar where they look like they're nursing a secret, burning passion for one another. (Spoiler: They were.) Alma swept into the protective embrace of the crown prince of Vorburg under a hail of gunfire (sort of). She still managed to carry on a State Visit with missing stockings and a smear of blood on her knee, but none of the optics have been as uncomplicated as *good*.

"What about giving an interview?" Noah suggests. "The palace can get out in front of the negative publicity by having a morning news show produce something sentimental and sweet about the undeniable power of love." His jaw works. "We'll sell Freja as a girl swept away by the greatest romance the world has ever known."

This is what passes as a reasonable suggestion within these walls, but Oskar stands, bristling with dignity, his voice a challenge. "My wife is not a product."

I grip Marc's hand and he leans close, warm and reassuring, as my gaze shifts to my sister, finishing her little snack. I wonder which identity will make way for the other. Is Freja foremost a princess, raised in the Summer Palace to do her duty, and willing to shrink her particularities for the needs of the monarchy? Or is Freja the wife of a commoner, a girl whose allegiances orient around the unremarkable flat on the other side of town?

Noah holds Oskar's gaze, a hostile static crackling in the air, until finally my proud brother gives a nod. "My apologies, Freja."

"You are forgiven. Oskar." Freja tugs her husband's hand.

"*Audicia*," he whispers to her, resuming his seat. *Mafia*. How can a man who frowns as much as he does also positively glow with how much he's into my sister?

Freja brushes crumbs from her fingers and looks around the table. "I don't mind being referred to as 'swept away by the greatest romance the world has ever known'," she dimples. "Where is the lie?"

Gag. My sister used to be a woman of few words and remarkably good sense. I glower at Oskar. "You did this to her."

Oskar gives Freja the kind of passionate, Pavian look we would kill to broadcast across the nation. He spares me a brief, not-a-smile smile.

Caroline clears her throat. "Constitutional scholars have been consulted." This brings another slide filled with damning legal implications which might finally settle the question: Who has ultimate authority, spiritually or legally, in Sondmark? The premier or the queen?

Marc leans forward, lips near my ear. "See? Your mother is already on top of it. You don't need to worry."

But I am uneasy, looking at these crisp bullet points. These questions have been battled out in bloody warfare for a thousand years. They were never supposed to be battled out in the courts. If my mother's power is forced to be measured in concrete, quantifiable ways, she is bound to lose.

"This family has many pawns, but only one queen," I say, lowering my voice. "This will end with Freja being sold for the Crown."

I escape as soon as the meeting concludes, and Marc jogs after me, hands in his pockets. Though I need time to think, I do have manners.

"I'll walk you to your car." I say it like this has been a normal afternoon and none of it was spent with my lips on his neck. In addition to the succession catastrophe, I need to think of that, too.

But he takes a left in the Great Hall and walks backward up the staircase, dragging me after him, step by step. "Are you trying to get rid of me?" he asks. "We're not done."

The implications tighten my stomach. His kisses turned me inside out. How much more unfinished business could there be?

"Hey guys," Clara skips down the steps, Max following in her wake. His rank allows him to grow a beard, and though it is neatly trimmed, he looks more like a Viking every day. Clara is on the fence about it.

"What's up?" she asks.

"I'm going to ravish your sister." Marc says it. He just says it, and heat washes through me, each oscillation like a tiny wave dashing over my skin. Clara laughs, choking off when she catches Max's expression.

"It's a joke. Stop looking at them like they're a thing. They're not a thing." Her nose wrinkles. "It would be like dating a cousin."

Max grins. "I thought that was one of the hallmarks of the Wolffe family."

"Babe. Not for most of the last century." She whacks his stomach and he traps her hand against his abs.

"Where are *you* headed?" I ask, shifting on the balls of my feet with this talk of my impending ravishment.

"We're babysitting Ava." Max's niece. "Are you gaming tonight?" she asks. "Do you want me to pop in after?" The idea of Marc and me being caught necking never crosses her mind.

"Don't bother," Marc says, continuing on his way up the stairs. "It's a two-person game. See you, Max."

When they disappear down the hall, I frown at Marc. "We're gaming? This is news."

He swings my hand. "We need to talk."

My limbs tense. What joy. None of Marc's "talks" are fun. I gallop up the stairs and he races after me. What will it be this time? That he's thought better of our kisses? That he's actually decided to start things up with Jang Mi? Does Marc want to tell me that I need to find some way of self-regulating that doesn't include having to touch him all the time?

"I'm changing." I lob my handbag into a chair, and escape into my closet. "Fire up *Heretics of the Blood Moon*, if you really want a game." Heaven knows I'm in the mood to go on a quest to escape ritual sacrifice.

I throw on a pair of loose joggers and a cashmere sweater, twisting a hairpin out of my tangled topknot as I pad into the room. He's discarded his jacket and shucked his Oxfords but his waistcoat hugs him and electricity dances along my nerves. When he hands me a controller, I sink to the floor at his side, braced against the sofa.

The game is a mix of puzzles and hand-to-hand combat. We problem-solve our way out of a palace dungeon, finding the cranks and levers to release as a blood-red moon rises, its sickly light framed by a window embrasure. As the metal door swings open, a cut scene pops up, the characters gently bobbing as stilted dialogue scrolls through text boxes.

"Our plan got us this far but there's an army on top of us and a murdering sect of priestesses beyond," my avatar explains. "We'll never escape."

"We need to talk." Marc tosses the controller aside.

My eyelashes flicker, but I scroll through the menu and skip the rest of the cut scene, nudging the controller back into his hands. "So talk."

After a beat, he follows my lead, shoving a torch into a crevice and leaning his digital weight against the door.

"We have to figure out how we're going to do this."

We have played this game so many times he shouldn't need to be told. "When the door opens, we head to the scriptorium for the map. Try not to get stabbed." Duh.

He dispatches a couple of lackeys with a well-aimed shove, sending them rolling down the spiral staircase. "Not the game. I kissed you today. We were in public." His hands still. Here it comes.

With flaming cheeks, I engage a hulking knight with an intimidating broadsword. I throw the torch, setting fire to his tunic, and observe his flailing immolation with some satisfaction. If only it were so easy to get rid of all my problems.

"We were at Minty's," I remind him. "You know how Arne has that place locked down." My heart is pounding in my throat and a sedimentary nausea, leftover from Freja's problems maybe, settles in my stomach. I smile it away. "You picked the right place."

"That's the thing," he says, slaying an attacker rushing in from my blind spot with the swing of a stolen sword. "I didn't *pick* anything." His breathing is uneven, full of catches and rushes as he sorts through his next words. "We could have been at the supermarket or the post office or in the middle of Frederickplatz. I would have found a way to kiss you no matter where we were."

The air thins and my lungs burn. "Can you imagine making out next to the Supernuss and pickle crisps?" I joke. "That would have been a first." Maybe being subjected to his surgical dissection of our kisses is how I die?

"Ells—" He tosses his controller. "We have a lot going on." His avatar gets stuck in a loop, hitting a brick wall over and over. Someone will probably come along to knife him in the back and he'll deserve it for doing this to me again.

"Too much for kissing at Minty's. I know, you moron." I know the list by my broken heart. "Han Heyden, Alix's wedding, the aid concert, Lindenholm, Noah in there somewhere, Freja's catastrophe..."

I don't expect anything different. I never do. From the time I was four, I could recite everything that took precedence over me. Standing up straight, Mama's tiaras, an Olympic bid we didn't get, an Olympic bid we did get, foreign tours, Freja's health...

"You already explained your to-do list." I lob this at him like a bowler in a backyard game of Sondish longball. Friendly. Easy. Pitched perfectly for him to crack it over the fence.

"I think..." His fingertips trace the edge of the coffee table. "I think..."

"Don't hurt yourself," I laugh, knocking his shoulder with my own. Always friendly. Never mind the pain. "I don't make dandelion wishes. It's not your job to be Prince Charming. It's fine."

He takes a breath and peels the controller out of my hands, erasing all our progress. I ball my hands into fists and wrap my arms around myself.

"It's not fine," he says. "Not for me."

The knife twists—stinging, intense. Mama thinks I have no genius for self-control, but she should see me now.

I cock my brow. "That's on you, because I am a very good kisser."

His mouth tips with a smile. "It's not fine because I need you."

My brows gather. I understand just enough science to deploy Occam's razor—the rule that states that the simplest answers are usually the correct ones. Things are never more simple be-tween Marc and I than when we are friends. More than any kiss—which was definitely good; I'll die on that hill—Marc needs my support and loyalty.

I hope I look like a cool girl. Cool with anything. "I get it. I need you, too. Our friendship is too important to play around with—we need to knock it off."

Even though Marc looks like a civilized spread in Business-men's Quarterly, he makes a low noise in the back of his throat. His eyes close for the briefest moment. "No, Ella. No. *I am not doing well.* This past month—and more—has been nothing but earnings projections, VP infighting, figuring out how to keep my workers employed in the face of ruinous tax regulations, and the logistics of putting on a benefit concert in the middle of the country. Do you know when I come up for air? The only time?"

I did not know there would be a pop quiz in the middle of this heartbreak.

"When I'm kissing you." He swallows, his voice dropping into a rough whisper. "All the things I have to do, all the roles I have to fill, all the people I have to answer to—it gets quiet."

I—I...

Suddenly it feels like I'm the one running into the brick wall over and over, caught in a loop.

He looks at me and takes a long time before choosing his next words. "What I mean is that if we want to turn this into a regular thing, I know our friendship is strong enough to stand it."

I shake my head but it doesn't clear. "Wait. What? I don't get— Marc."

In my confusion, he tumbles me back until I'm settled against the floor, and braces his hands on either side of me so that we are face to face. His expression is as serious as the Black Death. "Princess Ella Victoria Chiara Brunhild of Sondmark, should I repeat myself?"

My eyes widen and my hands curl protectively over my chest. I must look like a velociraptor. "Don't you think you should?"

He nods. "You are my favorite princess. Whenever you walk into a room, I do a little," he lightly pumps his fist in the narrow space between us, "because it's going to be a good time. Every time. That's not ever going to change. You got that?"

I think so?

"And you," he adds. "Are you going to suddenly find someone else to send your taco cat memes to?" he asks.

I shake my head. "You love those things."

"I do," he agrees, tone serious. "None of that has to change."

"What about—"

He settles a warm palm over my mouth and, with a quick jerk of his chin, makes a sibilant hush. I may be a princess, but I am also a normal, red-blooded Sondish woman. He can't keep touching me if he expects me to listen.

"I can't help the timing," he says, furrowing his brow. If I'm confused, he is, too, working it out in real time. He hasn't planned any of this. "And I'm not saying we date. I know we can't date." I wriggle but he holds me fast. "Noah would put my head on a pike if he found out I was…creeping around his little sister," he swallows, "and you're not looking for a relationship with someone on your mother's list." He's so certain. I made sure he would be.

"But." His breathing is labored. "But. We're going to start seeing each other."

I blush hotly. Is that a euphemism for sexy times?

I blink up at him, a million questions cascading through my head, and nip his palm. He darts his hand away and wipes it on the waistcoat.

"How far do you expect to take this?" I ask. Should my father demand pistols at dawn?

Marc hitches his breath and plants a soft kiss on my mouth, lingering long enough that the thoughts in my head evaporate.

"This far. Enough to take the edge off."

I'm a pain tablet? Take two kisses, put your feet up, call if symptoms persist.

The truth is that I'm tempted. I'm curious about the way he thinks we can confine ourselves to such narrow parameters of engagement and how he thinks we won't be hurt. I'm not foolish enough to think I can escape so cleanly, and the whole thing terrifies me.

"Isn't there something in the Geneva Bro Codes about kissing your best friend's little sister?" I ask, pushing back.

"We're not going to tell Noah. Or your sisters—or mine." Again, he presses a kiss to my lips. I don't know whether the soft, clinging touch should land in the plusses or minuses tally.

"What you're describing is ridiculous," I say.

He nods gently, repeatedly. "We have to do it anyway."

I take a steadying breath. Terrible ideas are my brand. Not Marc's. "Why?"

He kisses me again, lingering so long that he takes a ragged breath when he lifts his head. He looks like he's been running from the cops.

"Because it won't be Minty's next time." He brushes a curl from my face with a serious smile. "Think about how productive we'd be if we could regularize this, seeing each other—"

"Maximizing productivity requires kissing?" I scoff.

He's honest enough to make it clear that this will be something temporary, without the promise of a rosy future for the two of us. My throat tightens. *Have some dignity, Ella. Some self-respect.* I should say no—escape from the temptation of his proximity, and go back to driving him off with talk of cufflinks.

A thought intrudes. *And how did that work out?*

I've been trying to fall out of love with Marc van Heyden for more than a year and getting exactly nowhere. My strategy has been a failure.

He smells so good, and I wonder if going along with his reckless plan would be like cannonballing into a lake, going all the way to the rocky bottom, and pushing up to the surface as a new creature. No more flailing. No more wondering. Maybe it makes sense?

He leans forward, but this time I meet him, trying it his way. After a few seconds, he lifts his head and takes a large swallow of air. "Yes. It requires kissing," he gasps.

I trace the hollow under his ear, ignoring the medieval campaign music coming from the television. I'm tired of fighting this fight alone. I'm tired of being the only one to suffer. If I do this, I will become a turncoat to myself, willfully destroying the fragile peace I've won, but there will be compensations. "We'll go back to being friends?" I say.

"We won't ever stop being friends."

We'll end where we began. I can't say I haven't been warned. I hold my breath and peer into the future as far as I can. I can imagine ruin and heartbreak, but they somewhere are beyond the horizon. I see that I'm going to say yes.

I wedge myself onto my elbows, narrowing the gap between us, noting the way his gaze keeps returning to my mouth. *Vede,* how distracted has he been?

"Just kisses," I insist, feeling my power. "No scope creep." There are some things our friendship can't survive. I hold up my pinky between us, and he wraps it with his own.

"No scope creep," he repeats. "So it's a deal?"

Ignoring the stab of pain, I tip up my chin and whisper my answer against his lips.

"Deal."

21

HOPPED UP

MARC

"It'll be fine," I tell Ella, shrugging my suit jacket over my shoulders. I keep wanting to touch her—to say goodnight the right way—but we haven't worked out whether or not our deal includes affection, touches softer than passion but somehow more intimate.

So, I keep my hands busy smoothing my collar and straightening my tie, moving closer to the door as I attempt to reclaim some measure of control. "As long as we don't make it more than it is, both of us will benefit."

She leans over the arm of the sofa, resting her head on crossed hands, and chews on her lower lip. "Remind me what those benefits are?"

We went over this, but then we kissed each other like zoo animals released into a new enclosure—hopped up on curiosity, wild with it, running in circles. No wonder she forgot.

I return in five long strides and crouch, leaning against the arm of the sofa until we're face to face.

"I get to focus on being the CEO of Han Heyden and the master of Lindenholm without the considerable stress of wondering if I'm going to drag you into the bushes at one of your mother's garden parties." I'm going to start again if I don't leave now.

She nods, but her short fingernails rake against the texture of my tie and I feel the vibrations in the center of my brain. Does she understand the power she holds? "And I get—"

"Clear-headedness."

She quirks a brow. "You think this is giving me clear-headedness?"

I reclaim my tie. "You get to focus on the succession crisis without spending emotional energy trying to keep your hands off me."

She snorts. "I was doing just fine."

I'm fighting for my life and she's only having fun. I can't forget that.

"We'll be in a better headspace if we stop thinking so hard. Let's just show up for each other like we always do and let this happen in microdoses." I sound like a motivational speaker sent to boost company productivity by 3%, but I pray she buys it. This is the only way I see out of this mess. "We're in this together."

"You make us sound like Samwise and Frodo. Does our fellowship come with a motto?" Her hand sketches out an arc. "*The real treasure is the friend we made out with along the way.*"

I laugh when I leave her, but by the time I drive through the palace gates, I have regained enough sense to congratulate myself on this plan. Putting my attraction to Ella on a schedule is going to remove my major obstacle to moving through the world as a normal person.

It doesn't work out that way.

We start texting again—cat memes, wake-up calls, touching base—which manages to fill me with both restlessness and contentment, and I think about her more than before. This doesn't mean my plan is garbage. Once we're past the novelty of being allowed to touch each other, we'll go back to some baseline level of reasonable attraction. The problem is that I'm not finding the baseline.

I last two days before inviting her over to my sleek, sterile flat for dinner. "Nothing fancy," I text. It's not a date. We're very clear about that, but I put house slippers in her size by the front door and stock up on Vestfyn and extra throw pillows.

Ella arrives wearing a pair of joggers and my old *Two Strike* t-shirt I haven't seen in years under a zip-up hoodie. She passes my threshold and toes her shoes off while I grip the door handle, staring hard at the empty hallway with one thought in my head. It does not fit her like it used to fit me.

"Your hostess gift," she says, handing me a bag. I pull out a new *Two Strike* shirt.

"Did you steal mine or did I leave it at the palace sometime?"

She won't look me in the eye. "Steal is such a harsh word. What are we eating?"

I follow her into the kitchen with a laugh.

I show her the instructions left by the private chef, and we move comfortably around each other. I salt the pasta water according to the written notes that read, "like an angry toddler throwing fistfulls of sand," and wonder how I'm supposed to make this feel normal. Ella and I are not in a romantic relationship. We kiss and don't kiss. On. Off. The deal says nothing about nuzzling her neck while she stirs the bolognese or sliding my hands around her waist.

The problem of what this deal will allow works away in the background of my mind until I'm like an overheated laptop.

Ella cracks open a Vestfyn and syncs her phone with my sound system, cueing up a playlist of American jazz standards performed by a member of one of the larger Seongan boy bands. "Is he as pretty as he looks on my lock screen?" she asks, when I offer to introduce them.

I scowl. "If you like that kind of thing."

"Like an otherworldly creature with star-kissed abs?" Her eyes sparkle with laughter and she turns the burner down, dipping a clean spoon into the pot. She purses her lips to cool the hot liquid, tastes, and blows some more. "His skin is—"

She lifts the spoon for me.

My heart is beating hard and I push her wrist back, leaning in to taste her lips. Gentle and warm, with the faintest trace of bolognese. She giggles against my mouth. That's fine. She's welcome to find this hilarious. I drop the spoon in the pot, and banding her waist with my hands, I lift her onto the countertop where she's easier to reach.

Her fingers rake through my hair and I shiver. She's never the one to kiss me first. She's happy to follow my lead, but I feel a feather of discontentment. When I lift my head to catch my breath, she swings a foot and a slipper falls to the floor.

"I'm going to kiss you next time when I open the door," I tell her, voice roughened. "And maybe again when you put down your bag. I'm going to kiss you when you can't reach the upper cabinets and when you're looking for the lids."

She arches a brow. "How about when I'm asking about Park Hyeon Yu's skincare regimen?"

"Especially then."

Her lips twitch. "I wonder what kind of toner—"

She never finishes the thought.

We do eat eventually, after letting half the water boil out of the pot and replenishing it. Over pasta, she tells me about her last family meeting and how her mother threatened to cut off her wi-fi if she was late again. She swipes the warm olives off my plate, placed there in anticipation of theft.

This becomes our habit. When our schedule allows it—and even when it doesn't—we make dinner and talk about our day, then move to the lounge where there is an entire wall of glass and a view of the city lights. I scroll through a tablet with one hand, going over the accounts for Lindenholm or emails from the office, while the other arm anchors her to my side. She tells me about the intense logistics of Queen's Week and chats on her Friction server. She often works on the source code of the app she created for her family to track notable dignitaries ahead of royal events. I limit myself to careless, lazy kisses on the top of her head, promising myself more only when I've shifted a mountain of work.

As a result, I work like a man possessed.

It takes two weeks before she acknowledges that this was a brilliant idea. "It's like a personal chef," she tells me, placing a kiss on the underside of my jaw that has me gripping the leather sofa. This easy affection I decided I could not do without is murder. "There's an entire category of my life I no longer have to think about." She places another kiss, and I turn my head, stopping her mouth.

I absorb her approval with satisfaction. I'm brilliant. The first person in recorded history to have their cake and eat it, too. But I can't help feeling like we're fighting fire with drums of gasoline and tracts of dry, brittle forest. Ella and I are forever, but not like this. So I try to keep it light, and she tries too. There's laughter in the air every time we get serious, setting aside everything we've made ourselves busy with to do what we've been wanting to do all night.

We don't tell anyone, but some people begin to notice. Ella chats with my doorman Felix when she comes over, discovers his kid has a cough, and drops a small box of interlocking bricks off at the front desk to take home. The guards manning the palace security checkpoint have taken to opening the gates when they see my plates, and the night footmen stationed in the Great Hall probably have a betting pool about when I'm going to make Ella an honest woman.

It is sheer luck that Alix hasn't figured it out. When she video chats from a backyard cookout in Pennsylvania or a dressmaker's studio in Lebanon, Ella dives into my front hall, using the large blank wall as her backdrop. While she talks, I hold her free hand, lace our fingers together, and kiss them until she bats me away.

Caroline Tiele has seen me parking in the Summer Palace employee lot at all hours, and offers me a brisk nod when she does. She never asks where I'm off to, who I'm with, or how we're spending our time. I know she knows.

Tonight, I'm in Ella's suite, watching an episode of *Moonflower*. I drag her feet across my lap and answer questions about the complexity of historical Seongan wedding rites.

"But when are they *actually* married?" she asks. "When the bell rings? When they drink the nuptial wine? Or when they bow?"

I roll my thumb over the gold chain around her ankle and slide my hand along the curve of her calf. "It's a process," I answer, frustrated by these self-imposed boundaries. I have no one to blame. I drove the stakes into the ground and strung the fence myself. "In a way, they've been married since he sent the bride his first gift."

"That wouldn't make her married," she protests, crunching on a peppermint. "Not even in ye olden times."

"She kept his gift. That's the thing."

My gaze travels to her bed, heaped with stuffed raccoons, and the buzz of my phone breaks me out of a dangerous daydream. A text from Noah. "Basketball at the palace. ASAP?"

Ella rests her chin on me and reads over my shoulder. "Do you have to?" she sighs.

I grunt. "I should."

"Where are you supposed to be?"

"He probably thinks I'm at the office."

She looks up with an expression I've been calling her "math face" since I tutored her for the college entrance exams. "Five minutes to the car. Thirteen minutes to drive—"

"It's Friday night. The traffic is awful," I say, removing her glasses and setting them aside so I don't smudge the lenses. "It's at least twenty minutes to cross town."

"Another three minutes from the car park," I drag her around to the front of me.

She adds an extra five minutes to the timer on her phone. "You stopped to talk to one of the footmen on the way in."

She tosses the phone, and when I kiss her she laughs. She always laughs.

We're not laughing when we hear a tap on the door. I lift my head and scowl at the nearest clock. We have ten more minutes.

"Ella?" Freja's voice calls through the door and Ella pushes me off the couch. I land with a thud.

"It's fine," I whisper, "we're just gaming." We prearranged a cover story for just this eventuality.

"Have you seen yourself?" she hisses. Grabbing my face, she points it at a mirror, her voice low and urgent. "You look like you've been attacked by the dragon of Sondmark. Moreover, you're supposed to be fighting traffic."

"Ella." Freja's voice, slightly impatient, carries through the door and Ella drags me to my feet and stuffs me into her closet, really putting her back into it when I won't move as fast as she likes.

"Hey—" I catch her hand as she turns, tugging her in for a deep kiss, picking out her shape with my fingertips in the velvety darkness.

I get her to lose herself for a moment before she breaks free. Taking a huge breath, she kicks me in the shins. The low sound of my laugh dissolves in the shadows.

"Coming," Ella calls. I watch the sisters through a crack in the door. "Sorry," she says, her acting pretty plausible. "The mechanism must be glitching."

Freja is quiet and her eyes narrow on Ella's face. "Did you have shellfish?"

"What?"

"Your face is red and your lips are swollen. You know you're not supposed to eat shrimp when you're alone. Let me call Doctor Frum—"

"I'm fine," Ella replies. "I took a pill. I'm already past the worst of it." I sometimes forget how well she lies when I'm not looking for it. "What brings you to my lair?"

"Oskar and I had dinner with Mama and Père," Freja says, looking over Ella's shoulder. I shrink into the shadows, my heart beating loudly in my ears.

"Both of them at the same time?" Ella asks, resting her hand on the doorframe, blocking it.

"They're putting on a good show for Oskar," Freja answers.

"Of course. Putting on shows is what we do."

I frown at the bitterness in her voice. Ella is not like her sisters. If her nanny wrestled her into those little-girl dresses with the white collars, she'd march herself through the nearest puddle. She would make faces at the paparazzi and melt down on the tarmac whenever her mother's plane lifted off while everyone else was standing sedately. She used to tear through the administration wing, upsetting the royal order with a laugh no one but her mother could resist.

She's not laughing now.

Freja dips her head. "Can I come in? We could talk about it."

"I'm just headed out," Ella says. She reaches for a hoodie, shoves her phone into her pocket, and bundles Freja into the hall, staring pointedly at the crack in the closet before she goes.

I check my phone, the screen illuminating the closet. 20:49. I'm still supposed to be on the road.

I settle into a low chair and begin responding to work emails. This used to exhaust me but it's become more like a simple game of *Drop Bloks*. Every line I strike off my to-do list means more time to be with Ella. This part of the arrangement is working out, more or less as I hoped.

Eventually she returns and worms her way into my lap. "I had to walk her to her car, say hi to Oskar..."

I tug the ears of her hoodie until it falls away, nuzzling her cold skin. "You're keeping her at arm's distance."

Ella tenses. "Would you rather have me invite her in?"

I breathe against her neck. "Your family isn't doing well."

She releases a sharp-edged laugh. "Ten points for Team van Heyden."

"Reporters haven't worked out that your parents aren't the happy couple they present themselves as?"

She dips her head, planting a soft kiss on my earlobe, following it with the brush of her thumb. "Not yet. There isn't a whisper of it in the press. My sisters have them distracted with their ever-growing baggage train of calamities. Thank heaven for small miracles."

I catch her hand, holding on to my sanity. "What are you going to do about it?"

She lifts her head. "These aren't my problems. Mama and Père have been keeping separate quarters for more than a year. Every one of my sisters is going her own way. I haven't done anything but show up and do as I'm told."

My arms crisscross her back. "Family is everything. You can't abandon them when they need you."

"Marc." My name on her lips is threaded through with hurt. *Vede*, I didn't mean it as an accusation. "They don't want to be rescued."

I gather her closer, burying myself in the crook of her neck. "You're such a middle child, though. You're not happy unless everyone is happy."

"False. I want them to suffer."

"No you don't." I think of the Bible verses, committed to memory. *Love is patient, love is kind. It is not proud...* This is Ella.

"It's not my job to solve my family."

"We don't always get to choose the things destiny lays at our door." The words sound pompous but I kiss her neck to soften them.

"Destiny? I thought you were a thoroughgoing Lutheran," Ella says, taking this chance to turn to some less demanding topic.

I was raised Lutheran, my mother a great believer in equipping me with the tools to live in the world I would one day inherit, but I have just enough of a connection to my Seongan heritage to perform the ancestral rites and mean them.

"I can't dismiss destiny," I answer. I can't shrug away the idea of the heavens bending to some foregone destination. Leading me here.

The alarm chimes. Our time is up.

"My family is going to make their own choices," she says, tapping her phone. I should be leaving the car park by now, coming up the rain-soaked walk on the north side of the palace, but I don't want to leave Ella, especially now. "My hands are clean when it comes to my family. Their issues have nothing to do with me."

"I think you're better than that," I counter.

She looks deeply into my face. "Do you think I'm being selfish?"

I take a breath. "Your family needs you. With a little mercy, a little grace—"

"The Lutheran has returned." She shrugs off my arms and scrambles to her feet. "I could be one of those internet weirdos who goes no contact with their parents because they don't re-cycle used batteries or Pankedruss lids. But no, my great crime is leaving people alone."

"Ella—"

"We can't all be Saint Marcus, loyal liegemen to the crown, Martyr of Lindenholm," she mutters. The air crackles with hurt and frustration, but she's also really cute when she goes on a tear.

"Ells."

She points to the door. "Don't leave my brother waiting."

Vede. Noah. I give her a quick kiss and shrug on my jacket. "I'll text you when I get home," I say, helpfully unlatching her door mechanism when I pass through. The sound of the slam follows me down the hall and I grin.

22

RAMEN AND CHILL

ELLA

When I'm frustrated with my family, I'm tempted to set up a
Rube-Goldburg machine in the ballroom to make my feelings
clear. "Actions," I would thump them each on the head with
a long stick as the machine spun and lit on fire and rolled and
exploded at each stage, propelled by Newton's irresistible laws,
"have consequences."

No matter how much power Marc claims I have, I can't
change everything.

He said he would text. Why isn't he texting? I figure that
basketball takes an hour. When it's over, does he sit in the sauna
with Noah and the others and talk about his feelings? Is there a
trust circle and a talking stick?

It's almost midnight when I throw myself into bed. He
should be home, thinking up ways to tell me he's sorry about
how he left things. I stare at my phone screen, one of my trash
panda stuffies shoved under my head, and begin to type.

Are you home?

Delete.

Ramen and chill?

Delete.

I take a breath and type very slowly. *I'm sorry for calling you so many names.* I'm sorry for calling him even one. Feelings crowd the back of my throat and I bite back a curse. *Stultes es*, he always knows what I need to hear.

My finger hovers over the send button when a text bubble pops up on the screen. Marc. *I was telling you how to live your life. I know how much you hate that.*

Then, *Forgive me?*

I exhale, a weight rolling off my shoulders. I do not deserve his patience.

I type, *I didn't know being in a relationship would mean saying sorry so much.* I stare at the words. We aren't in a relationship. My heart hurts. Delete.

I roll onto my stomach and tap the video button, prepare my pleasant smile and smooth my hair.

"Marc—" It ends in a squeak. He's shirtless again.

I drop the phone and hear his laugh.

Our families have mixed for decades, taking summer holidays together at Outingen Huis and winter trips to Uncle Georg's private island for much-needed sun. He's been captured at beaches around the world by paparazzi using telephoto lenses. His abs are no foreign, undiscovered country, but I return to them each time like a long-exiled soul, kneeling on my native soil with tears of gratitude. I'm back. I am so back.

"Are you going to put something on?" I grit, righting the phone.

"I don't think I am." He grins, hitching up on one arm. He did a short stint as a male model after being scouted in Seong, and I've always been impressed by their impeccable hotness pipeline. One must admire an entire country dedicated to the proposition that they're not going to waste their baddies on a cubicle farm. Anyway, when he stretches like that, I know he knows what he's doing.

"I know you like it," he says.

"What makes you so sure—?"

Marc gives the phone a bland stare.

I look in the four cardinal directions and remind myself that there's no future in ogling Marc van Heyden. "How was basketball?"

"Noah had no idea I'd been making out with his little sister, if that's what you're asking."

My cheeks flame. I should be past this. I should be able to meet Marc on the well-lit ground we've decided upon—dead-end kisses, lots of fun, no complicated feelings. It's an arrangement as chic as a wedding reception I attended last year for one of the Saint Sissela girls where the only refreshments were bowls of cigarettes.

I tamp the blush down. "I was asking about basketball."

"We crushed him."

Okay, hot. "Do you always crush him?" I ask, snuggling into my bed.

He watches me, a hand kneading the back of his neck. "I wasn't in a mood to lose."

When Marc shifts the pillow, his shoulder rolls into the frame. I bite my lip to stop a second squeak. This chat should have stayed a text.

Speaking of... "I was in the middle of messaging you," I admit.

His lips tilt. "Yeah? Tell me what you were going to say."

He's flirting on purpose, certainly not part of the deal. That we're attracted to one another ought to be enough of a disaster, given how desperately I need out of the royal way of life and how committed he is to the oath he made to prop it up. He doesn't need to torment me with flirting.

"I called you names," I lie. "Kraken of the Silicon Sea."

"Oh, we're doing this?" He has a smile I never see when he's looking at anyone else.

"Hermit King of Lindenholm."

Marc squints an eye and his hand seesaws. "Mid."

"A man with gigabytes where his heart should be..."

His smile tips up, and the connection between us is so clear I see every pixel of his neck. "I said I was sorry. I am sorry. You were only trying—" I say.

"I know."

I know. With his words, my heart, like a watchful shield-maiden, lays down her spear and unbuckles her armor. She is unprepared for the piercing needle of grief that follows. Her knees buckle. Marc has said nothing about love. It's as it should be. This deal of ours—the emotional equivalent of strapping himself into a safety harness—includes a promise to leave, and I'm going to fight to uphold my end of the bargain.

"Mama is throwing a party for my birthday," I tell him, throat thick with feelings I can't begin to name. "Next week."

"I know when your birthday is. Is this an invitation? It better be. I have a thing with the birthday girl." His expression warms, and I clutch a fistful of flannel pajamas where my pearls would be. I can't sell my soul for a 'thing'.

"Is Freja coming?" he asks.

"We're a package deal."

In an attempt to stop thinking about Marc so much, I spend the whole week tracking the movements of the prime minister, logging the official information, and looking for patterns. If he has a say in where *we're* supposed to be, I want to know where *he* is.

On another screen, I break the source code for my app, re-configure the architecture, and scroll through ReadHe threads on AI integration. On still another, I nurture my *SquadRun* team, coaching dragonslayer2 through a tricky side quest and acting as a listening ear for Staggering_Indifference as she re-counts an effort to get rent money from her live-in boyfriend while maintaining her image as totally chill, fine with whatever.

Marc is impossible to put out of my mind. I gave him the security code for my suite and he abuses it. One morning he wakes me up with a hot pastry and an iced Americano from *La Baiser Chaleureux*, an upscale bakery in the heart of Handsel, nowhere near his office or flat. He slips up to my room and gives me such a fierce kiss that I'm clutching my bed clothes as he goes without a word. Later, he sends me an article about tech stacks for my app development.

I watch him in a broadcast from the Grousehof, standing in the ornate legislative chamber with the rest of parliament to hear the opening arguments in Freja's case. He wears his government robes—a heavy black cloak billowing back from a fitted waistcoat. Thick gold embroidery marches across the full sleeves and neck, and tiny buttons run from his chin to his waist, indicating his hereditary status as *Hochneerheid*—the High Lord of Sondmark. The costume should denote that he is ornamental—a throwback to a bygone age—or that he lost the power his ancestors wielded as their right. It should proclaim that the rest of parliament—elected properly and shuffling in with white synthetic wigs and short red capes, bowing to the empty, golden throne at the head of the room—are his betters. The idea is laughable.

They speak Freja's name and title, recounting her list of crimes, and present the formal petition to open an inquiry. The members of parliament murmur their assent with huddled heads, and I slam out of the media room, muttering my excuses to my family as I go. I am tense and suffocated and scared. I don't even question my destination when I log it at the security gate.

I drive to Marc's flat and wait for him in the front hall until he returns from the Grousehof. He opens the door wearing an ordinary suit and tie, and freezes on the threshold, a garment bag hooked over his shoulder. For a second, he looks at me in a way that clears the space between us, wiping away family obligations and old habits, future dreams and exit plans. My breath sticks in my throat, and I rush to fill the space with words.

"Your formal robes are wasted on the government," I say, stumbling back to lean against an entry table. "I had to come and see what they look like in person."

He shifts the weight of the bag, the intense, earth-shattering expression ebbing so slowly from his face that I wonder if I imagined it.

"Where else would I wear a thing like this?" he asks, wiggling the hanger.

"MangaCon? Dragon Summit?" For me? Around the house?

His eyes dance but he utters a soft complaint. "It took forever getting out of it. All those buttons—"

I push him toward the bedroom. "The sooner you start changing into your official robes, the sooner I'll be culturally edified."

He goes, but then sticks his head around the door-jamb—roguish now. "Are we renegotiating our deal?"

I lift my eyes. "In your dreams." In *my* dreams. "Make yourself decent and I'll help with the rest."

When he returns, he's shrugging the heavy article over bare, corded shoulders, and I gaze fixedly on the skyline of Handsel.

"Decent, I said."

"I'm decent for a swim," he laughs, halting less than a handspan away, counting on his proximity and hotness to do the rest. "And you promised to help."

It's a punishing exercise in self-control. I vow not to play so near to the fire next time as I push one heavy gold button at a time through its loop, up and up and up. His skin flinches away when I brush against it, and we breathe our laughter even though I don't know what's funny.

I didn't really race across town for this. I raced here because I needed to be with him. My skin feels singed and I want to burst into tears, but I slip the last button through and he hands me a thin black ribbon.

"Let's do it properly," he whispers.

The *Hochneerheid* doesn't wear a powdered wig. He wears the Sondish marriage knot to indicate his allegiance to the Crown. Marc's hair is not as long as it once was, but I perch on his stone coffee table and rake the sides back in the traditional loop, tying it off—three times around for health, safety, and fortune. A knot for fidelity and another for love. The action, one I have never performed for a man, carries an intimacy I'm not prepared for, and my fingers are stiff and unsteady. I ex-pected to get a little fashion show, some teasing—anything to get me away from the crushing tension of the palace. But this is the cord a Sondish Viking would wear as he went raiding—a pagan promise, carried from his hearth, that he would return to his woman. We all learn it in school. We make it into bracelets and draw it in the sand. We practice this as a game until one day—this day—it becomes a prayer.

He catches my hand as I tighten the loop, turns, and lifts me into a kiss. I thought I wasn't any good at discipline, but who else could leave Marc in such a state—tugging at my hand while I back out of his apartment. Who among my sisters in a similar situation could stop herself from undoing all those buttons again? Only me. Only just.

When Freja is called to testify before the committee, she wears a vintage Chanel suit. Oskar accompanies her to the door of the briefing room, handing over an insulated flask of tea and a package of cookies before giving her a light kiss. That image is splashed across the front page of *The Daily Missive* and *The Holy Pelican*. "FREJA PROPOSED". "Over My Dead Body: A Princess's Plea to Protect her Husband". Protests and counter-protests spring up. The next day, the papers carry photos of riot police.

My mother is tense. At all times, she is flanked by courtiers, secretaries, ladies-in-waiting, and lawyers. She checks my clothes before official engagements. If I don't meet her exacting standards, I am dismissed with the softest exhale of frustration. It drives home the point that I will never please her.

On the morning of my twenty-seventh birthday, I treat myself to a facial and manicure at Esther Hong's. When I walk out of the spa, my skin looks like the glowing sunrise of an alien planet, but I press through a gauntlet of paparazzi, cameras in my face, livestreamers asking about my twin, shouting about laws of marriage and succession they don't live under the unbearable yoke of. With my heart in my throat, I break a number of traffic laws to get home, arranging my expression into something that won't make headlines like, "Princess Ella Drives into Hostile Crowd" or "Stone-Faced Princess Contemplates Murder".

I tear through the doors of the Summer Palace like a cat emerging from an unexpected dunking. "What in the hell?" I gasp, tossing my keys to Anselm, one of our footmen. "What in the actual *flamen* hell has happened to Sondmark? Can we call in an airstrike on the satellite vans?"

A masculine laugh interrupts me, and I glance up to see Crown Prince Jacob, taking the stairs two at a time. He grabs me into a huge hug and I whoop in surprise.

"How?" I punch his shoulder, switching to English.

He grins. "I hitched a ride through the gates with someone in the renovation studio." He looks me up and down, with as much interest as a customs agent. "You clean up nice."

Over his shoulder, I see Max and Oskar sitting on the treads of the staircase.

"But why aren't you upstairs?" I ask, fetching up in front of the others.

Max carries on a low-translation for Oskar but Oskar shrugs him away and perseveres in English for Jacob's benefit. "She kick us out. Say tradition."

Max points at Jacob. "That one keeps bellowing for Alma, but she bellows back that she won't come down until you're all ready. Go talk some sense into them?"

Not a chance. A fizzing excitement races through my veins. Getting ready with my sisters for a birthday party is nothing like getting ready for a state visit—I thought those days were long gone.

Jacob breaks in, grumpy now. "Does she not know how long I drove?" He shouts for Alma's benefit, "Does she know I have to get back tonight?"

"Does he know he's being a baby?" my eldest sister shouts back.

I gallop up the stairs and race for my suite, trying to smother my expectations. It might not be what I hope for. It might be—

Before it can be anything, Clara scoops me over the threshold of my room and pushes a pink martini into my hand. BLUSH blares over the speakers. Freja is wearing noise-cancelling headphones, the band extended as high as it will go to accommodate the fat curlers in her hair, and Alma piles into the room with several dresses. Have I died and gone to heaven?

"Come see what we're working with," Clara says, clad in a silk robe and munching on a mini quiche. She leads me to a row of priceless tiaras laid out on the same console where I keep my ramen noodles, and runs a light finger over The Grenlaud, a multi-colored tutti-frutti tiara that was part of an inheritance donated by a social-climbing heiress who finally joined the cool kids club only after her death.

"This is mine. The sweatband is for Freja."

The sweatband is Princess Marel's Emerald Bandeau from the 20s. It's art deco, weird, and meant to be situated low on the brow. No one else has been brave enough to try it out, but we can always depend upon Freja to give aesthetic exuberances a crack.

"This is Alma's." She points to The Emir's Diamonds. The row of glittering stars was the gift of a Middle Eastern billionaire whose grasp of human rights is as tenuous as a gust of wind.

"Which one are you wearing?" Freja asks.

"I passed."

Her brow furrows and I lift one of her headphones. "I passed on Mama's offer."

Then I lift my voice. "Paige, turn it down to two." BLUSH subsides into background music and I watch Freja visibly relax.

For the next hour, my sisters pass in and out of my suite. We move like a bee hive—each of us acutely aware of the others. They grab tissues and borrow claw clips, pose with cocked heads while using curling wands. A fog of hairspray billows above Clara.

Alma leans over the sink, opening her eyes wide to apply mascara. "Jacob's mom is breathtaking. She pads around her flat barefooted, talks to her houseplants, and appears to be a completely normal American mom—until she looks at you. Then it's magic. She's not even fifty, and I'm willing to bet hard cash that King Otto will make a pass at her at Jacob's investiture ceremony."

I giggle. "Lock the cloak rooms."

"There are not enough locks in that castle." Alma nudges Clara. "How are things going with Max?"

Clara dimples. "I love his family, but their idea of family drama is ridiculous. The Maagensens planted sunflowers, which is going to throw the shade situation of the Andersen Garden Allotment into complete chaos. His mom wants to bake them a cake as a peace-offering, but I'm like, 'No—*war*.'"

"Diplomacy will only invite future incursions," I say with a wink. "Uproot the sunflowers and salt the earth behind you."

Clara nods. "See? You get it."

I slip into my closet to don my gown. It's the color of not-quite-ripe grapes and has a wide neckline with a fitted bodice. I struggle doing up the back, but hear, "I've got it," before Freja brushes my fingers aside. A tide of emotion rises so fast I almost choke. I blame it on the gin, but I know better. This feeling—anger? Grief? I don't know—has been here all along.

"How did you manage?" I ask, cursing the tremor in my voice.

"Manage what?"

"When you got married," I say, biting my lip. "Who zipped you up? The intern?"

Her hands drop. "The dress had ties I could manage on my own."

"Alone?" *Vede.*

"Who else would I have?"

Me. Clara. Alma. A knot of sisters. My throat burns with emotion, but I execute a little spin. "Well?"

She smiles. "You look like a fairytale."

Freja's dress has a tiny bodice, a long sweep of fabric falling from under her bust, and she wears Princess Marel's bandeau across her forehead. It should be shapeless and weird, but she has a kind of magical intuition about these things.

"You look like something out of a Russian novel," I say. Her brow lifts. "What? I've read *War and Peace*."

Her brow lifts higher.

"The manga."

Her lips pinch with a smile and she tugs the door of the closet closed, muffling the sounds of music and laughter beyond. When she takes both of my hands in hers, I fidget under the brilliant spotlight of Freja's attention, given to me all at once. It never happens like this. I'm the one always throwing myself at her chilly walls—ever so high, ever so thick—and I feel a momentary disorientation.

"Ella." Her breath hitches. "I've been trying to talk to you."

"We talk."

Her look convicts me. "It's my birthday," she tells me, as though I wasn't there for it. "You have to give me what I want and I want to talk."

Oskar has made her bolder. Teasing. More audacious. I try to blunt her intensity. "I guess I could return the fridge magnets."

She flicks my forehead, and I rub the spot before she recaptures my hand. "I'm never going to regret getting married exactly as I did. You can't wait for that." What did I expect? Freja is still Freja. She's still as abrupt as ever. She's still pushing me away. My feet shift but she goes on. "It might have killed me if Oskar had been deported."

"Killed you?" I scoff.

"I can't apologize for my wedding and mean it, but I hope you know I hated walking into that church without you."

I've imagined Freja a hundred times, marching away from me with brisk certainty, chin up, back as straight as she can manage, eyes clouded by the stupidities of love. I've imagined it like she smashed a jeweler's window and ran off with her bag of loot. I've imagined her posing for theatrical photographs, more concerned with a photo spread than having her sisters at her side.

Her smile wobbles and I look away. I know what the politics were. The prime minister was targeting *Neer* Velasquez. Time was running out, and there was no way the entire Sondish royal family could have packed into a Vorburgian church for a clandestine wedding without a national uproar. I know all that. But something frozen in my heart starts to thaw at the knowledge that Freja didn't charge into the chapel all sunshine and show tunes. She wanted us.

Her mouth pulls on one side. "I could not have done it if you hadn't shown me how. Remember when you told Mama you were going to school halfway around the world? You had the acceptance letter in your hand before you ever said a word."

"You're blaming this on me?" I choke, turning these tender feelings into something we can laugh at.

She resists my retreat, gripping me tightly. "I know I'm not always what you need," she says, taking a deep breath, "but I wanted you to understand me."

Not "forgive me". Understand me. *Dominanstid.* Freja has a way with her.

I want to run away from royal life but, holding Freja's hands, I hear Alma bellowing down the hall and Clara's answering laugh. The air is pregnant with our mingled scents, sharp and sweet.

23

CUT STEEL

ELLA

I kiss a folded over tissue and a knock sounds at the door. My mother's secretary, dressed in the depressingly plain black cocktail dress we've seen dozens of times that allows her to move around royal events and provide her own brand of unobtrusive organization, dips a respectful nod as my sisters pass out of the room. She enters with a tiara-shaped box.

I release a frustrated breath. Didn't I make it clear that I wasn't going to wear one of her clunkers, just for a private party? "Is this from the queen?" I ask.

"No, ma'am," she replies. "It arrived with a note."

I finger the heavy stationary, sealed with the wax cipher of *Neerheid* van Heyden, lord of Lindenholm, and open it with hurried fingers. To my slight irritation, the penmanship of the handwritten note is flawless.

My mother wishes to lend this to you tonight. You can't say no when I know how much you want it. —Marc.

I undo the latch and flip the top open. What I see makes me clutch Caroline's arm and suck in a measure of air. "Is that what I think it is?"

Caroline's rare smile peeps out. "I see a tiara, ma'am."

Not *a* tiara. *The* tiara. Gold-plated cut steel in a dandelion motif on a bed of dark velvet. The one I offered to place on Jang Mi's head when the words out of my mouth felt like a blade sliding over my skin.

"Will you be needing any assistance, ma'am?" Caroline asks, eyes speculative.

I nod and she scoops up the delicate metalwork, placing it on my hair. I close my eyes, savoring the sensation of featherlight material resting on my curls, and when I open them again, I find my reflection. The gold picks up the highlights in my hair and the added height makes me look like a character out of *Forced Marriage of the Fairy Realms*—a divine lawgiver, destined to save my people by forming an alliance with my worryingly irresistible enemy.

"Tell me if it's straight," I say, swallowing away the thickness in my throat.

Caroline adjusts the frame, and I decide that this is the most magical tiara that has ever existed. I love it, and it's just a loaner.

Alma pops her head in. "Oof. That's gorgeous on you. Is that the van Heyden tiara?"

"The good one. Is it time to head down?"

She holds her hand out and we join Freja and Clara in the hall. "Ready?"

Me and my sisters pause at the top of the staircase in an unbroken chain that seems to hum with feminine power. The menfolk turn at the sound of Clara's laugh. Max, Oskar, Jacob, and—my heart kicks into an unsteady rhythm—Marc.

My gaze skitters away from the intensity of his stare, and I dimly register a fifth man leaning lazily against the doors, brooding darkly as we descend the stairs with Caroline trailing behind us. Noah. Probably totting up how much this is costing the Crown.

Jacob curses under his breath, grabs Alma's hand, and peels off the wrong way with a shouted, "Happy birthday!" over his shoulder. I wonder if they'll ever make it to the party. Max, strides after Clara when she laughingly slips past him, his long legs narrowing the distance. Oskar meets Freja on the bottom step and puts his elbow out, bending his head to whisper into her ear. Caroline follows in their wake, her posture unbending, and Noah frowns after her.

"The dress isn't that bad," I say, reading his expression. "It's just that we've seen it a million times."

Noah drags a deep breath into his lungs, gives me an absent-minded glance, and crooks his arm. "Come along," he says, "I'll take you out."

"Don't overwhelm me with your enthusiasm," I answer, slipping my hand through his elbow.

Marc moves to my other side, one hand in his pocket, the other brushing mine as we walk, the slightest twining of our hands, his fingertips grazing my palm. My stomach tightens.

He's playing with fire in a hall full of reflective surfaces, and geometry is going to get us caught.

"Couldn't find a date?" Noah speaks over my head, taunting his best friend. I slowly shift my arm, my heart in my throat, but Marc resists my effort to make space between us. For a brief moment, his fingers lace through mine, sending a shiver up my arm.

"Still living with your mother?" Marc grins.

"I have my own cottage," Noah counters.

Marc places two fingers behind his ear, bending it forward. "On the grounds of where now?"

Marc catches my look in one of the mirrors, eyes blazing with how much he has kissed me this spring and how much kissing he still intends to do. He bumps his chin. "Later," he mouths, moving forward to the party.

Eventually, the path narrows and Noah and I follow the row of torches to the lower gardens. We've been lucky with the weather. The day is cloudless and warm enough for a garden party around a long stone swimming pool dating from the 18th century. Spring-fed and wild, the pool contains frogs, newts, and all manner of slimy things. Clusters of wildflowers, reeds, and marsh thistle provide a soft border against the cropped, velvety lawn, where ruthlessly-manicured trees dot the perimeter. Lights crisscross high above the water, and the sun dances into the horizon, kisses it, and eventually sinks.

A more lavish event wouldn't strike the right tone in the midst of Freja's succession crisis, so there won't be fireworks or dancing, but the party has a string quartet playing a succession of songs sampled on Pixy videos. Wondering glances linger on the Dandelion Tiara, but I say it's a loan from *Amma*. Nothing to do with my mother's dynastic matchmaking. Princess Ella hasn't swept Marc van Heyden off the market. I can almost hear the sighs of relief.

When the early stars begin to peep out, Oskar finds me talking with distant cousins. "Can we cut the Kindercakes?" he asks. "Freja is tired."

"Have you tried giving her a canape?"

"Of course." His lips twitch into almost a smile and I follow him back to a low dias where Freja stands before the monstrous cakes.

The old Sondish dessert is baked in the shape of a person and decorated with no regard to the night terrors it might give me. Mine has peppermint curls and a gown of black licorice, while Freja's is filled with Pankedruss custard.

We call for silence, and the crowd gathers. Clara lights candles on each cake, and the crowd begins to sing—nothing bright and simple. The people of Sondmark salt every celebration with a heavy dose of Calvinism.

Welcome tomorrow, goodbye today
Last of the sunset flying away
The dark will unmake us, Then usher the dawn
Goodnight, my old self. A new self is born.

We blow our candles out and pose for a quick photograph. The softness of Freja's cheek lingers on mine; our hands are tightly woven. There is no seeing into the future, but I taste the bittersweetness of unity, just for tonight.

When Freja and Oskar slip away, I mingle for two. The crowd thins, and I spot Marc standing on the other side of the pool. My eyes fasten on his suit, really lingering now that the light has fallen and my own expression isn't so easily read. Is he wearing—

He tips his head. *Come here.*

Slowly enough that it doesn't look too obvious, stopping to greet and laugh and kiss cheeks, I dance around to the other side.

"You look stupid hot," I tell him. My eyes are trained on the pool, and Marc's smile is slow and easy. "I didn't realize—"

I have a thing for *Intelligence Force*, a kind of Seongan James Bond knock off, insanely better than the original IP. The drama poster hangs in my closet and Marc must have seen it, given how often I've stuffed him in there lately. In addition to the dead black suit, he's wearing a sparkly brooch and a pair of aviators, achieving the perfect cosplay. I doubt anyone else has noticed. Happy birthday to me.

"If you're not careful," he says, gaze arcing over my head like he's checking the perimeter or preparing to neutralize a hostile target, "it'll be obvious."

"What obvious?" I ask, plucking two flutes of champagne and putting one into his hand. Now he's got a weapon in the event someone needs to be stabbed in the shoulder.

"That you want to have your way with me." I choke but he takes a smooth swallow.

I frown into my glass. "Can I call you Je Ha? Just for today?"

"You may not."

I give a brisk nod. "Right. Best to keep the identity secret."

"How's the tiara?" He scuffs his shoe against the rough stones.

It's only a loaner. It's only a loaner.

"Any chance *Amma* wants to sell?" I ask, touching the delicate metal. "She hasn't done me any favors, lending me this. Everything else is going to be second best."

"You can visit the tiara whenever you want."

I smile, but it hurts, right up under my ribs in a way that makes me want to dive into the pool and swim down, down, down until I emerge in some other timeline in some other land. In a Sondmark that never heard of Seong, as an Ella who never loved Marc.

"With my nose pressed up against the glass, fogging it up?" I laugh. "It's not the same as being mine."

Marc slides his hands into his pockets and I watch the play of muscles. "You don't want a future that involves tiaras."

"Right." I blink in rapid succession. I'm leaving. I'm still leaving. Sooner or later.

The string quartet breaks into the national anthem, and Marc removes his sunglasses while the party stands at attention and sings. The assembly bows or curtsies as Mama and Père retire, making a show of unity as they walk hand in hand towards the old family apartment.

"Are things better there?" Marc asks, looking after them.

"That's just a pretty picture," I say. Warm lights dot the garden, and floating flowers are reflected in the dark waters of the pool. I smile and nod as guests begin to trickle away. "Are you going, too?"

"Should I?" he asks, his tone a lazy invitation. But I'm not about to drag him off to the shrubbery for a little light necking. There have been too many close calls.

I swallow. "You look tired."

"You said I looked stupid hot."

I grin. "With you it's not mutually exclusive. Why are you tired?"

"Alix is making one of her passions my problem."

I can hear the exhaustion in his voice as he holds the ragged ends of his responsibilities in too-few hands. Everyday I expect him to say he's too tired for me, but he brushes his fingertips over my cheek and I flinch against the temptation to lean into his touch. Who is watching? I don't even know.

His hand drops and I wave to Lady Greta, getting caught in another round of farewells. When I find my way back to him, it's just me and Marc and a moonlight garden.

"You need to get some rest," I say, holding his hand in mine, wondering if we could melt into a dark shadow and I could steal a proper kiss before he goes.

He slips his arms around my waist. "I can't leave yet," he says.

"Oh." My hand goes to my head. "You're going to want your tiara back."

Midnight comes for every princess. There's no magic strong enough to stop pumpkins and field mice from assuming their natural form. I'll go back to what I was, too. A restless girl looking for a way out of this mess.

"That's not what I meant." He bends down to where the edge of the pool turns into cattails and native grasses, plucks a large, near-perfect dandelion, and holds it between us.

"What's this?" Our deal doesn't include gifts and dates, but this is the first flower he has ever brought me. I take it between my fingers, careful not to disturb the trembling seeds. Dandelions don't last. This isn't something I can press into a book of remembrance, even.

"It's a wish," he says. "I want you to close your eyes and wish for the one thing you've wanted more than anything else your whole life."

It's a wonder he can't feel my pulse through my skin. In the darkness, I let my heart break wide open. *Dominanstid*. He asked me what I want, and the answer waits like an unstable snowpack before the crack and collapse—the wrecking slide and the billow of ice. I grip the delicate stem, and the wish forms before I grant it permission to exist. *Give me Marc van Heyden and I'll never ask for anything else.*

I open my eyes, take a breath, and blow. The seeds fly in the cool air, glinting in the light like tiny flecks of silver.

Maybe this can turn into something real. Maybe I'll kiss him really well. No matter how many commitments he's made to his best friend and the Crown, he turns into pudding when I do that.

I take a breath.

"Ella—" He gets there first, his voice amused. "From the first time you ran away to Lindenholm, you wanted one thing."

I nod. Yes. One thing.

"It's probably a terrible idea—" he continues.

Gravity holds me with the lightest touch. *No. It isn't. It's a very, very good idea.*

"—but after everything you did for Seong, I wanted to find a way to make you happy."

This is not the most romantic confession. Still, he's a man, and allowances must be made. Making me happy is a good place to start.

He holds my face with his hands, pushing his thumbs over my skin. "So tonight..."

My heart beats loud in my ears.

He grins. "...we're breaking you out of the palace."

24

CRACK TEAM

MARC

Ella emerges from the pool house, clad in black from the light turtleneck top to the curve-skimming leggings. I look away. These last weeks have felt like climbing a sheer rock face. When I started, I was confident in my ability to scale the heights, but now each handhold is more narrow and unlikely than the last. Bits of gravel scrape my fingertips and skitter to the ground. I can't see the next grip, and I can't see my way down. So I hold myself here, every nerve and muscle screaming, waiting for death or rescue.

No matter how much Ella likes my kisses—and she does—she is always in control. I've been wrestling with my attraction for her almost from the first moment I returned from Seong, but at the end of every night, cheeks flushed and lips swollen, she is very much the master of herself. She's still looking for a way to escape, and when I have to let her go for the last time, I'll do it. I promised.

I shoulder a black backpack and take her hand, threading my fingers through hers. "Caroline will pick up the dress and tiara."

"Are we really doing this?" she asks.

I nod. "Nils agreed to let us do a security test. He's giving us thirty minutes to try and cross the wall," I say, pulling her behind a sculpted bush. "Think of it like war games. If the palace guardsmen tag us within ten meters of the perimeter, we lose."

Ella cranes her neck. "What's in your backpack?"

"Rope, folding stool, voltage tester, laptop."

She reaches up and kisses me. "Do you want to renounce your title?" she asks. "We could run away and become a crack team of hackers, righting the wrongs of a corrupt society. We could spend our winters in a non-extradition country, sipping cocktails on a beach, and wreaking havoc with the locals."

The dream of me and Ella in a lonely shack in Lijuela takes up residence in my brain like a mountain shrine, overgrown with moss and vines, echoing with desperate prayers. I wheel away and run a shaking hand over my face. "First, let's get over the wall. How do you want to do it?"

She gauges the distance between us and the fence, and settles on the grass as she logs into the laptop. "I assume you brought this because you already sent a phishing email?"

I crouch down. "I wanted to be prepared," I say. She grabs me by the collar and jerks me forward for another kiss.

"Put some knots along the rope at intervals," she directs. Her fingers begin to fly, and I busy myself with the assigned task.

"We're going to do it along this stretch," she says, pointing at a schematic of the perimeter, deciding so quickly she might have spent the last decade casing the palace for this moment. "The bushes will cover our approach."

Ella and I zigzag across the palace grounds, sticking to the shadows, pausing to evade security. "Are you ready?" I ask, folding her against the trunk of a tree, my breathing ragged.

"I'm worried about the glowing screen," she whispers. We'll have to use the laptop to override the electrified wire, and we don't have time for more elegant solutions. Ella looks around my bulk. "Let's get to some dense vegetation," she says. Her body tenses, ready to run across open ground, and then checks. "My family won't be unprotected if we—"

Ella never forgets her family. She can't.

"They're safe," I reassure her. Nils and I have been thorough.

We silently sprint across open ground and break through the hedge line. I pull her under a large ornamental bush, where she opens the computer and turns the brightness all the way down.

"I don't like our odds," she hisses.

I grin. "They promised not to taze us."

We have fifteen minutes left. I unpack the rope, coiling it on one side, and snap the stool open.

"That's three cameras down," she says, tapping the keyboard. "Now they know we're coming." A rush of activity sounds beyond the hedge, the pounding of shoes along the perimeter fence. "I cut the cameras on the south side and another one by the workshops to divert their attention. If we're fast enough here, it won't matter that the cameras can see us."

A guard slithers between the narrow gap between the hedges and the wall, and we hold ourselves absolutely silent until we hear the heavy beat of retreating footsteps.

"What about the electrical wire?"

She gives an outraged squeak. "Nils is trying to change his password. I can keep him out as long as my hands are on the keyboard." She grins. "He can't reset it because I keep slipping an exclamation point in when he tries to duplicate it. If you go right this second, you can get over."

I perch on the stool, touch the voltage tester to the line, and it beeps loudly. Nils promised to dial the voltage back...

"Okay, not *this* second. I'll get it," she swears, her fingers performing magic. "Now."

I slip the looped rope over a fencepost when a noise sounds in the distance. Someone has spotted us.

"You go first," she whispers. She grabs the front of my shirt and hauls herself up, convinced my strength is enough to hold us both.

I give the rope a tug, and test the wire. The voltage device is silent. "Brace your feet at the top, step over the wire, and rappel down," I say. Two and a half meters is not so high.

"I'm still keeping Nils out," she insists. The guards will be here any moment and I shut the laptop almost on her fingers.

"You're going *now*." I scoop her onto my shoulder and she grabs the rope.

"Come quick," she commands. "Nils—"

I shrug her onto the wall and she steps over the wire, gives a delighted, roguish salute, and rappels down the opposite side.

Soon, the rope lands on my head. I hear Thor barreling across the meadow and scramble to the top of the wall. I step over and lean back, but my greater bulk makes the rope unstable. I swing suddenly and knock against the wall, my knuckle grazing the wire. A current flies up my arm as a hot, sharp sting.

I land hard, and air gusts out of my lungs. Ella sinks to her knees, running her hands up and down my limbs. "I'm fine," I tell her, my voice tight. Sondish, English, and Seongan curses ricochet through my brain when the head of palace security pulls up in a golf cart. "Nils, you *vailys*, you were supposed to turn the voltage down," I grit.

He crouches, pokes my chest with a stick, and waves away a clutch of interested officers.

"It was the tiniest little zap," he says, moving the stick up under my chin. "Did we scrape your pretty face?"

"Why did you let me talk you into that?" I say, struggling to my elbows. Blood oozes from a scratch on my hand, and I have no one to blame but myself. "Ella could have been hurt."

Nils laughs. He actually laughs. I'll have him sacked—

"I never worry about Her Royal Highness when she's in your hands," Nils observes. "You would die rather than see her hurt. If you need patching up, I guess we could call the surgery." In horror, I watch as he lifts his shoulder and pinches the short-wave radio.

"You wouldn't dare," I grunt.

He laughs. "The rope is a little low-tech. I expected better."

"*You* were the soft target," I grind out. "You and your hunger for scalped Dragons tickets. You threw the gates of the Summer Palace open yourself."

Nils scowls. "You made it over the wall *and* I'm not registered for the FC Motovia game? *Flamen* hell. *Flamen*. Hell."

"I promise you can finish this discussion tomorrow," Ella chides, blowing gently on my hand.

Nils wedges himself into the golf cart. "We're turning that all the way up now," he says, pointing at the electrified wire, "so don't try anything stupid. I'd better see you walking past the south gate in a timely fashion." The cart rolls away again.

The night is soft, and a gentle breeze follows us up the hill and through the golden gates. At this hour there are no news vans, protestors, or tourists, and I nod at security. "Was that everything you ever wished for?" I ask, lights from the palace illuminating the gravel drive.

Our shadows trail behind us, following where we lead.

"Better." She smiles and lifts her fist. I tap her knuckles, and our hands make the form of tiny explosions, falling away from one another. "When you're ready for your life of crime, let me know."

Ella follows me back to my car and digs out my emergency kit, looking for a band aid. She leans me against the bumper like I'm really injured.

"I can—"

She clicks her tongue, and I think of Atlas and his lichen-covered stone, groaning in my walled garden under the blazing sun and in the bitter cold. No one ever lifts his burden. No one ever tends to his wounds. Ella holds my hand and dabs on a salve, blowing gently. She applies the too-large bandage and gives it a kiss. I tilt her face up and follow her kiss with a warmer one.

We part when *Vrouw* Tiele comes tripping through the lot, jangling her keys in the midst of a suspiciously timed coughing fit.

I spend the next week on a business trip to London and have to content myself with late-night texts and mid-day check-ins. I speed home on Friday because Alix messaged me not to bother. She was only having her bridesmaids in and out for dress fittings.

It's been six days since I saw Ella, and I take the stairs two at a time, tapping on Alix's door. "Is it safe to come in?" I ask.

Before I enter, I force my expression into lines that read, "This is boring. I'm a little bored. I'd rather be doing double entry bookkeeping." My plan is to cross the room, lean on the back of a sofa—pick up a book or something. Every word out of my mouth is going to sound like a chore.

But when I see Ella standing on a dressmaker's platform, my plan is blasted to hell. "What in the name of Erasmus are you wearing?"

Alix giggles. "You sound exactly like the housematron at Saint Sissela's."

I don't see what's funny. Ella is half naked, while the seamstress seems to be doing a very poor recreation of a traditional Seongan dress with its close-fitting, wrap-around top and billowing skirt. The usual shape skims the ground, but Ella's shapely legs are on full display.

"Is there a bottom to that dress?" I growl.

Alix rolls her eyes. "Marc, you are being elderly."

"Queen Helena will have something to say about this," I insist. "One little breeze and you're going to launch another succession crisis."

Ella glares at me. "We can weight the hem."

Alix taps her lips. "No. That will drag the shape out of it." She gives a throaty sound of irritation. "I hate it when he has a point."

"Truly the worst," Ella agrees.

Alix snaps her fingers. "So let's give this look to Dahlia," she directs the dressmaker, "and reverse the effect for Ella. It'll be full-length but low-cut and we'll give you something strappy up here." Alix's hand flutters in a way I consider wildly irresponsible.

"She's a princess of the blood," I say. "For the dignity of the nation, she ought to be covered."

Alix's brows gather. "Now he sounds like Noah. Honestly, Marc, you'd think Sondmark was on the brink of collapse. Our country won't rise or fall with her neckline." She sweeps her hands at me. "Turn around while I get Ella out of this."

The sound of fabric dropping bores into my brain, but the dressmaker works quickly, creating a quick mock-up of the traditional silhouette married with a summer dress.

"You want to know what else I hate? How much I love this," Alix says. "You can turn, Marc. Dearest, you almost look tall."

Ella twists a strand of hair, tucking it into a loose updo. "Sold," she laughs.

"Not sold. Not. Sold. Nobody is selling anything." I shake my head. How is this better? The skirt is long, but the crisscross top should be a dozen centimeters higher. I drag air into my lungs. Where in the Sondish Sea have the sleeves disappeared to? I want to pound my head against some antique woodwork.

Ella's eyes linger on my face. "I've always wanted to be tall." Has she missed me as much as I've missed her? I try to detect a trace of it.

"Let's have a pair of narrow straps tie right at the point of her shoulders," Alix murmurs to the dressmaker, her focus elsewhere.

Why doesn't anyone care that Ella is brewing a national scandal? "This is so much worse. It exposes—"

Alix lifts her head, nailing me with a look *Amma* would surely recognize. "This is my best friend, Marc, and I won't have your loyalty to Noah ruining this for her. She has to dress like a middle-aged public health minister when she's doing her job, but this *isn't* a job. It's a wedding, and it's completely reasonable. It just is. I refuse to send her down the aisle looking like she's wearing a sack."

I take an unsteady breath, and Dahlia pokes her head around the door. "Is this where the party is?" She gets one look at Ella and whistles.

"Come in, come in," Alix gestures, swinging her gaze to Ella, her hands pressed in supplication. "Be the best maid of honor and take him off my hands for a few hours before he shrouds all my bridesmaids in shapeless bedsheets? I'll sort it out with the dressmaker. I'm so sorry to inflict him on you," she adds, glaring at me with narrowed eyes.

Ella smiles. "Anything to make you happy."

After a few tucks and measurements, she's sent to change, and she emerges from a curtained-off area in a pair of jeans and a Lao Hu Zone t-shirt. The members of the eternally youthful boy band look out at me from the graphic t, each dripping with jewelry, each sporting a different hair color.

I am hit with a wave of emotion—a tsunami.

I have a memory of how Ella turned from an awkward fifteen-year old with a posture problem into an unhinged Lao Hu Zone Lioness with a posture problem. I remember the slide deck she forced me to watch so I'd understand each nuance between her bias, her bias wrecker, the main visual, and rap line. "They're so pretty, Marc. So pretty." I still can't keep the members straight.

"Is it June 28th already?" I ask, remembering the anniversary of their debut. "Were you up when they went live?"

"So early," she smiles, "sitting up in bed, waving my lightstick in the dark like a maniac."

I am hit with another wave of wishing I had been there, arm hooked around her waist, face buried in a pillow, trying to sleep while she watched on her laptop.

My time in Seong taught me something about tsunamis. They aren't just a rush of water. When they roll in from the ocean, they thicken at the leading edge, the wave frequency stacking and building up layers while picking up debris. Everyone has been knocked over by a wave at the beach, but when seismic conditions alter the sea floor, the wave carries all the flotsam it encounters—the past piggybacking on the present, everything arriving at once. When a thing like that smashes into you, there's no coming back.

That damned shirt.

Vede. I have to get out of here because Alix isn't blind.

"The weather is gorgeous," I manage. "Wanna inspect some fences?"

Alix makes a sound of disgust. "Teach him some manners, friend, or he'll be a monk until he dies."

I hold the door for Ella, and as soon as she walks through, I shut it behind us, catching her by the wrist until it's just her and me and the ancient paneling of Lindenholm. It's been a week and I can't live this way. She gives a light laugh and returns the kiss, amused by my urgency, perhaps. I don't apologize. Contentment, heavy and sweet, settles in my limbs because she belongs here, our strange edges somehow fitting together.

"Marc," she whispers, when I come up for air.

I know. We're taking too many chances. I pull away but hold her hand, leading her to the mudroom, where I supply her with a change of footwear and a rough coat. She hops on the back of my quad, and we set off, first touring her past the BLUSH excavations and then driving deep into the parkland. The weather is windy, and I head straight into it, skirting fields with Ella's arms banding my chest and her head nestled between my shoulders.

"Are we really inspecting fences?" she asks when I come to a halt atop a rise and cut the engine. A cool breeze from the North Sea buffets against us, and she buries herself into me, snuggling against my back. "Nothing else?"

My arm covers hers. "I can multitask."

"Why are you irritated with Alix?" she asks, nipping at my waist. "Is it really the dress?"

I shake my head. "It's not a dress. It's scraps of fabric that barely cover—"

Ella laughs, slipping under my arm, and negotiates her way to the front of the bike. It's not seductive—not with messy hair and a muddy jacket—but she never has to try to make me want her. I just do. We're like kids on a swing, rubber boots making us clumsy. Her nose is rosy, and I press a kiss on the end of it, wishing I could bend time back to the moment I told her this wouldn't be serious.

"Stop being grumpy," she scolds, smoothing the line between my brows. She burrows her head under my chin. She cuddles. "Alix values your approval."

"She has it."

I pull away and give in to the desire to kiss her. The wind gusts against us, but I hold her tightly, wrapping her into my jacket and warming her where we touch. As usual, I lose my head, but Ella lifts hers.

"Marc, what if someone—"

She shouldn't be thinking at all. I should be capable of kissing every thought out of her head or I'm not doing it right. I glance around. There are Jutland cattle a few pastures over, but I'm not going to be thwarted by cows. I pull her close again and try to make her forget herself.

She does for a time. When she breaks off, she rests her brow against mine. Shaken. Finally.

"You're supposed to be teaching me manners," I say, tracing her jawline with the edge of my thumb.

I realized some things in London, filled with long days without the promise of seeing Ella at the end of them. In another minute, I'm going to cross a line and tell her what they are. But Ella hops off the quad and wades through knee-high grass. For a second, I think she's going to say something serious, but she only laughs. "Will you miss me when...when I'm gone?"

"What is it this week?" I ask, catching her from behind. "Are you going to move to Florida and launder money through real estate?"

She sinks against me, and the beat of her heart seems to sync with mine. "California has better weather. I'll wear muumuus and clacking jewelry, and drink the same cocktail everyday at precisely 4 PM."

My arms tighten and I look over the wide horizon. If she wants privacy, I can give it to her. If she wants a place away from the glare of the Summer Palace, Lindenholm is right here. If she wants to sunbathe in her birthday suit, I could plant a thick stand of trees and sue any intrusive paparazzi back into the stone age.

I open my mouth to say so, take a breath, and close it again. Ella doesn't want me—not forever—and the great wish of her life is to leave Sondmark. How can I fail to grant it when I love her?

I swallow thickly. I'm in love with Ella. The thought is new enough that it isn't painful yet, though that will come. It's been building this whole time, crashing like a wave I can't escape.

"You're going to be lonely." I soften my words with a kiss on the top of her head.

A gust of wind buffets against us, and I hold her tighter. "I have a pile of stuffed racoons to keep me company."

She hasn't said anything about missing me.

"Marc?"

"Yes?"

"Are you a vault?"

"Hmm?"

"You won't go tattling to Noah?"

How do I tell her that my loyalties have shifted so decisively that Noah hasn't entered my mind? He hardly ever does anymore. "I'm as secure as a Swiss bank."

"I'm looking into the prime minister," she admits. My breathing checks, but she continues. "I was leading a *SquadRun* campaign this morning." Oh, I know. I've been sneaking into her sessions. My avatar has been a lone wolf, grinding for experience. "We were shedding life points until this little runt on our team realized the final boss was so focused on protecting the treasury that he was leaving his flank open. We found his weakness."

I wish my worst enemies the singular experience of having the woman they love describe them as 'this little runt'.

"The prime minister is only after Freja because her husband is an immigrant," Ella continues. "If there's any hope of getting him to change his focus, I need to know what he would lay his life down to protect."

I turn Ella around. "You don't think his political opponents have tried to find his weakness?"

Her jaw hardens and her eyes narrow until I see the medieval queens she descended from. "I think they aren't me."

Why is it that the more murderous she looks, the more irresistible she is? "It's dangerous, getting involved in politics. Someone is going to find out who you are."

"No one knows who I am online," she says, like I haven't been tracking her progress as trashpandaprincess from *BRIx* to *Runaway Wagon* to *Eldritch Crown*. If someone else finds out and exposes her... *Vede.* I'm so worried about her that I don't even think about the monarchy.

"I'm careful," says the girl who has been sharing her Friction server, her voice, and her expertise without hesitation for the last month to someone she assumed was an anonymous internet stranger. "I'll lay so many red herrings over my tracks that they'll think they stumbled on a fish packing plant."

"I don't like it."

Her smile wobbles then firms. She goes on her toes and gives me a quick kiss. "I'm not asking permission."

25

Deliberate Kiss

ELLA

Nothing has changed. Yes, the old crush has returned, damn it all to hell, but it will go away. It always has before. I just need those old, homespun virtues Mama is always talking up—diligence, grit, better posture. As I practice these qualities, I've been distracted by days of dangerous headlines.

"May I Have the Honor? How Princess Freja Popped the Question"

"The Queen Caught Flat-Footed on Christmas Eve"

"Lies, Royal Lies, and CCTV Cameras"

"The Guest List: The Security Guard, The Photographer, The Secretary, and The Intern"

Even Alma's as-yet-hidden love life gets a look in.

"Vorburg's Crown Prince Spotted Crossing Border"

The palace is a hive of activity. Mama's staff crafts strategies that get discarded and statements that never go out, busily winnowing the words down to their most essential, potent elements.

I stay out of it like the agreeable princess my mother needs me to be, but it's time to get serious. The hour has arrived to make the prime minister pay for destroying my sister's peace.

I can be diligent when my mind is bent to something I'm passionate about. I wake early each day, hastily brush my teeth and shower, bowing to the knowledge that I'm one of those people whose mental focus correlates with how wild her hair is on any given day. Opening a brand-new laptop, I check the VPN connection, check it again, check it thrice, and take a deep breath. No more idle threats.

There's no such thing as being incognito when you hold the title to your own personal duchy, own a bright orange Mini, and appear in the press wearing jewelry sourced from your mother's underground vault. Online, however, I am a shadow.

"Okay, loser," I say, flexing my fingers. For hours I dive into the life of *Neer* Jakkon Torbald—the nineteenth prime minister of Sondmark—following his rise from a posh private school and into public life as a backbencher for the Blue-Greens, a political party best defined by its electoral flexibility rather than any deeply-held policy goals.

Along the way, he entered into a marriage to Gerda Raukema, the daughter of a political benefactor. The birth of two daughters, now aged eleven and nine, followed.

The family—blond, matched, and wrangled—gives off a cyborg quality in official portraits, although informal pictures paint a softer image. There's a snap of Torbald walking his girls off to their first day at school, scooping the younger one into his arms to dart across a busy street, while listening to the older one who looks like she never shuts up.

Relatable.

I wheel through a cascade of photos captured by the press pool photographer, where he is seen glad-handing constituents, hobnobbing with heads of state and oligarchs, and kissing babies. I read articles and follow footnotes, discovering *Neer* Torbald's station within a vast network of connections.

I expect to find a shady underworld and secret organizations. Instead, upon breaking down the polling on a granular level, I discover that his constituents love him for delivering on promises to bolster local manufacturing firms and streamline simple healthcare wait times using telehealth portals. I toss down a pen and plow fingers through my hair. *Vede.* If I didn't know how unctuous, insular, and petty he is, maybe he'd have my vote.

If I voted. Which I don't. One of Mama's policies.

My phone emits a low chime—the first three notes of "Love Crime." Marc. "May I bring my homework over?" he asks.

I glance at the dozen odd tabs open on my computer, and the long list of notes on my desktop.

"If you want," I answer, voice calm even as my toes dance along the rug. After hanging up, I twirl out of my computer chair and peel off my t-shirt. I dive into my closet, tearing it apart in my quest for something cute. My latest denim looks relaxed, but hugs my backside as lovingly as a sloth mom. Should I pair it with a sweatshirt? Something silky?

My thoughts collide, and I drop to the floor in an explosion of high-end loungewear, bathed in the glow of the light over my limited edition *Intelligence Force* poster.

Dust motes twirl in the air, sparkling lazily as they descend, each one like a memory of me and Marc. I was there when he tried to grow facial hair and looked like a weedy gangster. I remember how he drove across San Francisco during rush hour to pick up Sondish herring when I made the college honor roll. I choke on a laugh. There was the time he was dating an academic communist who used to raid my toiletries bag when she ran out of personal hygiene products. My response was to buy ten boxes of jumbos, stow them under his bathroom sink, and label it "The People's Collective".

I look down at the chaos of clothes, reading the signs as I would a scattering of tea leaves. I pick up a light sweater in forest green—three-quarter sleeves with a subtle pattern picked out in the same fine wool—shrug into it, and give myself a hard look in the mirror. The seers are troubled.

This is too much. Not the sweater. It's a perfect blend of comfortable and flattering. My business has never looked better. This. Marc and me.

"It's just fun," I mutter, wandering over to the bathroom sink and applying a quick swipe of eye liner. Maybe some mascara, too? I glance at the clock. I've got time.

I keep falling for Marc, but I always get back on my feet again. It's a whole cycle, and I can repeat it again to get us back to what we decided this was going to be at the outset. Fun. But I'm gently working a few dots of blush tint over my freckles, making slower and slower passes.

Is this fun? I glance down and the blush applicator clatters into the sink. This is a date. I'm dressing for a date.

Vede.

A light knock sounds on the door, and I take a hard, assessing look in the mirror. Marc has seen me in the full royal get-up without ever once dropping to his knees and promising half his kingdom. He'll survive a flattering sweater. I take a deep breath, willing myself to inhale rationality and sense with it. I've been falling in love with Marc for a dozen years and, in all that time, he's never fallen back.

Another knock. He has the code, but he's being polite.

If I meet him at the door, I'll look like I'm bounding up for my scratch behind the ear, so I punch the door mechanism, take a beat, and wander out when I've had time to collect myself.

"Hey," I manage.

He looks tired when he walks in, but he loosens his tie, scoops me into his arms, and brushes my lips with a kiss. It's easy and careless and makes me want to burst into ugly tears.

"I like this," he says, nipping the fabric at my waist.

"Are you hungry?" I ask, slipping out of his embrace.

He shakes his head. "I took my team out for a work dinner."

"To celebrate? Did the EC sign off on the acquisition?"

"The approval came in before markets closed." I take his jacket just for something to claim my attention. "Are you mad at me?"

I aim a look of amused incredulity at the floor. "Of course not. Why would I be mad at you? Did anyone see you on your way up?"

"No." He rolls his shirt sleeves past his forearms. "But anyone could check the visitor's log."

"No one will check. I'm not one of my mother's special ducklings. As long as I'm not causing trouble, she's not interested in my comings and goings."

He breathes a laugh and touches my face. "No?"

I swallow. "I've been tracking Torbald's whereabouts all day." Best have it out now.

Marc's hand falls. He leans on the arm of the sofa, gathering me close enough to stand between his outstretched legs. "I wondered if you were."

"You're not going to tell me to stop?" I look past his shoulder, but he tips his head into my line of sight.

"Would you stop if I asked you to?"

My eyelashes flicker. I wonder if there's anything I wouldn't do for Marc. I work my fingers under his heavy palms and his hands slip from my waist, trying to keep some kind of distance. "What are you working on tonight? Seong, Han Heyden, or Lindenholm?"

He digs into his bag, powers up a tablet, and settles into the sofa. "Come here," he says, stretching one arm out. "I want your opinion." I slide into the crook of his shoulder, slotting in as smoothly as a new graphics card into a motherboard. He scoots me closer and presses an absent-minded kiss on my temple. I weave my arms over my stomach to keep myself from holding him.

"It's Alix," he says. "She approached me about turning part of Lindenholm into a boutique hotel. Five suites in all."

I turn my face up to him to find our lips a breath away. I want to kiss him as lightly and easily as he kisses me, but he laid out a deal with guardrails and guidelines to protect himself from the danger of taking this further. To protect himself from me. So, I train my eyes on the screen, frozen on a slide deck. "Do you need the money?"

He turns my face up and takes the kiss I held back, slowly, thoroughly, until the voice of warning in my head drops to a barely audible whisper and my skin whispers like a field of grass bending in the wind.

He lifts his head and clears his throat. "*Amma* left the estate in good shape if we carry on exactly as we have been. I want Lindenholm to be self-supporting, and the numbers don't leave room for risks."

"So you tell her no."

"Look at this proposal," he says, scrolling up and down a slide deck full of footnotes and pie charts.

"Is this Tom's work?" I ask.

"She says he only provided her a list of things any good investor would want to know. She collected the materials herself."

Alix's intellectual life reminds me of Clara's sorority sisters—girls who did their projects with hot pink glitter pens, but still had their flowcharts locked down. I take the tablet and skim through the proposal. "Cons?"

He wraps a finger around one of my curls, rubbing it against his lower lip in thought, and flips to slide seven. Alix hasn't been sparing about the costs of her scheme. Her vision doesn't include a few AKAE bunkbeds thrown together on a weekend.

"It complicates the estate," he murmurs. "We'd have to add an actual carpark instead of the temporary one we're putting together for the concert. Then there's the installation of a professional kitchen... Here's the footnote detailing local regulations. They're not insignificant."

"Lawyers can help you manage that."

"She included the name of a local legal firm." His hand drops over a hip and he wedges me closer. "But we'd have strangers coming and going. Weddings every weekend all summer..."

"In a sliver of the estate." I brush my finger across the tablet, taking in the bigger picture. "She's capable of doing this, if that's what you're asking. It's smart that she wants to work out the kinks by starting in the walled garden," I say, "adding a suite or two as she goes." I nudge him. "It's only the east wing. There's nothing really important over there."

"There are the woods," he says.

My cheeks flame and he catches my chin, planting another slow, deliberate kiss on my lips. I look down again. Marc is in a mood tonight, and I fear California won't be far away enough to ravel up the tangled threads between us and snip each one.

I clear my throat. "Pros?" I ask.

"*Amma* wants to relocate to Seong full time. There's an old friend who wants her to stay. He—"

"He?" I grin.

"He's helping her navigate government agencies, getting aid into the right hands." Marc is happy for his mother, I can hear that, but he's uncertain, too.

"Tom is based in New York," I say. Where does that leave Marc? Alone. Chained to his ancestors in Sondmark.

"Alix says he's willing to relocate." Marc chews on his lip.

"Handsel could use an investment banker of Tom's caliber."

He nods. "Alix would be close. Her children would be close. I wouldn't be running this place by myself."

A hard knot forms in my throat, thinking of baptisms. Of flying into Handsel to stand at a font next to Marc as godparents, a tiny baby between us. Of Marc having his own babies after I've gone to California to enjoy endless MangaCon and the weightlessness of immense wealth.

I tuck a hand against his chest and think long thoughts about the path that led me here and the one that promises to lead me away again. I trace a button, flicking the edge of it with my thumb, and feel the steady beat of his heart. "Why don't you say yes?"

The button slips through the hole—an accident—and he does it back up. His laugh shakes through me and he taps the back of my hand, trapping it with his own. "No scope creep."

"What about Alix?" I remind him. He needs people, even if he doesn't need me.

He releases a breath. "I'll think about it."

26

SEPARATE ACCOMMODATIONS

MARC

Noah leans against Minty's mahogany bar, fresh from an urban revitalization summit in his suit and tie. A pair of crystal tumblers rests in front of us, each with a single sphere of hand-carved ice clinking against the glass.

My friend releases a breath. "This succession fight..." he says, when we've exhausted the topics of sports and weather. "I know how busy you are. Thanks for keeping your eye on things." He tips his glass and takes a swallow.

Though my parliamentary duties are supposed to be strictly ceremonial, I have been seen stalking down legislators in the halls of the Grousehof, my robes billowing around me like the wings of a black dragon. It's not difficult to perform any office that might take that tense, anxious look off Ella's face.

"How are things at the palace?" I ask like I don't know.

Noah makes a juvenile noise. "Alma is worse than useless. She goes jaunting off to Djolny every other weekend to crash on Jacob's mother's sofa."

I smile into my whiskey.

"What?" he clips.

"The idea of Alma, of all people, going all that distance to make out on a couch. It's funny." I shake my head.

Noah glances around the shadow-blurred interior of the private club. "It's not funny."

I nod, mock-serious and he punches me in the arm.

"I don't think she even cares that he's the crown prince."

"People *do* fall in love," I counter. It's no longer an abstraction for me, but Noah has an answer for that, too.

"Alma isn't people. I'm not people. None of our family is. Love is not a reason to lose your head, and you know the rule. First comes the crown, then comes the consort."

"That's some highly refined Wolffe garbage," I say, stretching my back. "You're going to pick a wife by how well she knows her place?"

His brows gather. "Don't be a *vailys*."

"Who's the lucky girl who gets to walk two paces behind you for the rest of her life? One of those models?"

"What is your problem?" he asks, but there isn't much heat in the question. "You know there will be compensations for accepting the role of a future queen. Connections. Jewels. A title. Respect."

I cough through a laugh. "Chilly bedfellows on a frigid Sondish night."

"What's that supposed to mean?"

I am in a mood to kick down some doors. "I mean that it's stupid how hard your family runs away from happiness. Love matters, even if you're a future king."

Noah and I were both born into the privileges of wealth and the pressures of rank, but I don't understand a man who could be happy and won't.

I stare into my glass. "Did she not care for your compensations?" I ask.

He knows exactly who I mean. I can see it in the stone-carved set of his shoulders. I don't even have to say Caroline's name, but still, she's there.

He'd like to think he's too good for love, but even the heir to the House of Wolffe can't practice emotional austerity all the time.

A hum of light conversation lays over a lazy piano melody, and the atmosphere of the bar is warm, inviting patrons to sit and talk. But between me and my oldest friend, the air seems to shimmer with heat.

His voice is almost too low to hear. "You're crossing a line."

I reach for the tumbler and take a swallow. Noah draws a sharp breath. A reset. We're dissecting his love life, but what would he say if I told him that I need to figure out a way to keep Ella from leaving the country?

My responsibilities spread across several businesses, trade organizations, and the estate, and I used to think it would be impossible to balance and bear them all. With Ella, everything seems easier.

"My sister mentioned Alix's proposal for Lindenholm," Noah says. This isn't my biggest problem, but it's simpler to let him think it is.

"Ella wants me to take Alix up on her offer." I lean back in the bar chair, swirling the amber liquid against the ice, and let myself feel the drag of temptation. "Lindenholm is too big for a dozen families, never mind one bachelor."

"But?"

"But my mother sacrificed decades to the running of it, and what is it going to look like when I put it on my sister's shoulders now that it's finally my turn?" I shake my head. "It's selfish."

"Alix wouldn't be taking on all of it, and she is a grown woman—"

"Hey, now."

Noah laughs, raising innocent hands. I couldn't do the same. "Duty doesn't have to be a bitter pill."

I release a cynical grunt and wish I could take him back to that moment on the beach we're still not talking about. The moment when I saw everything he wanted and wouldn't let himself have.

"Say yes to your sister and, if you really want to solve all your problems, go get that girl from BLUSH while you're at it," he says, always the matchmaker.

"BLUSH? What are we talking about?" Ella fetches up to us, and I scramble to my feet like a child caught with his hand in the Kyriekager tin.

She's wearing a perfectly ordinary outfit—a pair of gray slacks, conservative hoop earrings, and a creamy blouse with inspired draping. Her gaze darts to a booth—*the* booth—and a warm flush works up her neck.

Noah settles deeper into his bar chair. "None of your business."

I cuff Noah with the flat of my hand. "Show some manners to the lady."

He rubs the spot with a grin. "That's no lady. That's my sister."

I turn my bar chair out, and Ella slides in with a brief smile, her scent trailing after her. Her curls drag along my skin and, when she leans back, she traps my fingertips where I grip the chair.

I twist myself free, discreetly tugging a curl. Now *she's* going to get us caught.

"What brings you down to Minty's, little sister?" Noah asks, nodding at her soft-sided laptop case.

Color washes the freckles high on the ridge of her cheeks and she scuffs the toe of her shoe on the brass footrest. We're about to be lied to. "Change of atmosphere. I had some work to do."

"Is your suite too cramped?"

The toe traces a pattern on the metal as she cooks up another lie. "I was hoping to run into Marc. He promised to teach me how to play Fate."

I almost laugh. Over the years, I've spent hours trying to teach Ella the game, played with a deck of illustrated cards depicting, among other things, the rising moon and flying cranes. They say there are as many ways to play as there are citizens of Seong, and while she has a knack for the forehead flicking—willing to do it even when she hasn't earned the right, holding a man down, even—she's never developed a sense of when to bid and when to hold.

"Don't you know how to play by now?" Noah asks.

"Listen," she clips. "There is a world of difference between a game invented by corporate focus groups and one that evolved in the hills of Seong for a thousand years."

Noah knocks back the rest of his drink. "As fun as this is, I've got to get going," he says. "I have to walk the dog and Mama wants to finalize the itinerary for Clara's tour."

"San Sabao, Tzeke, Kleingeshaft," Ella recites, leaning up for a kiss. "I wondered if Mama was going to cancel Clara's Tour of Middling Matrimonial Prospects now that she's met Max."

"It's a chance for her to get some practice. Coming?" he asks me. "Or are you really going to play my sister's games?"

With a shrug, I lift my drink.

"What kind of answer was that?" Ella laughs when he goes.

"Was I supposed to tell him that I can't wait to play your games?"

"Even when I'm dressed like a grandmother?"

Even in ripped jeans and a hoodie. Even in flannel pajamas. "Stop acting like you don't know I'm wrecked by your work clothes. Is your mother happy about this change?"

She looks down, frowning at her trousers, and twists in the narrow chair, her pointed heels peeping from the wide-legged hems. "She's too tense about Freja to be happy about me."

I lean against the bar. If Noah doubles back he'll see me standing too close and this game will be over. I reach past Ella for a pistachio, feel the leap in my blood as the distance between us narrows, peel the shell away, and tuck it between her lips.

"You don't look like a grandmother," I tell her.

She chews quickly and swallows. I watch her lips purse and want to kiss her. Nothing new. "A Lauza Erdo blouse is not exactly earth shattering."

Lauza Erdo deserves an Order of the Dragonslayer.

"Maybe it's the glasses," I say.

She half-removes them, looking at me over the tortoiseshell rims, and the wooshing sound in my ears must be all the air being sucked out of the North Sea Confederation.

I brace my hands on the arms of her chair until we're practically lip to lip. "What are you doing? Put them back on. Or take them off. You look like—"

She laughs. "Someone with mild astigmatism?"

A light cough sounds, and we look into the urbane, faintly disapproving look of the head waiter. His expression reads, "I had hoped it would not come to this."

"Will you be needing anything, ma'am, sir?" His tone is dry. "A room, perhaps?"

Ella's nose wrinkles at the 'ma'am'. "I could use a private booth to work, Arne." She glances at our booth.

"Work?" he echos, a little squint in his eyes. "Of course."

He makes a discreet series of movements with his head, summoning staff forward to clear the place settings and situate her workspace. A notepad is placed at one side with a sleek fountain pen. A bottle of Vestfyn is decanted next to a tall-necked glass. A pillow is brought forth to support her back.

She flips it down and sits on it instead, adjusts her ergonomics, and looks up with a smile, "Thank you."

I move forward and the head waiter shoots me a quelling glance. "For you, sir? Will you be needing separate accommodations of your own in another part of the club, perhaps?"

"It was a one-time thing, Arne," I insist. "I can be relied upon."

His head tilts up, as though deep in his memories. "I wish I had the innocent, trusting nature of a younger man," he observes.

"I could do with a coffee," I say, sliding in next to Ella as she opens her laptop.

"What are you doing?" she whispers. "You're going to get us in trouble again, and I really am working."

I slide my arm over the back of the booth and let gravity do the rest. My hand lands lightly on her hip. "In Minty's? What are you up to?"

"You won't like it," she warns, adjusting herself to my embrace.

"This is pretty basic tech," I say, tipping the computer up, examining the brand and specs. "Is this...a burner laptop?"

She nods and I continue my examination. "You're being awfully careful and you're nowhere near the palace."

Again, she nods.

"Ella." My tone is level but she lifts her chin.

"Here's the thing..."

27

SOMETHING ROTTEN

ELLA

Marc's voice drops. "Why are you using an anonymous, untraceable computer on the grounds of a private club with a long track record of keeping its secrets? What mischief are you up to?"

I swallow thickly. Mischief. That's the way to sell this. A prank. Bringing about the downfall of a popular elected official is barely a step up from circling the toilet ring with snapping fireworks, setting the seat gently in place, and waiting for a furious sister to burst from the loo.

"Listen," I begin.

"Oh no." Marc looks up to the dull metal ceiling where our reflections live in blurry contentment. "It's more than a few Pixy comments, isn't it? It's more than just 'looking into' the prime minister."

I clear my throat. "A little more."

He closes his eyes, and I wonder if this is one of the early warning signs of a heart attack. "Have you hacked into the national security database?" he asks. "Are we talking about something that big?"

Is it wrong to feel flattered that he thinks I'm capable of it? "I don't need to hack anything. You would not believe how much dirt you can dig up simply by tracking how busy nearby takeout places are during a national security crisis."

"Explain."

"If there are lines at the döner kebab place, they've got a problem with the Navy. The top Army brass prefer an American pizza chain." His hand tightens. "The point is that culling through publicly accessible information is not a crime."

"I tremble when you use that tone," he says, dragging the laptop closer. "If you're not doing anything wrong, explain the remote location and VPN."

"I wanted a measure of discretion."

"Discretion," he mutters. "Show me what you're working on."

I don't know how to keep secrets from Marc. My brow wrinkles. That's not entirely true. He doesn't know how much I would give to memorialize this booth for posterity, to put up a historical plaque that *Neerheid* van Heyden and HRH Princess Ella made history on this spot. Continents shifted. Lives were changed.

He navigates with the touchpad, emitting a series of grunts.

Finally, his knuckle brushes the underside of my chin, urging me to face him. "I thought you were trying to untangle yourself from your family. To run away and never look back."

Arne probably has his eyes locked on us now, prepared to spray us down with a fire extinguisher in the event of another public incident.

"Neutralizing their greatest threat is my parting gift," I murmur.

"*Vede*." The word seems to hiss through his skin, and I drag my gaze away.

"I'm tracking his position," I say. "The prime minister's office has a daily rota of activities and lists of meetings anyone is privy to, but there are consistent gaps." I pull up a spreadsheet, divided up in quarter-hour segments. "Once a week, he drops off the grid."

"It doesn't have to be anything nefarious," Marc argues. "Maybe it's pickleball. Maybe it's church."

My eyeballs almost roll onto the table. "Can you see him bending to the will of the Almighty without alerting PAPZ?"

A smile flits across Marc's mouth.

"Look at this," I press, lifting my phone. "During one of these dark spots in his itinerary, he posted a 10 second video of himself, promising a review of the Provisional Residency Card system."

Until his marriage to Freja, Oskar was a Provisional Resident. For Ella, the subject is personal.

"You might not like him, but he has to visit his constituency and address their concerns." Marc pushes back, but I don't mind. He listens, his questions always sharpening my thoughts, forcing me to articulate my reasoning.

I shake my head and Marc brushes a curl back, tucking it in among the others. "He's not in his constituency."

Marc taps the screen and watches the snippet, running through it several times. "You have no way of knowing that. This is a ten second video of his face and a bit of pavement."

"Watch and learn," I say. "He claims to be in the Nordoest district, but he walks by a sidewalk cafe."

"We see a few tables and chairs, *elskede*," he counters with a laugh.

"Don't call me that." The words snap from my lips like an icicle in a high wind—unexpected, shattering. *Elskede. Beloved.* My reaction to the most common endearment in Sondmark freezes the air between us. If he doesn't mean it, I don't want to hear it.

I hitch a breath. "There's also a flash of a little sandwich board."

He takes a beat then follows my lead, zooming in on the image. "It could be anywhere."

I've already done much of the legwork for this. Still, it looks like magic when I lean into the keyboard, navigate a series of images, and cross check them against online reviews. "The crack in the sidewalk matches up," I say, toggling back and forth from a still.

A review from JohnnyMarrsThirdFret declares that *Le Pain Kat* has, "The best washrooms in Frederickplatz." Further digging reveals an American tourist and a travel influencer who tagged the cafe for that day. One of them posted a photo of the sandwich board with the same font. Special of the day: Pankedruss pancakes.

"We got him," I say, flashing a look of triumph.

Marc leans back, his hand sliding to my waist. "Impressive. What does this prove?"

I tap the screen. "He went to all that effort to make it look like he was in Nordoest. There has to be a reason why."

"You think he's going to tell Princess Ella?"

"I don't care for this tone," I reply, wiggling out of his grasp.

His face sobers even as he redoubles his hold. "I'm worried about you." I feel the lowness of the ceiling, the wandering plink of a piano, and a storm outside the windows close in on us. Time slows, glimmering as softly as the lighted votives dotting the room. A kiss. This time, I'll let myself mean it—

"The weather is inclement," Arne murmurs, setting a tower of desserts on the table with a flourish. "The lounge has become full of people who know your mother, ma'am." His smile is all lemons. "A happy thought, is it not?"

Arne is hardly a fussy man but he arranges the tower with unusual care. "I would not wish Your Royal Highness to be made the subject of gossip."

When he leaves, words slip through set teeth. "You have got to keep your hands to yourself."

I can't blame Marc. I have lost my sense, too. It's increasingly difficult to keep things light. If I forgot myself in his arms, he would feel the change—and then he'd feel responsible. For a man on my mother's spreadsheets, bound to Noah by chains of ancient duty and deep friendship, that could only take one form. Marriage. He'd be trapped. Both of us would be.

Not that Marc would ever admit to feeling trapped. He might even see an alliance as convenient, formalizing his ties to my family with a bride he knows isn't interested in his money. I know he'd work to make me happy. Is that enough?

Not even a second passes before I dismiss the dangerous idea. I could never tolerate a marriage with that much math, balancing a long list of pros and cons like a game show where contestants attempt to slice a soft pretzel into two identical pieces and weigh them up at the end. My parents are evidence enough that a marriage of convenience is convenient to no one.

Marc lifts his palms, but there's a playful curve on his lips. He likes kissing me, but his exits are plentiful and clearly marked. One of these days, he's going to take one.

"What are you going to do with the prime minister's information, *elskede*?"

I press my lips. Challenging that word again will only lead to questions. "Now that I know he's hiding something, my investigation is about to get serious."

He looks at me for a long while, takes a breath, and brushes a kiss on my cheek which Arne couldn't possibly disapprove of.

When I return to the palace, I have just enough time to throw myself into a cocktail gown—glittery sequins in a rosy mauve—and present myself in the salon for Mama's inspection.

Clara intercepts me. "You look just right," she decides after a long look, nodding over to our mother.

It's not exactly a compliment to my beauty. Clara's boyfriend, along with the entire crew of his naval vessel, is receiving a special commendation for the heroic rescue of foreign nationals (and two goats) on the high seas. Her nerves are probably in shreds and she wants to make sure I don't cause a scene.

"It's a big day for Max's big boat," I say.

Her eyes narrow. "Ship, Ella. You won't—"

I giggle. "I'll be as good as a saint."

"I need you to be much better than that."

The fanfare sounds, and we enter the long reception room to the applause of government officials, leading citizens, and scores of military personnel in their dress blues. The lone press photographer snaps continuously when Mama receives Max's correct bow—the first recorded meeting between the naval officer and the mother of the nation. Max carries it off without a hitch.

Alma approaches with a glass of champagne carefully half-full. "I miss having your app to help me memorize all the names," she says.

"It's down for repairs."

"So many uniforms tonight," she murmurs, glancing around the room. "You could use this time to go shopping for a future husband Mama won't entirely disapprove of."

It never even occurs to her that I'm seeing someone. That I'm at the bottom of a hole I dug myself and am digging deeper every day. That everything hurts. I take a tiny sip of government booze and force myself to laugh. "Brody—my soulmate—is mining cryptocurrency for our California acreage as we speak." Brody will do as a nice, fat red herring, but talk of soulmates makes me want to detonate the golden palace gates.

She tips her glass into mine, setting off a tiny chime. "Here's to true love. Oh!" The word squeaks out of her. "There's Marc. I'm surprised this is important enough to take him away from business."

Same. "Fancy meeting you, here," I say when I finally make my way to him.

Though crisp military uniforms abound, Marc holds his own with a sharp suit and a silk tie. "That dress," he starts. When he looks at me this way, even the press won't be able to ignore it.

"Scope creep," I murmur. With effort, he hauls himself into line. "This isn't your usual scene," I observe. The event is not big enough for someone who doesn't have to absolutely, positively be here. "What brings you?"

"I hated the thought of you and all these officers."

I smile into my champagne flute. "As much as I would love to believe that... Are you spying on me?"

His expression is one of outraged innocence. "I'm not lurking behind a potted palm."

"Marc," I repeat.

He exhales and puts a hand to my elbow. "Things are getting too serious. As one of your oldest friends, I'm begging—"

Oldest friends. After all this time and all those kisses, he makes no other claim on me. I swallow past a knot of pain. "The prime minister is threatening my family and I'm supposed to smile and pretend that he isn't? What did you think I meant when I said I was taking him down?" I glance around the room with a fixed smile. "Poems? Petitions?"

"Freja can take care of herself."

My laugh draws attention and Marc leads me down the long gallery, away from the dense crowd. We pause under a life-sized portrait of Malthe III, dressed in black and wearing his murder ring. He was the one who began writing *The Red Book*, a how-to guide for kingship, recording all the bloody deeds of the earliest rulers of Sondmark down to the present day so that the House of Wolffe would know how to win a crown and keep it. We didn't get here by playing nice.

"Freja couldn't push her way through a moist towelette, but I know how to throw a punch. You want me to accept whatever Torbald dishes out without fighting back? Thank you," I curtsy, "no."

"Ella, you can't go this alone."

"Hypocrite," I whisper, rounding on him. "Look at you. Exhausted, carrying every burden you think you have to carry, and then some. *You* won't take any help, so don't tell me I'm not allowed to look out for my sister. And don't go thinking of me as one more problem you have to take on either. I didn't ask for it."

He calls after me, but I'm on the clock, perilously near tears, and I promised Clara I wouldn't cause a scene. I melt into the crowd, nodding tightly to the guests, when another voice intercepts me.

"Something rotten in the House of Wolffe?" Prime Minister Torbald. His words are low, meant only for me.

I turn, composing my face. "*Neer* Torbald. What a pleasure it is to have you at the palace."

He waves this away. "Let me offer a friendly warning," he says.

I will die happy if I never hear the word friend again.

"We keep a dossier on you at the Grousehof—on all of you. At first, we didn't have much luck. Your mother keeps a tight grip on her family. But random pieces of information began to dig their way to the surface, and now your dossier is worryingly thick."

He glances around at the gilded hall with its majestic artwork and heavy curtains, like a new tenant measuring for drapes.

"I have something you could add to it," I bite out. "There are these odd gaps in my official schedule. I'm in Frederickplatz when I say I'm in Nordoest. Why would I lie about what I'm up to or who I might be meeting?"

His pasty face drains of color, and he scoops a mop of hair from his forehead, checking for bystanders.

"I don't know who you think you are, little girl."

I am the terror of the North Sea. "I know you don't want me as an enemy."

It's a good parting shot. In that brief moment, I feel like the leather-clad heroine of *Intelligence Force*. Cool. Dangerous. Always in command. But Torbald stares at the alcohol swirling in his glass. "You majored in computer science at that American university. Good at tech. Addicted to gaming."

This is nothing.

"It would be strange," he continues, "if you had no digital footprint. I wonder if you've been meddling where you shouldn't."

A thin trickle of ice runs through my veins, but I retrace my steps over the last months. He's bluffing.

He smiles. "Have you always been as careful as you are now?"

"I wish you luck trying to find out."

"I won't need luck or skill," he says, "Not when I have an entire intelligence service at my beck and call."

My heart is clanging, but I paste on a smile. "The opposition party would be fascinated to hear your thoughts on the limits of ministerial power."

"Opposition?" Torbald chuckles. "The only candidate who even bothers opposing me is a crank who's been running on the same anti-monarchist platform for thirty years. I've got the safest seat in Sondmark. Your mother, though. Heaven willing, by the end of my administration, she'll be plain *Vrouw* Cavallero," he murmurs, soiling my father's family name in his foul mouth, "and paying five *markke* to visit the royal jewels with the rest of the tourists."

Torbald slips his glass on the tray of a passing waiter. "I hope I can count on your vote, ma'am. Have an exceptional evening."

ALLOW IT

MARC

Ella.

My thumb slides across the screen. Send.

I spent half the night online, traveling from *SquadRun* to *Runaway Wagon*, finally finding her in *BRIx*, building a pixelated castle, one cube at a time. She doesn't engage my character, but pauses long enough in her work to see that I've fought off an army of zombies. She sends a short message of thanks to my anon account but returns to her work.

I'm newly impressed with how my queen managed to bring her second daughter into adulthood without ruin or catastrophe. I run down to Lindenholm at the weekend, still wondering where I stand.

Alix has returned from the U.S. for the wedding, and she drags me out to her reception venue in the soft morning sunlight, wearing a summer dress and an oversized cardigan slouching around her elbows. The ground, on the edge of a test orchard, is torn up in several places to allow the placement of complex utilities for a massive wedding party and a future BLUSH concert. I have a meeting with a local planning commission after lunch to convince the burghers of Aunslev to accept a generous donation to make up for inconvenient spikes in electricity use, but my thoughts are not on utilities or crop yields or Q2 earnings.

I kneel, brushing a dew-soaked dandelion glowing in the sunlight. The transformation of this flower, somehow both sturdy and delicate, is a wonder. The bright yellow face of it is turned up, soaking in the sun, but soon the flower will furl, delicate petals twisting up tighter than two hands clasped in prayer. It will hold there, waiting until the stem bursts into seed to become something else entirely. Then is it time for wishes.

"Have you made a decision about the hotel?" she asks, hand gripping a branch, swinging lightly.

"Not yet." Alix goes very still, and I try to explain. "It's a big step."

I take no joy in disappointing her. Alix is a child of Lindenholm as much as I am, but because I'm the firstborn son, my vote is the only one that matters.

"We don't have a farm shop," she says, shading her eyes. Her disappointment is tucked away.

"Now you want a farm shop?" I smile.

Alix turns away from the muddy field and retreats into the orchard. "If you're not ready to trust me with a hotel…"

"It's not about trust," I insist.

"I have a backup plan that won't cost you a *fennig*."

I don't deserve this much graciousness. I tip my head, listening.

"We could host market stalls, the kind that sell healing crystals and beeswax candles, and start out self-sustaining. In a year or two, we could afford an actual shed." She passes me her tablet showing an image of a stone and beam structure

"That's a lot of crystals."

"I know the public. They're starving for aesthetic jars with tiny useless spoons tied on." She smiles, but her expression grows serious. "The Crown Estates is breathing down our necks, and this would be a good place to sell the Lindenholm label directly to the customer."

There are a thousand decisions to be made, and I feel the weight of every one of them.

"I'll think about it," I say, not wanting to dim her smile. It dims anyway. A feather-light cloud passes over the sun.

"I can do this, you know."

"Of course you can." I answer too quickly.

"*Amma* was a model," she says, "same as me. She dabbled in performance art and eloped with a drug addict she met in a club. She didn't emerge from the ether as a force to be reckoned with."

She scoops up a thin, flexible twig and swipes the heads off several sodden dandelions, scattering her wishes with brute force rather than a soft breath. "You were a uni student when you financed your first startup. I remember telling you what to wear to the meeting."

"You always know what to wear."

She aims another swipe at the weeds. "I know more than that. I may not have every step mapped out before I start a project, but I know the vibe."

I will not laugh. "I can't run my life on vibes."

"You should. Haven't you ever wanted something you couldn't explain with a task management tool? Something you felt in your gut before you ever worked it out in your head?"

She means business, but my mind slips to Ella. My brain was the last one to get the memo, and when it did, it set about putting a ring of sturdy seawalls around all the things I felt in my gut, keeping that unreliable organ out. *It's a temporary thing. Just physical. We're just friends. Forever that.* The walls are ruined now. A pressure forms in my chest, but I shake my head, bringing myself back to Alix and her aesthetic spoons.

"I know what I want—know it's reasonable and right to want it," she says, "and I trust myself to do the creative problem solving and collaboration it will take to get me there."

I can't believe this is what she really wants. "The estate isn't your responsibility. I want you to be free to live your life wherever it takes you." I look around. "Not in a muddy orchard, thinking up ways to bribe the local authorities."

She shrugs the cardigan over her shoulders and stuffs her hands into the pockets. "You think you have to do it all yourself."

"It comes with the title."

Alix shakes her hair, turned to silk in the morning sun, out of her face. "Grandfather used to tell *Amma* he was the head of the family. When dad was on a bender, shaming the ghosts of Lindenholm, Grandfather would remind her that she was under his wing."

"As you are under mine." I hunch against a tree and look down at the mud. My mud.

She crouches low enough to look up at me. "As you are under mine." The reminder comes with a smile. "Grandfather tried to get her to see that the van Heydens were a family linked together. That even if a link failed, the fabric would hold. Her Seongan heart understood it." Alix touches my arm. "You're not alone, Marc. You don't have to shut yourself up at Lindenholm with all your responsibilities while everyone else gets to live the lives they want. Let me help you."

We turn back to the house, and a soft wind ruffles the leaves behind us. Alix has unconsciously added her voice to Ella's, rooting me out of the notion that my role is to forever dispense aid and favor in my modest kingdom.

Driving into work the next morning, I give my sister the go ahead to plan a few farmer's markets. It's the smallest concession but, over the car speakers, I hear her delight.

At a train crossing, I scroll through my text messages with a frown.

Ella.

My text is unread and it can't be a matter of losing a charging cord or simply being caught up in the activity of the day. I check the House of Wolffe royal diary of official engagements. She's not busy. In desperation, I text Noah.

Game tonight?

His text comes bouncing back.

Pass. Ella is slated to testify tomorrow. We're prepping her.

I am uneasy all day, plowing through my workload, anxious for no reason I can put my finger on. I use that energy to burn through agenda items and wrap up a long, productive meeting. I turn from the executives to see Werner, hovering close by.

"Sir," he starts, clearing his throat.

"I thought you would be happy with me for once," I say, "spending so much time with the VPs."

He tips his tablet forward. "This isn't strictly Han Heyden business, but—"

I take the tablet, and read the chyron scrolling along the bottom of the screen. "Breaking: Princess Freja Renounces Succession Role, Royal Family Shattered".

I emit a low, explosive curse and pull up a video—a short interview of Freja and Oskar, sitting down with Sondmark's most trusted news reader, *Neer* Hjefdal.

Freja, wearing a sober blue dress, is blinking too much, but Oskar reaches over and takes her hand. She flashes him a smile and turns her gaze on the interviewer who asks, "Why have you chosen to halt the parliamentary process, ma'am?"

Her voice is steady. "Because no investigation will clear me of disregarding protocols established in the wake of the Marriages and Succession Act. I married, seeking neither the permission of my mother nor her government and, while such rules may seem outdated and strange to anyone outside the royal succession, my wedding was against the law and carries clear penalties." Her expression is serene as she paints herself into the tightest corner. "Though I believe I chose the correct course of action, I also agree wholeheartedly with the prime minister. The law makes no allowances for the intensity of my feelings."

Dominanstid, Freja.

Neer Hjefdal leans back, his reassuring presence like that of a favorite uncle. "Are you asking that the Marriages and Succession Act be abolished? Is this not the logical conclusion of your refusal to bend to parliament? Do you suggest, ma'am, that having entered the modern age, the need to control governmental policy through strategic alliances has evaporated?"

Oskar is silent, but he clasps Freja's hand. It's strange. I've known her since she was born and she didn't like to be touched, even in her pram.

"I make no such claims," Freja says. "I have no wish to influence the Sondish legislative body. I have always felt that certain marks of antiquity allow us to understand our past."

Deep grooves bracket *Neer* Hjefdal's mouth and he looks like he has a stomach complaint. "Do you propose, as some have suggested, annulling your marriage and going through the approval process? Starting at the beginning, as it were?"

When she turns her gaze to her husband, Freja glows. Unease ripples over my skin. A thermonuclear warhead glows in the moment it wipes the map clean.

"I wish the prime minister well in every good thing he hopes for Sondmark, but I cannot bend to this request. It's much too late for that," she says, her smile tucking her cheek. "I have been in communication with the palace and have notified my family that I am surrendering my HRH title effective immediately, and will no longer be a working member of the royal family. When I am spoken of in the press, I wish to be known simply as *Vrouw* Velasquez."

Boom.

"This will come as a surprise to the country, ma'am," the newsreader allows.

"You think?" I roar. "You think?"

Neer Hjefdal turns to Oskar. "How can you allow such a sacrifice on your behalf? Would it not be better to allow the approval process to proceed? Your acceptance by parliament would signal a new Sondish approach to the royal family, one welcoming of diversity."

Oskar lifts his brow. "My father-in-law is Pavian. Is he not welcome?"

Freja nods—her smile is more certain than reality.

Still *Neer* Hjefdal presses. "*Neer* Velasquez, how can you allow it?"

Oskar doesn't smile readily, but his features shift with subtle amusement as he glances at Freja. "Perhaps you do not know how formidable a princess of Sondmark can be." A small silence follows and Oskar leans forward. "I will be guided by my wife. She has chosen to make this sacrifice, and my task, for as long as I draw breath, is to make her feel it's been worth it."

Oskar looks at Freja and she looks at him, gives him a quick nod, and turns to *Neer* Hjefdal. "I would like to add another piece of news, if I may." Freja clears her throat and I brace myself for more bombs. "We hope that each citizen of Sondmark will add their prayers to ours for the safe arrival of our little one. We're expecting our first child."

Dominanstid. I whisper the oath.

The interview fades to black and the emergency broadcast returns to a newsdesk. "Surprising news from the newly-minted *Vrouw* Velasquez..."

I shove the tablet into Werner's hands and bolt from the room, taking the stairs three at a time. I call over and over again as I go.

"Pick up, pick up, pick up," I say, pressing on the accelerator, and race out of my executive parking stall. I bypass the ornate main gates of the palace, already thick with news teams staking out the best shots, and choose another entrance.

"How are things?" I ask Thor, briefly lowering my window.

"Princesses causing all hell to break loose." He lifts the gate with a grin. "It's just another day at the Summer Palace."

29

GRAND PASSION

FOUR HOURS EARLIER

ELLA

I spend the morning in the Chevres Salon, where Alma runs me through several interrogation scenarios, both friendly and hostile. Freja enters just after Alma has posed the question, "Do you expect us to believe that your twin sister kept this relationship secret from you?" She tugs Clara after her.

"Where did you come from?" I ask, eyes darting to their linked hands. Voluntary touching isn't Freja's thing, and it always means big feelings when she does.

"Oskar and I had a meeting with the Management," she says. Noah, Mama, and, to a lesser extent, Père are at the apex of the Wolffe family hierarchy, and all major decisions are shunted through their command structure.

My most reliable tool for discovering Freja's emotional state, buried under layers of her natural reserve, is her clothing. You can't hide clothes. She's wearing one of Mama's old frocks and I cock my head. "Where have I seen that dress before?" I ask.

She kisses my cheek and grips my hand, leading me to a long sofa—more sturdy than a true antique. When she sinks in, I am pulled after her on one side, Clara on the other. With a tiny jerk of her chin, she indicates Alma's place at the end. "Mama wore it during the nuclear warhead crisis when she was expecting us," she answers. "Remember the footage from the press conference?"

How could I not? In every documentary about the Crown, there are clips of our mother standing at the gates of the palace in the burnt orange light of sunset, addressing the people directly and challenging the international community to keep their eyes on Sondmark—all as the great powers conducted a tense standoff in her waters and threatened her sovereignty. Everyone knew she was pregnant, but no one has ever looked less vulnerable. That was the night the North Sea Confederation was born.

I expected this dress to be on display at The National Museum someday, not on my sister's back.

"You look good," I say. My eyes drift down. "It's actually giving you business up top. Wait. Did you get a boob job?"

Freja stifles a laugh. "I did not."

"Well, you're doing a lot of touching," I say, "and it's freaking me out. Hurry up and tell us what it is."

She swallows and nods. "Oskar and I are going to be interviewed this afternoon. We cleared everything with Mama. We're giving up my place in the line of succession."

Clara makes a tiny, wounded noise, and Freja tips her head to hers for a moment. "I wanted to tell you in person."

This is growth. Freja is growing. My throat hurts, my head starts pounding, and everywhere else is numb. Moreover, I have failed to keep Freja in so that I could get out. Nothing will ever be the same again.

"I guess I don't have to prep myself for the legislative committee anymore," I offer, making light of the situation. It's a poor attempt to give Clara time to pull herself together, but we can get through this. We can.

"I have one more piece of news," Freja starts.

Stultes es. She never was able to read a room. "I don't know if this is the time for more news."

"It's the time," she breathes. "I can't keep it private for much longer."

"Oh hell. How bad is it?"

"Not bad, even if it is difficult." She touches her cheek against mine and I breathe in her scent. We were born this way and it is a gift when she lets me feel it. Her voice is soft. "I'm pregnant."

In Seongan dramas, white box trucks come out of nowhere, smashing through the plot in the blink of an eye, and throw characters into disarray. They are responsible for everything from meet-cutes to death. You just never know.

At her words, I feel like I've been pushed under the wheels of one. We are happy for her. We can't be anything but happy. But Clara cries and Alma fusses, asking pertinent questions about due dates and prenatal nutrition. I try to catch my breath. I hug my sister as long as she allows, but I still can't catch my breath.

I'm still trying hours later when the Management watches Freja's interview behind the closed doors of Mama's office. Me and my sisters crowd around Caroline's desk, cautious and winded. Nothing Freja says comes as a surprise. Not the renunciation of her role as a working royal or her pregnancy. Thank heaven for that.

Clara, the new Number Four, is heartbroken in a way no one else can understand.

"She looks calm," Alma says, leaning into the screen and fidgeting with her button. "Doesn't she?"

Clara nods. "Ella?"

Their eyes turn to me and know what I look like. Pinched. Tense. Like one more shock will disintegrate my bones. I close my eyes and bite the inside of my cheek as my sister calmly explains to the entire country her reasons for throwing away her first identity, the one stamped on the birth certificate issued by the private nursing hospital where we were born. *Her Royal Highness, Princess of Sondmark.*

There are photos of the day: Mama, looking astonishingly well-made-up, holding Freja. Père, his finger held by a tiny fist, smiling down at me. Princesses. Twins. The House of Wolffe was doubly blessed.

My stomach roils, and I press a fist against my midsection. This reminds me of the video feeds from the Seongan earthquake showing areas of liquefaction—of sandy soil turning into water and rigid building foundations beginning to flex and buckle. Unthinkable destruction followed.

I knew this was coming. Knew it was possible as soon as Freja ran off to be married, if I'm honest. If she did that, she might do anything. But the knot in my throat grows harder by the second, and I feel a wish form at the cellular level. Marc. I need Marc.

"It's fine," I manage, sounding like this happens every day, talking around the painful ache. "This is what she wants."

Caroline looks over her shoulder at me. Her glance flicks to my fist before retreating in discreet, sympathetic silence. Does she also know what it's like to have emotions that have no easy outlet?

When the broadcast concludes, Noah pokes his head around the door of Mama's office. "Come on in," he says, leaving it ajar even after we stride past him. There's likely nothing we could say that Caroline hasn't heard already.

Mama's hand is tucked into Père's steady grip, knuckles stark white against his tan, but I don't make the mistake of getting my hopes up. She has been a giantess my whole life, and if the last several years have made her hard, the last hour has made her fragile.

She leaves it to Noah to guide the discussion.

"The interview didn't do any more damage than Freja's departure will," he says. "It probably helps in the long run that it appears to be her own idea. The press will make itself ridiculous for a few weeks, talking about the baby, but the main thing is that we need everyone to lock in. No elopements." He looks at

Alma, who utters an outraged gasp, and moves on to Clara. "No gloating when you win your lawsuit."

I am on the edge of losing it and his aggressive certainty makes me bristle. "You know what would be really helpful?" I reply. "If you picked a girl, got married, and gave us an heir." It's easier to have these kinds of spats than face the storm of emotions brewing in my chest.

Noah's jaw sets, but Mama raps her knuckles on the desk. The air shivers with power.

"Your brother is correct. We have asked for circumspection time and again this year and, *dominanstid*, we've had little of it. The press will run with stories sourced on the thinnest material. We can't afford to give them any."

Père releases a breath. "I'm proud of our *donnina* for putting her marriage first."

Silently, pointedly, Mama slips her hand out of his. She aims a blind nod to no one. "There are to be no comments to the press. No leaks." She aims a scorching glance at me. "It's certainly not the time for levity, Ella. You are all dismissed."

While the administration wing is in fight mode, my sisters elect to raid the kitchens for ice cream bars. I tell them that I'd prefer to blow off steam by exploding space lizards on my computer.

I run up to my suite, and instead of reaching for the gaming controller, I kick off my shoes, frozen in place. The ancient wood floors creak under my shifting weight and I feel...I feel...

Every tear crowding my throat comes wrapped around a nucleus of knowing that Freja is right.

I jump when an urgent knock sounds. "I know your code," Marc calls through the door. "Just let me in there."

Vede. Painful pressure gathers behind my eyes and in the roof of my mouth. I open the door a crack. "Where is security when you need it?" I mutter.

He scoots me backward and presses the door shut. "They think I'm harmless."

He's not harmless to me. We watch each other across a short expanse. The pressure builds and builds. "You saw the broadcast."

"You knew it was coming," he says, narrowing his eyes. He's figuring this out now. "And you didn't tell me."

I wave a hand, but the careless effect is ruined by the stiffness of the motion. "I didn't know anything four hours ago. Didn't Noah tell you?"

He shakes his head.

"Then you should be banging at his door."

I swear he growls. "It's not Noah I've been kissing."

My eyes burn, but I think of how my mother will appear in public tomorrow, as cool as ice.

"That's no reason to babysit your best friend's little sister," I say, pushing him towards the door. He doesn't budge and my feet slip.

"Ella," he protests.

He's a wall of muscle and vastness, impervious to my attempt to shift him. I think seriously about investing in a moat or posting snipers at the head of the staircase.

"We're friends," he says.

Stultes es. The ground beneath my feet is shifting and my fist rests against his heart. My own is going to break into a million pieces.

"We help each other," he continues. "Don't throw me out." He reaches over and locks the door.

I hold his gaze and flick the lock free before retreating to the sofa. I take position in the corner, holding a pillow across my chest like it's some kind of shield.

"Freja let us know before they went public. I'm not mad." Thoughts cascade through my mind. I am a leaf howling through a hurricane. I don't know what all this means for my future. I'm proud of my sister—I swear I'm not mad. But I want to scream and scream and scream.

"You didn't think to text me?"

I thought about it every second, but I need to stop needing Marc. "It was just family business."

Marc sits on the coffee table, elbows braced on his knees, eyes level with mine, and his mouth tightens. "Hypocrite," he whispers. It sounds like an endearment more than an accusation. "Trying to hold it together by yourself." He grips the edge of the pillow and pulls it from me with no effort at all.

"You come to me when you're in trouble," he says. "That's the deal." I glance away, but he tugs my knees until I look at him.

I know. I know. This arrangement we have comes with an exit, but our friendship doesn't.

His grip tightens and he touches my forehead with a light finger. "What's the worst thing you're thinking?"

My lips part and close several times. He knows me too well—the wrangled public princess part and the trash panda gamer part and the shieldmaiden for my sisters part and the part so mean I don't show it to anybody else. "I should never have taught her those camera tricks last year. See what it got us?"

His mouth tips with a smile, and the sense that it's all going to be okay envelops me like a forcefield—conjured by him, but containing us both. "Oh no. A happy marriage. A future child. Not that." I deserve this gentle mockery. "She saved The Nat with those camera tricks, you know. In a way, it's more like *you* saved The Nat."

This gets me to laugh but it's like popping the tab on all the emotions. I open my mouth to say something even more awful, but instead, I feel the knot in my throat slip loose and keep slipping. A tear slides down my cheek. Then another. Then another.

Marc presses a handkerchief into my hands, but I'm too far gone for a quick mop up. Each of my sisters has come to me when the royal wrecking ball has blasted through their lives. I dole out sage advice and fancy tissues that have soothing lotion. I never... I don't... *Vede*. Crying is not my thing.

My shoulders shake with an unwanted sob, and Marc gathers me to him, scooping me up and appropriating my corner of the sofa.

We seem to step out of time and I make a deal with myself. I'm only going to allow myself a few more tears. They'll be like Clara's, slipping gently down my cheek, and make me prettier, if anything. I'll count them, and then I'll stop it already and say something funny. These plans are obliterated by the feeling of Marc's arms tightening around me. It should calm me down, battening down my emotions, but it does the opposite.

I don't think about what he'll think of me or how I'll explain myself. I fight the frightening sensation of freedom, and then I surrender, gripping his lapels to weep against his shirt. It is as though an ancient palace wall has collapsed, rendering every private space exposed. Anyone might see the odd collections and childish memorabilia. Anyone might glimpse how everything is turned inside out and strewn across the floor. Anyone might note the incongruity of a stately home and a shattered princess. Anyone might—but only Marc does.

My door opens, spilling light across the floor. Marc reaches for a stuffed animal and lobs it at the intruder.

"Who was that?" I ask, my bottom lip shaking.

"Celine of Anjou," he says, blaming our restless palace ghost. "She's looking for a place to kiss her lover."

I breathe a laugh and sniff. My tears have stopped, my face is pinched, and my head is achy.

"Feel better?" Marc asks, pushing my hair back.

The sharpness of my emotions has blunted enough for me to regain my footing. "We will not speak of this again," I say.

"Then we'd better speak of it now."

I try to climb away from him, but he holds my waist. I try to maintain a dignified posture, but when he won't let go, I wrap my arms around him and burrow into his chest. The truth is that I would like to buy property, hire an architect, and live here forever.

"What's the stupid thing you're telling yourself?" he asks, guiding my face up with his palm.

"Freja doesn't need me anymore. My family doesn't need me. I should revisit that idea of becoming a Lutheran nun."

His mouth tucks in a smile. "You like kissing too much."

A weary curse forks through my brain. It's not kissing that I like. It's him. I sniff again. "Maybe when you visit, I can take a Lutheran nun sabbatical."

"I draw the line at kissing a nun." He scoots me closer. "You're allowed to be upset. Freja is an idiot."

I scowl. "Don't call my sister names."

He rests his cheek on the top of my head. "How was she?"

"Resolute." I worry the edge of his button. "But I like—" I start. "I like that she refuses to apologize about loving Oskar. I would never apologize if—

I train my eyes on his shoulder, on the solid strength of it. Of course my emotions don't arrive gently. When I finally realize what's happening, it feels like an alien mothership emerging from a thunderhead. I swear there is lightning spiking to the ground, splintering trees and illuminating the dark center of the cloud. I hear the roar of my heartbeat in my ears and I hold very still in the awful majesty of it.

No, no, no, no, no, no. This wasn't supposed to happen. I take a ragged breath.

My feelings for Marc had come back, but they're supposed to fade again. The pendulum swings. I could always count on a reprieve, no matter how brief. Eventually.

Not anymore.

I will never fall out of love with Marc van Heyden.

Marc anchors me to him, but panic crawls up my neck. There is no one else for me. This is the end of the line, and it's the worst thing that's ever happened. *Vede.* I need to get him out of here so I can think.

"Even if you approve of Freja, you're still allowed to be sad," he says, continuing a conversation that doesn't even matter anymore.

Vede. Freja is forgiven for running off with Oskar and throwing her whole life into disorder if *this* is what she was feeling.

I want to find some semaphore flags and signal a message from the palace ramparts to her flat. S-O-G-L-A-D-Y-O-U-G-O-T-Y-O-U-R-M-A-N. Stop. S-E-N-D-H-E-L-P. Stop.

"I'm over it," I say, surprised to find that I'm speaking the truth. This whole day has been a revolution but Freja behaved beautifully. "The tears were great." I give Marc a double thumbs up I immediately regret. "Thanks for facilitating."

He smiles. "Anytime." He presses a soft kiss against my brow. "I'm sorry I can't stay long tonight. Werner's spreadsheets are urgent."

I've never been caught in an actual flood, but the common advice is to grab onto the first floatation device that passes. The one that passes me now is the jankiest life preserver I've ever seen, but I can't afford to be picky.

Spreadsheets. I push myself away, putting a few millimeters of space between us. "Speaking of, now that I know where Freja stands, I think it's time for me to consider my mother's spreadsheets," I laugh. Marc came to me today and how did he get me to open up? *We're friends.* It's a reminder and a warning. "It's time I find some clapped out Motovian aristocrat to drag down the aisle of Roslav Cathedral."

"Hm?"

"It's time."

He threads a curl around his fingers. "Where is the princess who said she would never marry anyone her mother described as appropriate?"

Have I made him nervous? With my plans to leave and my threshold for marriage set, he probably thought he was safe from being seriously considered as a future husband. Safe enough to kiss. "With my sisters otherwise engaged, I'll have my pick of the crop. The Motovian aristocrat doesn't even have to be clapped out." I smooth my skirt.

A line forms between his brows. "No. You're going to leave. You have a plan. The endangered species tracking. The Bond lair."

I swallow, picking my way through thoughts that begin to slowly organize themselves. I have to make him believe me. "When Freja told us she was pregnant, I thought that there was no way. She loves her personal space too much. She likes order and quiet. She couldn't possibly trade all that to nurture a tiny human. That kind of sacrifice..."

My nose prickles with more tears but I wrinkle them away. "You should have seen Clara when Freja stepped out of the line of succession on national television, moving her up one rung. She's devastated and she probably won't even tell anyone but Max. The thought of doing that to her again..." I shake my head.

And Mama. She looked vulnerable in a way a giant never should. I can't do that to her, either.

I see the balance of my life. The dress codes and proscribed behavior. The public-facing masks and the friction of working with my family. I'm not blind or ignorant. These don't disappear just because I decide to stay. But I think about Freja being brave and Clara being scared and how much I want to protect everyone who shares my blood.

"I thought I was a runner." I lift my shoulder. "I guess not."

What follows is a tense second. Then Marc holds my hand between his palms. Does he feel caught? Does he feel bound to say something? Offer something?

"Anyway," I jerk back and clap my hands lightly, "Noah doesn't have a family yet, and I can read the writing on the wall. It's time to open the spreadsheets. Mama can't afford to lose another HRH, and I know when to surrender."

His smile fades and he lowers his head for a slow, deliberate kiss that leaves me in pieces. "You've been nursing the same *SquadRun* team for years. You don't know anything about surrender," he insists, pulling me in for more.

When he kisses me, I feel like crying again.

Marc and I promised that we wouldn't take this any further, that acting on a sliver of the physical attraction between us would satisfy, tiding us over a rough patch. We sealed it with a pinky swear, but something has shifted in the last few weeks. I've learned to take his kisses as my right.

I break free and take a deep, shuddering breath. It's time to move along. I see my future unfolding before me. It belongs to Entirely Reasonable Spreadsheet Guy who doesn't expect a grand passion—or, if that's too heartbreaking, I could lean into being the cool aunt forever.

Why can't it be Marc?

Freja and I aren't anything alike. She is tall and I am short. She is self-contained and I am a trash panda. She likes fashion and I like gaming. But it seems that we both love deeply and irrevocably. She got her happy ending with Oskar, but I love Marc van

Heyden and he considers us to be—first and foremost—friends. Everything else can be traded away.

"I have to go," he says, planting his feet firmly on the ground. "We'll talk about it later."

I reach for the tail of his shirt, worked free from his waistband, and move to tuck it in. He jerks back, finishing the job. I stare at my hand, suspended in midair, then let it fall. See? I can't do this halfway. I need all of him or nothing.

"There's one good thing about finally knowing what's going to happen with Freja," I say.

"What's that?" he asks, straightening his tie.

"We don't need this arrangement anymore."

30

SHE CHEATS

MARC

My hand freezes on the knot of my tie. "Excuse me?"

Though the tip of her nose is still red, Ella smiles. "We met our goals," she says, sounding like a *flamen* quarterly report. "You said that the aim was to provide ourselves with a much-needed outlet for," she waves her hand dismissively, "rampaging hormones while we handled various dramas. But Alix's wedding is less than three weeks away. Most of the organization for the BLUSH concert is done. Now that Freja dropped the hammer on the succession crisis, I don't need to worry about what might happen anymore. It's happened and—"

"The fallout is going to be significant," I counter.

Ella walks around the room, fluffing pillows, straightening the coffee table, and erasing any signs that I was here. "I told you my plan for that."

"The spreadsheet." The *flamen* spreadsheet. The cursed spreadsheet.

She nods. "It's only fair to give it a look. Maybe," she kicks a stuffed raccoon out from under the bed, "I can find an undiscovered treasure. Someone who checks all of Mama's boxes and all of mine, doesn't have any pending paternity suits, and still has his original hairline."

I run my hand through thick lustrous hair, one of my best features, but Ella isn't hinting that I'm one of her options. I don't even occur to her. "You'd really marry someone you were matched with?"

She scoops her ponytail over her shoulder. I kissed her there. "No one ever guessed Freja would run off with a commoner or that Alma would choose an American." Her eyes dance. "Surprises abound."

"Why stop now?" I ask. I am not cool. I don't carefully calculate my choices. I sound desperate. "We're getting along pretty well with the current arrangement." A lie. Every day I have to hold myself back. Every day it gets worse. I've been like a wolf in a trap, chewing at my leg. "I'm getting mountains of work done." That much is true.

Her nose wrinkles in thought. "You're easy to kiss," she says, doling out the compliment like the Order of the Dragonslayer, pinning it to my chest. Impersonal. Rigid. "But what this...incident on the couch taught me is that you're too important to play around with. Who else would I have cried all over? No one. We are such good friends, and I had a lot of fun," she assures me, not meeting my desperate gaze, "but we both know that doing damage to our friendship is a real possibility. I can't take that risk anymore."

Her words whistle through the air and sink into my heart like arrows. Thunk, thunk, thunk. In another moment I'll drop to my knees and bleed out.

She stows a pile of things in a cabinet. "It was nice—"

Nice? I sniff like a wild bull elk. This was *nice*?

"—but things have changed. The way you are with Linden-holm—" She lifts a shoulder. "You never run away from responsibility. And I—it was good for me to see what that means, up close. Is that the lesson you were trying to teach me all this time?" she asks.

She thinks I had control? That I was doing anything more than holding on to her because I had to? With every word, she turns me to stone.

"When everything was happening today, I had to think about what sacrifices I was willing to make to protect what I love. The more I thought about it, the more obvious it became that I have to choose my sisters, Noah, my dumb parents, every great aunt that visits for Christmas—even the scandalous cousins. All *you* do is protect what you love. You involve yourself. You fight for it. I don't know if I would have seen my duty without you showing it to me."

Well, I am an idiot.

"I know I'm going to be frustrated," she concedes. "I'm going to complain like there's a shortage of whiners and I'm filling the deficit. But my place is here, and since I'm going to stay, I have to start building my life around things that matter."

She knows how to deliver a punch.

"Freja and the baby?" I hazard.

She nods.

I finish tucking in my shirt as I absorb the information. "You won't resent the choice to stay?"

"Once a month, at least." She talks as she potters. "It will take some time to settle into the idea. In the meantime, I'm going to make sure Freja and her family are secure," she says.

I slip my arms around her waist and gather her back to me. We don't have to break things off. I inhale, arms banding her waist, the scent of her working deeper and deeper into my lungs. "So you're signing up for the whole royal program? Dress codes, comportment lessons, arranged marriage..."

She breaks the ring of my arms and goes to straighten a stack of books that don't need straightening. "Yep."

I lean back on the console, bracing my hands on the smooth wood surface. This is the deal I laid out for us. When we ended things, she'd take it with cool detachment, more secure in her own ability to fulfill the role she was born to play. This has happened exactly as I described it, the runes tumbling from a cup on a lucky roll.

For myself, I wanted peace out of this arrangement. I would finally stop thinking of Ella at wildly inappropriate times and in extremely inappropriate ways. I would get so much of her I'd be sick.

I follow the curve of her cheek, the sprinkle of freckles over the ridge, and the slight pulling around her mouth. I will never be sick of her.

There's a trace of irritation in my voice. "You're just going to do everything your mother tells you to?" I ask, frustrated that she's so calm about this when, for the love of Erasmus's cap, my frozen bones are screaming.

She answers, a tuck in her brow. "You taught me how to make deals."

She's blaming this on me? Suddenly I want her to suffer. I want her to fall to pieces. I want her to be up at 3 AM, wanting me as much as I want her.

She turns, plucking at her lip with her teeth. I kissed her there, too. I'd lean down to kiss her now if her expression wasn't so earnest. She's obviously preparing for a monologue.

"I was headed for a disaster," she says, "after Freja eloped. I was furious and heartbroken and ready to smash the monarchy. I wasn't talking to anybody. Not really. If you hadn't come home—" Her chin dips and her glance slides away before she recovers. "I don't know how you knew I needed this kind of distraction."

This. Her hands move back and forth between us like we bartered a basket of potatoes for a pound of butter. I'll never forgive her.

Her hands still. "It was a crazy idea but I needed it. I hate it when you're right."

I swallow hard. "I'll get that admission framed. You can sign it."

"Deal. Now, are you ready to make this break official?" she asks, raising her hand between us, pinky extended. She straightens her shoulders so there's no mistake that this is anything casual. "Marc van Heyden, will you be my completely platonic friend?"

It's not a bad deal. She'll still come to me with her problems. We'll text. We'll talk. Because Ella keeps her promises, I know it will last forever.

It's not enough. Before all this, I was stuck in the narrow channels of duty—always choosing the right but slowly suffocating. Does she even know what it feels like to pull her into my arms and experience all that heaviness falling away? *Dominanstid*, I answered emails from her closet. I broke her out of the palace. I've been sneaking up the Grand Staircase and lying to my best friend's face and having more fun than I've ever had in my life.

"Marc," she prods, poking my hand with her pinky.

She isn't running away from Sondmark. There's got to be a way to work with that. I wrap my finger around hers, and seal it with the press of our thumbs. Friends forever. Promise.

"Okay," she says, brushing her hands against each other now that the oath is made. I don't know how to say goodbye anymore without a tangle of hands, a tug on my tie, and one last kiss, but she walks to her door and turns the handle. "I guess I'll be seeing you?"

Do we have to learn how to do this again, reversing our way out of weeks of intimacy and easy affection? Mechanically I pass through the door and down the staircase like I'm on my way to be hanged for crimes against the Crown. The pavement is slick with a spring shower, and I'm halfway to the car park before I come to myself. No. Hell no. Hell. No. I double back, but my pace is arrested at the sound of my name.

"Marc—"

I smother a curse and turn to see Noah emerging from one of the trails ringing the royal estate, hands stuffed into his pockets.

I grip my keys and close my eyes briefly. I jog over and his well-trained dog—a biscuit-colored hound of indeterminate breed—waits for me to greet him before nuzzling my hand with a wet nose.

"What brings you to the palace?" he asks.

"I saw the interview. I thought—"

He drops a hand on my shoulder. "Sorry you didn't make it in. I gave orders to *Vrouw* Tiele to keep everyone away from the admin wing. It's been a firestorm." I follow Noah to the west lawn. "We worry that the government will use this incident as an excuse to wrestle more power from the Crown, but the upside is that we don't have to figure out how to integrate Oskar as a working royal. And there'll be a baby. I love babies."

"Did Oskar want her to bail?" I ask.

Noah shakes his head. "No. He loves her." He says it like it's an emotion one shouldn't encourage. "They're falling over each other to make the greater sacrifice."

"He's just going to let her make it?"

Noah takes a tennis ball out of his pocket and chucks it. His dog waits and waits until he gives a brief command, then bounds onto the lawn.

"There's no 'let' with the women in my family." Noah retrieves the ball and sends it sailing away again.

"What about Ella?"

"What does Ella have to do with anything?" When I don't answer, Noah continues. "Do you have any updates? You must have talked some sense into her. She's been pretty decent, even if she's mad that it's Freja who gets to leave."

My skin electrifies with the memory of holding Ella in my arms, crying her eyes out, but determined to understand her twin. Barely giving herself permission to be upset about something that is going to affect her life in ways she can't even guess at. Deciding to stay, to make her peace, and to put down her weapons.

I'm so proud of her, and I don't think I've ever wanted to punch Noah more. "We talked a little."

My crown prince throws the ball again, lobbing it in the direction of the grace and favor cottages. "She'll get over it. Ella can't hold a grudge."

I ball my hand into a fist. *Stultes es*, if he knew about her plan to unseat Torbald… "Would it kill you to take care of her for once?"

"Take care? She's not exactly a delicate flower," he laughs. "She can wrestle any of us to the ground—and she cheats."

I know she cheats. She bit my shoulder once when I was holding one of her school notebooks just out of reach. What was she afraid I was going to see? Girlish scribbles? But she also worries over everyone's happiness in a way I wish just one member of her family would worry over hers.

I suppose this is what you get when you hold your own against the most powerful monarch in the North Sea Confederation. People forget you need taking care of.

"She'll forgive Freja, you know," Noah says. He must see hostility in the set of my jaw. "Not because we force her to, but because no matter how many threats she makes, Ella's heart is as soft as butter. If anyone she loves is hurt, she'll go to war."

My hand unclenches.

"What is your mother going to do with Freja?" I ask.

"She'll make a big opening demand from Torbald—something like keeping the HRH, even though that's already a lost cause. Then she'll follow up with a more reasonable concession like having Freja still attend key royal functions. She might get to wear a tiara and sash, but she would have to sit at the bottom of the banquet tables with the unwashed masses."

"That's long term. What's Her Majesty's plan for the short term?"

"The pregnancy helps." Poor little Hiorulf or Annika, already hard at work in the royal mines. Noah's smile is cynical. "We're going to have to shift the public's attention."

"How?" I already know how. I've been playing this game almost as long as Noah has.

"You know the playbook. We need to find someone suitable for Ella and me."

He's not being callous, merely clear-eyed. This is how the monarchy has gripped Sondmark in an unbroken line for 800 years. There is enough of it in my blood to understand.

But the idea of Ella being served up on national television as a blushing bride in a dress dazzling enough to hide Freja's legal troubles... My hand clenches again.

"I'm on the list," I say, my voice hoarse with tension.

"It wasn't a threat." Noah slaps me on the back. "I wouldn't let them do that to you."

It's not too late to push his teeth in. "When is it your turn for marriage?"

"I'm ready now."

I grunt, and the cool night air ruffles my hair. "So what's stopping you?"

The hound comes bounding back with the tennis ball in his mouth. Noah works it out of his jaw and lobs it again. "Nothing, when I figure out how to get what I want."

His words echo in my mind all the way back to my flat—past Felix, up the elevator. They stay with me as I discard my tie and twist open the top button of my shirt, through the first tumbler of whisky and into the second as I burn through work. It's late when I finish. My view is spectacular, set in the modern quarter of Handsel and surrounded by metal and glass, but opening up to the ancient parts of the city and the glowing palace on the hill. What's stopping me from Ella?

Nothing, when I figure out how to get what I want.

My gaze shifts from the lights on the hill to my reflection.

Ella accepted me as an occasional distraction, but I take a long, deep breath. I can never go back to being just friends. On that, my mind is suddenly very, very clear.

I barge into my home office and tear apart the room until I find a legal pad, *the* legal pad—the same one I used when I sketched out my plans for getting into Stanford, founding Han Heyden, and relocating it to Sondmark. I don't use this for grocery lists. I scrawl her name at the top of a page, slightly crispy with age.

Ella. I strike two lines under it and tap my pen. I add an asterisk. **Girlfriend, Wife,* Vrouwheid *van Heyden.* I can't be half-hearted or chase myself into dead ends. Losing her will drive me insane. I drum the pen on the page. What's it going to take to get my girl? Ink spools from the point.

Deliver Torbald.

If that's what she wants, that's what she gets. If this involves a little light law-breaking? Well, what a time to be alive.

Offer freedom.

The monarchy has narrow rules and she is determined to follow them, but I know Ella—and I know what she needs to be happy. The sacrifices she's willing to make for her family are always going to hurt if she doesn't have a certain degree of freedom.

I chew my lip. She tells me she's considering someone suitable. I grin, remembering how many kisses she stole behind her family's back. Ella says she would take a—what was it?—clapped out Motovian aristocrat, but I don't buy it. Suitable is not what she really wants.

I scrawl the words.

Be unsuitable.

When my head finally hits the pillow, I am resolved. A photo of *Amma* and Alix rests on my nightstand, but a strip of black and white photos tucked into the frame draws my attention. I never gave them to my sister. Even then, I had no intention to. Ella's face laughs up at mine and I take a large breath. I have a plan. I know what I want. My arm falls across the massive bed and I feel an invisible weight.

Her.

Here.

Forever.

31

CHEAP WINE

ELLA

I thought I was prepared for the pain. Breaking things off with Marc was always going to hurt, but tonight was far worse than something a few processed snacks and bed rot can solve. Relegating our relationship to the chirpy, heatless boundaries of friendship isn't a paper cut. This time, it feels like a folded steel blade dividing my flesh from my bones.

My first thought is to numb these emotions with gaming, rounding up enough of our team to do a late-night *SquadRun* campaign, and sacrifice an unheard-of number of life points as I drive pitilessly toward the goal. Rescue the princess. We're always after the *flamen* princess.

No one is happy when we log off, and the night stretches ahead of me with nothing to do but think. No, thank you. So I shrug on my hoodie and reach for my wallet. I race down the staircase and almost crash into Caroline Tiele crossing the Great Hall.

She curtsies, apologizing for my clumsiness, and her gaze sharpens on my face. I will not cry.

"Ma'am—"

"Ella," I snap. "You're older than I am."

She's silent so long that blood drains out of my cheeks and guilt rises out of my mouth. *Vede.* "I'm sorry, *Vrouw* Tiele. I didn't mean— I'm not in a good place and...and... I'm sorry."

My voice rises higher and higher with each word.

She should accept the crumb and retreat into the hedgerow of propriety, pretending she doesn't see anything that goes on around here. Instead, she plucks at her lip with a row of endearingly uneven teeth and steps beyond the clear boundaries separating a royal princess from the palace help. "Caroline," she corrects. "Where are you headed?"

"To get a drink somewhere."

"The palace has quite a lot of alcohol."

"I can't stay here. I know what you're going to say," I start, heading off her judgement.

"Really?"

"Yes. You're going to tell me I can't shatter the illusion that we are a family who has its crap together."

She laughs. It's small but it's the most human sound I've ever heard from her. "No one following the press reports this year is laboring under that delusion." She sighs and tucks her hair back. "Listen. I've had a long day doing crisis management for your sister. I don't really want to spend tomorrow managing the headlines if you get smashed in some club."

There's another human admission. I thought there was no royal mess Caroline Tiele wasn't prepared to clean up. "No. You're right. You are. I should return to my suite and go back to being Sondmark's favorite princess."

She glances over her shoulder. "I live at the bottom of the hill if you want to do it at my flat. The choices aren't special—some cans of beer and a few bottles of cheap wine—but I know how to keep a secret."

Caroline and I aren't buddy-buddy. She's both indispensable to my mother and a completely unknown quantity, but standing here, I feel all the things I've messed up flooding in around me. I can't message Alix about her own brother. My sisters are cocooned in frothy bubbles of romantic contentment, I don't want any of the Saint Sissela girls to remember this, and the rest of my friends are chronically online. The thing is, when things get this bad, I usually text Marc.

"Cheap wine?" I ask.

"The perfect vintage to drown your troubles."

"You have troubles too?"

"I meant generally," she says, shaking her keys. She turns on her heel and I follow.

Everything about Caroline is modest—the length of her skirt, the height of her heels, the color of her car, an elderly gray Ciprio kept in immaculate state—and I feel a little like a forest troll trotting after her. My red hair is wild, my jeans are ripped, and my emotional state is best described as "Smash Everything".

We drive in silence, and she turns into a square lined on three sides with tall, beautifully-maintained townhouses from the time when Sondish cloth merchants ruled Europe. Along the fourth side runs a shallow channel of the Handsel River, improved by mature plane trees and a stone riverwalk. I've been here before. Several schoolmates come from this neighborhood, and Dahlia's flat is on the south side of the square.

Caroline slots her car into a narrow mews and leads me to a rococo townhouse, the stone exterior shell pink. Bypassing the grand entry stairs, she steps down to a narrow landing where an old servant's entrance has been improved with a door of heavy beveled glass panes, the woodwork painted glossy, expensive black.

She slots a key into the lock and pauses. "Listen," she says, her chin dipping towards her shoulder, "I can be whatever you need right now. Would you prefer it if I pretended I didn't know about *Neerheid* van Heyden and how much he shows up on the palace security logs? I don't have anyone to tell," she says, pushing through the door.

"I can't pretend," I say, following her.

I don't know what to expect of her flat. Maybe a crisply modern space with a few personal touches. Maybe a version of her tasteful office at the palace, but on a larger scale. It is neither of those things. We squeeze past a tiny entry table, and Caroline drops her keys into a pretty teacup with blue and yellow flowers. We enter a small sitting room where there's a row of windows, framed with net curtains, above a slouchy sofa. Tucked in a corner is a tiny kitchenette: just a short bank comprising a few cupboards, a sink and a stove. A small refrigerator hums on the end. I recognize from my time in college that Caroline's flat is how you decorate when most of your furniture has been dragged off of the street or sourced second-hand from online sellers who give you a pick-up window from six to seven on a Wednesday night.

"Give me a second to change and wash up?" she says. I nod, and she moves through a doorway into her bedroom while I inspect the flat. It's more relaxed and cozy than I imagined Caroline would choose. She has a round table with three matching chairs and an orphan, a bookshelf stuffed with paperbacks, and a wall of family photos I don't have time to inspect before a knock comes from one of the interior doors.

I should probably dive behind the sofa and hide, but Caroline is a closed book—padlocked, tossed into an underground vault, and guarded by a cadre of loyal assassins. I can't resist the chance to peek behind the curtain.

Will this be a boyfriend? Mr. Discretion Is My Middle Name? A landlady popping down to warn against gentlemen callers? I open the door to reveal a man about my age with sandy hair, a paint-splattered graphic tee that reads "Question Your Questions", and a turtle.

"I cleaned Boris's enclosure," he says. Then he looks up, "Oh, sorry." He shoves a hand in his pocket and looks over my shoulder. "Is my sister around?"

My jaw drops. I jab my finger at the turtle. "Wait—Boris? As in, 'You gotta clean Boris's enclosure or your sister—'" I stab the air in Caroline's direction, "'is going to open up a can on you'? *That* Boris?"

"How did you—" His voice sinks into a shocked whisper and he looks wildly around. "You're Princess Ella. Wait—you're...Trash Panda Princess?"

In a panic, I drag the door almost shut and speak through the narrow gap. "You never saw me," I hiss. "Definitely don't tell your sister. *Stultes es,* does she know about us?"

Does my mother know?

He salutes with a fist to his heart. He actually salutes. "My liege." He pushes the door open. "How could my sister know? *I* didn't know. What kind of filthy traitor do you think I am?"

"Linus," a voice cuts in. I scramble back to see Caroline emerging from her room in a matching lounge set. "Out."

Linus lifts Boris. "I cleaned him. It smells like roses up there. Come up if you want something to eat."

"Pass," she says, swiping a wildly expensive controller from her shelf. She tosses it to him with the carelessness of someone who didn't spend weeks researching the specs, and he gives me a look of outrage. *See what I'm dealing with?*

She aims a nearly identical look at me when he goes. "Sorry," she says, pouring out a glass of wine and handing it to me. She pours a small measure for herself and settles into the corner of the sofa, one bare foot tucked under her, the other swinging to the ground. "I don't think he has any real friends," she continues, describing one of the revered founding members of our squad. Dragonslayer2 is a legend.

"He won't tell anyone you were here," she assures me. "Do you want to talk about it?"

Caroline is no one's idea of a soulmate, but I don't have a better option. I close my eyes. "I did a deal with Marc van Heyden but I cut it off and now I'm dead inside and sure I'll be alone until I die."

"Deal?" She zeroes in on the most important word and a shudder rolls across my shoulders. Caroline can be terrifyingly like my mother.

"It was like a...a friends-with-benefits thing." Ugh. Putting it into words is a nightmare. "Just kissing. Anyway, if my future is here in Sondmark, I have to start building it in healthy ways. I can't do that with a man who isn't going to choose me."

"Here's to wise choices," she says, tipping her glass against mine with a clink. "You're celebrating by getting drunk at my flat?"

I scowl. "I fell in love with him—"

"Again?"

"How much do you know?" I shake my head. "Yes, again. It's the whole wheel of cheese this time, but the second his lips aren't on mine, he's like, 'You're the best. You're such a great friend. Let's play catch.'" I sock Caroline in the arm and she takes it pretty well. "I don't feel friendly."

"Maybe you're just caught in an old habit," she ventures. "Have you tried dating anyone else?"

"Every time I do date some guy I find myself really irritated because I have to explain my ramen order and carry around Vestfyn because he doesn't keep a dedicated fridge in his office for me, even though he hates it." I faceplant into a downy pillow, my words muffled. "How long am I going to be mad that no one else kisses me like he does?"

"He's a good kisser?" Caroline asks.

I lift my head. "When I tell you how good," I say, touching the tips of my fingers in the same Pavian gesture Noah uses.

Caroline glances away and my gesture dissolves. "The future Mister Duchess of Sorstorm, if such a man exists, will just be some guy on a list—some low-rent, spreadsheet version of what I really want—and I hate him." I take a too-large swallow from my glass. I don't have any more tears.

Caroline watches me for a long time, and finally she takes a breath. "People always call it a spreadsheet," she murmurs, "when it's more of a series of alphabetized summaries, arranged by rank. I could get them for you. Maybe it's not as bad as you think."

The side-eye I give her could shift the earth off its axis, but she laughs.

I was expecting homespun advice and a call to rectitude. Instead, we talk. I leaf through her paperback collection, heavy on romance, and recommend a few Seongan dramas. I fish for information and discover that her whole family lives upstairs. I reveal just how long this thing with Marc has gone on, and she admits that her social life is limited to a Vorburgian diplomat who looks her up now and then.

"When he's in town?" My brow cocks. "What is this? Are you a side piece?"

Her hand tips in a seesaw motion. "I think he's trying to sort out whether or not a Sondish royal secretary is a benefit to his career or not."

"He sounds like a drip."

For a moment the ladylike, professional facade drops away and a laugh lights up her face. In the next heartbeat she remembers herself and twitches the neat net curtains of her soul back into place.

At midnight, she drives me back to the palace, completely sober in contrast to my slight tipsiness. There's too much time stretching ahead of me and I'm thinking very seriously of crying myself to sleep or perishing from a broken heart like a character stuck inside a 19th century book.

Well, the ones turned into graphic novels, anyway.

"You can come again," Caroline says, standing in the doorway of my suite, watching as I fumble my way out of shoes and hoodie. "Anytime you need to hit the sauce."

I grin. "You saved me from public humiliation, Caro." A night in a bar wouldn't have stopped at two glasses of wine and a sip of *hjemmebrændt.* "It's good to know one of us has some sense when it comes to love. Thanks."

She leaves me to a night of dead ends and spiralling reflections, the beginning of a mourning period for my love of Marc van Heyden. I wake to the pounding of the door. *Vede*, the *hjemmebrændt* has a kick. I flail blindly, finding a button under my bedside table, and press it before I think. I sink into the pillow and wait for death.

"Good morning, *elskede*." Marc bends over me, sun shafting across his hair, kissing his dewy skin.

I scowl against his easy endearment—and then yelp. Our deal is over, and Marc is in my bedroom. I bolt upright, gathering a down coverlet up to my chin.

"How did you get here?"

He leans forward, and I scoot back, winding the wild hair away from my face. The sleeves of my oversized *Mermaid in Moonlight* t-shirt fall back, and I feel his gaze warm my skin.

"I took the roundabout out of Frederickplatz, shot up the E12..."

I pinch him and he grunts.

Why is he here, looking like Saint Leofdag's gift to Sondish maidens? Was last night a fever dream? Didn't I end it?

I press the back of my fingers against my forehead and work my tongue into the wells of my mouth. No fever.

We're over. It happened. He can never find out I got drunk.

"What's this?" I ask, watching as he unpacks a bento box.

"Side dishes."

"I don't know what it is you want, but I'm not Freja," I say. "You can't tempt me with food."

He removes several lids, unveiling warmed up hangover soup, kimchi, and seasoned tofu from Lindenholm. His mother installed a Seongan chef first thing and bribed her to stay for decades.

"The assortment of fruit was ordered in from Minty's and the rolled omelet is me. I'm an early riser," he adds, answering the unspoken question.

I tip my chin, inspecting all the dishes, the warmth in my chest like a nuclear reactor. "You should have texted. I wouldn't look like such a mess."

He looks at me for a long time and silence stretches into a thin, transparent tissue.

Finally, I wind my hair away and clip it back. "If you ever wonder if I'm fishing for compliments, the answer is always yes."

"I didn't trust myself to comment on your appearance. You look—" he starts.

"Too late," I reply, the words like the extension of a hand at a work college so they don't go in for a hug. I can't cross the same boundaries I promised to fortify. "Give me a minute to pull myself together."

I toss on a pair of dark slacks and a blouse, brush my teeth extra well, and quickly wrangle my hair in case I'm pulled into a family discussion. We eat on my narrow balcony overlooking an ornamental garden and he leans against the railing, catching me up on news from Seong and preparations for BLUSH. With a face like his, I'm sure he's never been on the losing end of a break-up. I surprised him yesterday, and I suppose this is his way of wrapping things up on his own terms.

"Come out for a walk with me," he says, pulling me to my feet.

I follow him through the hallways of the palace and watch his back as he steps into the sunshine. I can't have him, so I shake my head and train my sights on the grounds of the Summer Palace, cultivated over centuries. We have a rookery, a couple of follies, and a copse of ancient oaks planted during a bloody reign. There's even an ornamental English garden, dotted with statuary, and a wilderness big enough to sustain several herds of white-tailed deer.

I shy away from the wilderness. Marc and I have a track record when it comes to wildernesses. Under the bright sun, my head throbs with the after effects of cheap wine, and I walk as carefully as possible.

"How are you feeling? About Freja's thing," he clarifies. Not ours.

I lift my shoulder. "I'm not the main character in this drama."

He reaches over and hooks a finger through a belt loop, catching me, and his eyes travel over my face. My heart kicks up a traitorous rhythm because I know he's capable of seeing nearly every part of me—happiness for Freja, worry about the future, the persistent friction with royal life that has receded from a wild keening to a low hum. Progress.

He touches my face. Then he leans forward, kissing me softly on the brow, my temple, on my cheek. Still friendly locations. Just.

"Is this you fishing for compliments?" he asks, slipping his arm around my waist. He did this a thousand times when we were only friends. It's fine. "Does your family know how miserable they'd be without you?"

The soft spring air brushes between us, and I place a hand against his chest.

His hand slides up my back, and I don't know anymore if I'm leaning or he's pulling. I am poised on the sharp edge of wishing I could undo yesterday, right on the cusp of going up on my tiptoes and saying things that might reverse this delicate truce. Then there comes a crunch on the gravel walk and a surprised, "Oh."

We spring apart under the interested, amused regard of my father. My heartbeat clatters in my chest, but Père waves Marc's bow away.

"I am fizzing with curiosity," he says, "but I'm in no condition to be lied to." He rubs a palm over his flat stomach, a line between his brows. "It upsets the digestion."

I slip my arm through his. "We've had an upsetting few days. Marc was telling me how sorry he was."

"With his lips?" Père asks. Marc holds his gaze when he should have the decency to look ashamed. Père smiles. "I dare say there's not a square meter on the whole grounds where I didn't get into mischief with my bride."

"It's not like that," I insist.

Père glances past me, but Marc shoves his hands in his pockets, cheerfully hanging me out to dry.

"What's the agenda for today?" I ask him with a newfound commitment to schedules and timetables.

"The prime minister is meeting with your mother now," Père says, brushing his knuckle on the end of my nose with a look that is both happy and sad.

"Is he accepting her proposal for Freja's position?"

"She will handle him with such delicacy that he'll think it was his idea all along," Père grunts.

"He's dangerous," I venture.

Père touches my hand, the dull gold of his Pavian signet ring glinting in the light. "Your mother is a world-class diplomat," he assures me. "Shall we go see how she is getting on? I'm her greatest support, you know."

I feel a tug of pain at his words, lifted from countless news articles and opinion pieces. This sentiment—once sacred and true—he's turned into a joke.

We enter the palace through the administration wing and find it oddly deserted.

"Where is everyone?" he asks, peeking into Caroline's office. "The prime minister's security officers should be—"

We hear a sharp exchange from the sitting room where Mama customarily receives the prime minister, and Père gives me a look of surprise before he moves swiftly into the room, ready to pour a little Pavian charm on the situation.

The door is slightly ajar, and Caroline isn't here to keep me from doing it, so I creep closer. Marc is on my heels, and I lean closer to the wood paneling because the voices are frustratingly low. I leap out of my skin when Mama shouts, "How dare you, you bureaucratic reptile. You dirt-sucking snake."

Through the narrow crack in the door, I see Mama rush the prime minister. I gape, but Père swiftly intercepts her, scooping the Mother of Sondmark and the Sonderlands up and striding her away a few paces. She struggles to free herself from the arm banding her waist. Wordlessly, Marc slips his arm around my waist, holding me fast.

"Your Majesty," the prime minister shouts. "Madam, contain yourself!"

"You threatened my child," Mama roars.

I take it in, frozen in disbelief. Where is the diplomat? Gone. There is something primal in the way words tear from her throat. A line of the national anthem runs through my head. *None will bridle the dragon of Sondmark.* Her fury is powerful enough that she might even recover Freja's HRH—but, *dominanstid*, if it ever gets out that she shouted at an elected official…

"Did you expect me to take that meekly?" she thunders, completely unhinged. The sound of her voice rattles the walls as Père holds her.

My mother's priorities might be disordered, but it is a rare joy to hear her voice, billowing with ancient power and royal rage, fighting for the Crown and its prerogatives.

"Her online activities are outrageous," the prime minister blusters, snatching up his briefcase. I roll my eyes. Freja's Pixy videos encouraging more visits to The Nat aren't a scandal. He points a shaking finger. "If you have any hope of holding your present role, Princess Ella must be sacrificed—"

I straighten, bumping into Marc's solid mass. Princess Ella is me. They are talking about *me*. I grapple with the arms around my waist but Marc's hold tightens as Mama's voice, low and menacing, carries through the door. "How dare you speak of my precious child."

I gasp, and Marc puts a hand over my mouth, whispering a hush against my ear.

Slowly, his restraining arms become an embrace, holding me tightly. *Precious?* I turn the word over, examining it for flaws and conditions as a jeweler would search for fractures and clouds. Mama doesn't put anything before the Crown. Not herself. Not her family. Certainly not a child who battles her at every turn.

But through the narrow opening, I see evidence that tells another story.

Marc folds me against his chest, keeping me steady and secure even as my mother rages. "If you threaten my daughter, you will get a fight."

32

Scruples Evaporate

MARC

"And you, Madam, should prepare yourself for a press conference," Torbald spits. "I intend to reveal her online identity tomorrow."

Ella tears at my fingers, trying to get me to release her. No chance. The exposure of her gamer tag and social media handles will be a dark day for the monarchy, but it wouldn't be in the same league as strangling her mother's minister. I pick Ella up and throw her over my shoulder, jogging silently down the hall. When a door opens behind me, I dive into a supply closet, shutting us in.

"You can't fight him," I say.

"Did you hear?" she says, trying to get past me. She dodges. I weave.

I shake the flashlight on my phone, illuminating the narrow space, and catch her close.

"Sorry, Ells. There is not a prayer you're going to get past me." She starts scaling my height, which would be the right time to tell her that she's the love of my life, and that we should get down to sorting out the logistics—if she would just stop moving for a second.

She wedges herself over my shoulder with a grunt, pushing against my shoulder blade, and brushes the doorknob with her fingertips. I carry her out of reach. "You can't beat up the prime minister."

I slip her forward until we're eye to eye, and sense the moment her breathing shifts from murderous to physically aware. She's attracted to me, and maybe we could use our time more wisely. I could press my luck and—

No. I shake my head and peel her off me, one limb at a time. There is a risk of rushing her when she's in the wrong frame of mind. I have to be strategic.

"Did you hear?" she repeats, sinking on a stack of cardboard boxes, her mouth trembling. "She's going to fight. For *me*."

She toys with her fingernail, rubbing the smooth tip against her thumb. I catch it and she lets me hold her hand a minute while her thoughts are elsewhere.

"I didn't think she was capable of that." Her lips twist. "She hasn't forgotten, right? That I'm not even one of the good princesses?"

Ella looks up when my fingertips skim her cheek. "She knows she just destroyed her bargaining position to protect a mouthy, online gamer, right?"

Excuse me. *My* mouthy, online gamer. We've wasted too much time already, and I want to skip to the part where she realizes she loves me.

"I have to do something," she says. "Now."

I look around the cramped closet. I mean, my lips are right here.

"Take me somewhere," she says, grabbing my wrist. "I have to think."

We end up at a coffeehouse on the road to Lindenholm. The building has the spare modern lines of a frame house, with black cladding in stark contrast to the brilliant green of the sun-dappled grove. The interior is warmly lit, and a single barista—backed by high shelves filled with vinyl records—takes one look at our faces, briefly registers Ella's princessness, and puts on a Coltrane album. She takes our order and directs us to a private booth next to a large window. I ought to feel like I've caught my breath, but when Ella is sitting opposite me, I am not calm.

The coffee arrives with a plate of warm danishes.

Last week I would have been pouring advice about diplomacy into her ears, but now the prime minister is targeting my princess. In the last hour, I went from feeling a duty to keep her from killing Torbald to wanting to dig the hole she buries him in. Apparently, I inherited the ruthlessness—and the limited imagination—of my Hanaya ancestors; always with the burying.

"He's winning," she says, watching the sunlight shift through the window.

"He's not winning."

"No? Freja is out of the succession. My position will be gone or radically curtailed tomorrow. Alma is going to have to be so careful to roll this thing out with Jacob, because having bagged a couple of hunting trophies, the prime minister won't stop trying for more."

I don't tease her about the dream of California sunshine and bottomless mimosas. If Torbald wins, that *could* be her future. I brush her cheek. She doesn't lean into it as she used to, but leans back and takes a drink.

"So what's our plan?" I ask, dropping my hand.

"*My* plan," she corrects.

I ignore that. "How do we take him down before he takes you down?"

"There's no need to involve you in my ruin."

I lift the mug and blow a cooling breath across the coffee, ruffling the surface "Hypocrite," I whisper.

Her back straightens. "That's the second time you've called me that."

The window frames a green and delicate wood, reclaimed from wildness with careful tending.

I repeat the words I've been hearing for months. "'Marc, you have to get Alix onboard with running the estate. She's dying to help you.'" I smile. "You've been like a broken record all spring. 'Don't do it alone, Marc. Don't carry it all on your own shoulders.' If that advice is so good, why aren't *you* taking it?"

Her lips curve with the shadow of a smile. "I only meant—"

I reach across the table, lacing my fingers with hers. She lets me touch her still. "The deal is that, when you have a couch to move, the people who love you are going to show up." I want to say more, but there are too many briars between me and this princess to hack them away in one afternoon.

"Those sound like the words of a man who's going to let his sister help manage his ancestral home," she says, brushing her thumb across mine. These marks of affection are unconscious to her, but I'm like an overheating server room with no kill switch. When they open up my insides, everything will be melted.

Ella is right, though. I can't palm Alix off with farmer's markets when she could be doing more. "Okay. I'll do it. I'll accept my sister's offer to help if you accept mine."

"I don't need—"

"Or I could send her to America. I'm sure Alix will find fulfillment sitting on the board of an HOA in Miami, handing out citations for improper lawncare."

She clicks her tongue and I tighten my fingers. "We both agree that the prime minister needs to be taken down a notch," I insist. "You need help."

She rolls her eyes, but she doesn't let go of me. "I thought you said it was insane and reckless to consider toppling a democratically elected government, which (a) is weak sauce—Torbald's governing coalition controls more than 57% of parliamentary seats, and they aren't in danger of anything but boorish leadership—if anything, I'd be doing them a favor; (b) we live in a constitutional monarchy, and he's undermining the monarchy part; and (c) you don't really want to help."

I grin and glance away, my eye caught by a piece of framed artwork hooked to the wall. The bright red embroidery floss looks like a string of fate. It curves and tangles back in on itself in a bold, graphic typeface. *Home is where them haters ain't.*

I release a laughing breath. From a narrow cot in Seong, to an oversized bed in a Handsel flat, to the cozy antique in Lindenholm, Ella has been with me all along. *Home.* When her walls are under attack, my scruples about what I owe my government and my oldest friend evaporate.

"You're getting help whether you want it or not," I say. She gives another light *tsk*. "I could execute a series of assignments tailored to my unique skill set."

"You *are* a very good kisser." She winks.

I love her.

"Anytime, of course," I say, rocking our hands. "I mean that I can hide your digital footprint behind so many firewalls and false leads that they'll still be looking for it when the glaciers melt."

"Alright," she surrenders, giving me a teasing two-fingered salute. "Do your duty. In the meantime, I'll close out my *SquadRun* account and wrap up this business of Torbald's whereabouts. Tonight, if possible."

"How?"

"I've got an idea." Her brows pucker and she takes a sip of coffee. "I wonder if Dahlia is in town."

I take notes of our plotting in an app, giving her editing privileges (practically a declaration of my intention to love her forevermore, if she cared to notice), when a text message pops up on my phone. "PM Announces Noon Presser to Reveal Identity of Trash Panda Princess". I turn the screen around to show her. We have less than twenty-four hours and we can't afford to waste time. When I drop her at the doors of the Summer Palace, I resist the urge to press a kiss on her lips.

Before my car makes it onto public roads I'm on the phone with Alix. "Listen closely," I say. "The woods next to the walled garden are to be regarded as hallowed ground—untouchable. Otherwise, you have the go-ahead to develop this hotel idea." She squeals and I punch the volume down. "Celebrate later. I have a bigger problem and I need your help."

"I'm suited up," she laughs. "Tom, too, of course."

"Ella is in trouble. Her online activities are about to be exposed. Can you convince her team to mop up her *SquadRun* history?"

"How did you know—"

"You know the anonymous runt who keeps running interference in the castle sequences?"

The silence stretches and stretches until she makes a strangled sound.

"Alix," I break through her questions. "One more thing. I'm trying to convince Ella to be my girlfriend, so any brainstorming you can do in that direction would be great."

33

COUNTERPOINT

ELLA

Well?

Send.

Dahlia hasn't checked in since receiving her assignment last night and I am chewing my fingernails.

Finally, the text bubbles bounce.

Edward didn't get in until 2 AM. Lights out at 3. I'm uploading some screenshots now.

What I asked of Dahlia is not technically illegal. Edward was a rotten boyfriend, always using her as a chauffeur, chef, and personal assistant—and I gambled that he'd be lazy enough to leave his cell phone connected to her car's Bluetooth. He could have disabled it at any time, but chose not to because he is a sloppy, cheating prat. You can make a fortune betting on the fecklessness of an aristocrat.

The plan was wonderfully simple, as all good plans are. Dahlia drove over to Ed's house in the middle of the night, waited for his Bluetooth to automatically connect—and scrolled through sensitive texts between him and his boss—the prime minister—on her dashboard screen.

You're an angel, I tell her.

Are you kidding me? she answers. *I am your faithful hench-man. We ride at dawn.* She signs off with a yawning emoji.

Père strolls into the breakfast room, and I navigate away from a donors list for the Blue-Greens to a webtoon called *Peach Blossom Billionaire and His Feral Fox-Bride*, idly swiping through the panels.

"Good morning. What are your characters up to?" Père asks, giving my screen a glance before making himself a tiny cup of espresso.

Be normal. Act normal. "The billionaire is sleeping on a bed of leaves outside a haunted mountain shrine with his new wife. I don't know how they're going to keep warm."

"Very good. Is he," he snaps his fingers for the correct word, "*tsundere*?" Cold and aloof until very much not. It's darling that Père keeps up on my interests.

"The *tsundere*-est," I answer.

Père sets his espresso aside. He leans back in his chair, crossing his legs at the knee, suddenly the picture of southern European elegance.

"You've been remarkably civilized this spring," he says. This is less a scold and more an observation.

I play with a stack of rings on my finger. This must be what Pavian detective work looks like. It's not an interrogation, but merely a chat, his urbane unconcern seeping into my vulnera-bilities, inviting me to talk.

"I'm trying to mind my own business."

"Not so, *adana*." *My girl.* "You are, how is it said, up to your barrettes in family business."

"That is *not* how it is said." I take apart a roll and spread chilled butter on one side, tearing at the soft substance. "You always pretend your Sondish isn't very good when you want us to be particularly attentive."

"Why would I do such a thing?" he asks, reaching for a news-paper, his eyes sparkling with amusement.

"It makes us feel like we're supposed to make allowances for your message and excuse the blunt speaking. I know you, Père."

He shrugs, his suit jacket moving with his body. "And I know you."

I glance up and feel, for the second time in as many days, a deep and unexpected contentment with my parents.

"I admire Freja's loyalty to Oskar," he says, shaking out the pages, turning them back. "You'll need it when you marry. Total loyalty to your spouse." He reads a headline aloud. "'Royal Order: Queen Helena Shrugs off Civil Control of Monarchy'. Your Mama made her formal offer to the government. She pro-poses that Freja will still attend official functions as a guest and wear the tiaras, but she will not take precedence over Clara any longer. It will be an arrangement that suits her social peculiari-ties."

Peculiarities? "That's not how you should speak."

"Yes, yes. God is Sondish and the only correct way to exist is Sondish." Another shrug. "But Sondmark steps so delicately around some truths that they never arrive at them. Freja has to work twice as hard to feel half as comfortable doing what you do so easily."

"Easily? I'm always fighting."

"About the smallest details. At your heart, you take to this like breathing…just like your mother. Tell me about Marc." Père pivots with deadly accuracy, catching me off guard.

"He's bringing Alix on board to manage Lindenholm."

He closes his eyes against the slanting rays of the morning sun and gives his head a little shake. "Sondmark likes to step so delicately around the truth," he repeats, his tone bland. "Contrive to understand what I mean."

My mouth goes dry. "I don't think this topic is appropriate to have with one's father."

Père smiles. "That sounds promising. Would you like me to take the boy aside and have a talk?"

I wish somebody would. "It wasn't like that."

Père, having disappeared behind the newspaper again, flips a corner down. "*Adana*, I am not a child to listen to fairy tales."

"We're friends. We decided to be friends."

"A good tactic."

My mouth is firm. "It's not a tactic. I admit it. We had kind of a thing…"

Père snorts.

"...but he's Noah's best friend. He would never take me seriously." I shake my head. "It's over now, and he's not acting like he's desperate to have me back."

"Counterpoint; I saw his hands." I blush hotly, and he retreats to his paper. "I know a good deal about loving someone you don't know how to say it to."

My fingers curl over on the table. Through a crack in a door, I saw how much my father still loves my mother. It was there in the easy way his arm held her around the waist, his whole frame absorbing her fury. I don't know if they will ever get back to the marriage they once had, but it is as clear as day that my father never left.

I shake my head. "Marc and I— Our lives are complicated."

"*Adana*, space is complicated. International diplomacy is complicated. What you were doing—" He slaps his hands together in a glancing blow. The case has been made. It's finished.

No. What Père witnessed was two friends and an old habit. If Marc wanted me forever, wouldn't I know?

I've been running myself ragged, trying to keep these feelings at bay, and I am tired. When this is all over, I'll ask Uncle Georg for his private island. I'll march over the whole of it, wearing a straw hat the size of a small yacht, and curse the day I fell in love with Marc van Heyden. I'll scrub out the intractable feelings with copious amounts of salt water and beachy cocktails, returning every year until those feelings are so small it would take an electron microscope to see them.

In the meantime, I force a laugh. "Be serious, Père. You know me. Sailing off into the sunset with Marc would make all the wrong people happy."

Père arches a brow. "You don't want him because he's a name on a dreaded marriage list?"

"That's it." My cheeks burn with the lie. My mother screamed at her prime minister about my preciousness and I can't unknow that she loves me, whether I make her happy or not. Still, I try to herd my father away from the truth—that I want Marc too much to accept a chummy, friendly kind of love. "You were caught in an arranged marriage, Père, wedded to a woman you hardly knew and packed off to a country you'd never seen. You would choose differently, I'm sure."

Père slaps the paper down in a sudden storm of irritation. "I would never have chosen another woman to be my wife. I knew it the moment I stepped off the plane and every day since."

The details of this meeting have faded into family myth. The grieving young queen, bound by a marriage contract signed by her parents, and an embattled young prince, fleeing his homeland with only his life. My curiosity is piqued. He knew it the moment he arrived?

I lean forward, but Caroline appears in the doorway and dips a curtsey. "Your Royal Highness," she says, speaking to Père. "Her Majesty requests your presence."

"What about?"

Caroline flicks a glance at me.

Père waves her off. He brushes my cheek with the back of his hand before he goes. "No matter what happens today, *adana*, your parents will fight for you."

Webtoon billionaire shenanigans, even of the always entertaining "oh no, we have to keep each other warm in this narrow bed of dry leaves all night even though I hate you and your impressively sculpted abs" variety, can't keep my attention. As soon as my father leaves, I open another tab to my *SquadRun* Friction server, and begin to type.

"Re: Death of a Trash Panda Princess

Dear Squaddies, we've had an amazing run but it's time to hang up my leather flack jacket. Please know that marauding with this rag-tag group of scoundrels and turtle-dads was the best part of my week when I needed it most. Love, TPP."

Send.

These were only digital connections. I don't know these people. Not really. Aside from Alix and Linus, I never met them in real life and wouldn't recognize them if we passed in the street. But they're the reason I've lasted the better part of a decade in the royal fish bowl without going completely insane, and I feel tearful as the connection is cut.

A distant grandfather clock chimes the hour and I take a sharp breath. There is no time to waste. I dive into my email cache, scrolling through Edward's text messages to find that they contain reminders about interviews, appointments at the spa, and meetings with Girl Trackers groups. I look for patterns and keep every name on a list.

A message pops up on my phone. Marc. "Sent Werner to check hotel logs and restaurant reservations in the Frederick-platz vicinity every Tuesday. There are some names that keep popping up. You might want to crosscheck."

The most notable name is Valdemar Stennum, a possible match to 'VS' in Edward's texts. Valdemar is the younger broth-er of Sondish Petroleum CEO, Anker Stennum. I know him well. For the next hour, I keep my head down, doing more digital footwork, digging into social media accounts until it becomes so complicated that the sticky notes spread out on the table start to look conspiratorial. I uncover a report he submit-ted to Parliament proposing drilling in the wildlife reserve near Max's cottage. He authored a press release for Sondish Petro-leum's new government contract—just before environmental activists flooded the company parking lot and planted marsh grass in protest.

Torbald and Stennum.

I think about what I know about the prime minister. His wife comes from old money, but I double-check his address, bringing up the street view. Yes, the family home is relatively modest, all things considered, and I calculate the projected sale price and what kind of income it would take to sustain a place of that size. This is the kind of math they teach you at Saint Sissela's.

I do a mental sum of his expenses, including tuition bills, voice and dance lessons, and family vacations. It's close, but there might be shortfalls. Perhaps Torbald's corruption is as simple as accepting bribes from business leaders for access. Or maybe he's having an affair?

My finger scrolls back and forth on a photo of him walking his girls to school. I zoom in on his happy face and strong grip. Something feels off. For all his faults, Torbald is a family man.

I stand on a dining room chair, trying to make sense of the explosion of information spread across the table in the few short hours left before the press conference. Being a government official doesn't pay extravagantly, but connections are made and palms are greased. Egos become inflated.

I can see a number of avenues for corruption, but I can't bug a private dining room. There's only so much information I can lock down before I outrun my luck and get myself caught. Do I have enough to spook him away from going after my family?

I begin synthesizing the information into an iron-clad timeline, looking for ways to use rock-solid information to make it appear as though I have the whole story, when my phone buzzes.

Marc. "Turn on the news."

My stomach slithers. Has the story of my online activities leaked ahead of schedule?

The computer screen shows *Neer* Hjefdal sitting on an upright kitchen chair across from a man sprawled in a massive beanbag, a riot of framed art over his shoulder. Is that—I lean closer—Linus? Dragonslayer2? He has my secrets, that little worm. I trusted him.

Neer Hjefdal is using his hard news voice. "You're telling me that your online persona—"

"Avatar, my dude." Linus straightens the nearest canvas.

"—is Trash Panda Princess? *You* are the princess everyone is looking for?"

I drop into my chair with a thump. Linus is not exposing me. He's providing cover.

"Yep." He grins. "I'm your Cinderella. My job is to inspire the worthy to perform noble sacrifice." I recognize the words of Staggering_Indifference, tossed off so casually. "Anyway, reality is a construct, my dude."

Neer Hjefdal declines to fact-check the metaphysics of that. "Rumors spread that the identity of the person who leaked Hereditary Grand Duke Pietor of Himmelstein's affair—the scandal that turned Sondmark on its head last month—might trace back to Princess Alma herself, another senior member of the royal family, or a notable public figure. Can you explain how you gained access to the photos?"

"First off, I *am* notable. You can catch my art at the Aunslev Public House on the north side of the village, a couple of kilometers from the ring road right now. They acquired a piece I made featuring Queen Helena." He leans into the microphone. "The bottle caps were ethically-sourced. Second of all, I admit it wasn't cool, messing with my sister's phone but, like, I lost the remote and needed to download an app. It's not my fault she had that stuff on there."

"And your sister is?"

"She works for the man up at the palace."

"The man? She works for the royal household?"

"That's what I said. She had this folder on her phone and I put two-and-two together." He waves a hand. "It's not like I broke them up. People can blame me all day because the economic treaties are in peril or whatever, but a hereditary grand duke who couldn't keep his hands to himself was never going to bag a hottie like Alma."

"Never?" *Neer* Hjefdal follows his subject right off a cliff. "How do you know?"

Linus cocks his head at the newsreader's ignorance. I swear he was—within the range of a turtle-dad—completely normal. Nothing like the California surfer persona he's serving now. "The guy from Vorburg—Crown Prince Jacob—he's a Scorpio. You can see him practically panting on his knees when she walks into a room. You think a guy like that is going to let a cute little Leo pass on by just because a Libra placed dibs? Think again."

Bless *Neer* Hjefdal. He's fighting for his life.

"You broke into your sister's private files pertaining to sensitive royal matters and uploaded it to a popular internet forum. What did you hope to accomplish with your actions?"

"I'm no monarchist. As a matter of fact, those people can—"

A crash is heard from an adjoining room, startling both interviewer and guest, but they soon shake it off and resume their discussion.

"It's lame the princess had to hide her break-up just so some unionists wouldn't freak out. It's lame Torbald is trying to dig up something about my avatar and pin it on a princess." Linus's gaze flicks away and back, like he's scared of something over

Hjefdal's shoulder. "And, while we're at it, it's kinda lame of a prime minister to be harassing Freja for locking down her man, you know?"

34

BRIBERY

ELLA

Things have never been better.

In the following days, the palace is busier than ever. The machinery of monarchy pivots deftly around Freja and her delicate condition, but, for the first time, I am absolutely certain that they would pivot just as carefully around me.

When Fairy Godmothers, my patronage dedicated to fulfilling the wishes of critically ill children, asks me for an urgent favor, I attack the assignment with the dedication and intensity of one of my *SquadRun* raids. Once upon a time, I would have argued that I could show up for "tea with a princess" in trainers, sweat-wicking fabrics, and a pair of stretch trousers. I would have settled for a shirtwaist dress and a pair of flats. Now, I reserve the Chevres Salon, arrive in a quinceanera-sized ballgown with two extra crinolines, every medal and badge pinned to my sash, and balance Alma's murderously heavy Lowenwald diamond kokoshnik on the best tiara hair this family has ever seen.

If any palace brickwork needs repairing, my make-up could be scraped off with a trowel and applied in place of mortar, but I pass out plastic scepters and tiaras, drink tea with my pinky sticking straight out, and show everyone the proper way to curtsey. The press eat it up, giving the rest of my family a breather for the day.

This is the life I choose now, and I'm very nearly perfectly happy about it. Anyway, I've stopped living with one foot out the door.

Alix invites me out for a pre-bachelorette party hen night. "Just us," she says. "We'll do karaoke."

I could use an outlet. I underestimated how effective Marc's kisses were at taking me out of my head, and I feel his absence in ways too numerous to tally. In lieu of being seen and understood by the man I've been in love with for ten years, an off-key rendition of BLUSH's "Possessed By a Maiden Ghost" will have to suffice.

Nordic people prefer to escape the bleak contemplations of death by going to the sauna, withstanding the rigors of brimstone preemptively, so karaoke bars are a novelty. Alix books us a private room at the only good club in Handsel. I flip through the music offerings until she clears her throat.

"Here's the thing," she says. "We're not here for karaoke." Alix takes out a tablet and taps a few keys, connecting her device to the massive screen on one wall.

"What's this?" I ask, though it's obviously an empty video conference. Her username, LoveShush, displays in the corner, and she fiddles with the camera until we are properly centered. Soon, other members pop in. Staggering_Indifference patches in from Washington D.C. Her name is Jess, and she's a graduate student who doesn't mind gaming in the middle of the night. Dragonslayer2 I recognize as Linus. His room is a jumble of art supplies and large, half-finished pieces. The outrageous mannerisms from the interview have vanished. BeastlyDutchOaths is Willem, a secondary school teacher in the Netherlands. These are my oldest gaming friends, with me from the beginning.

"Hi guys," I wave. "I'm Ella, I'm a princess in Sondmark."

"No kidding," Jess says. "Your voice has been in our headsets for years and you know a freakish amount about constitutional monarchies. Some of us already figured it out."

"I didn't," Linus breaks in.

"How are you all here?" I ask, my heart tightening. I've been through the hardest breakup of my life, and I haven't been able to take solace in destroying a medieval warlord with the best squaddies a girl could have. It hurts from morning to night, and I've been holding on to sanity with sheer grit and the threat of disappointing of my ancestors.

"Alix got us together," Willem says. "She rounded us up on another Friction server and sent out a message to scrub your history. You needed help and we came."

My smile is wobbly, but it's the first real one I've produced in what feels like forever. "Saving the princess?"

He shakes his head, the connection glitching and smoothing. "Helping a friend. Linus did more than anyone."

"Who knew assuming your identity would be so lucrative?" Linus laughs. "I've sold three art pieces, and I'm in talks to do more."

"Don't give him too much credit," Alix cuts in. "His sister made it worth his while."

"Caroline?"

Linus shifts in his computer chair. "Your mom told Caro that you were behind the gamer tag, and she recognized it from my computer. Later, my sister approached me... Approached," he grunts. "She pinned me down."

My mother's secretary? The one who never steps a toe out of place? I remember the interview on national tv, the crash after it looked like Linus was about to launch an anti-monarchy rant... Was Caroline swinging a rolling pin?

"I would have done it for nothing, but I negotiated up to a year of her cleaning Boris's turtle enclosure and keeping her hands off my controllers."

We laugh, we trade stories, and we almost convince Jess to ditch her loser boyfriend. When Alix drives me back to the palace at the end of the long night, she asks if I'm dating anyone.

"My social calendar is as empty as the Felslot plains," I say. "No one is interested in," I clear my throat, tight with emotion, "capturing the castle."

"Keep it like that, will you?" Her gaze is sharp, but I can't meet it. "I might have someone..."

"Sure," I murmur. Another finance bro. Maybe Tom has a cousin. My future has to start sometime.

I throw Alix a proper bachelorette party on a riverboat, complete with an elaborate drone show of exploding hearts, revolving hearts, and arrow-pierced hearts overhead. Half the population of Handsel turns out to watch, and there is talk in government circles of making this an annual event. We are wearing sequined rompers, but Mama commends me for threading the needle between innocent, girlish fun and excessive displays of wealth.

Things have never been better—except that I am constantly checking my phone. Marc texts and it's strictly platonic. He sends cat memes and the occasional GIF. He informs me that my trashpandaprincess accounts can now be linked to a dizzying number of dead ends. So this is really it. We're really over.

Several days after the cancelled press conference, I arrange a secret meeting at Minty's to tie up my loose ends. I work through Arne, relying on his discretion, and I am comfortable in the knowledge that there is no record of my request anywhere. I am situated in a tiny anteroom on an upper floor when Prime Minister Torbald enters.

"Your Royal Highness," he says, delivering the briefest bow. "Last week's interview... I don't know how you got that crackpot to stand in your place, but you've only kicked the can down the road. It's going to be all the worse when it blows up in your face."

"Tea?" I ask, lifting a pot. I hate tea, but I had to set a stage. Mama has taught me a thing or two about dressing for your audience. I am wearing nondescript business attire—not so well dressed that it will offend his democratic sensibilities, but not so casual that he will think I don't take him seriously. If this does blow up in my face, it won't be because I showed up in a graphic hoodie.

Torbald settles himself at the table, and I begin.

"I have credible evidence that you have been engaging in a bribery scheme. We—" My cheek tucks. He probably thinks I'm being pretentious and using the royal we, but I haven't been alone. I've had Dahlia and Yasmin on my team, as well as Marc, Alix, Caroline, Linus, and the rest of my squaddies. "We have enough information to make things difficult with the press."

"Bribery?" he laughs. "You think I'm being bribed?"

I release a breath. "No. No more than your average politician, actually. Your wife's investment strategy is beating nearly every other model on the market, but that's not enough to get you thrown out of office. It took me a while to work it out. I've got you showing up at secret locations and attending some suspicious meetings affiliated with Sondish Petroleum."

"The Stennum thing is not what it looks like." He takes a hasty swallow of tea. I am correct. This is where his weakness lies.

"I agree," I answer. "Since you were kind enough to share your plans for my family, I've been tracking you, digging into your past… One of the constants is how much you love the press."

He shrugs. "A politician has to manage his image."

"True." I take a tiny sip and try to hide how much I hate it. This tastes like licking a football pitch. "You know what's so unusual about you? You never use your family. They would be a powerful political asset if you put them in front of the cameras more often. Pretty wife. Cute girls." His eyes are watchful but his body goes very still. "You daughters attend a private school. Brunhild Academy, yes?"

His hand turns into a fist. "You'll leave my girls out of this."

"You've been meeting Valdemar Stennum. Did you know that his wife is the chairman of Saint Sissela's board of governors? Jeneke. Their daughter Yasmin is one of my oldest friends. I was in and out of that house growing up—having stay-lates, braiding each other's hair, gossiping at all hours. I imagine she has a lot of sway when it comes to admissions."

He shifts, and the chair creaks under his weight. "It's true that I want to get my daughters into a better private school. Is that a crime? Citizens of Sondmark like to pretend we live in an egalitarian paradise, but I still have to bow to a queen every week, don't I? Someone always comes out on top. Why not my girls? I have nothing to hide."

I take a sip of tea and promise myself that the next time I corner a politician, I'll plan the beverage situation better. "You're hiding because there's nothing more socially contemptible than someone who knows he's not good enough for the company he keeps. Do you think they can smell the desperation?" *He* can smell it. That's why he went to such lengths to conceal his locations. That's why he couldn't approach the Stennums with a direct bribe, cloaking his meetings with Valdemar behind the less humiliating veneer of political back-slapping. That's why his eyes shift uneasily. He wants to hide, even now. He hates this—being seen for what he is—and I let him twist in the sensation for a few moments.

I'm human and schadenfreude is delicious, but that's not why I'm here. I take a card from my clutch—more adult than a paper torn from a BLUSH notebook, removed from a *Roar's Mansion* backpack—and scrawl on the back of it.

"When you threatened my mother's children, this," I point at him, "is exactly how she felt. She can be difficult. She's ruthless and hard-edged. She buries her virtues under layers of protocol and duty, but she won't make deals that target her children. She will never let what happened with Freja happen again."

He sputters. I would have loved it if it had been bribery or an affair—I would have tossed the information to the press and relevant government oversight bodies without a second thought—but people are complicated. Even terrible prime ministers are allowed to love their children, and I won't turn them into pawns.

I am my mother's daughter.

I pass the card across the table, and he turns it over to find Jeneke Stennum's private number. "Whether it comes with my personal recommendation is up to you," I say. "Your poll numbers are tanking this week because it looks like you ran a vulnerable young mother-to-be out of her job. My offers don't get better from here."

He flicks the corner of the card with the pad of his thumb, his face a war of emotions. "What do you want?"

"I want your support for the monarchy."

His mouth sets. "Does that require my resignation?"

He might do it, if pushed. I've seen the embargoed pictures—those girls are his sun and moon. But I close my eyes and mentally chant *telehealth portals, telehealth portals, telehealth portals.*

"You're fortunate my sister is content to leave behind the life of a working royal," I say.

He releases a thread of air. "But?" He's not new at the negotiating table.

"You're going to leave our family out of your politics. You're going to stop speaking as though Oskar Velasquez has damaged the purity of Sondmark, and that a few thousand immigrants are a boot to shove your children down the social ladder." I take a breath. Freja doesn't need my help, but I am in a position to help the people she loves. "I understand that there are debates worth having about all of these topics—and that it is my duty to stay out of them—but you're going to propose a fixed citizenship test with clear, understandable rules. Make it as difficult as you want, but stop moving the target."

"What's the catch?" he asks, wary.

The Ella I once was would have staged a public takedown, embroiling her family in weeks of drama and weakening the monarchy. The Ella I've become this spring makes a more strategic choice. My deal is inspired by Marc. Everybody wins. Rivals become allies. "No catch," I assure him. "As long as you keep this from my family, we can both leave this room with what we want."

He *uhms* and *ohms*, but in the end we shake on it. His daughters are Saint Sissela girls now. They are under my protection forever.

I catch glimpses of Marc on public access television during this time, entering the Grousehof in his parliamentary robes on business I can't guess at. When he doesn't have to keep running home to see me, I suppose he has loads of time for extracurriculars. The sight of him makes my heart hurt.

Clara and Alma, possibly noticing that something is off, take me running—which is about the meanest thing they could think of. Worse, it doesn't even keep my mind off Marc. I think about how he would have made me climb onto his back a couple of kilometers in and jogged me up to my suite and told me how brave I am in between giving me kisses.

It's three days before Alix's wedding when I corner Caroline in her office, desperate for some occupation. "Are you in trouble," I bump my chin at my mother's door, "since your brother admitted to leaking the photos of Alma off your phone?"

Her lips press. "She knows it was really you because of the prime minister."

"Yeah, but I've not been—" I slice a thumb across my neck. "Why?"

Caroline lifts her palm. "She asked me if you knew Linus, if he had a drug problem, and if you two were...seeing each other." Her lips twitch with a barely-suppressed smile. "I told her she had nothing to worry about on that score."

"They're talking about you in the press," I whisper. Caroline isn't important enough to be a headline on the front page, but the social columns are full of items like, "The Queen's Right Hand," "The Power Behind the Throne," and "What Else is on *Vrouw* Tiele's Phone?"

She waves her hand. "They'll move on to somebody more captivating."

"We all have reasons to pray that Noah will get serious about somebody," I smile.

I hear my mother clear her throat with a tiny cough, and I just about leap out of my skin. From the doorway, she beckons me into her office, and I take my spot on the carpet while she leans against the front of her desk. She tells me I've been endangering the monarchy, and that I've been irresponsible when it comes to my online activities. She tries to put some of her old bluster into it, but it rings hollow.

"The gamer...name?" she says.

"Tag," I supply.

"The gamer tag is dead, and you're suspended from social media until further notice. A member of staff will run your account until you rediscover what little sense you were born with. Have I made myself clear?"

It's adorable, really. I can't take any of this *Queen Helena wielding a bloody sword* stuff seriously anymore. I *know* I am her precious child. I know that sword will be turned on my enemies. I nod and give her a big squeeze she isn't entirely comfortable with. "Sure thing."

I return to my suite, but there's a lump in my throat and my chest feels hollowed out. It feels like grief. I don't know why. Torbald has been neutralized, my mother has let me off with the smallest rebuke, and I have taken on my royal role with a new sense of purpose and determination.

A tear slips down my cheek.

Things have never been better.

35

KISSED AGAIN

ELLA

I open the door to an insistent knock, and Clara bursts into my suite, dragging Freja behind her. Alma slips in and shuts the door, locking it for good measure. "We saw you leave Mama's office," Clara says. "What's going on?"

I sink against the arm of my sofa, more lost than I've ever been, and twist the toe of my shoe on the floorboard. "Nothing."

"There it is," Alma says, pointing at my foot. "You're lying. She's lying. Marc told me what to watch for."

Traitor. I kick off my shoes and grab the remote, powering up the television.

"You've been weirdly punctual," Freja says, right on my heels.

I scramble onto my bed and sit with my back on the headboard, scrolling to that one episode of *Unwritten Destiny* where the female lead kisses the male lead upside down really thoroughly before he goes in for triple bypass surgery. The way the camera lingers on his craning neck has never failed to pull me out of a crisis.

Alma and Freja crowd onto the bed.

"You showed up to that tea party in a ballgown," Alma says, tossing a bag of peppermint puffs into my lap.

Clara piles on last, chucking a box of the good tissues I keep in my bathroom into the middle of our circle. "You're getting low."

I miss Marc. My heart hurts. I can't talk about it to anyone.

I throw the box of tissues across the room. "It's been a rough couple of days. I'm not dying or anything."

"Of course, dearest."

"We know you're not dying."

"I came for snacks."

Their words flop over each other like a net full of fish, awkward and disquieting, and I take a breath. "Why are you treating me like I've got days to live?" I ask, pointing to my wrist where Freja has hold of me.

"You are exhibiting an unhealthy amount of royal compliance," Clara explains.

"I have a theory." Alma blushes and clears her throat. "It's a crackpot theory—"

"My favorite," I return.

"You were upset the other night after Freja's announcement, and when I came in I saw that you and—"

A small plink against the windowpane interrupts her.

"I saw you and Ma—"

Another plink. Another. The Summer Palace is old and emits many noises, but these are too regular for chance.

"Go see what it is." I shove Clara off the bed, and she trots to the window, throwing back the French doors to the cool night air.

A shout rises from below. "Princess Ella Victoria Chiara Brunhild of Sondmark!"

"Ella." Clara chokes on a laugh, turning a surprised face to us. "You're going to die."

I know who it is. It's Marc. My good pal Marc. His recent text messages have been full of GIFs of Seongan actors making a fist with the caption, "*Whui-ho.*" I take them to mean "Hang in there, little buddy." I take them as a daily punctuation mark to signal the beginning of Marc and Ella's Friendship: Phase Two, Electric Boogaloo. My throat thickens with tears, and I want to tell my sisters to put a cauldron of pitch on the boil. We have to drive him off. I can't see him when I still don't know how to pretend I'm not in love with him.

"Ella," Freja prods me in the back, her touch as gentle as the business end of a pike. "He's calling for you. It's polite to answer."

"Thank you. I'm just learning that," I shoot back, my tone acid.

She prods the sensitive spot on my waist and shoves me off the bed. "What do you want?" I shout, flouncing to the window in my huffiest huff.

I'm not prepared for the sight of Marc on the terrace, leaning against a balustrade. A thousand lifetimes would not have prepared me. He's wearing a navy blue polo shirt and one denim-clad leg is crossed over the other. Ordinary enough. But, when he catches my eye, he pushes a hand through his hair, and the muscle of his arm strains against the cuff of his sleeve. The motion lifts the hem of the shirt, exposing a shocking amount of abs to just be flashing themselves in my great-grandmother's ornamental garden.

I choke. "Couldn't you find a shirt to cover you?"

"You like it better when I don't." He grins, lifting his arm a few more centimeters.

I clap my hands over my eyes. I know exactly what this is. Marc is recreating the cover of *Seongan Vogue* from nine years ago. August edition. I have ten physical copies just in case solar flares wipe out global data storage and civilization has to start from scratch. One of them is in the drawer of my nightstand.

"What are you doing here?" I ask, doubling my hands over my eyes when I catch myself peeking.

"Don't pretend you don't think I'm hot," he says, loud enough to alert half the country.

"I don't," I insist, feeling the sudden rush of my sisters all around me.

"*Elskede*," he says. In my thousand lifetimes, each version of me pauses, longing for that word to be said in just that way. This is your turn, they seem to say.

"*Elskede*," he repeats, "the time stamp on your latest install-ment of *Temptation of the Elf Prince* would suggest otherwise."

My cheeks burn and my hands drop. This week has been difficult and lonely. There was no *SquadRun*. Alix is busy re-ceiving her first guests. There was no Marc.

To keep myself out of trouble, I wrapped up that old, episod-ic story. My readers have been waiting for years and deserved some kind of resolution. My throat tightens as I mount a bril-liant defense. "That fanfic has nothing to do with you."

He nods, casually, easily. "It's a coincidence that your Elf Prince is Asian-coded and has my forehead scar—and he's better at kissing than your red-haired heroine imagined he would be."

I squeak, but I don't have an answer. The Elf Prince is defi-nitely Marc.

"Wait." Freja's soft voice cuts through my mortification. "Wait. When Alma came to us with her genuinely insane theory that you and Marc might be a thing, I thought maybe, just maybe, your old crush had resurrected itself. I was prepared to feel sorry for you," she says, her words vibrating with outrage. She aims an accusing finger down at our brother's oldest friend. "Have you been dating Marc van Heyden? Is that what's been happening all this time?"

It doesn't feel like the right time to explain that it wasn't really dating. "We were keeping things low-key," I grit, shooting a glare at Marc.

"You were keeping things secret," she shouts, loud enough to drive the bats from the attic. "You yap about everything. You have dragged secrets out of me I wouldn't give up under torture, but you didn't breathe a word about Marc this whole time? You pushed me out of your life for a man?" Freja appeals to Alma to settle our dispute. "I came to smooth things over and she practically shut the door in my face."

Alma slides me a "For shame, Ella" look.

"I didn't have to loop you in because this wasn't ever going to go anywhere," I protest.

I look down at Marc, who slides me a "For shame, Ella" look. Then his eyes shift with subtle intensity, and I shiver with the effort of holding his gaze, every nerve humming with some promise, not yet satisfied.

What game is he playing?

"She shoved me into the closet, Freja," he says, never glancing away from my face. Arrogant. Taunting. "Forgive her, though. She wasn't thinking straight. I'd been kissing her senseless."

How long have we been keeping our secrets—our hands grazing in the fullness of my gauzy dress, our eyes meeting across an ancient pool, our lips— There have been more kisses than a whole decade of lonely nights. Now he's telling everyone.

"This is my great-grandmother's ornamental garden," I blurt. "You're being inappropriate."

His mouth tilts with a dangerous smile. "Freja, I'll bring her around when she's ready to grovel," he calls up to my sister, "but we've got some things to work out. Are you coming down, *elskede*, or am I coming up?"

"Stop calling me that," I shout, curling my hands around the wrought-iron railing. I can't survive this if he doesn't mean it. I can't. The sheer terror of not knowing bubbles up as fury. "Send me a cat meme if you want to talk. A chirpy little *whui-ho*."

His brows gather. "How can you be upset about cat memes, woman? I was busy this week and I couldn't chance saying too much over text. I wanted to be encouraging. I hoped you would understand—"

"Understand what? That we're definitely friends still?" I give him two aggravated thumbs up. "We're definitely that."

"Ella," he scolds, crossing the terrace to the base of the palace walls. Thick vines curl up the ancient structure and he tugs on them, testing his weight. What is this? I shake my head. Marc has a profound respect for the monarchy and an impeccable public image. He's bluffing.

My certainty evaporates when he lifts his foot.

"Any news from the prime minister?" he asks, hauling himself onto the first string of foundation stones.

Still bluffing.

"He's going to get his daughters into Saint Sissela's," I say. "That's what he really wanted."

"Your doing?" Marc hauls himself to the next string of stones, his hands gripping a mass of vines. The upper branches quiver, but he's going to stop any second. He doesn't have a safety harness and he can't mean to climb all the way up.

I swallow away the dryness in my throat. "I only gave him some contact info."

"What did you get in return?" He leans away from the walls with one arm, testing and rejecting several handholds, and looks up at me in a way that sends heat through my veins.

My voice is thick. "A standardized immigration test. I've been turning my app into a general quiz about Sondish culture and history which should boost the pass rates. It's an elopement gift."

Marc tips his head back, craning his neck. "You could use some help with the interface and roll-out. Your involvement would be untraceable. When you commit your crimes, I'll always clean your fingerprints off the glass."

I inhale suddenly. Hope hurts. Time without number, it has splintered through my heart with the swing of its sword. Stomping in with heavy boots, ransacking, destroying. If I let it in again—

Marc holds my gaze, and the seconds stretch between us. This time, hope comes as a friend.

Freja makes a strangled sound in her throat. "The immigration thing? Ella, I love you for this. Oskar will love you for it, too." She leans over the balcony. "Be good to her, Marc, even when she's beastly."

"I like a challenge," he grunts, his face suddenly serious.

My breath catches and my hands feel unsteady. Is this possible? Marc and I are nothing alike. He wears linen suits, dark sunglasses, and silk ties to boiling-hot tennis matches. He deserves a self-contained goddess whose clothes are always crisp and whose angles are always right.

I try to imagine this perfect woman, but she won't material-ize.

My mind is busy remembering all the straw hats he brought along just in case I burned, his laughter at my improper jokes, and the way he would tuck my flyaway curls behind my ear. I think of all his crumpled programs, used to fan the back of my neck.

Watching his progress, my thoughts are like a herd of cat-tle, preparing to ford a stream, bunching up at the riverbank, watching the rushing water, terrified and dizzy with excitement at the same time. *Vede.* This is it. Marc is coming for me where everyone can see. He deserves a goddess but he's getting a grem-lin. There's no taking this back. I swear, if he falls I'm going to kill him.

Just as I'm getting used to the idea of being kissed again, a shaft of light falls across the terrace and my brother strides into view.

"What in the hell are you doing?" Noah's thunderous gaze bounces from me to his best friend, and I have never wanted to assassinate the future head of a government more.

But Marc's attention remains fixed on me, gaze warming my skin. His tone is mild. "I'm going to kiss your sister in another minute. When she's had enough of that, I'm going to ask her to start dating me with a view to matrimony."

"She doesn't need you to make a noble sacrifice," Noah growls. "She's got spreadsheets."

"He's *on* the spreadsheet, you idiot," I shout.

"I'm at the top of the list." Marc looks at me again. "*Elskede*, don't turn me down just for that. I promise you I can be profoundly inappropriate."

My eyes dance. He's already doing a bang up job with the flashing abs and the climbing walls. My heart is beating so hard I can feel it in my palms.

"Stop making passes at my sister," my brother barks. "And come down so I can knock your teeth in—" Noah reaches for the vines but Caroline, appearing out of nowhere, canons into him.

They stumble back a few paces, and he holds her, the both of them panting with surprise. She scoops a fall of hair out of her face and seems to regain her footing. When he moves to the wall, Caroline reaches for him again, placing her hand on my brother's sleeve.

"Noah," she whispers, shaking her head. The gesture is so little and yet it carries the weight of a command. Clara gasps.

Noah checks. I wait for him to pour out his royal wrath—using words like *temerity* and *presumption*—but it never comes. When he drops back, Caroline retreats through the open door.

My brother straightens his tie. "We'll settle this later," he clips.

"It's already settled," Marc says, sparing his best friend a glance. "Ella is my girl. You should go find your own."

I imagined Marc's loyalty to Noah and the Crown as a genetically altered gorilla, rampaging on a remote, skeleton-littered island. I thought it would end up destroying me if I got in the way of it, but it's only grumpy and human-sized now. Noah fixes his jaw, inhales sharply, and departs.

Marc continues his climb until he's within kissing distance.

"Watch out," he tells me. My sisters shuffle back, eyes wide, holding hands like finalists in a beauty pageant, and I don't breathe until he lands the vault onto the balcony.

I rush into his arms. "You idiot," I breathe.

He holds me like he has done a thousand times this spring, and I feel like the door of a vault when the tumblers fall into place. Secure. Safe as solid gold. When I'm here, I never worry if I'm not enough or way too much. For this man, I am just right.

"Cat memes?" I remind him. "Nothing but cat memes and *whui-ho* for a whole week?"

He nuzzles into me. "I was afraid I was going to tell you that I love you over text," he says. He lifts my face for a soft kiss. "I do."

I close my eyes and burrow into him, reading the signs secreted in between bottles of Vestfyn and first-thing-in-the-morning selfies.

I touch the soft flesh of his side and he claps a restraining hand over my fingers. "Don't be mad about the cat memes. I've been busy getting you something you'll really like."

My room is filled with Marc's gifts. "I like *you*," I breathe.

He rewards me with another kiss. "Don't stop there."

"My sisters need to leave," I say, laughing against his lips.

"Not yet." He lifts his watch to check the time. Half past the hour, and a little bit over. "Alma, be a dear. Look up some parliamentary news I embargoed until about a minute ago and read it out."

She's already scrolling. *"In a stunning turn of events, Parliament voted for the repeal of"—"* She shrieks, tosses the phone to Clara, and pushes me out of Marc's arms, hugging him around the waist. Clara stares at the screen, then shoves the phone into Freja's hands. My littlest sister is bawling by the time she works her way under Marc's arm.

Freja, who hugs no one but her husband, passes me the phone and reaches for Marc's hand, holding it in a death grip. Her face is twisted with emotion.

I pull up the news and read. *"Hereditary peer* Neerheid *van Heyden introduced an act of parliament to overturn a significant portion of the Marriages and Succession Act of 1798..."*

I fan my face with both hands, eyes stinging with unshed tears. Does he know what this means? No man could possibly understand as he does. A massive boulder, pressing in on me and my sisters with each breath for as long as we have been alive, has shifted.

Even with his hands full, Marc reaches out to me, brushing his fingers across my cheek. I catch them, kiss them, and continue to read, leaning into his palm. *"It passed with overwhelming support, bringing the number of royal personages who must secure government permission to marry from five places in the line of succession down to one. Parliamentary watchers suggest it was due, in large part, to recent overreaches by Prime Minister Torbald,* Vrouw *Velasquez's pregnancy, as well as an interview with noted*

Sondish artist, Linus Tiele, also known as Trash Panda Princ ess.'" I choke with a laugh, the words tumbling from my lips. *"'Though the heir to the throne, Crown Prince Noah, must still, by law, seek Her Majesty and her minister's permission to marry, the amended act will allow the royal princesses to choose whom they wed,'"* my voice has risen to a shout, *"without the consent of the government.'"*

I squeeze my eyes shut. All my life I imagined my wedding as a gauntlet of legalities. I imagined that my tender feelings, if I was allowed to have any for my future husband, would be smothered by article this and subsection that. I imagined myself in a sheath dress and pearls on the steps of the Grousehof, emotions withering under the dark, unblinking glare of a thousand cameras. But now— I take a breath and then another, my lungs burning as I try to wrap myself around this new freedom.

"What about Freja?" I ask.

"It's not retroactive," he murmurs, his words carrying regret. "I tried. I—"

"I don't care," Freja declares. "I don't. Oh, Marc. Ella is crying."

Marc rubs a thumb over my cheek, chasing away tears. I scrub a hand under my chin, catching more.

This is the life I choose. My family is still difficult—and I still have to get up next month, wrangle myself into heels and stockings, and sweat through every kind of ridiculous engagement. I shake my head. But this life— I can love it now.

Another tear slips down my cheek.

"There are too many people on this balcony," I say, peeling through my sisters, aiming strategic kicks to get them moving. "You all need to leave, right now."

Alma grimaces as I slip into Marc's arms. "I can't get used to this."

"*Get* used to it," I tell her, working my way in more deeply, only truly content when I hear the soft close of the mechanized door.

"Did you mean it?" I ask. "Do you really want us to start—" He climbed up the side of a palace for me and I can't even complete a sentence.

"Yes." His tone is firm. "I want to date with a view to ma-tri—"

I slap my palm over his mouth and my face flames. "We haven't even been on one date."

The words ring false as soon as they leave my lips. Of course we've been on dates. It didn't matter what we called them. It didn't matter what little story we told ourselves about our motives and goals.

I think of my avatar in *BRIx*, hefting one block at a time, each pixelated segment mined and moved. It doesn't look like anything up close, but when you stand back, you see a castle. All spring, kiss by kiss by kiss, Marc and I have been building a future.

He peels my hand from his mouth, lacing our fingers together. "I'll give everyone a minute to adjust to the idea of us. When we seal this deal, I don't want to be tearing out of the Grousehof just to beat the news. I don't want to be in a rush."

"Rush?" I laugh, placing a kiss in the smooth hollow of his throat. He makes a low sound and curls against me. I look up and hook a slim finger under his sleeve. "You made time to find the tiniest shirt in Handsel."

He grins. "I didn't want to risk showing up in a suit and tie, bearing roses and your mother's stamp of approval. You would have run me off."

"I wouldn't," I say, suddenly serious. Here it is. No more trying to be cool. "I would have told you I love you." There is a catch in my throat. "I do."

I thought I knew Marc's face, memorized its lines and expressions over years of patient study, but I've never seen it like this. Like a saint at his prayers and a child on his birthday. Like he has counted the days of his life and found them too few. Like he believes in forever. Like he has to.

"I thought you were going to get me out of your system," I say.

He releases a broken breath. "I thought you wanted to run away and never come back."

I go up on my tiptoes, wrapping my arms around his neck. "My father is going to ask about your intentions."

"Scope creep," he answers, giving me a wolfish wink. Then he holds his pinky between us. "I want dates and family dinners and being hounded by the press to make it official. I want to be caught kissing where we shouldn't. Do we have a deal?"

"We have a deal." I wrap my pinky around his and press his thumb. "I would take you if it meant tiaras and military parades every day. I would take you if I had to wear sky-high heels to serve school lunches. If you want me," his embrace tightens, "they'll have to wrestle you out of my cold, dead hands."

"Tiaras everyday? You do love me." His smile is lopsided. "At least the Dandelion Tiara won't give you headaches."

I do a little internal squeal. Very chill. Sort of chill. My spiritual fingertips are prancing. The Dandelion Tiara will be mine. Oh, yes, it will be mine.

Marc leans down until we're forehead to forehead. His breath comes with a shake. "I have missed you so much. I had Werner start shopping for an island."

"Why do you need an island?" I lead him to the sofa. Sealing this deal might take some time.

"For whenever you need to run away."

Marc has covered all his bases. "What else should I ask for, since you're in a mood to grant my every wish?"

"Hurry and decide," he tells me, placing soft kisses on each eyelid, and on the end of my crinkled nose.

I don't think about how much Mama will approve of this or what Alix might say. I have mentally consigned Noah to the end of the long meadow where he can overlook the dark ocean and consider what he owes his Viking blood.

I sink against Marc, and his hands band my waist. My eyes drift closed as his mouth covers mine. When he holds me, he keeps on holding.

I think, *Whui-ho*. We've got this. There's nothing left to wish for.

Epilogue

ELLA

On the day before her wedding, I break the news to Alix while we're sitting in side-by-side pedicure chairs at Esther Hong's. When I say, "I need you to know that I'm dating your brother," her massage feature switches to "vigorous," and it sounds like I've induced a seizure.

"How did he manage to talk you into it? Do you know that he paints miniature *Siege Blade* figurines to relax? Never mind," She shakes her head. "He's perfect. You're perfect. The important thing is that we're going to be sisters," she declares, her voice pitching up into a near-squeal.

"Alix, we're just dating. You can't put the cart before the horse," I say. Of course, there's a bonus feature in *Runaway Wagon* that absolutely allows players to do such a thing.

It doesn't matter where the cart is. I see the future as clearly as I see my own toenails, painted Seongan Spring just for the wedding. It's always been Marc, and it will always be Marc.

To her credit, my mother is trying not to appear elated. Her official position is that her daughters will be the death of her. That this is a difficult time to manage yet another boyfriend for the House of Wolffe, and could I please think of the monarchy and keep things well in hand over the coming months? Her unofficial position peeps out in the form of a dimple whenever his name is brought up or she crosses his path and he gives her one of his courtly, old fashioned bows.

"What?" she asks, when I catch her eye on these occasions. "It's rare to see a young person do it correctly."

Amma doesn't make a scene when we tell her, but she gently edges Marc out of her way and holds my hands tightly, brushing my cheek with her own. The thin crust of her Lutheranism must have evaporated during her time in Seong, because as soon as Alix told her such an event was possible, she collected the precise moment of my birth and consulted a shaman. When we pass her in the halls or gardens of Lindenholm, in the midst of these last minute wedding preparations, she murmurs things like, "Next summer is an auspicious season."

Marc handled Noah. I am not privy to the particulars. I don't know if anyone wrestled anyone else into submission. The only thing Marc will say is that no punches were thrown. He must have given Noah something to think about, because my brother paces the halls of the Summer Palace with his "Isn't there a foreign country we can wipe off the map?" face and growls irritably when Marc walks through the Great Hall like he owns the place.

"Don't worry about him," Marc says. "This really isn't about us."

I promise Alix that Marc and I will keep things private until well after her wedding, but she begs us go public. "I can't buy that kind of buzz," she says, which isn't even true. She hired a pair of juggling fortune tellers off of Pixy Shopfront for the reception, and invited acclaimed artist Linus Tiele to recreate the bride and groom in bottle caps as her guests watch.

Marc and I are another kind of spectacle. We hold hands and don't let go, not even when *Vrouw WOW's* photographer trains his lens on us. I feel the moment we're captured. Marc scoops me into his arms and lifts my hand to kiss the back of it. I straighten my shoulders and give the camera my best angle, but I can't stop smiling long enough to look elegant. It was a nice track record while it lasted, but I very much doubt I'll be winning any popularity polls with readers of *Vrouw WOW* next year.

When Yasmin sees us, her mouth forms a tiny cupid's bow of shock. Soon, though, her expression shifts into the determined look of a town crier, bent on sounding the news through every hamlet and village in Sondmark that Princess Ella has thrown her cap over the windmill at last.

By morning, everyone in Sondmark will know that Marc and I are a couple.

Tom gives a speech and presents his bride, now on her fourth wedding outfit, a *Creature Catching* account, filled with all the life points he's collected while taking business calls. "I'm never not thinking of you," he says, dipping her into a kiss.

I move my hands in a series of tiny claps, my shoulders lifting in a happy sigh.

"Think about the private island, Ella." Marc leans over and gives me a *whui-ho* fist.

I look up at him. "All that time, Marc. Think of how many digital butterflies he had to catch when he doesn't even like video games. I think I love him."

He scans the room. "I can do better than that."

Marc takes my hand and secrets me out of the wedding tent, leading me deep into the orchard. He shrugs out of his tuxedo jacket and throws it across my shoulders before I have a chance to feel the chill, and when the sound of the party is low and distant, the stars winking brightly overhead, he pauses.

At the base of a cherry tree, he finds a dandelion and brings it to me, holding the delicate puff between us. The seeds glow in the moonlight, full of promise, a dozen possibilities shivering on one slender stem. This is our new tradition.

"I'll give you all of your wishes," he says, secure in the knowledge that I won't wish to be anywhere that he isn't.

I blow, and the seeds drift in the night air, glinting under the moon. I think back on a moment I've been turning over since it happened.

"What is it this time?" he asks.

"You'll laugh," I say. I'm laughing myself.

There is no such thing as a Lutheran shaman, but I can see the future. I can see my roots planted deep in the soil of Lindenholm. I can see Marc and I weaving our lives together, the threads strong and unbreakable. I can see the generations to come, stamped by the both of us. I don't waste wishes on a sure thing.

I have vowed to work for the monarchy as long as my family needs me, even if I prefer living on my own terms. It will happen naturally as I become a peripheral member of the royal line, and there's only one way that's going to happen. "I wished that Noah would fall in love and get married."

"Why would I laugh about that?" he asks, swaying me gently to the distant sounds of an American ballad, something from Sinatra.

"Because I wished he would do it with Caroline."

I laugh and expect him to laugh with me. I expect him to say, "Caroline Tiele and your brother? Try wishing for the moon."

Instead, he pulls me into a kiss and whispers against my lips. "I'll see what I can do."

Author's Note

Dear Readers,

The germ of *The Dandelion Princess* came because I was thinking about the tension between community and individualism (as one does). One of my fantasies is living in a 19th century cottage—with magically beautiful plumbing, a roof that never needs replacing, and wild animals that stay safely away from my pantry—but my dreams are always tempered by the idea of what people who lived in small villages owed to one another for all that tight-knitted-ness. Privacy? Never heard of her.

I liked the idea of confronting Ella with these same questions. Though she would love to wear cracked-out clothes and go to endless fan conventions, she's not so thrilled with the rootlessness and lack of purpose that can come with total independence. On the other hand, living in a tight-knit community stressed her out. Everyone was up in her business, even if the strength of her sisterhood was undeniable.

I didn't know what Ella would choose when I went into this book, but the fun is in asking questions and being surprised when your characters answer them in ways that are totally unique. Freja answered very differently, and there are no one-size-fits-all solutions.

As ever, my beta readers are heroes. Debbie West reads everything—always, anytime, repeatedly. Kylene Grell is outstanding when I need an incoherent, cheerlead-y squeal. Paula Thacker sat outside a Starbucks with me and gave me the push to rewrite the prologue. Afton Nelson read an ugly early draft when I was lost—so lost—and gets the most desperate Marco Polos. Stephanie McRae read *The Dandelion Princess* when she was busy putting out her second book (*The Hero and the Patriot* is a gem, and you will love this well-researched Revolutionary War romance). And J.D. Rogers (author of the suspense romance *Midnight on the Tigris*) listened to some very stressed voice notes and returned the calmest, most chill advice in the middle of a terrifying second draft. Without these ladies, this book wouldn't be what it is.

Jacob Hanna, who also composed the Sondish National Anthem, patiently answered a variety of questions about his years in Taiwan. He is the best.

Leni Kauffman created the most wonderful cover—she always does. That light coming through the window of Ella's room makes me want to scoop it into an ice cream cone. The nod to Hayao Miyazaki's *Ponyo* adds just the right note of whimsy. I can't say enough about what a dream she is to work with.

Karie Crawford is my fairy godmother. In the last months, she has been my sounding board, accountability partner, and marketing friend, too. Though I work with her extracurricular-ly, you may find her editing services at CookieLynn Publishing Services. I owe her so much for how coherent my newsletter and website have become. I wish her a whole display case of warm, glistening, sugar-flecked pastries.

Jessica King is every inch a delight. She worked hard to untangle my grammar and sent the most encouraging messages as she edited my manuscript. My books straddle British and American English conventions, feature a slew of made-up words in a variety of made-up languages, and contain a lot of gamer slang. When I write, I tend to carpet-bomb the page with unnecessary commas. I don't make it easy to edit. If you see something that slipped past us, just assume it was me, tinkering behind her back. It's always me.

Though the East Asian country of Seong is fictional, my love and appreciation of the media coming out of that region are not. Seong is not-Korea in the same way Sondmark is not-Denmark. I've hidden little nods to Korean, Chinese, and Japanese pop culture in every available nook and cranny of this manuscript—from brooding shower scenes to white box trucks to drama titles to Seongan pop stars. Please do not mistake me for an expert. I, like Ella, am a fangirl.

Let us discuss my family. Like everyone else, I live in tension. On one hand, I would have finished this book faster if I didn't have to pick up Maren after school—listening to BTS as she talks me into going through the McDonald's drive-thru. Faster if I didn't have to make Zac's beloved pork chops and noodles for dinner. Faster if I didn't have Sunday School lessons to prepare or church camps to attend. Faster without phone calls from my sisters, texts from my college kids, and loads of laundry. But without these things, my books just wouldn't be any good. The things that take my time (and drive me bananas) are the same things I'm in love with. Nathan, Jonah, Jane, Spencer, Zac, and Maren are my favorite people, and you meet my love for them in my books.

And you, dear readers, are the best. I feel lucky to have the nicest ones. I hope that spending time with the very human Ella gives you a little nudge to love the life you've chosen. She did that for me.

All my love until next time,

Keira

P.S. My Asian drama recommendation is *Hidden Love*, a brilliant, Chinese drama about a girl in love with her big brother's best friend (there are mild, closed-door sexy times, fyi). Chen Zhe Yuan and Zhao Lu Si are beautifully paired. The thing I love best is that it shows every tiny step from hero worship to grown-up love, with all the messiness and mortification in between.

About Author

Keira Dominguez graduated from BYU with a B.A. in Humanities and lives in Portland, Oregon with her husband. She has five children, but they're no good. They keep leaving for college.

She likes Asian dramas, those Trader Joe's toffee rectangles, black licorice, the smell of babies, walks in the forest when it's not too hot and not too wet and the likelihood of her car being broken into is low, her precious sisters, the brothers, too, scripture study when everyone has something to say, a really good pot roast, apple cider, and historical facts that remind her that the human family has ALWAYS been banana-crackers.

Keira enjoys being seized by sudden enthusiasms and gets weepy about how much beauty there is in everyday life if we live with our eyes open to it.

For writing updates, you may sign up to Keira's newsletter at, her website, keiradominguez.com. She is often found on Instagram under the user name keiradominguezwrites, discussing all manner of nonsense.

ALSO BY

KEIRA DOMINGUEZ

MAGICAL REGENCY

Her Caprice

The Telling Touch

The Sweet Rowan

ROYALS OF SONDMARK

The Impossible Princess

The Winter Princess

The Midnight Princess

The Dandelion Princess

NOVELLAS

Stay Close